Louisiana Rogue

Louisiana Rogue

The Life and Times of Pierre Prospère-Tourmoulin,
Picketpocket, Thief, Gambler, Fugitive, Undertaker, Barber,
Doctor, Priest, Prisoner, Bandit, and Count; Latterly penned in
his hand for the gentle reader of leisure
Spanning the years 1831-1839

Translated

by

Peter Tourmoulin

ISBN: 978-0-9852552-7-5
Library of Congress Control Number: 2013934302
Manufactured in the United States of America

Lamar University Press
Beaumont, Texas

CONTENTS

Translator's Foreword

Among the heaps of papers my Great Aunt Miss Agnes-Marie Tourmoulin jealously guarded during her lifetime, but left in disorder at her death in 1995, was a curious memoir in French which she claimed was written by her Great-Grandfather Count Pierre de Tourmoulin, also known in English as Peter Prosper during the early years his life (1813[?] -1895). Despite objections raised by several members of our old and very Catholic Louisiana family, who were scandalized on several counts by these revelations, it was always Aunt Agnes-Marie's hope to translate and publish at least the first part of the huge manuscript, "even if it harelips all of Louisiana and half of Texas," as she put it, annoyed by her finicky kinfolk. But though feisty to the end, she tarried more than she talked, and by the time she finally got serious about the project, age had so eroded her health, as English had weakened her French, that neither was up to the task.

Since I was perhaps the last of the scattered descendants who still had a fair command of French and also some proficiency in Spanish through my father's side of the family, she prevailed on me to complete the work. Swayed by my deep affection for Aunt Agnes-Marie and done in by deathbed sentimentality, I could not refuse her.

Meanwhile, without telling the rest of the family, my Cousin Evette made off with the memoir in the chaos following Aunt Agnes-Marie's passing. How it wound up back in my hands is a bizarre story in itself, but this is not the time or place to tell it. Once into the project, however, there were moments when I wished Evette had kept it. For instead of a straight-forward narrative, my ever-so-great Grandfather's "Memoirs" turned out to be a water-damaged, bug-eaten maze of notes, scribblings, erasures, smudges, marginal rewrites, and puzzling omissions.

To make matters worse, my French was often overmatched by his rich archaic language and flowery nineteenth-century style in all the languages he wrote. I all but wore out several large dictionaries trying to chase down some of his antiquated vocabulary. Nor did his marginal comments in Spanish in the latter chapters help matters. In fact, without the generous help of Prof. Eduardo Mindiola of Southwest State University those portions would have stymied me. Not that this admission is an excuse for any errors of translation. These are my sole responsibility.

But beyond all these problems, I have my doubts that my ancestor actually did many of the things he describes. To give him some benefit of the doubt, I will concede that there is a thread of truth in his narrative. He did study briefly for the priesthood, and it is a fact that he fled New Orleans because of certain "indiscretions." Years later he returned and became a man of wealth and influence. Where he went and what happened in between is a matter of conjecture.

All this being said, at least I have kept my promise to Aunt Agnes-Marie by offering for your enjoyment or horror, gentle reader, as old Pierre would say, my version—*faute de mieux* (for want of a better one) —of these adventures of a LOUISIANA ROGUE.

Peter Tourmoulin
St. Martinville—New Orleans, Louisiana

Part I: Touching on Peter's early years; his parents and family, companions, education and circumstances; the curious tale of Alain DuClos (Sixfingers) and his odd demise; his mother's story; how he avenged himself on brother Henri and escaped the slavers

Perhaps none, or few, of my misfortunes about to unfold in this tale would have happened had I not betrayed my brother Henri to the slavers. Yes, you heard me aright, dear reader; I delivered my brother into their hands for the lucre of a few coins, thereby setting in motion a series of events and their consequences beyond any capability on my part to foresee them. But I will repeat to the end that if the blame was mine, the fault was his, or so I felt at the time without any sensible sting of remorse. You may judge the affair differently but I hope fairly. At least have the patience to hear how the matter was circumstanced against me before you issue a condemnation.

The only likeness ever I saw of my father Joseph Prosper, or Prospère, as it was written in our French tongue, was a framed artist's sketch my mother kept hidden in a drawer by her bed. With cosmetics or crayons she had completed as faithfully as she could the approximation of his features. Whether in truth he was or not my father, God alone knows of a certainty, but with this public claim my mother inscribed and baptized me in St. Martinville parish as Pierre Prospère, adding as a second name Tourmoulin in memory of a relative, her father, if her account can be believed.[1]

Picture then, if you will, a gaunt, long-necked Frenchman sunk into weeds too large for his lean frame; fierce blue eyes; untrimmed, blond hair—and by the look of it all but virgin to comb and brush—descending to his shoulders; a high forehead; bristly yellowish eyebrows; large, wafery ears set at a low, wide angle to his head; ruddy, freckled skin too fair for browning in the New Orleans climate; an uncommonly large nose hooked over a thin-lipped mouth etched by exuberant red mustachios; and a wispy, reddish pointed goatee that completed a long, narrow face. With these features you will have his true image.

I was long incuriously ignorant about his origins and whereabouts, for before I reached the age of memory and sensibility, he fled New Orleans for the Spanish territory of Coahuila-Texas, clutching a bag of purloined funds, lashing a lathered stallion, and—so it was rumored— taunting pursuing constables.

No description could be more unlike my youthful recollections of Mother's appearance. She was soft of feature and form, saffron in complexion, and the apex of her fair glory was her waist-long hair that undulated in lustrous and luscious ebony over her smooth arms and shoulders. Her dark eyes sparkled as her high merriment and extravagant charms earned her entry into the passions and purses of old New Orleans. Her voice was melodious with the accents and words of the languages we all spoke and commingled with casual fluency: French, Spanish, and Old Quarter English.

Though beyond the meridian of her life at the time of this telling, yet she retained charms sufficient in their effect to rouse the patrons to whistling, thunderous applause when she played the harp and sang French and Spanish songs. At times in a more ebullient spirit she danced Spanish boleros and fandangos and French contra dances and waltzes with selected partners in Père LaChaise's venerable cabaret or, later, in Madame Sonnier's more raucous Sojourner Inn and Tavern. She had a passion for the minuet learned in her years in St. Martinville but for want of accomplished partners and stately locale seldom danced it in New Orleans.

On fair afternoons as she customarily issued forth into the streets of the Vieux Carré men halted to view her passing, hats doffed and hearts secretly or openly offered to her feminine splendor. As she glided by staring male onlookers, serene in her seductive beauty, skirts and petticoats a-rustle in short, form-hugging and puffless cirsaca and matching casaquin, many an angry lady berated husband or companion for his helpless bewitchment. Outwardly indifferent to their silent or spoken provocations, which she accepted as the natural homage men pay great beauty, yet she seemed to enter into a tacit complicity with each gentleman by leaving him with the singular impression of having been favored by a fleeting smile, a subtle hand signal, or an inviting tilt of her head. As a poet of the English tongue has sung:

> Grace was in all her steps, heav'n in her eye,
> In every gesture dignity and love.

Notwithstanding this intense masculine admiration, it brought no honest courtship, much less solid offers of matrimony. Her remote admixture of African blood, though diluted by Spanish, Irish, and French ancestry, was too ecumenical for old Creole families, and as American influence grew in Louisiana, the same traits that bewitched the men of New Orleans also forbade her intercourse with prudish Anglo-Saxon society. Moreover, she had three children of uncertain paternity, Henri, Monique, and me, offspring of illicit loves and liaisons that were the

6

grist of gossip and scandal in the Old Quarter.

As we return to the year when this writing commences—the Year of our Lord 1831—in the fifteen or so years since her arrival from St. Martinville she had reigned in near legendary supremacy over rival entertainers who exchanged their soft charms and amorous interludes for the hard coin of eager patrons. Unlike others of her condition and profession who flashed meteor-like in lurid, ephemeral glory only to fade as quickly into diseased or alcoholic obscurity, with superior cunning and beauty my mother evaded this tragic dénouement by becoming the mistress of a series of affluent and powerful men. In this way she avoided perilous traffic with drunken sailors, lawless rivermen, riotous frontiersmen, and vicious riff-raff that drifted in and out of New Orleans.

You may think it disrespectful and unnatural of me to speak of my mother as I do. But since she showed us no natural affection and talked as freely of her lovers and liaisons as one might speak of a hangnail or a bout of catarrh, I grew up assuming she had as much right to her personal immorality as a less audacious woman would have to her prudish virtue.

She took only the scantiest interest in our material welfare and upbringing. Indeed, she once concocted the fable—acknowledged by all but believed by none—that Henri was the son of wayward sister Cécile who, supposedly, abandoned him to elope with a French sailor from Marseilles. In any case, she forbade us to show ourselves in Sojourner's Tavern and punished us severely if we disturbed her during the hours when she customarily entertained her present gentleman. We were barely past toddler age when she shoved us out to fend for ourselves in the streets of the Old Quarter, there to beg, steal, lie, and deceive with the consuming passion and singular cunning that hunger breeds in the human race. My siblings and I learned early and felt often the hard truth of a common Old Quarter saying:

> La faim rend tout pain délicieux
> (Hunger makes any bread delicious)

Possessed of a certain natural shrewdness, I excelled in larceny and soon became the leader of a motley band of young ruffians who preyed on visitors and shopkeepers in the Quarter, quickly becoming delinquent masters at lifting purses and coin, merchandise, wine, food, and whatever else of profit and gratification we could lay hands on. As the years passed, the few survivors of our band—Jules Petrie, Joseph ("Pouches" [pockets]) Ducoeur, Ignace Bossier, Julie Cheveuil, and I—rose to the

7

higher ranks of thievery, mastering the intricate nuances of pick-pocketing and slight-of-hand tricks with cards and dice and acquiring consummate skills in many a time-tested ruse for separating fools from their money and beauties from their virtue, as we, beginning with sweet Julie's willing help, were precociously parted from ours. We overproved the truth of the adage:

> So long as the world lasts, there will always be a plenteous supply of knavery to meet the ample demand of folly.

Gentle reader, if you are sharp of hearing and chanced to be walking along the river side of the Vieux Carré on a certain Tuesday afternoon in May of 1830, you may have overheard Jules, Julie, and me planning our latest swindle.

"I have caught his eye and he follows me now like a puppy. We have talked and he is ripe for the taking," sloe-eyed Julie whispered to Jules and me as we strolled by without looking at her. "And his purse looks to be as thick as his belly," she added gleefully.

"Then see to it that he follows you to the room behind the alley before some strumpet plucks him," Jules instructed her without glancing in her direction. "And be ready for me. I will do the rest. Pierre will stand lookout."

As I guarded the alleyway, the corpulent victim wasted no time stripping to his underdrawers and making ready to mount his delectable prize. At that very moment Jules burst in, waving a gleaming knife and screaming his outrage.

"You scoundrel! You swine! What are you doing with my wife? Have you no decency? When I finish carving you into a capon, you'll service no other woman! And you, woman, so you thought to cuckold me with this fat pig! Have you no shame?"

"Mercy, God's mercy, dear husband! This man spoke to me in the Plaza then followed me. I rebuffed him, of course, but he took me by surprise as I made for the market. He dragged me into this alley, and tried to have his way with me! I swear by all that is holy that I speak the truth!"

"I heard no screams of protest, but we shall learn the truth of the matter, and you will answer to me later. But you, son of a diseased harlot, you will pay now for this outrage!"

"Gentle, good sir, spare me! I had no idea the woman was married. She mentioned no husband, but led me to think she was willing to ... But let me make amends, I beg you."

8

"In what way can you repair this outrage to my honor?"

"Sir, I have money," the man said, sweating profusely and dancing on one leg as he donned his trousers. "I will pay you all I have if you will let me go, as I beg you."

"Money cannot restitch a man's torn honor," Jules responded in a milder tone but still waving his knife.

"I would offer more if I could, but what I have I offer with apologetic sincerity."

"I will take your money, since I do not wish to add my own crime to the wrongs done here today. But my grief against you remains. I counsel you not to cross my path again, lest upon seeing your face again I regret my action and decide to take vengeance."

The man hurriedly buttoned his trousers, emptied his ample purse on the bed, and fairly ran out the door and down the alleyway. As for us, we celebrated one of our finest swindles with wine and song. The money was considerable, but as soon come as soon gone.

Such was our life on the street in those far off days.

As I revere the memory of Father Branigan—of whom I shall speak later—for the understanding I have of letters, Creed, and faith, so now I render a perverse homage to Alain DuClos for polishing my larcenous skills. He always wore gloves, and when asked why, told us it was none of our affair. One day by accident when his glove caught fire in his bakery, we learned the truth. To his five exceptionally long, dextrous fingers and, we assumed, his toes, nature had added a shorter sixth digit. Despite his threats and protests, this abnormality quickly earned him the unskakable nickname of Sixdoigts (Sixfingers) and became the object of fixated wonderment to all who had business with him.

With only rare exceptions, these dealings proved to be as ruinous to his fascinated customers as they were profitable for his purse. His portal to the world and the legitimate shelter for his many unlawful enterprises was his *épicerie en tous genres*, or general store, located near the crossing of Bienville and Dauphné streets. In Spanish times its smaller, primitive forerunner was known simply as the Bodega of Spaniard Jacinto Vigo. When Spanish rule in New Orleans ended in 1803 don Jacinto decided to return to his ancestral Galician terruño, as he nostalgically called it. Rumor had it that the astute Sixfingers duped the homesick gallego into sailing for Spain with only an officially notarized but worthless promissory note and the grandiose expectation of receiving double his invested money within the year. As far as I know, he is still waiting.

Once in possession of the store, Sixfingers launched a series of enterprises well beyond the outermost legal bounds. From my band of young thieves he redeemed stolen items worth many times over the paltry sums he paid us. To our complaints he responded with huge, sweeping gestures with his extraordinary hands, rolling his eyes in mock exasperation and pointing out the risks he took and the bribes he was obliged to pay to deflect constabulary investigations. Although we grumbled and tried to think of ways profitably to dispose of our stolen items elsewhere, in the end we always came back meekly to Sixfingers, hanging our heads as he scolded us for our disloyalty and lack of trust. For like most thieves, we were as inept in the merchandising of stolen goods as we were skilled in their removal from rightful owners.

Notwithstanding our whimperings respecting our meager returns, we dared not consider betrayal of any sort, for we were singularly mindful of the suspected demise of one Jacques Grandpré for a breach of the thieves' code. Outraged over his paltry receipts and Sixfingers' comparatively handsome returns, Grandpré formed a scheme to deliver the object of his spite to the authorities. But learning of this intention through his suborned agents within the constabulary, Sixfingers moved first. Lured into the *épicerie* on a promise of making amends and rectifying underpaid accounts, Grandpré did not emerge and indeed was never seen again in New Orleans. Sixfingers was suspected of a homicidal crime and became the object of an official investigation. But inasmuch as no cadaver was found, no charge could be made. The case remained unsolved, even though gossip and conjecture abounded. For a brief time neighbors avoided Sixfingers and his épicerie, but in no great lapse of days his abundant supply of uncommonly spicy and conveniently cheap sausages and tallow candles brought back his old customers and earned him new ones as well. His customers commented on the peculiar tang of the sausages, to which Sixfingers responded that the savor was traceable to a rare African spice unknown in the Western nations. I suspected without saying so that it had to do with the unfortunate Grandpré. You, dear reader, will understand why I consumed none of the spicy sausages.

Even as I treated Sixfingers with fearful circumspection, I recall with admiring gratitude his help in avenging myself on one Patrice LaChaise, son of the venerable Père LaChaise who so nobly came to the aid of my mother and her family. In personal qualities Patrice so differed from his noble father that it strained my belief to accept his filial kinship. For Patrice was as miserly as his sire was generous, as vicious in instincts as Père LaChaise had been noble in impulse. I speak of Père

LaChaise in this way for he had passed to a better life some years since and Patrice inherited his enterprise.

Now in response to certain petty thefts, belligerent Patrice declared war on my band, and so severely did he press us in a coordinated campaign with the authorities that for a time he all but rendered us ineffectual in our larcenous commerce. The sudden dearth of merchandise alarmed Sixfingers who complained that he was unable to satisfy the requests of his best customers. I explained the cause to him, but instead of responding with his customary exaggerated gestures and melodramatic oratory, his lean face took on a thoughtful cast as his six-fingered hand drummed on the sordid counter.

"This requires a plan," he muttered finally to our quizzical looks, "and I have the makings of one. Monsieur LaChaise, my lads, will find that we are not so easily bested. Get along with you now, but you, Pierre, return tomorrow. I shall have a task for you then."

The next day I did as he bade me, and no sooner entered I apprehensively than he called me behind the dirty curtain separating the store from his squalid living quarters and handed me a bag with twelve gleaming Spanish dollars.

"Now, *mon petit ami*, these are your instructions. You are to take one of these new dollars to LaChaise's Inn where you will ask for wine and food. There you will apologize to monsieur Lachaise in your best manner and vow by all that is sacred that you have renounced your former life of thievery. Say no more, but the next day you will repeat the purchase with another new dollar; and the next, and if necessary, the next. And mind you, spend none of the change. Understand you fully my instructions?"

"Yes, of course, but what is the scheme?"

"You will know in due time."

Though thoroughly mystified by my instructions, obediently I followed them. No sooner had I entered the inn than Patrice came towards me so menacingly—for he was large of frame and stature—that I fell to my knees in genuine terror and sobbed out my abject apologies and the grievous error of my ways. He looked down on my groveling posture, arms on his sides, and his face took on a look of smug self-satisfaction.

"You have stolen your last from Patrice LaChaise, and only if your apology is sincere may you yet avoid imprisonment for your thefts."

"Oh, sir, but it is, it is!" I pleaded. "Never again will I take anything not earned by honest labor."

"Then what is your business here?" he asked suspiciously.

11

"Oh, sir, I came only to purchase wine and food. As a consequence of my new resolution, I have found employment that pays me well. See, here is my money to pay for my purchase."

Patrice took the dollar, eyed it suspiciously, and muttered, "It looks newly minted. Few such coins circulate in New Orleans."

Puzzled by the newness of the coin but unable to prove its falsity, he pocketed it and served me wine, bread, and stew. The next day I repeated the act and the request, paying with another handsome new dollar and receiving my coinage in change. By the third day, Patrice was overwhelmed by morbid curiosity.

"Where and how do you come by these coins?" he asked. "I cannot believe in their legal provenance. Yet if counterfeit, they are ingeniously done."

"In my ignorance of the matter I cannot respond to your doubts, sir, only to your question. As I explained earlier, my employer sees fit to pay me in such coinage, and it is not for me to protest the wage."

"I would like a word with this employer about these dollars. Where can I find him?"

"In truth, sir, I have never set eyes on the employer himself. He has his reasons, I take it, for protecting his privacy. Both the instructions regarding my work and the wages so earned come to me from his aide. Perhaps I could speak to him, sir, on your behalf."

I reported to Sixfingers what Patrice had said. "Tell Patrice that the aide will speak to him out of gentlemanly courtesy, but for reasons of his own, he prefers a private setting for their conversation. Give him these instructions if he desires more information. If he agrees to the meeting, then your part in this matter is done, and you will return the remaining dollars—all of them and every cent of the change, mind you—to me."

Indeed Patrice eagerly agreed to the secret rendezvous, and I had no choice but to surrender the lovely coins to Sixfingers. Only later learned I what transpired.

Petulant Patrice, Sixfingers laughingly reported, had pressured the aide—in reality one of Sixfingers's accomplices—until finally he confessed that the coins were counterfeit, but so genuine in appearance that not even expert bankers were able to tell the difference. The problem was not in producing the coins, anybody with the proper ingredients could do it, but in putting the dollars into circulation without arousing constabulary suspicions about their origin. If they had a business like Patrice, it would be much easier and greatly lucrative.

The vision of stacks of undetectable counterfeits aroused the profoundest greed in dear Patrice's bosom, and he commenced to inquire how he might come by a supply, which consisted, he was told, of a mold, secret metal alloys, and finishing acids. The aide resisted his insistence, and it was not until Patrice hinted of possible communications with the constabulary if access be denied him that the aide relented and agreed to let him pursue the affair.

At the appointed time after the next midnight hour, the eager but outwardly calm Patrice and the apprehensive aide knocked on the door of a dilapidated hovel on one of the back alleys of the Quarter. A mulatto man peered through a crack and told them to go away, for he did not know them or their business.

"What do you mean, you don't know me, Fletcher? Is this any way to treat your old friend Louis?"

Fletcher swore and opened the door a crack. "But I don't knows the man wid you and I don't deal with no strangers. Ain't no good business go on at dis hour. Now you tells me what you wants."

Apprised of Patrice's stubborn intent, Fletcher shook his head. "No, sir, man, I can't let the stuff outta my hands. You knows what da boss man say, Louis. Besides, it's awful 'spensive."

"How much for enough to make a thousand dollars?" Patrice asked impatiently.

"A thousand dollahs!" Flethcer said in a shocked voice. "No, sir, no way I could sell you dat much—even if I was selling it. And I ain't."

"How much?" repeated Patrice.

"Well, about ... Naw, man, it cost you too much."

"How much?" repeated the implacable Patrice.

"Well, normal, we gets three hundred dollahs. But we be a little low on stuff and it aint easy to slip it in from Coahuila. So I says what I said de first time: can't deal wid you, mister. Now why don't y'all jist go on 'bout yo' business and let me go back ta ma bed?"

"Four hundred," said Patrice, visions of shining dollars stacking up in his excited imagination.

"You say four hundred, mister?" asked the incredulous Fletcher, almost choking at the offer, "four hundred dollars?"

"Four hundred dollars, that's what you heard. Now how about it?"

"Well now, dat gitting to be a hoss of a diffent color ... but ... I dunno, Mister, it take me some little time to git it ready fog you. But ... tell you what, man, you go gets yo money and come back here in a hour. I reckon we'll see if we can do us some business, though I be considerable fretted bout the whole thing."

Well, as DuClos told the story, Patrice hurried back with four hundred dollars, slyly including the three counterfeits since no one could tell them from the genuine coins. For this he was handed a heavy bulk containing, so he was assured, the precious mold, acid, and enough of the secret alloys to mint a thousand milled dollars. But just as Patrice turned over the coins and was about to inspect the purchase, a man appeared in the alleyway with a lantern. "A constable!" Fletcher whispered, running away down the alley with the bag of coins. His panic was contagious and Patrice followed on his heels.

Safely back in his establishment, Patrice discovered that he had bought a roll of copper, a jug of mere vinegar, and a rusty, unworked block of cast iron. He seethed with rage but was powerless to call for the authorities and thereby reveal his own intent to defraud. Needless to say, neither party to the fraudulent transaction was to be found. As for me, I purchased no more wine or stew in his establishment and took extreme care to see that our paths did not cross.

Yet I was still mystified about the counterfeit coins duClos had given me to lay the trap.

"Counterfeit?" laughed Sixfingers the next time I delivered items to him. "No, *mon petit ami*, they looked genuine because they were: dollars I had laved to make them shine like new. We only had to make him believe they were counterfeit and trust to his greed to do the rest. Remember this, Pierre: successful schemes require dishonesty on both sides."

Not long afterwards, however, Sixfingers came to a foul end, perhaps by the hand of vengeful Patrice himself, but I suspect his passing had to do with a much older grudge.

In the years before he acquired the épicerie, Sixfingers and accomplices Love Vaughn and his brother Sommer organized an extensive network of horse and slave thieves from New Orleans to Kentucky. Love Vaughn posed as a traveling preacher, holding what the infidel Protestants call "revival camp meetings" along the frontier. As American settlers flocked to the meetings, at which liquor and religion flowed in similar copious amounts, brother Love and his wife Bertha examined the crowd so as to spot the handsomest horses and owners of the best slaves. They then relayed this information to Sixfingers and Sommer who connived to make off with horses and Negroes. In many cases the latter departed willingly, seduced by Sixfingers's promises to reward them with freedom and send them north, provided they would allow themselves to be auctioned to gullible new masters. Once purchased, he would help the Blacks escape. Once a number of such auctions had been made, the slaves were then to be set free.

Often DuClos broke his word to the Blacks. He promised a certain slave, by name Uncle Harry, that for his willing compliance he would purchase his wife Sallie and young son Zion, slaves on a neighboring plantation. But once the slave family was in his possession, Sixfingers reckoned that the comely Sallie and sturdy Zion would fetch a handsome price on the New Orleans slave market and thus refused to release them to Uncle Harry. The latter pleaded and begged for his woman and son but to no avail. Furthermore, another ex-slave hinted to Sixfingers that Harry's former master had given him many privileges, allowing him to make items such as foot mats, ingenious cypress carvings, and cotton baskets and to keep the money earned from their sale. It was rumored that he accumulated a sizable hoard with which he hoped to buy his family's freedom. No sooner was Sixfingers the greedy possessor of this information than he and his men commenced to torture Uncle Harry, cutting off his ears and fingers and gouging out his eyes. Finally, when it became apparent that no human cruelty could persuade Harry to reveal the whereabouts of his treasure, in frustrated rage Sixfingers plunged a knife into his chest and left the old Black to die in a deserted grove.

Before he was dragged away, Zion, a lad of eight or nine, rushed to his father's side to embrace his sire and utter these words:

"Now I be a boy, but someday I'll be a man and I promises you I'll get even!"

Uncle Harry whispered something to the boy and breathed his last. Zion and Sallie were carried away to auction on the New Orleans Slave Market. Years passed and the incident was all but forgotten.

But then one day Sixfingers was found murdered in the same grove where Uncle Harry died. The cadaver was missing ears and eyes and all twelve fingers were cut off and placed in a bloody stack beside the body. A large oak had been felled near the body and from the appearance of scuff marks and chipping it seemed that something had been removed from its hollow core. Speculations abounded about Patrice LaChaise's complicity in the murder, but for want of proof they amounted to fruitless suspicions. Moreover, Patrice furnished constables with a reasonable alibi backed by eyewitnesses who attested to his whereabouts at the time of the crime. Few remembered Zion's promise; even fewer took it seriously, and thus the murder remained unsolved and forgotten. The consensus was that DuClos had made many enemies through his unsavory schemes and any of them could have have killed him.

Besides my dubious dealings with Sixfingers and my cronies, I learned from my mother the art of tarot fortune-telling, cheiromancy, and various astrological readings; arts, she said, that a gypsy fortune-teller taught her in St. Martinville. In truth, these latter arts I rehearsed but little, believing them to fall more properly under the purview of hags and witches and unworthy of my serious and prolonged attention. Nor did I delve into the darker realm of Voodoo divination, for I witnessed its ravages and feared the taint and grip of the black arts. I claimed no estimable estate in this world yet I was as proud of my soul as any other mortal, and though my life only sparingly brushed on Church dogma, I had no disturbing doubts of its efficacious truth.

In any case, few and fleeting were the gains and pleasures afforded by our nefarious lore and mischievous skills and frequent and harsh the punishments for our delinquencies. Ah, if you could but see, dear reader, the scars I bear on my limbs and back as sad souvenirs of my foiled stratagems! For not even our considerable skill was able to change our evil luck; each time we found ourselves on the verge of a quick gain from a master theft or swindle, fate snatched it away and instead often left us bruised, beaten, and occasionally jailed for our effrontery and contumely. From a very early age I formed a notion that indifferent Providence was no match for my unpromising fate. What a cruel sarcasm my purported surname came to be, for though I risked all, in nothing did I prosper!

Perhaps because of a mild stirring of that same Providence or my mother's passing interest in rehabilitating her life and family, she enrolled me over my profanity-laced protests in Father Branigan's school for orphans and foundlings, which convened on Tuesdays and Thursdays in a dilapidated structure hard by the Convent of the Ursulines. In the three years of my sporadic attendance I progressed in my letters and ciphers, even to the point of mastering some elements of Latin, which if not always fully understood were at least imperfectly fixed in my memory. It was a matter of pride on my part that Father Branigan soon came to admire my elaborate cursive lettering and entrusted to me certain recordings of parish activities and the penning of his epistles in French, a language that resisted his best efforts to master it. The formal rudiments of the Faith, however, were less to my liking, and since clumsiness is ever the boon companion of indifference, therein I displayed only the most mediocre of aptitudes. Often the good-hearted but short-tempered Father soundly boxed my ears for stumbling and yawning through the Catechism.

I was possessed of a high, pure voice that settled nicely in my adolescence into a good tenor, or so I was told. This and an ear for music were qualities that Father Branigan wished to cultivate for service to the Church. Accordingly, for the duration of my stay in the school I was a member of a small choir that betimes he had sing at ordinary mass—

16

when enough of us could be gathered—and render service in certain other church ceremonies at the Cathedral.

Though possessing no formal musical knowledge, I learned on my own to strum quite handsomely on a stolen guitar I kept for myself under my bed. I was particularly fond of the tempestuous Spanish manner, but regardless of the style or the language of the music, the worldly songs of human passions were much more to my liking than the Latin hymns of divine love. Every now and then my mother would blend her wonderfully modulated soprano voice with mine, and in those occasional moments I truly believed her to be the most talented and beautiful woman in the world. At these intervals my love for her revived, but to no avail: she showed her offspring no natural affection.

These remarks about my mother are perhaps as good a prelude as I could wish, dear reader, to provide intelligence about my maternal ancestry. I tell it as it was told to me, yet I must add that it is but one of several versions my mother related. For her imagination was as lively as undisciplined. Therefore, I caution you beforehand to remember the source of the tale and, if you please, ask you not to cast your blame on me for any transgressions she makes against truth or history.

My Mother's Tale

In 1782 when France, Spain, and the Americans were leagued against the perfidious British in the last year of the Colonial Revolution and the much-admired Governor Gálvez guided the destinies of New Orleans and la Louisiane, unrest and revolt were already beginning to seethe in the French colonies of the Lesser Antilles. It was then that King Louis XVI, of tragic memory, sent the young Count Antoine de Tourmoulin to pacify Haiti and certain islands. This at first and for two years he did to the best of his ability with the few forces placed under his command.

But before three years had passed in this impossible task—for the infestation of revolt against France was already secretly spreading like the creeping tentacles of an octopus into the huts and hovels of the oppressed and wretched African slaves—, before three years had elapsed, I say, the dashing young Count from Normandy, whose wife and daughter Celeste had remained at the ancestral château in Rouen, conceived a tempestuous passion for a mulatto woman named Rosa Montes O'Malley, the daughter of a Spanish adventurer and an Irishman's bastard daughter on an African slave. So powerful was his love that he betrayed King, family, and country and cast his lot with Rosa and the rabble. For this treason he was hunted, captured, condemned, and

17

garroted in the Spanish manner. But of their illicit love were born two daughters, myself and Cécile, who—a curse be on her—eloped to Marseilles with the French sailor. I have told you her sordid story before.

The French then redoubled their cruel persecutions of the rebels. Still mourning my father's death but finding herself in grave danger of imprisonment or death for her complicity in his treachery, my mother fled with us, first to Port au Prince and thence across the perilous straits to Santiago, Cuba, where a legitimate half-brother Enrique Montes y Marchán had preceded her some years earlier after his father's death. Married to doña Begoña Escardó de Montes, a comely Cuban woman, he had fathered by her two children, Roberto and Rosaura. They were near in age and temperament to us, and even though Cécile and I were of mixed ancestry, our cousins were oblivious to such differences and we became inseparable companions. There we lived several happy years, undisturbed by the troubles we thought to have left behind us forever.

But then my aunt's brother Carlos Escardó y Losada returned to Cuba from Spain where, it was rumored, he had amassed a considerable fortune, modestly by commerce, mostly by marriage. With him came his Spanish wife, doña Asunción Segovia de Escardó, a dour, embittered creature several years his senior, as I recall, who bore him no children and offered him no happiness, but fetched an enviable dowry to her handsome young husband.

Only a short time elapsed before Carlos was smitten by the charms of our still beautiful mother. She did not refuse his advances, and their love affair became the scandal of Santiago. Confronted by doña Asunción, my mother told her *cuatro verdades* (four truths), as she put it, meaning that she insolently boasted to her face of her conquest. Such was her fiery character.

Mother did not reckon, however, on the power her rival was capable of bringing against her in the "Pearl of the Antilles." The affronted shrew's uncle was an army general and a cousin was adjutant to the Spanish Governor in Havana. These personages exerted pressures against Mother and ordered her to dispense with her property and either leave Cuba within the year or suffer grave consequences.

She turned to her brother for aid and protection, but, alas, Uncle Enrique was in precarious circumstances himself, having lost his money in gambling and foolish sugar speculations. Nor had he sufficient influence or will to nullify the vengeful cabal of his concuñada and the Spanish officials. Finally and most painfully, Carlos her lover, fearful at the prospect of confronting his wife's outraged family and perhaps losing his fortune, repented of his adventure and would have nothing further to do with her.

In desperation but with her characteristic impetuousness, my mother appealed to the Tourmoulin family in Rouen. It was now late 1793 and France itself was a ruin of revolutionary horror. Her letter arrived at a critical moment, as she subsequently learned, for a few weeks later she received in the post a letter from Madame Celeste, widowed mother of the executed Count. Her correspondence read as follows:

18 décembre 1793
"Ma chère Rose:

[*Autrefois* ...] In another time surely I should not have acknow-ledged your epistle for reasons that are clear to us both and need no belaboring. But these are different and desperate days and mayhap your letter be a godsend that will open a door to us both when every portal seemed closed to hope. The death of my beloved son Antoine amidst circumstances that were never made clear to me, followed not long thereafter by the demise of his grieving widow, reduced this once proud family to a sentimental calamity, as you may imagine. Yet that was but the early foreshadowing of a larger public disaster now engulfing all of France and threatening this household.

It is imperative, my dear Rose, that my granddaughter Celeste be removed from this evil conflagration to a place of safety. It is a miracle that we have survived as long as we have. For the godless brigands that have outraged law and decency throughout France daily issue threats against the Tourmoulin estate, and I doubt not that soon they shall put torch to its edifices and sword to its occupants and by these base acts proclaim themselves to be the principled liberators of their fellow rabble. May God's full wrath fall on them for their unspeakable mischief! The world is truly turned upside down and wrong is everywhere triumphant.

My concern is not for me. I am a widowed old woman with but few days remaining and no fear of death. My one abiding earthly hope is the safety of my granddaughter Celeste, now nineteen and for nigh on two years married to Viscount Louis de la Motte. She is four months with child but now bereft of husband, for the Viscount deserted her and now cowers in fear for his wretched life in Turin or its environs, so we have learned.

I was gladdened beyond words to say, dear Rose, by news of my two precious granddaughters. Alas, I shall never know them in this life, yet I send them my love and pray God's blessing on their innocent souls.

19

Describe Nicole and Cécile to me, I beg you, so that I may hold their happy image in my heart and pray for them daily.

It is because of them, dear Rose, and a grandmother's love that I appeal to your generosity of spirit on behalf of Celeste. For she is half-sister to them. Half, say I? Nay, whole, for she loves them tenderly without knowing them. Such is her sweet disposition and nature.

In the direst of straits and threatened on every side, yet we are not without means. I have in my hire certain trustworhy men who, under promise of considerable gain, assure me that they can spirit Celeste out of France through the Low Countries and escort her safely to London. Money and possessions mean little to me now and I would gladly give all to ensure the safety of my Celeste and her child. And though it is unlikely that she shall be able to take with her valued treasure or jewelry —for she must travel disguised as a peasant woman—yet with a degree of prescience at the beginning of this unpleasantness I deposited in London a considerable portion of the family fortune, sufficient to see her safely to America and once there to establish herself comfortably in that strange and distant land.

You speak of your own pressing need and the gross and unjust manner in which the Spanish officials in Cuba have treated you. I have no doubts concerning the accuracy of your description, for it is said that the Spanish are a fanatical lot, wanting in the ordinary decencies of civilized French folk. But perhaps we can combine our efforts in a common desire and purpose. With Celeste's help and the means I can furnish her, you may leave the benighted Spanish lands and perhaps make your way to Louisiana where my dear cousin, the Baron de la Fontaine, lives in exile in St. Martinville with many other nobles who once frequented the Court of His Majesty and were its spice and charm in a happier time. Ah, ma chère Rose, as Monsieur Tallyrand says so well, those who have not lived in Paris around 1780 cannot know how good life can be! The Baron is a generous man and will accept Celeste as his charge and look upon you and precious Nicole and Cécile as his protégées. If you are in agreement, from London she will book passage for Santiago, or failing that possibility, certainly for Havana. There she can gather you and my precious granddaughters and thence proceed as a family through New Orleans to St. Martinville and safety. This is my hope and soon, I pray, it will be yours as well. For I have a horror of leaving Celeste and her unborn child alone and without family.

With God's blessings upon you and my precious granddaughters, I leave you in the earnest expectation of receiving welcome news from you. Etc. etc."

(signed and sealed by la Comtesse de Tourmoulin)

My mother displayed the greatest ennui imaginable until the old lady (la vieille) commenced to speak of treasure and jewels. Then her solicitude for "chère Celeste" warmed to a veritable passion and she could not wait to welcome her and her treasure into the bosom of our family as another beloved daughter. Forthwith she posted another letter to the aged Countess that fairly gushed with false generosity and repeated assurances of her love for Celeste and her child who henceforth would be as her own.

Meanwhile, as impatiently we awaited news from the old Countess, Enrique's finances crumbled into so much ruin and debt and so threatened was he by his implacable creditors that he conceived the notion to join his family with ours in common flight from Cuba. Cécile and I were delighted by the prospect of having Roberto and Rosaura with us on the journey.

Several weeks passed and a second letter arrived from Countess de Tourmoulin informing that indeed Celeste had reached London safely and should embark within a fortnight for Havana, the only port in Cuba that still permitted English ships to dock. She thanked my mother with a veritable litany of senile blatherings, the promise of a thousand prayers for her generosity, and other such simpering sentimentality that afflicts the elderly as their common sense deserts them.

At Enrique's urging we hastily departed Santiago under cover of darkness, taking only a few items promised to his creditors. My mother had dispensed with her modest furnishings, and with this limited capital we thought to travel to Havana, there to await our salvation in the person or more truthfully, the purse—of our noble half-sister. Our Aunt Begoña wept bitter tears at the prospect of leaving family and friends in Santiago. Furthermore, even though she detested her sister-in-law, at the same time she harbored considerable resentment against Mother for having seduced her brother. But in the end her aged mother declared: "Such is the law of life; for better or worse, a wife must accompany her husband wherever he will."

The long journey in the diligence produced no undue problems besides mosquitoes and occasional torrential rains, and as though in compensation for these discomforts, it offered us youngsters a thousand excuses for wonderment and excitement. Arriving in Havana several days later, we lodged ourselves in an inn with such lowly pretenses of decency and cleanliness that Cécile and I sent up howls of protest and even gentle Tía Begoña, normally the very soul of demure meekness, raised her voice and openly questioned her husband's judgment and soundness of mind. My mother diminished our distress by reminding us of sister Celeste and her fabulous wealth, which grew with each telling.

Ten days later to the murmured displeasure of native Cubans, who remembered the English aggression of 1762, the British ship rose on the horizon and presently navigated past the Morro fortress into Havana harbor. The chusma, as they call the dock riff-raff, caught and tied its ropes, secured the gangplank, and waited, hat in hand, to receive a gratuity for their efforts. Both our families had come in full number to welcome sister Celeste, and you can imagine the high excitement and anticipation with which we greedily awaited her appearance.

If we were already fixated on her purse we soon became enamored of her person. She was in the full truth of the words, a splendid blonde young woman who radiated warmth and charm. Her gravid state was more obvious than we expected, yet instead of detracting from her youthful beauty her approaching motherhood enhanced it with the rosy cheeks and robust carriage of exuberant good health. Despite our difference in coloring, age, and temperament, Mother noticed at once my resemblance to her and schemed to extract profit from it.

It took but little wooing on our part to turn Tante Celeste (as we preferred to call her) entirely in our favor, for she was strangely devoid of jealousies and, indeed, as kindly disposed towards us as her grandmother had described. She was especially taken with me and indulged my every whim and notion in dress and dainty bonbons, much to the displeasure of Cécile who, the truth be told, materially at least fared no worse than I for her attentions. And she was equally kind and attentive to Roberto and Rosaura.

No sooner had my mother insinuated to her our impecunious circumstances than she, with incautious trust and naïveté, responded with largesse to our several needs. Seeing the ease with which we had presumed upon her purse, our Uncle Enrique was emboldened to present a similarly favored request, always with ardent and convincing promises to repay her consideration with even more generous interest.

Having circumvented for the moment our financial embarrassment, we then moved to the best accommodations in Havana. My mother and Enrique now thought to forego the voyage to Louisiana entirely and instead to reside indefinitely in the city. But upon making a covert inventory of Tante Celeste's fortune, Mother was startled and angered to learn that it was exceedingly finite and would be exhausted ere many weeks elapsed. It seemed only a matter of time before we should be obliged to resume our journey to St. Martinville.

Henceforth my mother's enthusiasm for her lover's daughter commenced to wane into contemptuous indifference. Tante Celeste seemed not to notice or take offense but appeared delighted to spend even more time with her younger half-sisters. Cécile and I passed hours in wide-eyed fascination as she showed us her clothes and told of the royal banquets, gay balls, and glittering events of her girlhood. The costumes and dresses she described seemed to be the magical stuff of fairy tales, and our provincial imaginations were taxed beyond their limit to picture the high and handsome marquesses, dukes, counts, and princes and the fabulous dresses, jewels, and charms of marchionesses, duchesses, countesses, and princesses at the royal court at Versailles and Paris. Occasionally she would stop to sigh and tears would come to her eyes as she remembered her perfidious husband.

Enrique got word that his creditors were bringing formal charges against him for absconding with the compromised items he had failed as promised to surrender earlier. He was desperate to leave Cuba, but a problem prevented it: Tante Celeste was now too close to delivery to travel. We had no choice but to wait until she gave birth. Never a paragon of courage, Tío Enrique was reduced to nervous panic by this contretemps, whilst meek Tía Begoña surprised us all with her calm manner and steadfast determination to save her husband and family from disintegration. She marched husband Enrique to the confessional and thence to mass. Having thus repented of his misdeeds, under her unrelenting insistence, he wrote to the creditors with the lie that servants had packed the items by mistake but that he would soon restore them to their rightful hands. It was a sad thing to see Tío Enrique's star sinking in the eyes of his family, but a wonder to behold how unassuming Tía Begoña displayed much unsuspected strength under the prod of adversity.

Weeks passed as our collective fortune shrank ever closer to a catastrophic reckoning (though caught up in our games we children fretted little about such things). Finally, on a Sunday in late May of 1794, I believe it was, Tante Celeste was delivered of a darling, blue-eyed boy whom she named Antoine—to my mother's private consternation. A fortnight later, with Tante Celeste nicely recovered from her travail, we quitted Havana harbor aboard a creaky, rat-infested ship, having expended nearly all her funds and ours for passage to New Orleans.

The first two days of the voyage through the Florida Straits and into the Gulf of Mexico passed without undue incident, though for us children our first remembered experience at sea was thrilling beyond telling. Meanwhile, however, uneasiness grew amongst the adults, for the captain and his two lieutenants spent much of the day locked in his quarters drinking whilst the surly, sweaty crew treated us with gross rudeness. Their premonitions were justified, for the third afternoon at sea we—and half a dozen fellow passengers—were surrounded by the heavily armed and mutinous crew and ordered to surrender all our money and possessions. Resistance was out of the question and we had to comply. They searched our trunks and finding no money proceeded to pummel and strip the men with the most callous disrespect. Nor spared they the women a similar indignity, though as I recall, for the sake of modesty, as I supposed, at least they conducted the search in the captain's quarters, spending a considerable time with each female. Some, like Tía Begoña and Tante Celeste, emerged flushed and tearful but without facial bruises or visible signs of physical abuse. The crew found little but left us less.

Then in their foul anger and drunken disappointment, they commenced to debate the fate of the passengers. Some thought it expedient to slit our throats and toss our corpses to the fishes, but the decision that finally prevailed was to cast us adrift without water or provisions in the ship's two boats. One of the younger men whispered to mother that we were now not more than forty or fifty leagues from the delta of the great river and that with luck we might make landfall in two or three days. As bad as our plight was, the captain and his lieutenants fared worse, for no sooner were we crowded aboard the boats than we heard screams and curses and saw their bodies tossed overboard. Not all the officers were dead upon impact, but after a few gurgling cries and spreading crimson on the water they sank into the deep. Thereupon the mutineers hoisted sail, set a course southward and soon disappeared from view.

This horror goaded our men to a rowing frenzy. But, alas, all that day and the next passed without sight of land. Our situation was becoming desperate for want of food and water. But then late in the afternoon of the third day we spotted low-lying treeless marshes to the north and rowing frantically to our encouraging cries, the exhausted men brought the boats to a deserted shore where we sank to our ankles in dark, foul-smelling ooze. We slaked our thirst with stagnant swamp water and the men slumped in the muck in utter weariness and fell soundly asleep. The rest of us soon joined their slumber.

We were awakened not many hours thence by terrible cries that seemed not the issue of human throats but were as the roaring of wild beasts. Tía Begoña and Tante Celeste clasped their children to their breasts as the other women huddled about them, but mother armed herself with a club and with the men prepared to confront the worst. We found ourselves surrounded by howling, near-naked savages armed with knives, hatchets, and tomahawks. At their first rush one of our men, a German by the name of Vondenberg, dove into the water and swam away in the darkness.

We were not so fortunate. The first to fall were Tío Enrique and Tía Begoña, and in the course of a few minutes none of our men was left standing. Indeed, we had all surely perished in the first assault with our fellows had not my quick-witted mother gathered us—Tante Celeste and baby Antoine, Roberto and Rosaura, Cécile and me—and under the cover of darkness pushed us into one of the boats. Taking up the oars, she was casting off when the Indians spotted us and with murderous whoops ran to block our way. At that moment Tía Begoña, still clinging to life, screamed the names of her children. Roberto turned and hesitated, but Rosaura leapt from the boat and ran crying with outstretched arms towards her. One of the savages grabbed her from behind and decapitated her with two strokes of his hatchet. Tante Celeste turned on impulse to aid her only to have the Indians jerk Antoine from her arms. One of the monsters took the baby by one foot and swinging him in a circle several times smashed his tiny head against the boat. Tante Celeste screamed and fainted. The Indians now completely blocked our escape, and fighting off my mother's valiant efforts to defend us with an oar, soon overpowered her.

But instead of slaughtering us as they had our family and comrades, they dragged us inland for the better part of a league and tied us to stakes. There we witnessed the ultimate horror: the savages eating human flesh, among the parts—unless I am mistaken—the plump white limbs of little Antoine ...[2]

The savages stripped us and felt our bodies. One of the men who spoke some French told me that because I was young and plump they intended to reserve me for the dinner of their chief, who would arrive in two days. In due course, Cécile and Robert would be served up at banquets for honored guests. As for my mother, such were her courage and strength that she was worthy of a full tribal feast.

At length Tante Celeste retrieved her senses and with returning consciousness came the full realization of her awful circumstance and loss. As she screamed for her slaughtered Antoine, a sub-chief approached and indifferent to her sobbing cries, drew his knife and from the inside of her ample thigh, sliced off a generous piece of her flesh. Thereupon she fainted again as blood streamed down her leg. Without a backward look the savage returned to the fire where he spitted the flesh and when it was roasted to his satisfaction devoured it with relish.

We doubted not that our end was near. My mother, whose rage against the heathens had turned her spirit indomitable, exhorted us to pray and be strong. Above all, she told us, if die we must, then we shall spit in the face of our tormentors and perish with pride. Nevertheless, Cécile whimpered in terror and even though I wanted to respond to my mother's example, what little bravery I could muster shrank before the horror at hand.

Having gorged themselves on the corpses of our family and companions, the savages ignored us for the rest of the night, a night replete with nightmares waking and sleeping.

When I awoke to sunlight, I was surprised to find myself lying some distance away from the torture stake. My mother and Cécile were beside me, and not far away dazed Tante Celeste, her leg bandaged, swayed to and fro in oblivious disregard of her surroundings. The camp was strewn with dead savages and a young Spanish soldier was kneeling beside me. We learned that Vondenberg had, as though by a miracle, stumbled into Fort Latourette, which had just received a fresh contingent of mounted soldiers.[3] Without delay and with reliable prior intelligence of the location and movement of the cannibals, a remnant of the Attakapas tribe, the soldiers rode swiftly to our rescue.

The Spaniards took us to Fort Latourette and gave us every available care. A physician dressed Tante Celeste's wound and a chap-lain said a mass for the souls of the departed. Yet neither priest nor physician offered us reassurance that Tante Celeste would recover in mind though she surely would heal in body. Unhappily their prognosis proved to be prophetic, for even though she lingered amongst us for several more years, that very day she left us in spirit as surely as the souls of our slaughtered family and companions.

You have heard the rest of the story before. When we had recovered enough to travel, a company of soldiers escorted us safely to New Orleans. There we were obliged to remain for several weeks, accepting Père LaChaise's kind hospitality and arranging for transportation to St. Martinville. Père LaChaise's generosity and friendship were not forgotten and, as you know, years later when we returned to New Orleans after the Baron's death I sought in every way I could to repay the favor.

After a long, arduous journey by flatboat—you have heard me tell the story of that adventure—we reached St. Martinville, Le Petit Paris [little Paris], as it was called in those few years when it was filled with French nobility. There we received intelligence that it would be several weeks before Baron de la Fontaine returned from Abbéville and sites on Vermilion Bayou where he had gone to purchase plantations. We took lodging at Morphy's Inn, the Irish owners of which spoke perfect French. Having no children of their own and apprised of our recent ordeal, they soon became attached to Robert and proposed to adopt him. My mother was only too glad to oblige them and thus shed responsibility for him. We were not entirely at our ease amongst the native Acadians whose odd French at first offended our ears and whose rural customs we found crude. Nevertheless, their hospitality was genuine and in time we grew accustomed to their manners and speech.

Eventually Baron de la Fontaine returned and upon learning of our arrival, handsomely compensated the Morphys for their hospitality and removed us forthwith to his estate. I was saddened to live apart from Robert, but we consoled ourselves knowing that we should see each other nearly every day. Little was I to know that at that very moment our lives had taken different pathways and that in time we would come to look on each other disapprovingly.

There Cécile and I grew to girlhood under the Baron's solicitous tutelage and poor Tante Celeste received every possible attention and kindness. Her wounds healed though she always walked with a limp. The Baron's wife Madame Hélène, a sickly French woman, pined away for her homeland in what she called *ce pays sauvage et désolé* (this savage and desolate country). The Baron, long since wearied of her whimperings, soon developed a convenient relationship with my mother that lasted until her sudden demise—I have told you of my suspicions about poisons and what really happened to her. Now in young womanhood and already a mother—foster mother, that is—to Henri (for when Cécile saw his coloring and African features she would not care for him), I took my mother's place with the lonely Baron, who even spoke to me of marriage should he be so fortunate as to be some day shed of his carping wife. In truth, however, that proposal little appealed to me, for although I consorted willingly with him for material convenience (though I was very careful about my food), the thought of wedlock with a man now declining into senility was secretly repugnant to me. Besides, the young French cavaliers soon taught me too much of love and life to play nursemaid to an impotent old man.

It was then I met and, over Robert's prudish objections, gave my affections to Pierre's father, Joseph Prospère, a French adventurer who often practiced his English by reminiscing with the Morphys about Ireland, where he had spent some years in exile. Later he had fought, or so he claimed, in the young Napoleon's armies but found it convenient to flee to America for having killed an officer in a duel. Once in St. Martinville, he repudiated his revolutionary allegiance and entered the service of the exiled royalist Count Vincent Duvergier. I was careful to conceal my relationship with Joseph from the old baron, whose jealousy increased as his manly powers declined. Discovering myself with child again—I had miscarried before—I naturally convinced the Baron de la Fontaine that he was the father—a thing that if true would have rivaled an immaculate conception. Persuaded of his all but posthumous paternity, so vulnerable he proved to be to my schemes that he promised to settle on Pierre a considerable estate and perhaps even to recognize him as his son.

But, alas, my plans came to naught. So attached was the Baron's wife to her beloved illnesses that she outlived her husband. Upon his death, she and her two sons commenced to turn the community against us and to wreak their vengeance in many insidious ways. By now many of the French nobility were returning to France. At length finding ourselves without friends or means of livelihood in St. Martinville, Cécile, Tante Celeste, the children, and I were obliged to flee in disgrace to New Orleans where Joseph soon joined us. We bade a cool adieu to Robert, now changed in demeanor and speech into a devoutly Catholic Irishman who, embarrassed by our reputation and presence, joined the sanctimonious hypocrites opposed to our behavior.

Poor Tante Celeste did not long survive the move. She sank ever deeper into a childish idiocy from which only you, Pierre, could sometimes yet rouse her. Then she would stroke your hair and whisper "Antoine, Antoine" to you. But then she would peer at your dark hair, shake her head, and declare: "*Mais tu n'es pas mon Antoine. Où est mon petit? Ah, mon Dieu, où l'a-t-on caché?*" (But you are not my Antoine. Where is my little one? Oh my God, where have they hidden him?). Then in complete lunacy she would limp about the house for hours searching for her dead child. One night she died in her sleep. We found her the next morning her pale features frozen in a smiling death mask.

My disappointment in the outcome of events in St. Martinville was overshadowed by several other evil turns of my fate in New Orleans. My love for Joseph—the love of my life—was as deep as his affections proved to be shallow. For instead of a life together as he promised me in St. Martinville, he arrived in New Orleans with no other purpose than to betray my trust and abandon me, adding the theft of my money to the greater larcenies he committed. Not long afterwards, Tante Celeste died, a great bother and expense to me, followed by the scandal and inconvenience Cécile provoked when she ran away to Marseilles with that French scum, leaving me loutish Henri to care for. To add to my woes I discovered myself with another child and in the midst of miseries gave birth to Monique, Joseph's last legacy. Since then I have lived as I must, fairly detesting all men, and before any man or woman pass moral judgment on me, let them, if they can, walk the world in my shoes and live to tell the tale.

And on this defiant note her story, though frequently amended, always ended.

* * *

I am led to speculate, dear reader, how but for two reasons my life might still have taken a better turn. First, I had experienced too much of the lawless freedom of the streets to submit overlong to any discipline. Second, not many months later I learned that the Church had transferred Father Branigan to a seminary near St. Louis in Missouri. His successor, Father LaJeunesse, loved New Orleans society with a fervor equaled only by his distaste for the urchins Father Branigan had recruited for his school. We were disbanded in short order, much to the sorrow of most, but to my entire glee and my mother's evident relief. I was chafing mightily under the stern discipline and eager attentions Father Branigan imposed on me as his star pupil, and my mother, still beautiful but ever more shrewish and having long since repented of her good intentions, was rid of the burdensome resolution to improve my chances in the world. Thus at twelve I returned entirely to the streets, rendered no more pious by Father Branigan's tutelage but enhanced instead in mischief and cunning by my education.

Unlike me, my half-brother—or perhaps cousin—Henry, or Henri Étienne as my mother called him in her frequent moments of pique, could not hope to conceal his mulatto ancestry, and as we grew up and apart because of it, he came to loathe me, and I, to detest him. Now almost nineteen, he was taller and much stronger than I. Our disputes grew in intensity, and Henri, unable to match my glib tongue, from which volubly rolled every curse, calumny, slur, and insult in several languages known to New Orleans in those far-off days, took revenge for my verbal abuse with fisticuffs. So severe were the beatings and so great waxed Henri's hatred that I came to fear for my very life. I appealed to my mother as the thrashings became more brutal, but she, concerned only with her performances, dalliances, and survival, took little heed of our disputes, nor offered any recourse for their resolution. Denied justice in that quarter, in desperation I contrived a scheme to rid myself of Henri

29

in another manner.

In the days immediately preceding my eighteenth birthday I gained intelligence—for the news quickly spread through the Quarter—of a deputized posse from New Iberia in New Orleans to recapture slaves escaped from the sugar and indigo plantations upon the Bayou Teche. Moreover, I also knew—in ways better left unsaid—that not many days agone one of the runaways, a stripling of Henri's age and general appearance, had been foully murdered and, as was the practice of the time, his body dropped by night in the Mississippi River to sink or float away in the darkness. Although I assure you, gentle reader, that I had nothing to do with his demise, through my accustomed gaming chicanery I became the possessor of the slave's coat, a gorgeous garment overly large for my bony body, to be sure, but nevertheless excellent protection against the cold December airs of 1831. No sooner had Henri eyed the coat than he took it despite my abundant curses for the damnation of his soul and frantic struggles to keep it from his clutches. For my efforts he inflicted on me yet another beating that left me bruised and swollen.

With these facts and a plan forming in my mind, I made inquiries, and having gathered the necessary information, presented myself to the posse leader, Downes by surname, a fierce, squint-eyed, black-bearded individual, of Irish extraction to judge by his manner of speaking, who glowered down at me from what seemed from my inferior perspective to be a giant's stature.

"What botheration do ye bring to me, lad? Eh? Speak up, for I be a man with much business to attend." I recollect to this day his black-stained teeth and the gagging reek of tobacco, alcohol, and garlic as he cupped my face with his hand and leaned down to stare into my eyes.

"Sir, I know where you may find one of the runaway slaves," I gasped.

"Do ye now?" he grunted skeptically, splattering my exposed toes with a long, dripping jet of brown tobacco juice. "And why would ye be bringing me that news? Have a care that ye words be truth, for lies will bring on a caning iv ye scrawny arse sich as never ye had in all ye born days!"

"Oh, no sir, I shall say nothing short of truth and I mean no inconvenience to your person or mischief to your business," I replied, my liver turning to water as he clamped a huge hand about my throat.

"Ay, now, tis well-spoken ye are, though the accent falls strange on the ear," and his dark eyes widened in surprise as he examined me more closely. "Ye wear not the clothes iv a gentleman's son, and I spy yon toes peering from ye sorrowful shoes, yet ye speech be not that iv the Quarter riffraff. Whose son might ye be? Who sent you by and what be ye game with me?"

"Sir, O'Malley is my surname, and Owen my given," I lied out of habit but also in hopes by this ruse to appeal to his Irish sentiments. (Nor was it an entire lie, for O'Malley was—so my mother betimes claimed—her grandmother's surname. Owen was one of the several aliases I used for sundry deceits.) "And as for my late father, of the Black Irish, says my mother, he departed this present world before I had knowledge of him." (It was not an entire lie, for had he not fled to Texas-Coahuila, said to be hotter and drearier than hell itself?) "I live with my mother, a gentle lady whose means are few. We are a poor but decent family whose trust is in the Holy Trinity, the Holy Mother, and the true Church. That is what my mother says to one and all of our life and circumstances."

His countenance softened and he removed his hairy paw from my neck and stood erect. "Ay, now, and we have a lad iv Irish lineage, do we? Well spoken ye pious mother be, too, if ye words match the conditions iv life sich as ye have said. But tell me, darling lad, what knowledge do ye claim iv the accursed runaway?"

"As I said, good sir, we are poor and your help in exchange for the information I bring would be of great comfort in our lamentable destitution."

A flash of anger twisted his features and for a moment I feared the worst. "I've a mind to wring ye bony neck as 'twere a chicken's, Owen O'Malley, fer ye insolence. I am the law and enforce it as I plazes, and all citizens must heed me and assist me in my labors."

He glared down at me and then of a sudden his face wrinkled in an ugly resemblance of a smile and he proffered a coin.

"But since ye be poor and Irish and Catholic—for are these not one and the same fer our sorely oppressed race—this Spanish dollar is fer ye mother's needs, lad, if ye will but inform me as ye make claim."

"Could you make it two dollars, good sir? Our kitchen and cupboard are bare as dust and our stomachs empty, and last night we slept hungry." (It was not an entire lie, for my mother had expelled us without morsel into the streets when her present gentleman came in for the night.)

"One ye shall have now, and another upon retrieval iv the runaway buck, and if ye be not forthcoming and truthful as behooves you, I promise ye arse shall be forfeit and in a month ye shall not sit fer the soreness iv it."

Whereupon I described Henri's general appearance to Downes, detailing in particular the handsome coat which Henri wore everywhere with high pride made sweeter because he had bested me for it.

"Ay, tis true," nodded Downes, "the garment is known to us, stolen as 'twas reported from the Arceneaux plantation. And that with foulest effrontery, for the runaway ruffian removed it forcibly from the young Master Jacques Arceneaux. And there was further mischief: the rascal took certain coinage too from the lad. Know ye aught iv this second outrage?"

"Regretably nothing, sir."

Downes shook his massive head and let fly another stream of tobacco juice that speckled my toes.

"Tis no matter in that regard, lad. If ye can but direct me to the whereabouts iv the culprit, ye shall indeed receive the second dollar."

"In the evening he will appear here."

"Have a care, boy, that you pull on me no conniving trick. By what miracle can ye lade him to me? My business is earnest and my patience short with them what takes a notion to play me fer an ass!"

"Trust me, sir, and you shall see the truth of it."

At home in our quarters—two unheated rooms above Sojourner's Inn on Chartres Street—I found the remnants of a thin cold soup and a half loaf of bread left over from the dinner my mother had shared the evening before with her gentleman. Monique, shivering and thin to the edge of starvation, struggled with me for a share. I fingered the dollar hidden deep in my pocket and its very touch gave me fortifying comfort. Henri entered as Monique was licking the dish for the last morsel. Without a word he snatched the bread from me and shoved us both away from the table. As Henri muttered about our paternity and general worthlessness, I slipped the dollar from my pocket and commenced to flip it. On the second try, Henri suddenly extended his hand and caught it.

"Henri, it's mine! Give it back!" I screamed with feigned outrage.

"Think you to oblige me, spineless bastard that you are?" he grinned smugly as he pocketed the coin.

I cursed and fumed for a few minutes while Henri smirked at me as he chewed calmly on the remaining bread. Then I changed my tactic: *"De toute façon, j'aurai plus d'argent dès ce soir, parce qu'on en me doit encore,"* I said to him in our customary French, *et bien sûr ça ne sera pas pour tes sales mains nègres!* (Anyway, I shall have more money this evening, for they still owe me and for sure you won't get your dirty Negro hands on it!).

Henri reacted violently as I feared but expected, grabbing me by the neck and forcing me to the floor with his knee in my stomach. Monique screamed hysterically and ran to find Mother, out in all her finery for her usual afternoon stroll in the Quarter.

"Tell me now where and how much, cochon, or I'll break your arm off in the socket!"

Henri twisted my arm until I was nearly mad with pain. Finally, when I reckoned I had screamed and resisted long enough to satisfy his suspicious mind, I relented.

"Henri, please, please don't torture me any more! I'll tell you, I'll tell you! Just don't break my arm, please!" Henri, pleased by my groveling, relaxed the pressure on my arm but kept his knee buried in my stomach to maintain his control over me.

"Where, then, imbecile? You better tell me now or next time I won't be so gentle with you!"

I lied to Henri that in recent days I had run errands and performed other services for a merchant residing temporarily in the Quarter and departing the city on the morrow. Having completed my assigned duties, I was owed the remainder of my earnings—four Spanish dollars—promised for that evening.

"I'll go with you to collect it. Understand?"

"But the money is mine. I earned it by my honest labor!"

Henri began anew to twist my arm. "Honest, merde! If true, it would be the first time in your worthless life to do real work or earn honest money. Lying and stealing, that's all you're good for!"

I was in no position to debate Henri's summary assessment of my character, and after another twist or two and with whimpering submission led him to Downes's quarters.

As we entered I pointed an accusing finger at Henry and announced to Downes: "Sir, this is the runaway! See the coat?"

A grand commotion ensued. Too late Henri realized the trap I had laid for him and screamed out profane protestations of his innocence, to which Downes responded with thunderous profanity and thudding blows with his enormous fists. I thought it wiser to retire to the street until the matter was settled. Soon two deputies emerged with Henri in tow, bound, bloodied, and minus his coat. I could not resist a chance to smirk at him on my way to collect my wages. But as they dragged him away, cursing and struggling mightily to deliver me one last kick of rage, I must confess it now after all these years that I felt a mild, momentary pang of regret. But this unaccustomed sentiment left me after a fleeting reflection on my condition. Justice, after all, I told myself, is what is being served tonight. And with that moral certitude I straightened my back and marched in for my money.

"Money?" growled Downes, "money ye say," still heaving from the exertion. "The buck names you as his brither and, more, sirrah, the master planner iv a deception to ensnare him. Come here, boy, and let me see you in better light. Be ye iv the nigger brood, too, as he claims, and as he says 'tis common knowledge hereabouts?"

I turned to flee but Downes clasped my arm with cruel pressure and put his ugly face next to mine, nearly overcoming my already reeling senses with the stench of tobacco, whiskey, and garlic.

"Oh no, sir! I do not know the ruffian except by his reputation as a liar and thief, for such has he been all his life!"

"All his life, ye say? And did ye not say that he be the runaway we seek? How be it, then, that ye know the fellow so long and well, if ye be not kith and kin to him? Answer me that, laddie!"

At that instant I felt the bitter truth of the saying:

Beware the trap that thou wouldst set,
Lest thou be snared in thine own net.

"Sir," I cried in terror, "you can plainly see that I have no trace of the African in me! My family is Irish and Catholic, as surely as yours must be. When I spoke in such terms, I supposed that the ruffian he is today speaks as the scoundrel he always was! This I meant and nothing more!"

"Tis true," mused Downes, ignoring my words, "that ye mortal appearance lends strength to ye claim, yet the hair be tightly curled and the skin a trifle sallow, the which, I deem, may mark the whelp iv a high yaller slut and kin to yon black. And I doubt not that there be truth in the suspicion, for he who denies all, confesses all." Then with an evil smile, he added, "Tis of no matter to me in either case. One slave will serve for another. As for you, one so silver-tongued and fine-featured will fetch me a fair price as a houseboy. Otherwise, ye be too frail iv body fer hard field work."

As well you may suppose, dear reader, I fell into terrified despair regarding my fate. My hope for revenge and financial betterment had turned into a most ominous prospect of total ruin. My mother and her ancestry were known in the Quarter, and my own career, though short in years, was generously peppered with cases of thievery and delinquency, the which earned me notoriety, though I assure you, gentle reader, these accounts were greatly exaggerated against my person and true character.

Howbeit, I do also confess that bluster and braggadocio were habits too deeply etched in my character to deny their expression in moments of crisis.

"You, sir, can bring no creditable reproach against me or my family," I protested. "The lout you have just arrested is, as you yourself know best, a thief and a rogue slave. Surely you cannot believe his lying words!"

Indifferent to my howls, Downes ordered me hand-bound and locked in the same chamber with Henri and seven Negroes dazed and bloodied by the beatings they had received. It was the dreariest sight imaginable. One of them, a woman with blood-soaked hair, moaned and swayed in pain and semi-consciousness throughout the night, whilst the men intoned intermittently in a low mournful wail filled with what I supposed were ancient African words, for I understood them not. At first Henri envenomed the air with threats on my life and curses on my soul, but bound hand and foot as he was, I no more acknowledged him than a street cur heeds the yapping of a house poodle. Eventually he fell silent. My mind labored to find an escape from my predicament, but as the hours passed and I conceived no prospect worthy of consideration or possible of execution, fatigue and despair stole over me and I dropped into a nightmarish sleep.

This fitful slumber was disturbed at three or four in the morning by the tramp of heavy boots. The door was thrown open and Downes strode into the room to kick us into alertness.

"Wake up, ye black dogs! The cages on yon carriages arc rcadicd to haul ye worthless carcasses away to fitting punishment and toil in the cane and indigo fields!"

Henri glared at me in silence, having exhausted his litany of curses and insults and knowing that further protests were useless in the present plight. Freed of their leg irons, the blacks rose, sullen and expressionless of countenance. Two of them helped to steady the moaning woman, but I pleaded for clemency.

"Oh, please, kind sir, release me! Plainly you can see I am no kin to these darkies. Let me go, for I am the only support for my dear, desperate mother, Mistress Nicole O'Malley." (It was not an entire lie, for indeed her name was Nicole and variously she gave as her surname Montes, Tourmoulin, Prospère, or indeed sometimes O'Malley also, depending on her mood and fickle memories of former paramours or family branches.)

"Waste no breath in further lies, whelp," Downes responded with a stretch and an enormous yawn. "I know now iv ye whorish mother and true parentage, not that it matters to me whose mulatto pup ye be. But fer ye disrespect of the law ye are arrested and soon shall fetch me a handsome price and live the rest iv ye mortal days a fancy-laced houseboy in some mansion yonder upon the Teche. Yet be not downcast in gloom, laddie, for tis not a better life I send you to than ever ye've known in this hard town? Here now, ye shall walk unbound so as to attend me as me porter." With that he untied my hands and handed me a heavy leather case filled with his smelly garments and vile personal effects.

Having recovered freedom of my limbs, I now dared with renewed hope to think on the greater freedom of my person. At first no chance seemed possible. Then as our sullen, manacled parade wended its way towards the waiting carriages, luck smiled and gave me an unexpected but welcome opportunity.

Three drunken Americans lurched out of a tavern with a painted trollop and, discordantly singing a foul ditty, staggered towards us. Downes and his men were not of a mind to cede the narrow wooden sidewalk, and the Americans, with the contempt of their race for the mixed citizenry of New Orleans, refused to step aside courteously into the muddy street. Insults were exchanged and shoving followed that soon turned to blows. One of the Americans pummeled Downes headlong into the muddy slime as his men clubbed down the drunken trio. The tart ran away cursing one and all.

I hurled the leather case in the mud and rushed in as though to help my stunned tormentor but in reality with designs on his watch and purse, which I lifted in deft, practiced style. Henri perceived my intent and lunged, manacles and all, to block my way. But one of the guards staggered him with a sharp rap on the head. By now Downes had cleared his senses and looked about to take stock of his person and possessions, but I had already taken flight down a narrow alleyway and into the avenue parallel to the wharves. I heard his bellowing and the splashing thud of heavy boots as the guards pursued me, which lent speed to my panicky career through the dark, silent streets.

Dawn was close, my hands and feet were numbed by cold, and my stomach was aching with hunger, but Downes's purse and gold watch felt substantial in my trouser pocket. Most glorious of all, I was free even as I imagined Henri and the runaways being carted away in chains. Yet the sweetness of vengeance did not wholly subdue my misgivings and I confess, dear reader, that I experienced a moment of contrition for Henri. But again I rallied against my stirring conscience by reasoning that it was justice that he be so punished for his wickedness towards me. So thinking, I straightened my back, screwed up my paltry courage,

36

climbed down from the roof where I had lain hidden and made my way towards my mother's residence.

The euphoria over my regained freedom and the expeditious way I had rid myself of Henri had all too brief a life. It was already being gossiped about the Quarter that Downes had placed a substantial bounty on my head for theft and resistance to his authority. Furthermore, Henri's mulatto friends in the back alleys of the Quarter took his capture as an affront and, already suspecting me, spread word that they would exact vengeance on his account.

To complicate these perilous matters even more, the very night of my ordeal, I soon learned that in a cursing, screaming confrontation that scandalized Sojourner's Tavern and roused the entire Quarter, my mother dismissed her erstwhile paramour so as to bestow her favors on a gentleman of much greater consequence and wealth. The financial advantages for her were exhilarating, including the conveniences of a promised new residence and wardrobe that she could lord over her envious rivals in the Quarter. The spurned paramour swore vengeance, but my mother dismissed his threat with a sneer and contemptuous wave of her hand.

Yet her new lover imposed a condition forthwith. My presence and reputation compromised the gentleman's delicate situation, and though he would tolerate Monique for the present, me he would not. Mother hastened to comply with his wishes, for as I made clear to you, dear reader, we offspring were impediments and a displeasurable reminder of her fading youth. Thus she instructed me to remain hidden at my rooftop location whilst arrangements were made for my removal and safety. When all was in readiness, Monique would bring me word.

Under the circumstances, Henri's disappearance was opportune, even though my mother lamented briefly so as not to appear heartless in the matter. And although she heard the rumors and had no doubt that I was implicated the matter, an accusation which, naturally, I indignantly denied, the truth was that by his very age and appearance Henri was an even greater embarrassment to her than Monique and I, for above all he was an unpleasant stigma of her family's humble mixed origins which she had repudiated, denied, and, in her cavalier manner, otherwise forgotten.

Monique and I were nearly as troubling to her, for we were annoying reminders of the only man she had been unable to dominate and discard. It was said that my purported father was the only one of her many lovers who used her cruelly and remained indifferent to her fabled charms. And the more he ignored her, the more she loved him in vain.

Thus when her new love issued his ultimatum she was visibly relieved to have a pretext for ridding herself of me as well.

I am tempted to lie to you, dear reader, by saying that her indifference, nay, her eagerness, for my departure wounded me deeply. But like filial bonds in the animal realm that vanish after a season, my natural affections for her soon dwindled, whilst her motherly care diminished in a similar manner. Thus seeing how we were indifferently circumstanced with each other, I fancy she no more mourned or remembered our separation than a wild bird thinks of her departed hatchlings of yesteryear.

Fearful of arrest by Downes, skeptical of my mother's help, and apprehensive of vengeful brutalities by Henry's friends, I descended from my hiding place in hopes of securing aid from my cronies. Sweet Julie was nowhere to be found, and even the hitherto loyal "Pouches" Ducoeur, scorned my pleas.

"*Je m'en fous! Laisse-moi! Va t'en!* (F--k you! Leave me alone! Go away!)," the moon-faced Pouches yelled as he spat and ran away, his filthy threadbare shirt flapping in the wind.

Roundly I cursed his ancestry as he treacherously left me to my fate, yet knowing that I should have treated him in the same manner in similar straits. Unable to find a helping hand, I scurried in panic back to my rooftop hideout, there to cower the rest of the day and all that night, pelted by rain and bereft of human comfort. On the afternoon of the next day—by happenstance my eighteenth birthday—Monique appeared with precious food and instructions to proceed that evening under cover of darkness to the corner of St. Louis and Chartres where a carriage would be waiting to transport me to safety.

I did as bidden and at the appointed hour and location identified myself to the driver of the waiting coach. Exhausted by my ordeal, no sooner did the coach begin to sway and creak on its journey than I fell soundly asleep. Not many hours thence I awoke to find myself sequestered several leagues from the city on a lonely cattle farm belong-ing to my mother's gentleman.

In this manner I escaped the city without further hazard or incident. Barely a month passed ere it was decided that I should depart for Memphis bearing a letter by my mother's new gentleman that would introduce me as apprentice to an undertaker in that city, a man by the name of Pollard. And I, weary of the ennui of rural existence and fearful of arrest or assault in the Quarter, welcomed the prospect.

I cannot deny, however, that I departed New Orleans with conflicting sentiments. In a furtive nocturnal parting my mother bade me adieu with only the briefest of embraces and facile wishes for my health and success in the world, whilst Monique regarded my leaving with tears and what I took to be genuine regret. Despite our differences and disputes, heretofore I had offered her a modicum of inconstant protection against the worst abuses. Now, at fourteen she thought herself past the greatest dangers when in reality she was just coming into the gravest perils. For even though thin to the point of emaciation, Monique was already commencing to exhibit a precocious womanly beauty, a prospect that aroused a jealous uneasiness in my mother.

I dared not board the riverboat in New Orleans lest watchful authorities seize me and turn me over to the vengeful Downes. Instead I determined to bend my steps along the River Road upstream towards Baton Rouge where, I hoped, their vigilance might not reach. Accordingly, I set out apprehensively some hours before the next dawn, carrying only a dry loaf and a few sausages, which Monique prepared for my nourishment on the road. I hoped to progress well beyond the city by first light and I hastened my steps to this end. I confess to feeling a few pangs of sentimentality as I set out. But no sooner did the city disappear from sight than melancholy vanished from my mind. Residing reassuringly in the front pocket of my trousers and unbeknownst to all were the fifty dollars lifted from Downes, whilst in an inner pocket of my greatcoat his erstwhile watch ticked away the hours until I should arrive at fair Memphis and the sweet future life that Providence—perhaps to atone for its past indifferences—surely had in store for me there.

Translator's Addendum

The highlighted item dated December 2, 1831, from the English-language The Gazette (New Orleans) was found inserted with others in the manuscript. Since the author himself makes no reference to it, I must assume that it was included after completion of the writing, perhaps without his knowledge. I include it for the different light it sheds on the events described by the narrator:

Items

Frédéric Duvosges, 49, a respected citizen of New Orleans, was kicked by a horse and killed last Saturday. He leaves a disconsolate widow and three grieving children to mourn his passing.

We regret to report that Mr. Guillaume Bourgeois fell from the roof of his house, breaking his arm, dislocating a finger, and otherwise hurting himself.

Pierre Lapin waylaid and shot his neighbor René Dumenier in the head one day last week. It is said they fell out over Dumenier's wife. Dumenier will die and Lapin and the woman have departed.

Miss Lilly Callahan, a young lady of respectable social standing in New Orleans, while crossing Bourbon Street, Monday ult., seeing Jacques Noyes at a distance, called out to him, drew a pistol from her purse, and shot him, the ball striking him in the lower extremities. She fired again without harmful effect, then surrendered her emptied weapon to constables. Noyes, she explained, ruined her under a false promise of matrimony.

A vigilant search is underway for the whereabouts of one Pierre Prospère. Known locally under the appellation Peter Prosper, 18 or 19 years of age according to police records, Prosper is a notorious wastrel, gambler, pickpocket, and known associate of the late Alain "Sixdoigts" DuClos of unhappy memory amongst the honest merchants and innocent citizens of this fair city. Prosper is featured as thin of torso and of medium stature with curly black hair. Dark of complexion and sharp of features, he often pretends by language and manner to be French or Spanish so as to draw attention away from his mulatto ancestry. He bears a two-inch scar on his left wrist and forearm and may effect a slight limp on his right leg, the just consequence of a fall suffered in the brazen execution of a felony. Jailed, fined, and punished several times for his offenses, Prosper, still young in age yet hardened in criminality, was, until his disappearance, the reported leader of the Petrie band of delinquents whose former leader Justin Petrie was murdered, a case that yet remains unsolved. It has been rumored, however, that Prosper himself is a suspected accomplice in the murder. This Saturday ult., Prosper, under arrest for interference in the proper duties of a law officer, escaped custody subsequent to assaulting and robbing chief deputy Ignatius Downes. A reward of $250 is declared to any citizen forthcoming with information leading to the capture of this notorious and habitual offender of public order, and all citizens are asked to aid law enforcement officials to this end.

Part II: How Peter fled to Memphis and fell among thieves; how he became an apprentice undertaker and barber; how he fell in love and heard the winsome tale of the marriage broker; how he was discovered and after the episode of the Spanish rain, how he took flight towards St. Louis in an unusual conveyance

Aside from my astonishment upon seeing the magnificent estates and plantations situated majestically along the River Road, my three-day journey to Baton Rouge was without incident worthy of detailed recounting. Once well beyond view of New Orleans, I donated the remnants of Monique's poor fare to a wretch I met on the road. Thereafter at Downes' unwilling expense I enjoyed the best board, food, and carriage transportation his money could procure. Upon arriving rested and nourished in Baton Rouge and having made the proper inquiries concerning river transportation to Memphis, I warily boarded a paddlewheel steamer, "The Memphis Lily," along with a score of other passengers whilst slaves trundled aboard deck six bales of furs, forty sacks of potatoes, several dozen sacks of flour, and various commodities and cypress lumber. Two days later, after a long stop at Natchez to take on more goods and four additional passengers bound for St. Louis, The Memphis Lily docked at its namesake early on a Saturday afternoon in late January of 1832 and thence continued upstream to St. Louis.

To seasoned river travelers the journey was doubtless uneventful, but to my novice eyes everything was new and strange and the deckmaster warned me more than once about leaning too far over the railing. I shall not forget the roiling, muddy currents and thick morning fogs, nor less the drowned animals, plants, and even uprooted trees that floated past our vessel. Occasionally southbound boats hailed us with their mournful horns. North of Natchez we steamed past lordly manors rising splendidly in sculpted, forested estates and oceans of cotton fields now winterbare and brown. A day and a half upstream as we neared the turbulent mouth of the Arkansas River, the captain pointed to a dozen mounted savages silently eyeing us from the forested west bank. Whereupon, much to the captain's displeasure but to the great hilarity and amusement of the other passengers, a portly, red-bearded gentleman by the name of Colonel Summerford pulled his pistol and fired a shot in their direction. Reacting with frightened yelps, the Indians wheeled their Spanish ponies and raced back into the dark forest.

Erected near the remains of earlier French and Spanish forts, Memphis, very unlike the settled refinements of New Orleans, offended my sensitivities and quickly dispelled the beautiful fantasies of the city conjured in my imagination in the days preceding my arrival. The snap of whips on animal rumps, the snarl of cursing drivers, splashing horsemen and muddy wagons churning the foul quagmire of the streets, pungent odors of hides, timber, gunpowder, tobacco, whiskey, offal, unwashed bodies, mangy hounds, squawking chickens, unruly children, and smoke from loathsome American cooking, such were the unpleasant sensory impressions of my first full encounter with the unbelievable energy and profound affinity for ugliness of the Anglo-Saxon race in its natural state.

I did not hie myself immediately to Mr. Pollard's mortuary/ barbershop (for he combined the two enterprises) but instead, eager to enjoy the delayed fruits of my remaining fifty stolen Spanish dollars, asked my way to an emporium with the intention of outfitting myself in an estimable wardrobe.

On second thought, dear reader, allow me to be more forthright with you and reveal my real intentions. The truth is I had made up my mind not to seek out Pollard at all. The more I thought about keeping close and continual company with the dead, the drearier that prospect appeared to me. With an uncommonly large sum of money already residing in my trousers and possessed of the skills I had mastered for acquiring more, it seemed unworthy for one so enterprising as Peter Prosper to pursue the unappealing livelihood of a mere undertaker. For as I surveyed Memphis and its vulgar, gullible populace, it seemed ripe for multiple and profitable swindles. And one must turn one's talents, or so I reasoned, to the pursuits for which Providence has intended them. Thus resolute in my philosophy, I bent my steps towards an emporium intending there to furbish my person with clothing suitable for a calling worthy of my elevated condition.

The clerk, a stooped, bald, and bleary-eyed dotard—a *vieillard* as we would call him disrespectfully in my French tongue—regarded my youth and general aspect with obvious suspicion and asked to see first my money. I produced ten of Downes's Spanish dollars accompanied by a tale that would convince the most skeptical of men of my highborn integrity and the legitimate provenance of my cash money. The old man hesitated, perplexed, as I reckon now, by my manner of speech, then shook his head in tired resignation and commenced to display the clothes before me on the countertop.

Subsequent to a close inspection of the available merchandise, I chose striped green and black trousers, spats, and coat, a trifle large for my frame, to be sure, but in expectation of abundant food and expanded girth. To these items I added the emporium's finest silk shirt and matching crimson cravat, red suspenders, leather gloves, new under-drawers, handkerchiefs with flowery crescents, the best top hat in stock, woolen hose, and, lastly, a pair of finely sewn leathern boots, also a bit large for my bony feet. I considered a walking cane for myself but then decided that my years were yet tender for its use.

Having been denied permission by the dour idiot of a clerk to change my attire on the premises, I hurried from the emporium, fearful of his suspicions, and ere long found a thick copse of trees overlooking the Mississippi River. There I furtively and quickly changed my garments, shivering in the frigid air, and, abandoning my old clothes as I thought to shed my former life, emerged from the wood transformed in attitude and aspect into the vainest young coxcomb ever to prance the streets of Memphis.

I now imagined all eyes to be trained upon me, admiring my new splendor as I walked in proud erectness through the motley town center, eyeing one and all with the natural hauteur of the rich young scion I now grandly imagined myself to be. Now and then I would extract from my pocket a handful of lovely coins, fingering them as if mulling some important purchase. And every fifty paces or so, I would remove Downes' gold watch from its fob pocket and ponder the hour with the seriousness of one engaged in the urgent business of the rich.

Nor was I entirely deluded in my musings. For not a few eyes turned in my direction. I shall not forget the sweet stare and dulcet smile of a blonde young lady of no more years than mine accompanied by her black nanny who tugged at her sleeve and scolded her for her improper distraction. Encouraged by her attention, I turned to follow them at a discreet distance.

But others of less attractive mien were also watching me, awaiting the opportunity to acknowledge my opulence in a more sinister manner. Having traversed the town square, I saw the girl and her nanny turn down a darkened side street. Night was falling, and I did not like the look of the surroundings in which my impulse had placed me, and as yet I had no lodging. Yet curiosity to find her residence led me on.

My apprehensions were soon justified. For no sooner had I advanced fifty or so paces along the darkened street than I was set upon by four burly ruffians whose strength and numbers rendered useless all opposition to their fell aims. And although I struggled as best I could, the while screaming curses at them, straightway the thieves stripped me of my money, watch, boots, hat, letter, and fine attire and left me barefoot, reduced to my underdrawers, bruised by their manhandling, and numb with cold. (Forgive me, dear reader, the indelicacy of my description.)

I got to my feet, mortified by my loss and shameful state and uncertain of my next act. At that moment a constable arrived, having been hailed by a citizen who witnessed the assault but could not describe my assailants who had fled into the night. The constable, a Mr. Bascom Harvey by name, secured a blanket for me, and I accompanied him (with a natural fear of authority I tried to conceal) to the office of the local constabulary. How differently, how piteously, the populace now eyed me! And how brief my proud strut! I was put in mind of Father Branigan's favorite Latin expression:

> *Sic transit gloria mundi* (Thus doth the glory of the world pass away)

But once inside the station and warmed by the fire and a substantial broth, I soon recovered my customary bluster and rhetorical powers and painted a picture of my circumstances and the aggression against me entirely to my advantage and favor. Finally, however, when Mr. Harvey relentlessly pressed me as to my origins and business in Memphis, my fabrications were stripped away and I had no choice but to tell him that I was come in apprenticeship to Mr. Lucas Pollard.

Luckily for me, the good constable remained ignorant of my cash purchases in the emporium, and I was spared the embarrassing explanations that intelligence of them would have necessitated. When an offer was made to furnish me footwear and clothing and to escort me to Mr. Pollard's residence where my unhappy circumstances would be explained, I acquiesced to the favor, and with heroic resignation accepted my rendezvous with the dead.

The clothing and shoes were altogether an abomination, no doubt stripped from some incarcerated or deceased wretch. The trousers, several measures too large, were patched and tattered in several junctures, whilst the boots afforded only the feeblest buffer against the frigid January air. My abandoned garments were far better, but at the moment to retrieve them would be to place myself under unwelcome suspicion. (Nor in truth did I ever see them again, for several days later when finally I had a chance to rescue them, they were gone, surely discovered and appropriated by one of the starveling tramps who lived in those woods.)

Thus I arrived at my undesired destination minus my rich purse and watch, and more miserably clad than when I departed New Orleans.

No doubt a moralist would draw his own lessons from my experience, but, if you will pardon the indelicate phrasing, hitherto morality had never filled my belly. I was concerned only with my material and physical state, the which I promised myself would soon rebound to my favor.

Convinced by the constable's account and thus untroubled that I arrived in Memphis without an introductory letter, Pollard admitted me without protest. He turned out to be nothing like my foreimage of him, displaying none of the winsome aspects of character ascribed to him by my mother's new gentleman. Instead of kindness, he showed asperity; rather than generosity, he revealed only avarice; and his abiding disposition was a shifting, treacherous miasma of cunning, cruelty, and choler. In physical aspect he was no taller than I, though much stouter of build and ruddy of complexion. I reckoned him to be about forty years old (though all such men seemed ancient to me at that age,) and his graying beard gave no signs of gentlemanly grooming. From these and other traits I correctly foresaw him to be a despotic and disorderly man whose servant and slave I was about to become. For he was generally apprised of my origins and knew of a certainty that black blood—miniscule in volume, I assure you, dear reader—flowed in my veins. I was not sanguine about my prospects.

These, however, promised to turn more in my favor than first I doubted. Pollard needed an accomplice more than a servant. Although he did his best to conceal it, I soon discovered that he was illiterate and could not manage even the simplest ciphers. My hopes mounted as plain evidence of his ignorance grew, for to my eager eye he seemed at first like a witless chicken ready to be pounced on and devoured by a hungry fox.

But he proved to be no easy victim. Though dense of mind, nature appeared to have compensated for his mental dullness with an abundant dose of intuitive cunning. His very inferiority caused him to distrust everyone and to remain as alert to deception as he was deaf to persuasion. Thus if I fancied myself a fox in his hen house, he was as sharp-eyed as an eagle in defense of his possessions. Chance was soon to place us in a distrustful collaboration, but dishonesty and suspicion began at once to corrode that tenuous, treacherous relationship.

Straightway I perceived that the apprenticeship as barber and undertaker, to which, you will recall, I was at first immovably averse, was in reality a fertile ground for my skills and aptitudes. With your leave and patience, dear reader, I shall lead you through the phases of my sojourn there, for by so accompanying me in the unfolding of events, you will understand better than I could otherwise relate my rise in fortune and the causes that eventually brought the episode of my life in Memphis to an end.

Pollard assigned as my quarters a diminutive, windowless, and unheated room attached as though by afterthought to rear of the mortuary, itself situated an irregular block north of the main town square. A frameless straw mattress, frayed, dirty blanket, small table with a single drawer and half-burned candle, and a straight-back hickory chair, on which an earlier inmate had carved the initials TG, constituted its only furnishings. He had installed a formidable padlock on the rear entrance to the room and gave me strict instructions not to tamper with it. Naturally, I ignored his command, and the lock itself was but a trifle to my practiced fingers that had outwitted some of the most cunning devices in New Orleans. In short, I soon had a private entrance that permitted me the freedom to roam the city at my leisure during the night hours when Pollard's snoring resounded from his quarters in the large rooms immediately adjacent to the mortuary in the east wing of the building.

The other door of my room opened to the carpentry shop where Pollard supervised Antoine, his Negro slave, in the manufacture of caskets of pine or cypress lumber hauled up from Mississippi, Louisiana, or the Arkansas territory. Antoine's woman, a slender mulatto nicknamed Poulette, as I supposed, though I never heard her claim any other name, sewed the velvet liners intended for stylish funerals, or for families of humbler means, bare cotton basting. She also served as cleaning woman and cook. Occasionally, when Pollard permitted it, she prepared dishes with piquant condiments and spices that stirred in me poignant memories of New Orleans which were rapidly receding into a past that already seemed far distant. They and their drooling, deaf-mute, and crippled three-year daughter Jeannette occupied a room only slightly larger and less impoverished than mine but situated in the south wing of the haphazard, heatless building and less exposed to the north wind, a fact that aroused some envy on my part on the coldest winter nights.

Yet Antoine and Poulette rather earned my sympathy for their plight than antagonism for their small advantage. Our common subordination to Pollard's fickle will and the punishments he was wont to inflict on us in his frequent rages soon goaded us into an ineffectual conspiratorial alliance against him. Furthermore we discovered that we shared a Creole past and, to our delight, a preference for French, our first and most heartfelt tongue. For a time it afforded us a coded channel through which to conceive and savor our intrigues. But Pollard, ever

48

distrustful, suspected our conspiratorial proclivities and soon forbade the use of French, muttering that it was the "language of the very Devil."

Despite his avaricious and violent nature, Pollard did not hesitate to refurbish my meager wardrobe with respectable clothing, observing that it was not seemly that one so solemnly employed should dress in a manner that impugned the dignity and high standing of the mortuary. I gladly accepted what he provided, though I could not dispel a silent but unfavorable comparison of this somber dress to the lavish and much lamented garments stripped from me by the thieves. And though it was to serve his own purposes and retain his mastery over me, he would say no word about my African ancestry so long as I served him faithfully. Naturally I swore my loyalty in the most profuse manner, though my inner thoughts were already fixed on my eventual freedom and aggrandizement at his expense.

My apprenticeship as an undertaker began a complete reversal of my natural outlook and understanding of life. Under Pollard's perverse tutelage I learned to take delight in mortal ruination. Disease was our ally, and death, our livelihood, he explained, for while others mourned the dead, Pollard was delighted by their demise. For this reason, nothing secretly cheered him more than the welcome news of a child succumbing to pneumonia, a youth dying of appendicitis, a woman perishing in childbirth, or an elderly person agonizing at death's door. Knifings and shootouts among the riffraff of Memphis were highly gratifying, for in addition to fees collected either from the possessions of these wretched delinquents or from the public coffers of the city, he earned the esteem and respect of the good citizens for giving these shiftless ruffians a Christian burial and thus bringing a proper end to their unprofitable lives.

I spoke of his secret cheer with good reason. For in behavior and demeanor he was the demure soul of hypocrisy. As death and profit drew inexorably nearer to convergence, in outward appearance he waxed as solemn as he was inwardly gleeful. With me in tow he visited the sick with punctual assiduity, outwardly to bring Christian solace to the suffering but in reality to estimate the material circumstances and mortality of these unhappy souls. Though illiterate, as I recall saying earlier, yet he kept a most wonderful log filled with a sort of hieroglyphic scribble comprehensible only to himself, in which he noted the probable advent of death, possible fee, and other details that might work to his advantage in the fatal hour.

The picture of circumspection at these fateful moments, he made subtle inquiries touching on the worldly possessions of the agonizing and planted in the minds of those close to the dying the sacred importance of a respectful Christian burial. "The body's the living temple of the soul," he would remind, skillfully improving on memorized Scriptures, "and it's our bounden Christian duty to respect it in gracious last rites jist like God tells us. It's the least we can do, and the most too, for God won't push us too fer or ask us to try what we ain't got the strength or means to do. But neither," he would add in grave, whispered tones, "will He forgive us for anything less. Now them's not my words, they's straight Bible talk, friends."

With soothing, cajoling words Pollard would usher the grieving families of the deceased into a small adjacent chapel and prayer room. This he did under the pretense of easing their distress but in reality so as to determine what useful or valuable items might be concealed on the corpse. At the cemetery Pollard often confiscated what he could before the casket was lowered forever. But if the solicitous family hovered to the very end about their loved one, then that very night, or at the earliest convenient opportunity, he would order Antoine and me to accompany him to the cemetery, there to open the fresh grave so as to strip rings, pendants, bracelets, necklaces, combs, knives, and even gold teeth and clothing from corpses. I blush to say that on several occasions before he could retrieve one item, my more nimble fingers had already placed several others in my possession.

I was not long in discovering that Pollard worked in secret or implicit complicity with Dr. Thurlow Cheatham, the most sought after— and for a time the only—doctor in Memphis. Cheatham, a lean, hawk-nosed man some years older and much taller than Pollard, always wore a black suit, cravat, stovepipe hat, and what once had been an elegant white silk shirt, now stained by innumerable gravies and liquors, and splattered by food and blood. His arms, already abnormally long for a man of the European race, were made to hang even lower by a pronounced spinal curvature that gave a certain vulture-like appearance to his person. He displayed a perpetual grimace that except for his harsh, unblinking stare and deeply furrowed brow might have passed for a grotesque smile. I do him an injustice perhaps in so describing him, but the truth was that I was uneasy in his presence and took as much care as possible not to be alone with him.

Despite my aversion, however, in one of his frequent rages Pollard thought to rid himself of me by assigning me to the practice of physic under Cheatham's tutelage. At first I lived in a state of subdued terror in the doctor's house, fearfully aware that I stood in awful proximity to the vile nostrums that served only to contravene nature's healing force and thus with undue haste bring many a wretch to his last breath. But as I watched him mix his medicines and write his conundrums, it soon became evident that my fears were overblown. Finally, I grew so bold as to disguise my suspicions as queries put to the doctor.

"These frontiersmen are hardy and lawless, sir. How have you lived among them this long with your bones still intact and your head yet joined to your shoulders?"

Cheatham gathered his unlovely features into a storm about to break over me. But then his frowning countenance relaxed and an ugly smile replaced his customary grinning grimace.

"Oh that. These ignorant people will believe anything I tell them, and despite what you or anyone else may think, I never give them anything really harmful, only gaily colored pills for minor ailments. I cannot help it, of course, if their nature has so weakened and diminished that human medicine cannot pull them back from the brink."

In our enlightened day I shudder when I recall the barbarous medical practices common on the frontier in that primitive time. The sworn enemy of heretical new theories just beginning to circulate in America, Cheatham practiced and prescribed bleeding as a universal remedy for all serious maladies. Those weakened by pneumonia or consumed by tuberculosis were quickly dispatched to the next world by his medical acumen and expert incisions. Birth labor often became the death agony of hapless women as his unwashed hands infected fetus and mother alike. To timid questions about his methods, he would rage, "Hell and damnation! What do these new doctors know about medicine?" Thus turning aside all doubts about his judgment, he managed with singular efficiency to keep his grisly record unblemished: under his expect eye and sure hand the nearly departed soon became, as the Americans were wont to say, the dearly departed.

But the deeper truth was, as I believed, that even if he had been convinced by the new medical theories, his real motive was not to save his patients but to line his pockets in profitable alliance with Pollard. He dispatched them, Luke buried them, and both shared in the spoils.

As for Luke, who was openly cynical about doctors and the medical guild in general, he was fond of quoting a saying inherited from his forebears:

> The doctor's blunder
> Lies six feet under.

Luke soon repented himself of his peevishness towards me and recalled me to his house and affairs. We were occupied anew with our ghoulish expeditions to retrieve buried treasures. If our nocturnal forays attracted attention, as once or twice happened, Luke explained to Hezikiah Barton, Harvey's chief deputy, who was summoned on one occasion, that he had second thoughts about the final disposition of the grave and chose to reassure himself under cover of darkness so as to spare the family undue distress. Furthermore, he went on to say that he had discovered an underground stream under the graveyard and that shifting and subsidence were becoming a problem. Eventually, he warned, the city might need to designate a new cemetery. A few people shook their heads in suspicion of Pollard, true enough, but most nodded in his praise, for his pretended concern seemed to the simple-minded, that is, to the majority, to be an act surpassing the call of his duty.

Following Pollard's strict orders, I remained silent during our initial visits to the dying, carefully imitating his placement of pious, folded hands, soft, sad voice, downcast stare, and most of all the mournful face contorted by grief for the dead or dying, concern for the bereaved, the depressing presence of death, and the sobering nearness of eternity.

One night, however, after several weeks of apprenticeship, fascinated by a sparkling diamond ring on a young woman's left hand, I felt compelled to offer her some words of comfort as she agonized in the terminal stages of consumption. "May the Holy Mother comfort and guide you through your ordeal," I intoned softly. The semi-conscious woman probably did not hear my words, but Pollard and a hard-featured lady beside him did. She gasped in the funereal silence and visibly recoiled at my words. As for Pollard, his reaction was as swift as decorum would permit. Pulling me aside and then into an empty adjacent room, he confronted me with a whispered vehemence and a slap across the face that caused my ears to ring and my blood to turn to water.

"Keep ye devilish popery to yourself, boy! These people ain't Catholic! Lord help us! They don't know nothing about no Holy Mother or her holy water or any of that there jargon of you heathen Catholics. The Scriptures, boy, the Scriptures, that is what you must spout to these people. They believe in the Bible maybe more than in God Hisself. Any more of that Catholic claptrap and it could hurt us, hurt my business! You understand me, boy?"

"I can quote some verses in Latin," I offered timidly, remembering a few passages Father Branigan had taught us.

"Oh, my-y-y God! Latin! Latin! Verses in Latin? You crazy, boy? The Bible in Latin! God help us! No, No, No! No Latin, you understan'? The Bible in Anglish, boy, the language God talks! You start talking sich

52

heathenish tongues as Latin or Franch to these people and they'll run you outta town or maybe hang you from the closest tree! Latin, who ever heard of sich a thing!"

Pollard ranted on about the evils of Latin, "Franch," and Catholicism more than I needed to understand the circumstances and amend my ways. That night he gave me a Protestant Bible called the King James, and though I prided myself on my quick mind and ready understanding, during the next few days I could barely make heads or tails of it. Pollard assured me that most people were like me and explained that many reveled in their ignorance, which they believed to be a reverse sign of God's greatness. The less you understand, he pointed out, the better. "Jest roll your eyes, boy, sorta church-like and quote the Scriptures. Don't have to understang nothing to get our job done. We ain't preachers, we're undertakers. We put 'em under, where the Lord sends 'em after that ain't our consarn."

Playing out their hypocritical charade, neither Pollard nor Cheatham ever missed a church service or prayer meeting, and Luke imposed on me the same ecclesiastical obligations. It was my virgin experience with Protestantism, and I must confess that I attended my first service with fearful apprehension. Father Branigan's fulminating denunciations of those he called apostates had affected me more than I knew, and I half expected the Fiend himself to seize me at the church door.

Instead a ritual began that was so impoverished in music and Christian aesthetics, so artless and plain in theological execution, that I wondered whether I was in a house of God or attending a gathering of lunatics. Were these poor, simple souls the same fearful enemies of God and the Mother Church Father Branigan had described with such fear and loathing?

But just when I was about to conclude that Protestantism was a spiritless and frail facsimile of the truth faith, a dour, lank, and black-clad pastor rose, coughed, and with a fixated stare at the congregation, read an incomprehensible Scripture, and then commenced a low, rumbling sermon that eventually rose to a shouting, squealing crescendo that all but frightened me out of my wits. What the church lacked in visible icons, communion, and inspiring music, the Reverend Jett Hale compensated for with lurid biblical symbolism. In apocalyptic language and expert scriptural references he described our execrable sinful state and hellish damnation and warned of the imminent end of the world. I was agitated to the verge of panic, yet despite occasional "amens!" I saw that Pollard and all but a few of the congregation appeared to be unmoved by the impending calamity. Indeed, he nodded and napped, and to my left Matthew Satterfield snored out loud as saliva drooled down his beard, both and all unbelievably heedless of the approaching Apocalypse and, as far as I could tell, indifferent to the gathering wrath of God. For his part, Cheatham sat unblinking, his features frozen in his characteristic half-smile. For the whole of that Sunday and the next several days I often turned my eye on the heavens lest its fabric should suddenly be rent and angelic heralds pour forth to trump the end of time. The nights were worse. In the darkness I listened to the accelerated beating of my heart, marking, as I imagined, the final moments before the world's doom.

Unwilling for the next few weeks to trust me on his funereal visits and probably reacting to pressure from Cheatham, Pollard assigned me instead to his barbershop, though I was not excused from Jett Hale's doomsday sermons, nor from my duties as gravedigger and grave desecration assistant.

I do not boast when I say I quickly excelled in barbering. My hands were nimble and sure from long larcenous practice, and though at first I owned no barbering tools of my own, with second-rate accoutrements I learned in no long lapse of time to clip the hair, eyebrows, and nose hairs; clean the ears of wax and grime; lather, shave, and trim beards; and massage the patrons in such a soothing and satisfying way that both the common run of men and those of standing and substance soon requested my services and abandoned Esmer Powell, the regular barber. Informed of my Louisiana origins, the town dandies in particular flocked to get my "New Orleans trim" and a splash of "Creole Cologne." (Unbeknownst to them, the trim had nothing to do with New Orleans but was a creature of my fancy: and as for the cologne, it was my own whimsical alchemy of alcohol spiked with certain of Poulette's exotic blends and spices and a dash of common perfume purchased at the Emporium.)

Pollard delighted in my success and even more in my earnings, though it is true that he grumbled even at the paltry cost of the perfume. Overnight Esmer became my enemy, yet for the moment his animosity seemed an empty and impotent rage, although I was to discover later that no enemy is to be lightly considered. So skillful did I wax in my new profession that Pollard soon was of a mind to turn me entirely to the strop and razor. This was convenient to my wishes, for I was more loath than ever to return to the care, tending, and desecration of the dead.

Notwithstanding my newly displayed talents as a barber, I realized no pecuniary aggrandizement from their exercise. Pollard's eyes were as blind to my plight as his ears were deaf to my entreaties. Downes's Spanish dollars that once weighed pleasantly in my pockets were a distant memory, never to be enjoyed again, I surmised, so long as I remained under Pollard's roof and dominion. Had I not ventured occasionally to lift a purse from an unwary soul, I should have been reduced to continual penury.

"You don't need money, boy," he admonished me. "All you'd do with it would be just to get into mischief, and we have the good name of my establishment to think of. It comes first. Now ain't that right, boy?"

In this manner several months passed, and one day I noticed with satisfaction that I was now taller than Pollard and that my clothes were becoming snug beyond comfort. Even though the insipid Anglo-Saxon food that Poulette was now obliged to prepare was nothing abundant, withal it was more substantial than the sparse meals and forced fastings in my mother's house. That same Saturday as I trimmed Matthew Satterfield's beard and moustache, he joked that I needed to tend my own peach fuzz. The mirror happily confirmed it: several curly black chin whiskers were discernible. I shaved them with virgin solemnity and pride. Nature was having her way, and I fancied myself already a maven of the coarse, common but always desirable status of manhood.

Pollard had long been puzzled by lingering gossip that a youth matching my description and demeanor had purchased with genuine Spanish dollars a gaudy wardrobe at the emporium the very day of my arrival in Memphis. Asked about the matter, I stoutly denied any knowledge of it, even when Gil Edmondson the store clerk fingered me as the purchaser and others claimed to remember seeing me so dressed. The matter seemed settled in my favor a few days later, however, with the arrest of a young hoodlum—probably one of my assailants—found to be wearing the trousers and silk shirt described by old Gil. Pollard pretended to accept the explanation, but I knew it was a mere ruse on his part. It was plain to me that he was far from convinced by my story and that his suspicions about my honesty and trustworthiness grew greater as he came to know me better.

It was a matter of considerable annoyance to me that he, judging me out of his own duplicitous nature, dismissed my artful falsehoods as common lies. For I was of the persuasion—and long remained so—that tales so skillfully crafted as to emulate, nay, even surpass truth in every way but homely fact ought to be respected above it. By what right did plain conformity to petty reality claim ascendancy over high creativity? The world I knew must be improved upon, otherwise life would be too cruel and drab to bear. For I sensed in my youth but realized only in later years that the true life is the one the world will not let us lead.

For reasons I am loath to divulge but which, nevertheless, I shall presently explain as a courtesy to you, dear reader, my need of money was growing more critical. My anticipated complicity with Pollard had not materialized and thus my early hope of sharing in the earnings afforded by his grave robbing and deceptions remained frustrated. For even though his enterprises were growing apace and profitably with Memphis itself, none of the benefits flew from his pockets to mine, much less to Antoine and Poulette. Indeed, their lowly condition as slaves kept my own at a similar level of misery. Our dissimilar talents and the unequal quality of the services we rendered him altered not in the least his contemptuous opinion of our African pedigree. It was God's consignment to our race, not his, he reminded me. Therefore, whilst we ought always to do better, we could never be better.

Pollard was devilishly secretive about his trove, but through Poulette I discovered that he kept his money and precious items hidden in an iron-reinforced chest in his living quarters. These he kept locked at all times, opening the doors only to let Poulette clean in his presence. With this bit of intelligence, I then turned my thoughts to the invention of a ruse or stratagem to gain access to treasures of unknown size and worth but which the more I magnified them in my imagination the more I determined to seize them as my own.

Meanwhile, pressed by the new circumstances that I have promised to explain to you, I thought to alleviate my penury through certain associations I had formed during my secretive nocturnal forays. Thus I gained provisional admittance to a circle of gamblers that convened nightly in the backroom of a disreputable tavern, one of a cluster of newly constructed hovels and random structures to which some residents referred derogatorily as "South Memphis," hoping to distance themselves and the reputable districts of the city from its unwholesome character.

I had no money, as I said, but a pearl necklace of modest value, which Pollard had removed from the corpse of old Gil Edmondson's recently deceased wife only to have it find its way into my pocket in a moment of distraction, served as my ante. Regarding my youth and feigned inexperience, my opponents thought to make quick work of my gaming innocence.

In this they were not disappointed. Before the evening ended, by premeditated design I lost the necklace but promised, if given the chance, to return on the morrow with an object of much greater value. My unsavory companions assented with sly smiles and knowing looks, and accordingly the next evening I presented as my stake the diamond ring retrieved from the finger of the young consumptive woman I mentioned earlier. (I recalled with pleasure how Luke Pollard thought to have dropped it in the grass beside the grave and crawled about for an hour on hands and knees searching for it by lantern light.)

This time a run of inexplicable luck appeared to offset my apparent gaming inexperience. My winnings mounted apace with the murmurings, curses, and dour grimaces of my fell companions. Though sorely tempted in the dim lamplight, I dared not dupe them to a point of having my tricks discovered and thereby inviting danger to my person, for all bore arms and knives. Therefore, once I had a respectable stack of coins in my favor, I made my excuses, promised to return the next evening, and took my hasty leave, running as fast as legs would carry me to evade assault.

My promise to return was as sincere as my inexperience was feigned and one I should have kept except for an unexpected turn of circumstances that happened as you will now hear. Having lost his money to me, the winner of the pearl necklace the previous evening attempted to exchange it for cash money, eventually presenting it to Gil Edmondson at the emporium. Much to his horror and grief, old Gil recognized it as the one he had buried with his wife at her request. Faced with Edmondson's apoplectic outrage and sobbing threat to have him arrested for desecration of her grave, the bewildered gambler ran for his horse and fled Memphis in a drumbeat of hooves and a cloud of dust.

Constables Harvey and Barton investigated the case, but fortunately for me, the other gamblers offered them few clues. Thieves and habitual offenders of public order, they displayed the natural subversions of wastrels and vagabonds who have known only the ugly and cruel underbelly of the law and consider it a virtue and an act of manhood to defy and thwart it at every turn.

But the hateful facts of my complicity could not be conveniently or wholly concealed. For one thing, I was now a familiar figure in Memphis. Other men had seen me enter and leave the tavern, and it soon got back to the constables that I must have had something to do with the infamous necklace.

This intelligence, which soon reached Pollard's ears also, caused him to fall into a cursing rage and near panic. The facts left no room in his mind to doubt that I had lifted the necklace, thereby not only depriving him of coveted property and mocking him in the act but also, by gambling it away, placing his enterprise and person at risk.

"Well, you bastard," he thundered, "you stole my necklace and now you'll be gonna to jail! That slick tongue o yourn ain't gonna hep ye now! No way you gonna wiggle outta this! I'll tell them yo momma is a high yaller! If you don't go to jail, I'll sell yore ass to the first slaver I find!"

I was unmoved. "If you do and I go to jail or elsewhere, then you, sir, shall surely fall with me, and for that matter, in punishment for a greater guilt. For if I am forced to tell the truth about my doings or my ancestry, there is much I shall have to tell about your activities: grave robbing, despoiling corpses ..."

Pollard turned pale. A frightened, sick smile twisted his ugly features and his unkempt beard quivered with conflicting emotions.

"Now, Petie," he muttered with false gentleness, "come on. Let's remember, it's jist an ol necklace, after all. I ain't gonna tell nobody nothin they don't need to know. And besides, you was here the night you was supposed to be gamblin at the tavern. Now ain't that right? You WAS here, wasn't you?" He seemed almost convinced by his own deceptive question, so strong was his hope that I was obediently and safely in my room at night.

"Of course, sir. I was here. I would not disobey your orders," I responded with practiced aplomb.

"Course not," he mused, now beginning to realize the extent and possible implications of my duplicity and disobedience. Whereupon with a shake of his head and the thud of his fist on the table, he added, "Then that's the way it is. You was here all the time. That's our story. We don't know nothin about dear ole Nellie Edmondson's necklace. We jist hope they catch up with that thievin rascal. He's the one that dug up her grave and stole it. How and when he done it, we ain't got no idea, but why else would he run off lickety-split like he did if he ain't guilty?"

I did not witness in person his meeting with the Bascom Harvey, nor hear the questions he put to Luke, but from what Poulette told me later, it was not a credible performance. Withal and to my good fortune and great relief, he clung to the story that I was at home the night I purportedly gambled away the necklace, a fact he would swear to in court. Needless to say, I told the same tale when queried, but I dare say to my credit that I was much more convincing than my dull master.

In the end, Harvey remained as skeptical as he was powerless to act. After all, Pollard was a pillar of the community, as the Americans put it, and his word would outweigh any circumstantial evidence of complicity in the outrage, to say nothing of the testimony of the tavern riff raff. The matter was temporarily laid to rest, though he did not discount certain unfavorable gossip that was beginning to circulate about

Pollard and me, and he remembered the night he had talked to him about strange activity at another gravesite. From that moment he was to keep a suspicious eye on his activities, which, to my annoyance, included mine as well.

But let us leave this unpleasant matter for the moment, good reader, and turn, as I promised, to the urgent reason why I needed funds. You do remember, do you not, the fair young lady in whose pursuit I fell into misfortune? During my nocturnal wanderings I found her mansion, one of the largest and newest of many being erected in fast-growing Memphis. It was located north on Thomas Road—an avenue named, or so I supposed, for her prominent father—in an elevated, wooded terrain overlooking the bluff and affording a grand view of the mighty Mississippi River. High iron fences blocked casual access and a pair of black mastiffs, rare here on the American frontier, snarled menacingly at pedestrians. On more than one occasion I heard voices calling to the dogs, and I deduced with a fearful shiver that human guards also patrolled the mansion grounds by night. Her family, I concluded with satisfaction, must be one of substance and therefore of possible profit to me.

I soon espied the thrilling object of my admiration and target of my scheming affections. The dreary winter had flowed into a delicious spring, and now warm summer was about to begin. As the days grew longer and the evenings warmer, Caroline Thomas—for such I learned was her lovely name—was wont to make appearances on her second-story balcony. At those moments I crept as close as I dared to savor the enthralling vision of her, yet my eagerness was subdued by fear of the vicious canines and their human cohorts.

One evening she failed to appear and I was turning to retreat unhappily to my straw bed when of a sudden a figure materialized before me, a hand gripped my sleeve, and an African woman's voice whispered to me.

"Young Massa Prosper, I would have a word with you!"

I recoiled in terror, correctly fearing that my secretive stalking had been discovered and assuming that I was once again due unpleasant punishment.

"Unhand me, woman! You frightened me half to death. Who are you? How do you know my name and what do you want with me? I have done nothing wrong!"

"Course you ain't—yet!" the Negro crone giggled. "But you just listen to me, 'cause I got a message for you from somebody you must want awful bad to see! And who wants to see you. Here's a memento she done sent you."

She handed me a delicate and lacy white handkerchief with the embroidered letters CT in one of its flowery corners.

"What is this? Why are you giving me this woman's handkerchief?"

"Man alive, are you so ignorant of romantical matters that you don't know what it means when a lady gives you her hankerchief?"

My heart began a pounding that all but overwhelmed my reeling senses. "Does it mean, then, that I find favor with your mistress?"

"Young Massa, you sure talk funny!" she giggled in derision. "Find favor! Is that what you call it? It means, young Massa Prosper, that my lady will see you in courtship, but I'm here to tell you that you got to behave yourself like a gentleman, for I'll be watchin over her—an you—like a hawk over a henhouse."

"I could not conceive of any other form of behavior in the presence of one so esteemed and so adored," I gushed with the inconstant sincerity of one moved to momentary false honesty by the prospect of amatory conquest.

"Uh huh! Un huh!" she responded with narrowed eyes and an old duenna's natural skepticism.

"Tell me, what am I to do?"

"Ain't nothing you can do tonight. Just have patience and when the time's right, I'll tells you what to do and when," she answered firmly.

"But when will that be?"

"You meet me tomorrow evenin just down the road, not in front o the mansion but down yonder by the trees. I'll tell you then."

And with that and refusing to accept any more questions, she turned and rapidly disappeared into the gloom.

You can imagine, dear reader, my state of elation, impatience, and high agitation—not without a warning note of fear, I must add—as I skipped and leapt and sang my way back to my room, stopping now and then to smell the perfumed handkerchief to remind myself that I was not dreaming. Darkest night had settled over Memphis, but my heart now lived in the magic illumination of love wherein no shadows dwelt.

Later, unable to sleep, I nearly exhausted my candle pouring out my inflamed heart in a passionate billet doux. I wrote of the celestial rapture of being in her presence, of swooning should I have the unmerited honor of contemplating her face, of the ecstasy of drinking in the heavenly beauty of her eyes and lips, of the unthinkable pleasure of winning her approval, of the vast poetry her sweet image stirred in me and, alas, of the failure of my poor words to express my feelings. To this

60

I added some remembered amorous verses, hastily and imperfectly translated from the French, aware of the magical procurement that even the poorest love poetry rehearses in the female heart.

On the ensuing day I arrived faithfully at the designated spot. The hag appeared not long thereafter and we retired into the grove so as not to be discovered by idle passersby. In physical aspect she appeared the same, but in attitude she was far different. For instead of professing a concern for the safety and virtue of her fair charge, she hinted and all but assured me of her willingness to serve my cause. Alerted to the greed that now began to usurp her nobler inclinations, I held up my hand to put an end to her servile protestations.

"Tell me, woman, what is the price for this help? And what do they call you?"

"They call me Audrey, just Audrey, ole Audrey," she answered with a nervous giggle as she fidgeted and pawed absently in the leaves with her sandal. Then she straightened, looked me in the eye, and gave me this rambling summary of her plight and preamble to her price.

"Young Massa Prospah, you listen to what I gotta say to you. The folks up yonder in the big house don't give me nothin but a hard life: whippins when they say I be bad, ole wore out clothes on my back, a cold biscuit an beans an some hog jowl now an then when they feel like it. An work, work, work. Lordy how I work! Treated just like an ole dog I am that can't hunt no more. Now that I be an ole woman, I expect one o these days they just might turn me outta the gate to starve to death out yonder on the road somewhere. So I need to make me some arrangements for the bad days that are acomin. You understand what I'm talkin about, Massa Prosper?"

"Indeed, I do, Audrey, and I'm ready to help you. But you must tell me how much it will take to ameliorate your condition," I insisted, sobered and saddened to realize how quickly my ideal love was being reduced to haggling.

She stared at me, apparently uncertain about my words. Then she said with deliberate slowness, "Well, sir, now I reckon I need about thirty good Spanish dollahs I see the white folks spend afore I can let you in to see my darlin Miss Caroline. Now that ain't a lot for a gentleman like yourself, is it? And she's worth a lot more than that."

"Thirty dollars! And what happens if I can't give you that much?"

"Sic the dogs and the Massa's guards on you next time you comes sniffin around here, sir, that's what I'll do," Audrey answered matter-of-factly. "Ain't no way you gonna get to Miss Caroline without my help, Massa Prospah."

The truth of her words was all too evident. "I do want to help you, Audrey, but it will take me a time to collect that much money."

I perceived that no purpose could be served by confessing to her that I had no money at all. Indeed, without my occasional pilfering and pickpocketing I should have been reduced to absolute penury. At that moment the many humiliations to which Pollard had subjected me during all my time in Memphis became accusations against me for enduring them, and I decided to resort to the most drastic measures to deliver myself from his loathsome dominion. The next day I ventured into my famous gambling escapade and by the second day I had amassed the necessary money and secured old Audrey as my accomplice in the conquest of fair Miss Caroline. I gave Audrey the thirty dollars and as her first service to me instructed her to convey my impassioned billet doux to Miss Thomas.

Two long days passed without word or sight of Caroline or old Audrey. Imagine, dear reader, the hourly increase of my agitation and daily multiplication of my impatience, the dark conjectures that grew about her absence and silence, the dreadful, swelling fear that our love had been discovered and that awful punishments could befall me at any moment. And I was tormented by the thought that perhaps my epistle was too bold of tone.

But the third night, I heard Audrey's familiar voice calling me from the shadows. "Over here, Massa Prosper! Come on over here."

I rushed to her but was disappointed to find her alone. "Audrey, what happened? I have been in a torment without news from you. Is Miss Caroline all right?"

"Why don't you ask her yourself, Massa Prospah? There she be, all modest-like, hidin behind that big ole tree."

I flew to her, falling to one knee before her radiance and despite my ardor determined to proceed with deliberation and choose my words carefully. Even at that tender age, I knew that many a suit fails because of unpremeditated haste and that once uttered, precipitous words cannot be recalled.

"Miss Caroline," I protested in my gravest tone, "I cannot tell you what an honor you do me to allow me into your presence."

She giggled nervously, put her hand over her mouth and coughed. "Mister Prosper, for that is your name, is it not, sir? A queer name, to be sure. I am pleased to make your acquaintance, but I must say these circumstances do us no honor and I must leave at once. And, Mister Prosper, the tone of your letter was way too forward, and besides, I didn't understand half of the big words you used. So we must be goin',

62

sir. Audrey! Audrey! Come on over here, we must be on our way!"

"Oh, dear Miss Caroline," I pleaded, "do stay for a moment to hear me out. I apologize with all my heart if my letter offended your delicate sensitivities. Be assured that nothing could have been farther from my true intentions. And you have my word as a gentleman that I would never conduct myself in a manner demeaning to your name and honor."

She smiled at my words and waved Audrey aside. "Your accent, sir, is strange to the ear. Is it true that you come from New Awleans and that you speak French and all? I ain't never met a body that speaks French, but they tell me it's a real sweet-sounding language. Is that right, Mister Prosper?"

"*Oui, c'est vrai que la langue française est très belle, une très belle langue pour une très belle dame.*"

"Oh that is sooo pretty, Mister Prosper. But now, sir, what did you say? You must mind what you say to me."

"I said that it is true that the French language is very beautiful, a very beautiful language for a very beautiful lady."

"Now, Mister Prosper, you mustn't be so forward in your flattery. I think we should go now. Audrey-y-y!"

"Oh, no, Miss Caroline! I want to know all you're willing to tell me about yourself."

"No, sir, before I tell you about me, you must tell me about yourself. What about your family, your parents? They tell me you work as a barber and apprentice to old man Pollard. Sir, how can you stand to be around dead people?"

"Miss Caroline, let me assure you that I share the feeling. It was never my wish to engage in either lowly profession and, thank God, I shall soon wash my hands of both. My inheritance is in probate and once the legal documents are processed and the formal hearing completed, I shall be returning to my estate in New Orleans."

"But being a gentleman of means, Mistah Prospah, how is it that you are doing this low kind of work? Now then, sir, are you telling me the truth, or just teasing and mocking me like you would any other poor witless girl? I've heard tell how some men like to deceive decent girls. My Poppa's done warned me about their likes."

Whereupon, protesting my honesty, good intentions, and high social state, I proceeded to weave a plot of family intrigue and deception that I dare say would have done credit to the sensational tales flowing from the pens of the great European novelists of the time. "And so you see, Miss Caroline," I concluded, "how, in league with other greedy relatives and unscrupulous barristers, my half-brother Henry aimed to swindle me out of my rightful fortune. Indeed, so deep reached his treachery that my very life was in danger, and I was removed to Memphis to escape their vile clutches. And—God be praised!—Providence has protected me. Henry's foul scheme has been discovered, his true motives unmasked, and he is being punished for his wrongdoing. Soon I shall return to claim the inheritance that is solely and rightfully mine."

"And I suppose, sir, that you will be well accompanied upon your return to New Awleans."

"What do you mean, Miss Caroline?"

"I mean, sir, that a man of your standing must have many supporting friends, relatives ... lady friends, no doubt ..."

"Family, yes, Miss Caroline, but lady friends, no. My heart will be forever captive here in Memphis."

"Whatever do you mean, Mister Prosper?"

"Ah, Miss Caroline, it means that my love for you enslaves me to your wishes."

"Now, now Mister Prosper, you mustn't talk to me that way. We have to go now. Audrey-y-y!"

Whereupon I threw my planned precaution to the wind and protested my love for Miss Caroline with all the desperate eloquence I could muster. Bowing before her, I compared her beauty—in truth considerable—to the fairest flowers of May and the loveliest stars in the celestial firmament. I described a heart surrendered to her divine enchantments, a life forever devoted to her service.

She pretended at first to be offended; but susceptible, as I rightly suspected, to adulation and having soon satisfied the requirements of maidenly modesty, at length she began to encourage my amorous tirade with shy smiles and provocative looks. Transported by my own fiery eloquence and emboldened by the palpable advances my pleas were making towards her heart, I reached for her dainty white hand. Hastily she withdrew it, but a second later it was again there for the touching, and her smile remained. Her eyes continued to fix on mine. A moment later, as I was gathering courage to essay another attempt, of a sudden she took my hand, placed it against her burning cheek, and then, to my amazement and delight, let herself fall limply into my enveloping arms.

What words we said thereafter or how long we stood transfixed by passion, I cannot with accuracy recall these many years later. I remember only our murmurings of love, mumbled promises of eternal devotion, and incoherent debate over the imperious demands of love and duty to chastity and decorum. I was bold to attempt a kiss on her lips, but she rebuffed me sweetly. Eventually old Audrey interrupted our idyll.

"Miss Caroline, we best be goin now, child. It's powerful late, and your daddy's men'll be lookin for us if you stay here any longer with Massa Prospah. You tells him goodnight now, you hear?"

"Oh, Audrey, it ain't that late. Can't I stay just a little longer?"

This unwelcome news and the fearful vision it produced in my imagination cooled my ardor, and I added my voice to Audrey's.

"Woefully, she is right, my dearest Caroline. We must part, and I shall not live until I see you next."

"Well, dear Peter, that'll be soon, if I have my way about it."

It was the first time she had called me by name. The effect was magically uplifting. I felt transformed and confirmed in my manhood. For as the saying goes:

> A youth is not a man until he hears his name from the
> lips of a beautiful woman.

A propitious opportunity to have our amorous tryst soon presented itself. By happenstance, not many days thence the famous General Andrew Jackson, one of the founders of Memphis and now President of the American Republic, was to visit Memphis. His name was well known to me, for all New Orleans told how he won the Battle of New Orleans a few months after I was born.

Now, gentle readers, as lovers are wont to avail themselves of any and all circumstances to be together, so Miss Caroline and I made capital of the public distraction caused by General Jackson's visit to plan our delicious rendezvous.[4] She pleaded an indisposition the day of his appearance, and reluctantly her parents left her in old Audrey's care whilst the entire household sallied forth with the Memphis rabble to welcome their celebrated hero and compatriot.

Pollard was likewise swept up in the common adulation of the great man, and since there were no corpses or customers needful of our services, he made no objection when Esmer, Antoine, Poulette, their daughter Jeannette, and I abandoned our tasks and joined the excited, motley mob.

Audrey was waiting nervously for me by the mansion gate. She quickly escorted me through the spacious grounds, assuring me that the horrific canines were locked away, the guards and other servants dismissed to join in the general festivities, and Master and Mistress Thomas gone to join other city worthies in welcoming General Jackson and his presidential entourage. Best of all, Audrey told me that she had prepared Miss Caroline to receive me. For days she had extolled me to the heavens, painted a picture of the delights of love, and labored to convince her sweet charge how foolish it would be to let the pleasure of this great love pass her by because of maidenly modesty. Chastity, she told her, is a convenient lie parents use to control their daughters.

Although I had burgled many splendid residences in New Orleans, I had never seen a more palatial mansion. My heart almost failed me as I gazed in admiration at its finery. From afar I could hear the triumph of trumpets, the crash of drums, and the roar of the mob as the presidential party made its grand entry into the town square, but here I was surrounded by such luxury and beauty as to reduce the public event of that day to mere noisome babble. Gilded portraits and paintings lined the high walls, thick draperies and curtains swayed in stately majesty, and ornate furniture spoke of wealth and riches far beyond my poor experience.

I could wax forth with greater eloquence about the surroundings, but these were relegated to a distant background by the acme and culmination of the wonders I beheld: Miss Caroline herself standing languidly at the head of a long spiral stairway, dressed in a crimson velvet dress that accentuated her pearly white complexion and flowing golden hair.

"Come on up here, Peter. Don't be afraid. Momma and Poppa and everbody else have done gone to see Mister Jackson. Audrey is the only one here, and she'll watch out for us. If were lucky, we'll have the afternoon to ourselves. Are you hungry?"

I recovered my reeling senses sufficiently to issue a bland gallantry. "Only for the sight of you, the most beautiful woman in all the world."

She smiled and corrected me. "For food, Peter, for food. Would you like some dinner—lunch I reckon maybe you New Awleans folks call it, don't you? You look like you could do with some." And without waiting, she called to Audrey. "Audrey, bring the tray up to my room. Come on up, Peter," she added, laughing at my hesitation, "don't be bashful. I won't bite you."

I could scarcely credit my good luck at finding myself in the very inner sanctum of my beloved's mansion. I seated myself uncertainly on a silk-draped divan whilst opposite me fair Caroline sat on a velvet-caparisoned stool at her dresser. Among its many curious and jumbled objects I spied a dainty looking-glass and other accoutrements of her morning toilette: rouge, perfumes, powders, pins, scissors,

66

ribbons, combs, brushes, and a silver-plated etui open and overflowing like a veritable cornucopia with rings, pendants, bracelets, and necklaces. On the wall facing me was an ornate oaken bookcase, but in lieu of books, in its shelves eight or nine dolls were displayed in the exaggerated and provocative postures and costumes of real women. In the adjacent corner stood their regal residence, a most elaborate dollhouse, complete with miniature doors, stairs, and furniture. Across the room my attention turned to her unmade bed lavish with pink pillows and sheets and a haphazard assortment of dresses and robes. The room, I recollect as though it were yesterday, was headily redolent with the wafting vapors of her lavender perfume.

"Cat got your tongue, Peter?" she purred, pleased at my discomfort.

"No poor words of mine could describe the heights and depths of my feelings at this moment."

"You do say the most gallant things, Peter, and I do love to hear them. But let's save all that foh later. I'm simply famished." Then she added with an impish smile, "I couldn't eat breakfast this mornin'—had to tell momma I was indisposed. And all for you, Peter. Just see what ordeals you make me go through. Don't you feel bad for making me suffer, you mean man?"

"Most wretched, indeed, Caroline, but touched more than I can say by your noble gesture."

"Noble, sir?" she retorted, "low down, that's what it is, Peter. I don't like having to deceive my momma and even less, fooling my poppa. You know what he'd do to you if he was to catch you in my room?"

A trembling terror seized me as I contemplated the wrath that would fall on me, and I remembered the horrific beatings I had endured for my larcenies in New Orleans. Often I was brave enough to be cowardly, seldom enough to be resolute. Yet courage was imperative in these uneasy but thrilling circumstances, and though my supply of this moral commodity has been ever small, I summoned what I thought to be a reasonable hypocritical facsimile.

"I would endure any lashings that fate or man may give me so great is my love for you, dearest Caroline."

"Peter," she giggled, "I don't believe half the things you say, but the way you say them is so gallant. But let's get busy now with dinner. I'm simply famished, ain't you?"

I nodded in eager agreement. Whereupon, we dispensed with further words and fell to our gustatory task with hearty earnestness. In our hurried competition for the best portions, a majestic roast was soon reduced to bone and gristle, thick slices of bread, rich butter, succulent gravies, and side dishes of okra, beans, and potatoes melted away before our eyes, a cool pitcher of tea was soon emptied, and generous helpings of apple pie straightway followed their culinary companions into blissful oblivion. When we had finished, Caroline instructed a protesting Audrey to bring us a bottle of her father's whiskey.

"Now, Miss Caroline, you know what you daddy'll do to you—and me—if he catches you with that liquoh. That be powerful stuff. He done warned you about that. Don't you remember, child, that other time you got in trouble drinkin your daddy's liquor?"

"Oh, hush up, Audrey, and fetch it," she responded with imperious annoyance. "Don't embarass me in front of Mister Prosper. Poppa ain't gonna know nothing about it, and Mister Prosper and me want us a drink. Ain't that right, Peter?"

Secretly appalled at her choice of beverage, yet I was too euphoric to disagree openly with anything Caroline might propose but instead laughingly seconded her proposal and enthusiastically joined her in urging Audrey to do her bidding. Naturally, wine would have been my choice, but it was rare among these Anglo-Saxons whose abominable whiskey I could barely swallow.

Withal, the repulsive, burning beverage elevated our good spirits; and I felt the need of music. I said so, and Caroline had Audrey bring me an old guitar on which I strummed and sang one of my favorite Spanish pieces. Ill adapted to the English meter, the words might appear something like the following stanzas:

The Maiden in the Tower

I spied a fair maiden in a lonely tower
While riding to Alora at the dawning hour.
In armor resplendent, with courage aglow,
I spurred to Alora to battle our foe.
But treachery stalked me that fateful day,
And she sang how still her lover lay,
At the rout of Alora by death laid low.

She tossed me a kiss and an azure flower
While riding to Alora at the dawning hour.
In armor resplendent, with courage aglow,
I spurred to Alora to battle our foe.

But treachery stalked me that fateful day,

And she sang how still her lover lay,
At the rout of Alora by death laid low.

"Good man, what maid sings in yonder spire?"
Responded the bent and venerable squire:
"Alas, sir, you have seen the beautiful Elaine,
Grieving these centuries for fallen swain.
She wanders the ancient, haunted tower,
Mourning whom she gave heart and flower,
Brave knight at the rout of Alora slain."

Caroline fixed her lovely blue eyes on me, her face radiating a sweet smile. "Oh, Peter, your voice is so beautiful! What do the words say, hon?"

"They tell of an undying love back in old Spain, the sort of love I feel for you, a love that will never ..."

"S-s-sh," she shushed, putting a finger to my lips to cut off my gushing declaration. "Put the guitar down now, Peter, and come on over here by me. Want to?"

I needed no further encouragement, but flew to her side in a transport of delight. This time she made no resistance as I showered kisses on her hand. Thus emboldened, I soon moved from hand to arm, and anon progressed from limb to lips. Thereafter, with kisses having been generously given and as lavishly returned, we paused ever so briefly, staring with sweet joy into each other's eyes, in startled wonder over the tender conquest we had so soon made of each other. Then the immobilized tableau broke and we fell to, as avidly consummating our love, I might say, as hungrily we had consumed the roast.

(Here, dear reader, I have prudently omitted details of my narrative. For me, I should have relished reliving them in their retelling, but I must think of the family as they read this. Thus we resume the tale after these delicious moments.)

"I'm so sorry about the picture. I'm afraid I broke the glass when I knocked it to the floor."

She giggled as she finished tying the blue ribbon in her hair. "You were, I recall, in a bit of a frenzy at the moment. My, lover, but you do get so impatient at times!"

"Forgive me. Are these your grandparents in the painting?"

"No, silly boy, they're my parents."

"Your parents? But they seem ..." I caught myself before uttering an imprudence.

"So old, you was about to say? Why yes, Peter, so they are, and there's a reason for it—and a story if you'd like to hear it. Would you?"

The truth was, I was becoming nervous, and mention of her parents reminded me that the afternoon was far spent and that they might soon return. I said as much.

"No, they'll be gone till all hours. When Momma gets with folks, she stays forever. And as for Poppa, he nevah gets tired of talking about business things—cotton in the Delta, the price of cypress lumber, land, and darkies, stuff like that. If folks will listen to him, he can talk about nearly anything. He reads all the time, you know, all kinds of stuff. You saw his library. Now, wanta here the story or not?"

I detected a note of disapproval in her voice at my reemerging pusillanimity.

"Of course I would, Caroline. And most of all, to hear your lovely voice," I answered a bit absently as I downed the remainder of my whiskey in the hopes that the searing spirits would steady mine.

"Well, you just get comfortable—here now, let me straighten that collar—and listen to my story. Momma called it 'The Marriage Bureau Story' and I ain't never told it to nobody. You're the first outside the family to hear it, dear Peter."

The Marriage Bureau

Back in old Charleston, in Carolinee where Poppa and Momma lived, she was the only daughter of Mr. Ambrose Purser, who made a sizable fortune, so they tell me, in land speculating or some such business. Momma was just a girl when her own momma died, of pneumonia, I reckon, and after some little time had passed—an indecently short time, most said—Grandpa upped and married a widow woman by the name of Mrs. Wilma Cunningham. Mrs. Cunningham had money of her own left by her grandfather. Her husband, though honorable, had no head for business.

Poppa was born in Carolinee but his momma sent him to be educated in the North. That's why he talks a little funny and teases momma and me about our accent. Course I don't have an accent at all, do I, Peter? That's what I thought. Now you do have some kind of accent that makes your English sound a bit queer at times. I don't mean to hurt your feelin's, Peter. You know I don't, love. No, I think the way you talk is so debonair and all. Here, Peter darlin', let me pour you a little more whiskey to settle your nerves. I declare you do fidget worse

70

than a scared chicken.

Now, to get on with the story, Mrs. Cunningham had a young'un, a son, Wilbert Cunningham, just a year or two older than Momma—Irene, that's my momma's given name—and the four of them formed a new family.

Things rocked on all nice like for a few years 'til one summer Grandpa and Mrs. Cunningham-Purser drowned on a cruise to New Yowk. It was a sad business, you can be sure, Peter, but Momma and Wilbert had lived together so long as brother and sister that they just kept on like that in the big ole house in Charleston.

Well, sir, the years passed and neither Momma nor Wilbert ever got married. Momma was a right pretty girl, they tell me. Still is, too. No, Peter darlin', she doesn't look like me at all. And there's a reason for it that I'll tell you directly. Just be patient, you hear me? Anyways, none of her suitors—and they were a-plenty, I'm told—met her expectations. One was too fat, one too thin, another one too poor, that other one too old or just too ugly. Whatever. Anyway, betwixt one thing and another, she got to be an old maid whilst folks shook their heads and wondered how such a pretty thing as Momma never got married.

As for Wilbert, if his life didn't entirely satisfy him, it was at least easy enough not to do anything drastic to change it. He was a bookish man; smart too; had a whole library of books. His sister—Momma—ran the household, saw to it that the servants cooked his favorite food and laid out clean clothes in the right order. He was as regular a man as you could ever imagine; for years he never changed his habits, even though his temperament had a hundred sides to it, and sometimes they had some pretty strong arguments over this or that. But afterwards things would settle down and run peaceable. They were both strong willed but bound to each other by genuine affection.

I guess things woulda gone on like so forever if one day Wilbert hadn't seen some gray in his moustache and a little salt mixing in with the pepper around his temples. After that, Momma says he started getting a lot more aggravating to live with. Moody, Momma says, and at times just downright bad-tempered. He took to spending more time away from the house and wouldn't tell Momma where he had been. Said it was none of her business. She thought the worst, and he didn't do anything to ease her mind. The word got around that he was a-drinking and carousing some, maybe gambling a little, too, and after that, the better Charleston families politely closed their doors and shooed him away from their daughters.

By this time, I reckon Momma's suitors had drifted away, got married, or the old ones maybe died. The pickin's got awful thin. When she found some steaks of gray in her own hair, which she was sure Wilbert had put there by his antics, she decided it was time to do something about it.

She heard tell that down yonder in Savannah there was a man called "a marriage broker." Now Momma was a proper lady and all, and normally she would never have even thought about consulting such a person or going to such a place. Certainly not in Charleston, what with her society friends and all. But there are circumstances I reckon that can push even a proper lady like Momma to do queer things.

Anyways, first thing you know, Momma's made up some kinda cock-and-bull story about an ailing cousin down in Savannah and booked herself passage on a ship to pay her a visit. Well–ha-ha-ha!–as you might guess, Peter, it was really to consult Mr. Marriage Broker.

It took a while for Momma to get up her courage. She used to laugh and tell me how she liked to wear out a pair of hightops walkin; round and round that place. But finally she got up her nerve enough to at least talk to the man. He once had been a proper lawyer and all, but then he found out there was more money in matchmakin'.

He seemed trustworthy enough and so Momma filled out some papers and such that he wanted—'cause Momma was right well educated, not so much as Wilbert, you understand, but it's a fact now that she did attend the female academy in Charleston and then journeyed to England for a whole month when she was young. Afterwards the man asked some questions about the kind of husband she wanted, though Momma spoke plainer about the kind she didn't want! The fee was considerable, but Momma had come too far to turn back. Besides, the money was the least of her worries at this point in her life.

The arrangement with Mr. Marriage Broker was that he would try to match her with likely suitors—all honorable, undivorced, and with means, he assured her—for Momma insisted on that. If anybody likely showed up, then there would be an exchange of letters—using some made-up name—a pseu-do-nym I believe they call it, don't they, Peter? The letters would be copied by somebody called an aman-uen-sis, or something like that. You know, a person who writes things down for somebody else. Thank you, Peter, an amanuensis, I thought that was the word. My, Peter dear, you are so smart! The reason was so the hand-writing couldn't be judged and all. You know, some say you can tell a body's character by just some little turn of the lettahs. It all sounds queer to me, and I don't believe it for a minute. Anyway, after that it would be up to the gentleman and lady to follow up on the romance or drop the whole thing. For Mr. Marriage Broker said in plain English that all he offered was confidentiality and his best efforts to follow Momma's instructions and match her up with a right proper suitor.

Well, sir, for several weeks she didn't hear a thing from Savannah and had about decided it had all been a big waste of her time and money. But a few days later a lettah was delivered from a gentleman by the name of "Robert." "Dear Miss Ophelia"—for that was the name Momma was using in this matter—"I have the honor to address you in this unusual way, and because the circumstances are exceptional, my first obligation is to assure you that I am a Christian gentleman from an old and respected Carolina family and, furthermore, that my intentions are honorable and my estate considerable. And I will tell you further that I chose from among several worthy possibilities to correspond with you." I remember the exact words because Momma recited them to me I don't know how many times when I would ask her about it. She was not happy at first over the thought that he couldn't decide which woman to write to. But then she realized two things: first, he didn't know her from Adam—or Eve either for that matter—and second, he was honest enough to tell her the truth.

In fact, Robert went on to describe himself "with candor," to use his words, "as a man who though no longer in the first flush of youth, was still far from the grip of withering age." That's the flowery way he wrote. "People say I am a man who speaks his mind, and if my words at times may seem a bit harsh, be assured that this perception arises, or so I believe, more from an awkward excess of honesty than a petulant lack of consideration for others. This is particularly true, Miss Ophelia, regarding the fair sex. You may, therefore, find fault with my opinions but never, I trust, with my conduct as a Christian gentleman."

It was then that Momma just about got cold feet. Had she plumb lost her mind? What in the world was she doin', accepting lettahs from a perfect stranger, a man who might be a delinquent, or touched in the head, or—heaven forbid!—married? And reading between the lines, Momma figuhed out that "Robert" had a pretty high opinion of himself, what she described as a proud, self-centered man, maybe just a little too conceited.

To make matters worse for her, about that same time Wilbert started acting strange, watching her, asking her questions, staying out till all hours, mixed up in Lord knows what. She noticed, too, that he had waxed and colored his moustache. and she suspected he had dyed the gray about his temples. About that same time, he started buying new clothes. And not from the Charleston tailors and haberdashers, mind you, but from New Yowk and London, England. Momma suspected he had gotten mixed up with some low-class hussy woman and was fixing to do something outright foolish. And even though she was distracted and all with her own strange business, she took it on herself to look into her stepbrother's queer behavior. But try as she might, she couldn't find out anything, no sir, not a thing.

Well, in spite of her many misgivin's, Momma did finally write to the gentleman called "Robert," and before long they had struck up a regular correspondence. Momma figured it would never amount to anything. He was probably just teasing her, and she got mad just imagining that he might be reading her letters to his low-down drinking friends. And all them laughing and carrying on with all their whoop-te-do about that foolish old maid sitting up there in some big ole house in Charleston town.

It went on like that for several months. Then one day Momma got a letter from "Robert" that liked to a scared her to death. "Miss Ophelia, the time has come for us to meet face to face. We have learned everything about each other our letters can convey, and I fear that if we confine ourselves to this means of communication and present only the favorable features of our character in our epistles, we shall form opinions and perceptions of each other so strong and positive that disappointment will be inevitable when—and if—we meet. Therefore, even at the risk of provoking this unwelcome sentiment in you and possibly losing a friendship that has become very special to me, I propose that we meet physically where we did so spiritually: at the entrance of the Marriage Bureau in Savannah on ***. I suggest that we each display conspicuously a red rose for mutual identification."

Here, Peter dahlin, let me take that glass. Want some more? Now, don't be so nervous. Momma and Poppa won't be back anytime soon, after dark, I reckon.

Well, Momma waited as long as she could before responding to "Robert." She was scared he would be disappointed in her, for Robert was right: they had said so many beautiful things in there letters that real people couldn't measure up to all those expectations. The truth be told, she shuddered to think that he might be a repulsive, degenerate man. Otherwise, why hadn't he found a wife on his own, especially if, like he said, he had "a considerable estate?" And he was probably thinking the same things about her.

But curiosity, you know, that killed the ole cat, finally just got the best of Momma and caused her to put aside all her misgivin's about Robert. To make a long story shorter, she agreed to the meetin'. So she told Wilbert that she was going to Savannah again to visit her ailing cousin.

Wilbert pitched a fit right then and there, but later when he had cooled off some, he announced that he would be away for a few days, too. Then they got into it all over again about some comments he made about her good looks, new dresses, new hairdo, and more rouge, powders, and perfumes than she ever had used before. Did she have a new suitor? he wanted to know. He didn't like the idea of her running off to Savannah to see some cousin she hardly knew. And Momma let him know it was none of his business whether she had a new suitor or not, or whether she went to Savannah, or to Chinee, for that matter. And besides, he was a poor one to talk. What about all the gossip about his new "lady" friend, if that was the right word, his mysterious comin's and goin's, and all the new clothes and such? Then she made a reference to his dyed moustache. He was terribly embarrassed and hurt, and Momma was genuinely sorry she had said such a mean-spirited thing. But that's what folks do when they get mad, ain't it, dear Petah?

It was the worst argument they had ever had, and even after they apologized and made up, it scared them both, and the sadness they felt just lingered and lingered. They pledged their affection and parted on good terms, but both knew in their hearts that things would never be quite the same again.

Momma was a bundle of nerves when she got down to Savannah. The sea was all stirred up by a summer storm, so the trip down the coast from Charleston had been rough and unpleasant. And to make matters worse, she ran herself ragged once she got there, trying to find a red rose. She finally found one, a droopy one, she said, but it was the best she could do. No wonder she was feeling a little sick to her stomach even before the hired carriage let her out in front of the Marriage Bureau. She couldn't bring herself to wait on Robert at the appointed place. So she sorta hid herself on a bench on the backside of a little park next to the Marriage Brokah's office. There she waited and watched. It was too far away to see people clearly, but she needed the distance so she could run away safely if she didn't like what she saw.

Foh a long time no likely prospects showed up, only townspeople going about their business. But then a tall, well-dressed gentleman strolled slowly by the Marriage Bureau, hesitating like he was looking for something—or somebody, and of course pretending not to, you know, like people do in these situations. Then he turned and looked in her direction. Momma said she was glued to the bench in pure panic, couldn't move to save her life. Then he started towards her, and poor

Momma just sat there like a statue. Can't you just feature it in your mind, Peter?

The first thing she noticed from a distance was the red rose in his lapel, and she knew it just had to be Robert. Finally she stood up and without thinking removed her own red rose. Then when he got closer, she got the fright of her life. For there as big as life was Wilbert acoming towahds her!

He was furious, Peter, just furious with Momma. Why have you followed me? he wanted to know. Do you have to stick your nose in all my business? Isn't it enough that you have your suitors and beaux and male admirers? Why do you have to run—and ruin—my life, too?

And Momma was just as mad at first, thinking that Wilbert had followed her all the way down to Savannah just to spy on her. And that meant that he had read her correspondence with Robert and knew about her dealings with the Marriage Bureau. She was humiliated and furious and about to let him have it with both barrels, as the saying goes.

But then she started thinking, and his words started to sink in. Suddenly it hit her. She reached in her purse, took out the red rose, and showed it to him. "Is this what you were looking for ...'Robert'?" Momma said there was no reason to hold back now. Her courage just came right back to her like it does to women when it comes down to things that really matter to them.

Wilbert stared at her in pure disbelief, Petah. Then the two of them just started laughing and couldn't quit for the longest time. So "Ophelia" was Momma and "Robert" was Wilbert! Then, after a while and just as suddenly they stopped laughing and got serious.

"But we're brother and sister," they both said at the same time.

"But not really," Momma then corrected him. "Before God and the Law there's really nothing to keep us from marrying, is there?"

"Only one thing," Wilbert answered with the saddest face you ever did see.

"And what's that?" asked Momma.

"You don't love me, you just think of me as a brother."

"Well, it's true that I have always thought of you as a brother, and friend, and protector, someone I care for and cherish, someone I admire very much, someone who would make any woman a wonderful husband. And just because I always saw you in another light is hardly a reason why I can't look at you from now on in a different way."

"But what would people say?" Wilbert wondered.

"Why, I reckon what they always say—the worst they can," Momma assured him. "But are we going to let our lives be run by what the gossips say?"

"No, by George, we're not," Wilbert answered with fire in his eye. "We've always been together and we're going to stay together." Then he added in a softer tone, "That is, if you'll agree to be my wife. Will you? Will you marry me, Irene, or should I say, 'Ophelia'?"

"No, sir, you should not call me 'Ophelia'," Momma answered him, "and I don't know whether I will or not. First, you have some explaining to do, Mr. Cunningham."

That really caught him off guard. Fact is Momma's always kept him a little off guard. Says that's one of the ways a woman has to deal with a man.

"Explain what, Irene?" he asked, bewildered by this unexpected turn of events.

"Your strange behavior these past few months, where you been agoing and who you been a-seeing and all."

Then he confessed to Momma that all that time he had been jealous—except he didn't recognize the feeling for what it was. He thought she had a new suitor, and it aggravated him like you can't believe. All that time he was in love with Momma, probably had been for years.

"There is no other woman in my life, Irene. Never has been."

"Well, sir, you just keep it that way, and I'll think about whether I'll consent to marry you or not."

Momma had gained the upper hand in their relationship and was enjoying it so much that she resolved never to lose her advantage. And I reckon she never has. But the smile on her face and the sparkle in her eye told Wilbert all he wanted to know. Momma blushed when she told me that they kissed right there in that little park, in front of God and everybody. And then they were so happy they just had to go in and tell that ole marriage broker the good news. He was happy, too, for you see, it was good advertising for his business.

"Then your parents are Mr. and Mrs. Wilbert and Irene Cunningham?" I asked Caroline. "I thought your family name was Thomas."

"Well, it is and it ain't, Peter dahlin," she laughed, amused by my perplexity. "You see, Momma was right, folks started a-gossiping like they had stirred up the biggest scandal in creation. What bothered them most was the rumor that they had been together all those years, you know, … living together … in sin and all. It got so bad that they got the idea of moving away from Charleston, going west somewhere and making a fresh start, and changing their name, to boot."

"So they just picked the name 'Thomas out of the air and moved on to Memphis?"

"Well, not quite outta the air, Peter. Thomas was Mrs. Wilma Cunningham-Purser's maiden name. But there's more to the story."

"How so?"

"Well, you see, Momma was too old, I reckon, to have any children of her own when they got married."

"But you?"

"Peter, I guess I'm what you might call an 'adopted' child. Only it didn't happen in the regular way."

"Then how?"

"Well, it was like this. About a year or so after they got married, people were so hateful to them that Poppa came west looking for a suitable place to resettle. And after he picked Memphis he went back to get Momma and their possessions—furniture, clothes, servants, Poppa's library, and other furnishin's. It was a sight to behold how much stuff they had, seven or eight wagon-loads, so they told me. Poppa sent Momma and her personal servants by ship—booking her as Mrs. Wilbert Thomas—plumb down around Florida and up through the port o' New Awleans. He said the overland trip was too hard for a proper lady to make. Oh, and I forgot to tell you that he had set up a decent house for her here in Memphis. That was before there was even a town in the proper meaning of the word and a good long time before our mansion was built. But Poppa said this whole country was gonna to prosper—just like your name, hon—what with the river traffic and all, and he predicted that some day a big town would start up right here where that old fort used to be. I reckon that was back in about 1818. Poppa still owns the propehty, down there on Poplar Street round the corner from where you live. Now in the meantime him and the men—the male servants and some help hired for the trip—started out with the wagons. I don't know how many weeks it took to make the journey, but several, I reckon.

"Finally, they got here with only one little mishap that I'll tell you about directly. Momma was waitin for them. But there was a surprise she hadn't counted on: a little girl, about a year and half old, or so they judged by her size and all."

"You?"

"Yessir, me. Now, Peter, don't start that again. We got us a little time, but I reckon not that much."

"And where and how did you come into the picture?"

"Well, that's the mystery, Peter. Nobody knows where I came from. According to Poppa, they were about two-thirds of the way here and had camped one night in the deep woods by a wilderness road called

78

the Natchez Trace. They had a big fire going when he said I just came walking in outta the dahk into their camp all dirty and scratched up. Luckily it was in the summer time, otherwise I don't reckon I would be here at all. I wasn't crying or carrying on, and Poppa said it looked like I had been cared for and fed and even though my little dress was all dirty and torn, it was a fancy pattern. I had chigger and mosquito bites all over, but otherwise was in good shape under the circumstances.

"Well, Poppa fed me and took care of me and the next morning sent some men out to find out who I was and what family I belonged to. They rode all over that countryside, but other than the Natchez Road, it was nothing but wilderness for miles and miles around. He sent men up and down the road, and they finally did find some other travelers. But they couldn't tell Poppa's men any more than they already knew, which was nothing at all."

"So what happened?"

"Peter, if you don't stop that! All right, I'll let you have one kiss and no more! There, now, that better? Now, to answer your question, Poppa did the only thing he knew to do, and that was to take me with him, in the hopes that somebody along the way could inform him about a missing little girl."

"And ...?"

"Nobody did, and by the time we got here, Poppa had built up such a love for me that he was detehmined to keep me. Leastwise, if somebody didn't come forward to claim me legally. He said I was his little angcl, 'cause the Lord musta sent me. Still calls me 'angel'."

"So that's how you came to be Caroline Thomas!"

"There's just one or two more twists to the story. When Momma saw me, Lord o mercy, she pitched the biggest fit you ever saw. You see, she thought I was Poppa's baby by some ole hussy woman back in Charleston and that he had made up that cock-and-bull story about finding me on the road somewhere."

"But couldn't his men vouch for his story?"

"Sure they could—and did—but it didn't matter to Momma. She just stuck her nose in the air and said in a huff that the men would say whatever Poppa told them to say. So Poppa had no proof, no convincing proof anyway, that I was a foundlin'."

"So what happened?"

"Well, time and a woman's mothering nature, I reckon, Peter. That's what happened. Momma just fell in love with me and claimed me as her very own, though to this day I don't really know if she believes Poppa's story."

"And do you?"

"Yes sir, I reckon I do, for my Poppa's too honest to lie. I think he would say right out if I was his natural child."

"So then you have no way of knowing who you really are or where you came from, do you?"

"Well, there is a detail or two that we know for sure. When I appeared in the camp I was wearing a peculiar little silver cross with a beautiful emerald insert around my neck, so I reckon that means I had Christian parents. Here it is. Want to see it?"

She extracted the tiny cross of curious design from her etui. It appeared to be pure silver and had certain miniature lettering and the initials C.T. delicately etched on the back. I pondered them, shook my head, as mystified as everyone else as to their significance. "You said there was another detail. What was it, if you'd care to tell me."

"Like I said, I was about eighteen months old, and I reckon I could already talk a little. Poppa said I kept repeating something like 'Momma otu, momma, otu' and looking around for something or somebody. They named me Caroline Thomas because it was now our family name and matched the letters on the cross, too."

"But there was nobody with you, was there?"

"Well, Peter, if somebody was with me out there in the deep woods, they never found them. Ole Bogeyman mighta got them. Every time I think about it, it scares me a little. I've tried to remember something, anything, but I was just too young for recollectin'. And that, dear Peter, is my story. Oh, just one more little detail. After we settled in Memphis the story got around that Poppa and Momma really had a different name from the one they gave out. I reckon some of the hired men blabbed and the truth came out."

"And ...?"

"Poppa explained that our name was, legally speaking Thomas-Cunningham, but that he preferred to be called just plain 'Mr. Wilbert Thomas.' And since he was a prominent man, everybody did, though we imagine that people still gossip about it behind our back."

Just at that moment Audrey burst into the room, ashen under her ebony skin and her eyes afire with terror. "Miss Caroline, they're here! They're here! Oh, Mr. Prosper, sir, you better run for your life! Mr. Thomas catch you here with Miss Caroline, why I reckon he'd just shoot you dead!"

I needed no second alarm to stir me into panicked reaction. As Audrey frantically hid the whiskey and extra plate and silverware, I heard the main entrance door opening and voices spilling into the parlor.

"Senator McCurtain," and "Congressman Duke," and a stream of other titles and courtesies now filled the mansion. I heard Mrs. Thomas excuse herself from the milling party and start up the stairs to look in on her "indisposed daughter." I considered my options, but now the window was the only way out. However, it was nearly a twenty-foot drop into the shrubbery below. With more dexterity than I could reasonably claim, it might be possible to leap to a branch of a mammoth oak that curved within a few feet of the wall. I judged my chances with a despair that diminished whatever odds I might have had in the best of circumstances. But the risks of being caught in Caroline's room were even more terrifying.

I hesitated only for a second, for I could hear Mrs. Thomas approaching. And just as she was opening the door, I made my flying departure.

Thereupon, my lowly terrestrial nature was made painfully evident to me. For even though my desperate lunge carried me within reach of the limb, like a wounded Icarus I was sadly unable to arrest my ignoble plunge earthward. Instead, my hands, lacerated and bloodied by the rough bark and protruding knots, lost their grip and flailed in gyrating desperation as I dropped in terror and ignominy into the stabbing bushes.

Dazed, out of breath, and with stars exploding about my head from the impact, I was forced to lie unmoving in the darkness as Mrs. Thomas came to peer out the window. "I coulda sworn I heard something out there. Didn't you hear something, Caroline? What about you, Audrey?"

"Why, not a thing, Momma."

"No, ma'am, I ain't heard nothing either. But maybe it was because I been too concerned with Miss Caroline here, trying to get her well again."

"Well, now, she does look much better, thank goodness. Her cheeks are rosy and her eyes've got a brand new sparkle to them, and, I swannie, it looks like she's had enough food for two people. And my gracious, how did you break the picture frame? I reckon there wasn't anything out there, or if there was, I guess it was just some ole possum. But nevertheless, Caroline, you need to keep your windows and shutter closed this time of the day to keep the varmints out."

"Yes ma'am ..." I heard Caroline answer before Mrs. Thomas slammed shut the heavy window and latched the shutters.

I got up tentatively and groped my way out of the jabbing hedgerow, fearful of what parts of my anatomy might be broken. But apart from a slight aggravation of an old wound in my right foot (the result of an injury I sustained trying to protect Monique from a runaway carriage), everything seemed intact.

My relief was short-lived. As I was hobbling toward the outer iron fence, I heard the terrible barking and thudding footbeats of the giant mastiffs coming for me. I ran, half-dragging my right foot that now throbbed in deeper pain. Yet panic goaded me to a final exertion toward safety. But as I scrambled up and over the fence, the men spotted me also and joined their excited voices with the bedlam of the barking dogs.

Again I had no choice but to fall from the fence onto a rocky surface now obscured by the growing darkness. My lame foot hit a protruding branch and I let out an involuntary cry of pain. "Over here, men! He's over here! Get in there and grab the sonuvabitch!"

And indeed probably they would have captured me if just at that moment my fortunes had not taken a fortuitous turn in the form of a passing delivery carriage returning from its rounds. I managed to intercept it and unbeknownst to its drowsy, nodding driver accommodated and concealed myself behind empty egg crates and wet straw. When last I saw the men and dogs, they had brought torches and were running back and forth outside the walls searching for me. Thus safely ensconced, I rode a goodly distance from the Cunningham-Thomas mansion before again dropping to the ground.

The immobility now made plain to me the pitiful and dolorous character of my scrapes, gashes, bruises, and abrasions. I limped painfully the quarter league back to my miserable quarters, my only consolation being the sweet conviction and wonderful certainty that Caroline's love was mine forever. I was exhausted, but before collapsing in agony into my crude bed, I took pains to place Caroline's mysterious cross—which, I confess, out of habit I extracted at the last second from her etui—in an undetectable crevice I had hewn in my wall for the deposit of such niceties. Later Caroline lamented its loss, but I feigned ignorance.

I soon recovered from my abrasions, deflecting curious inquiries as to their cause and circumstance. As usual, Pollard suspected much more than I would have him believe—a fall from a pecan tree—but resigned himself to the face value of my lie about the matter, muttering angrily only over the expense of replacing my torn trousers. Since the gambling episode we had entered into a mutually necessary but tense pact of silence. Neither of us could afford to speak openly and abroad about our respective doings.

As the soreness left my body, it was replaced by the pain of my separation from gorgeous Caroline and the imperious desire to arrange with Audrey's help a second successful rendezvous. For having found my way into her affections and gained entrance into her boudoir, I had no doubts about an early repetition of my first triumph.

In this happy expectation I was not disappointed. For several months our idyll flourished. With Audrey's paid complicity and astuteness, I savored fair Caroline's sweet companionship, in her room whenever entry into the mansion was possible, in the wooded grove where first we met, when it was not. The ardor of our love continued undiminished by greater familiarity, but to this grand passion Caroline added the alarming expectations of marriage, home, and family. I confess that there were moments when it pained me to deceive her with false accounts of my origins and former life in New Orleans. But to the dozens of lies I told her I would have added a thousand prevarications rather than have the cruel truth of my life and condition destroy our ecstatic felicity. She in turn wept at the slightest provocation and was given to odd whims and accusatory moods that puzzled and disturbed me.

But alas and alack, in the end not even my grand embellishments could save our love. How sadly unequal my fabrications were to the implacable march of events and the harsh light of truth! How grievously I misjudged the inconstant female heart! How deceptive its promise! How quickly withdrawn its fickle favors! For by now surely Caroline began to see through my ruses and to sense my grand deceptions. At first she protested with tears and frenzies but afterwards commenced to withdraw from me. Our trysts came less often and her pretexts for their cancellation multiplied apace.

One day Audrey met me without her mistress. "Miss Caroline can't see you no more, 'Massa' Prosper," Audrey explained sarcastically. "She's busy day and night with the high-faluting folks that been acoming over here ever since last yeah when they showed up with President Jackson. That ole Senator McCuhtain been after her ever since he first laid eyes on her and now he's done come back here from Washington to get her."

I was stunned by the news. "What do you mean, Audrey, 'after her'? Is he bothering her?"

Audrey giggled. "Ain't no bother to it, the way I see it. Miss Caroline's havin the ti-i-ime of her life, I reckon, all that attention from that rich ole senator and his crowd."

"But Caroline loves me," I protested. "She's mine!"

"'Massa' Prospah, you look here and listen to me," she rejoined, her tone turning serious. "Women like Miss Caroline don't belong to no-o-obody, for sure not for long. You best learn that right now and save

83

yourself a lotta misery. You and her done had your fun. Now you best just forget all that and get on down the road, 'cause that's what Miss Caroline's gonna do."

"I don't understand, Audrey. What's going on?"

"Well, to be honest with you, 'Massa' Prospah, talk is that Miss Caroline's gonna marry that ole senator and go to live up there in that Washington town, I reckon."

"But she can't! She loves me!"

"It's all been done already, I reckon, 'Massa' Prosper. Her daddy's done arranged everything with the senator, and Miss Caroline's done give her consent. And she done sent me to tell you not to come round her no-o-o more."

"But how can she do that do me! We love each other! We ..."

Audrey cut me off with a wagging finger. "The truth about you's done come out, 'Massa' Prospah, and there ain't no need for me to be proper with you no more. Some of them visitin folks are from New Awleans, and they've done put two and two together. Some of them gentlemen were needin a shave and haircut, I reckon. Talk come up about ole Pollard's barbershop and that young barber from New Awleans, and they say know about you and your family. Talk is you ain't nothin like you told Miss Caroline, that is, if you be the same man they been talkin about. And I'm reasonable sure you are. They're sayin there may even be a price on your sorry head. Sayin you family ain't got no money. And the stories they done told about your momma, lawdy, lawdy, I ain't never heard tell of such a woman! Why I reckon you're part nigger, too, if folks got it right, and one of them is a gentleman that used to keep her, I reckon. He ain't got nothing good to say about her—or about you, for as that goes. He say you arranged to have your own brother captured by the slavers. And here I been treatin you like white, and all the time you got African folks back yonder just like me! And a low-down rascal to boot! Anyways, you better be getting yourself on outta here, insteada strutting around all high and mighty tryin to pass yourself off as a white boy and messin round with white girls. Why they'll stomp you like a bug and kill you like a snake, they catch you hangin around here. I'm just tellin you for your own good cause I ain't got nothin against you. You helped me out and now I'm tryin to help you. And you better listen to me if you know what's good for you."

A clammy sweat of terror caused me to shiver, and my legs to buckle in terror of the calamities that might be about to befall me. Never was the old French saying truer:

The brave man dies but once,
The coward, with every danger he dreads.

It was true that I had clipped and shaved several of the visitors who, while lauding me for my barbering skills, questioned me about my origins and made sport of my accent. Even my eternally sworn love for Caroline wilted before the catastrophic dimensions of my dilemma. Suddenly Memphis, which briefly had bidden fair to be my Eden, now took on the ominous images of the infernal realm.

The events soon to be consummated in the Thomas mansion became the common talk of Memphis. Caroline's betrothal to the senator was announced, and the wedding set for the last week of September 1833. This news set off a flood of lurid innuendoes regarding the wondrous disparities between her exuberant youthful beauty and the advanced decrepitude of her aged suitor. The barbershop was the principal gathering point for these malicious tongues, and I was forced to endure the gossip with a straight face, an empty smile, and a very broken heart.

"Hope he's got some accommodating neighbors to help him out up yonder in Washington," smirked Matthew Satterfield, "He's gonna need some friendly folks, if you get my meanin'."

"Yeah, Matt," chimed in Colonel Rayford Summerford," his red beard shaking with wicked glee. "She's liable to be a widow afore she's a woman!"

"Well, now, you may be right," drawled Newt Powell with a lopsided grin, "but jist remember, fellers, that if thangs don't pick up, if you get my drift', they's always that there hard cash to make up for it."

"You're right about that, Newt," responded Matt. "Any way you look at it, she's gonna have it all pretty soon. And when she does she'll be a rich young widow and can have any man she fancies. Now, by damn, you can jist look at that old man and tell he ain't got many rows left to plow."

"Hell, Matt, he can't even get the plow point in the furrow no more!" guffawed Colonel Summerford.

The evening of Caroline's wedding I slipped away to the wooded groves overlooking the Mississippi, there to ponder my wretched fate. But I was too agitated to be consoled by mere bucolic surroundings and soon abandoned the attempt. But I returned with one vow: I had to leave Memphis, but I was even more resolutely determined than ever not to go empty-handed.

Only very rarely because of pressing affairs or out-of-town

journeys did Pollard cease his obstinate vigilance of his hoard, and despite my most earnest and expert efforts on those infrequent occasions, I was unable to open all the bolts and spring the locks he had installed to guard his treasure.

But Providence, which turns the world in strange ways, intervened in a series of unexpected happenings that would alleviate some of my present frustrations and open the door to other terrors, which I shall relate to you, dear reader, in due course.

Three occurrences converged to hasten my departure and change the flow of events. To begin with, Pollard returned from one of his journeys accompanied by a wife, the widow Bertha Bullard Vaughan whose first husband, according to Memphis gossips, was the same Love Vaughan, lately shot by constables in Natchez, who once trafficked in stolen horses and slaves with his brother Sommer and a New Orleans criminal called Alain "Sixfingers" DuClos.

"We got married in Natchez," beamed Luke, slipping a beefy hand possessively round her ample, shapeless waist. "Now I order you all, Antoine, Poulette, and you Petie, to show her all the respect due her as my wife and mistress of this house and establishment. Izat clear?"

"Yessuh, Massah," intoned Antoine and Poulette with bowed heads. I remained silent.

"And you, Petie? I didn't hear what you said."

"Oh, I said Mrs. Pollard will have all the respect she deserves from me."

Luke frowned, not quite knowing what to make of my double-edged remark. I was too frustrated and angry at the moment to suffer fools patiently, even if my sharp tongue placed me in danger.

For the first few nights, we were variously entertained and molested by scandalous squeals, giggles, and bangings emanating from Pollard's quarters. Then just a few nights later, the banging stopped, the giggles and squeals ceased, and the first thing we knew, Bertha had gathered her things and moved out into another room. Luke had nothing to say about this unexpected turn of events, but the grim set of his jaw and angry glares that passed between them told us that their former sweet love had quickly soured.

Distracted by my own misfortunes, I paid no more than idle attention to their oafish farce until something happened as a consequence of their estrangement that placed me squarely in the path of danger. Late one night, a Tuesday, as I recall, when Pollard was away, I heard a rap on my door. Peering out through a crack, I was startled to find myself staring eyeball to eyeball with Bertha in flickering candlelight.

"Petie boy," she whispered hoarsely, "I need to talk to you."

Her voice was thick with an alcoholic accent, for in her brief stay in Memphis, she had proved to be a most faithful and inseparable companion of the bottle.

"Mrs. Pollard, it's late and I don't believe it proper to admit you into my room at this hour."

"I need to talk to you, Petie," she insisted, her voice rising to an alarming volume.

Reluctantly, I cracked the door, whereupon she shoved her way inside. As she did so, the brusqueness of her movement snuffed out the candle and we were left fumbling in the darkness. Before I could secure and light one of the phosphorous matches next to my candle, her hands were already slithering over my body, introducing themselves with brazen abandon into my most private and forbidden precincts. I shuddered in involuntary revulsion, picturing clearly in the gloom her coarse features, bulbous lips, and black, rotting teeth with bits of food lodged between them.

Thereupon commenced a silent but earnest struggle in the inky darkness, for me to free myself, and for her to hold the indecent liberties she had taken with me and to gain new ones. Finally, I managed to remove her hands and, exerting great effort, to push her considerable girth out the door. Her only words were a snarling threat that let me know Pollard had told her about my ancestry.

"You'll pay for this insult, you little nigger bastard!"

I was too agitated to sleep the rest of the night, wondering what form her vengeance might take. And to complicate matters even more, the next Saturday as soon as I entered the barbershop with its customary crowd, a new menace confronted me.

Colonel Summerford arrived in a high state of excitement, his rosy cheeks flushed to a brighter red. "You'ns heard the news?"

"Whut? What've ye heard?" asked Esmer, ever eager for gossip and scandal.

The others feigned a manly indifference, but an involuntary tilt of heads in his direction betrayed their interest.

"Oh, just this and that," responded the Colonel coyly, not ready to release the succulent news.

"If you're talking about that boat sankin'," piped in Bluford Blevins who had just come up from the river, "I heard about that yesterday. Wasn't much to it, I hear, everybody done made it off and to shore, except a darkie boy the captain had chained up down on the lower deck."

"Ain't got nothin to do with no boat sinkin'," Summerford cut him off sharply, giving surgical attention with his pocketknife to a hangnail.

"What, then?" asked Bluford, annoyed by the colonel's game.

Summerford looked up suddenly from his crude grooming, snapped his knife shut, gave his listeners a knowing stare, and lowering his voice to a mysterious pitch released his news.

"You remember that little Thomas gal that got married to the senator a few days ago?"

"Yeah, course we do," said Esmer, "what about her? She done started complaining right in the middle of the honeymoon?"

A vulgar chorus of guffaws followed.

"No, and that's the thing. They say the ole senator's the one that be doing the complaining."

Esmer stopped shaving, his face still half-covered with lather, and all the men, seven or eight in number, moved closer to Summerford in conspiratorial curiosity, whilst I, listening to the pounding of my heart that fairly threatened to leap from my bosom, continued to strop one of the new razors Pollard had recently purchased for me. Word had spread about my mixed blood and past delinquencies, and although my talents as an expert barber were still sought and my presence tolerated, I was now treated with the contemptuous regard afforded colored servants.

"What about?" inquired Cletis Hardin. "That's about as fine a filly as any man would ever want to ride."

Heads nodded in agreement.

"Not the way I heard it," answered the colonel, peering again at the hangnail. "Why, way they're telling it now, he be aclaiming damaged merchandise."

I looked up to find Esmer staring at me.

"Damaged?" wondered Cletis. "What are ye talking about, Ray?"

"Well, just that it seems the little lady was already rode and broke in and maybe got herself a little play-pretty in the doing of it."

"Like what?" Ossamus Hargrove wanted to know.

"Like a baby, I truly reckon," drawled the Colonel, a sly, evil grin spreading across his round face. "Word is she had done gone and got herself knocked up somewhere, and the old senator's aripping and asnorting and athreatening bloody murder soon's he finds out who bigged her. And Mr. Thomas is jist as mad."

"Who you reckon it was?" wondered Esmer's brother Newt Powell.

"I ain't got the least idee. All I know it wasn't me, though I wouldn't've minded performing that little favor for her, the truth be told."

"Yeah," chimed in several voices.

Esmer was staring at me again.

"But they'll find out who done it," Summerford said confidently, "and when they do, I'd hate to be in that bastard's boots."

"Amen to that," everybody agreed.

Imagine, dear reader, my agitation, my despair, my terror. On the one hand, I experienced feelings entirely new to me as I contemplated the alien idea of fatherhood. I who had never known a father could only look upon the prospect as the deepest mystery imaginable. And amidst these strange new provocations there surged as a newly stoked flame my old love for Caroline Thomas. I was moved by an unpremeditated impulse to rush out to defend her and the life she bore within her.

But on the other hand, I quaked in fear for my very life. Colonel Summerford was probably right: It was only a question of time until they discovered my complicity and devised my ruin. Caroline herself might confess who her lover was.

The malicious gossip about Caroline's plight was overshadowed only by the excitement caused by the third fateful event that was to shape that episode of my life. Around noon that same Saturday a carnival caravan arrived in the town square with trumpets blaring and barkers enticing the townsfolk with promises of wondrous amusements, miraculous medicines, and magic shows in the coming days. Bascom Harvey directed the carnival master to set up his tents in Henson's pasture, several acres of level, grassy terrain east of the town center within walkable distance. There the traveling carnival commenced its deployment to the gawking stares and excited commentaries of onlookers. The barbershop quickly emptied.

As for me, I now calculated that I had only a few days—and perhaps only a few hours—to escape Memphis with my life. I must move swiftly. Caroline was beyond my help in any case and any try on my part to aid her would condemn us both. Caught up in the carnival excitement and without corpses to tend or beards to shave, Luke and Bertha Pollard joined the townsfolk at the carnival. I neglected to relate to you, dear reader, that latterly they had reconciled their differences, and the nightly squeals, giggles, and bangings from his quarters had commenced again in full lascivious exuberance. Antoine, Poulette, and pitiful daughter Jeanette had also, or so I supposed, issued forth without permission from the distracted Luke to mingle with the gawking mob.

Thereupon, alone in the deserted barbershop-mortuary, I determined to risk all in a final, supreme attempt to force open Pollard's treasure chest and escape with its trove.

Wise from previous failures, I wasted no time trying to open the multi-locked door. Instead I took Antoine's auger along with a hammer and chisel, which he used to bore dowel holes in the cypress and pine casket slabs. Thus equipped, I crawled under the building, and at the location my measurements indicated, began my perforations with the auger

Unhappily, my calculations went awry and my first try was wide of its mark; for through the opening I could just espy the corner of the chest. Thereupon, I renewed my labors at a more promising spot, pausing at intervals to wipe my face and clean my eyes of dust, cobwebs, and shavings. This time the bit chewed eagerly into the soft underbelly of the chest and soon gained entry into the desired precinct. But the task was yet remote from completion. Several other perforations and considerable hammering and chiseling were necessary ere I was able to insert my hand into the opening. My first retrievals were disappointing: clothes and papers, which, I hoped vainly, shielded a considerable treasure. Anon, I began to reach garments and effects purloined from the dead: dresses, gloves, suits, ties, combs, pins, and an assortment of profitless personal items. These I extracted and discarded forthwith in frenzied eagerness to seize the expected coinage.

Extended to the utmost, my groping fingers touched and identified the iron-plated metal coffer into which, according to Poulette, she had once seen Pollard drop a handful of dollars. This observation had earned Poulette a severe thrashing, for obsessed as he was by the task Luke was unaware of her spying presence. But her painful witness now spurred on my hope and strengthened my conviction that I had found the money trove.

I conceived of no convenient method of removing the coffer. By extensive, prolonged labor I might succeed in enlarging the opening sufficiently for this purpose, but time was made precious by its limitation. I determined therefore to extract its contents by drilling and chiseling away a portion of its bottom panel. The labor was arduous and slow.

Suddenly the door banged open and Pollard strode in, followed by a panting Bertha.

"Honey lamb (gasp), I wasn't ready to come home (gasp)," pouted a half-drunken Bertha. "Thangs was just gitting warmed up out at the carnival."

"Now, don't you be a frettin', Bertha, I promise we gonna have us a fine time later on." (Bertha giggled as he groped her.) "I jist wanted

90

to come home a minute to check on things. I don't trust that thieving Petie as fer as I could throw a bull by the tail. Ain't nobody seen him since this morning and I just feel like he's up to somethin'. Just don't know what it is, and that bothers me."

"Well, honey, all I can say is you do need to keep a right sharp eye on him (gasp). I done told you what he tried to do to me other night while you was gone on that trip. Tried to have his way with me, he did, jist like I told you, and I didn't give him nary a reason in the world to git an idee like that in his nasty little mind. And you told me you was gonna put him in his place. I had to do it myself."

"And you hadn't oughtta told Bascom Harvey. I was gonna do it myself. All you done is cause me a big, big problem."

"Whut kinda problem you talking about, love? You didn't aim to let the little bastard git away with insulting me, did ye?"

"Just never you mind about my problems. And no, he ain't gitting away with nothin'. But I got my own way of doing things, and I don't need nobody to run my business for me. And that goes for you and everybody else in this town. Anyway, it's all being set up. Bascom and some deputies be alooking for him at this very minute. He'll go to jail for sure, and folks'll hang his ass from the nearest tree if word gets out about him trying to force a white woman. But they's still something about that there story o' yourn that bothers me."

"Whu-u-ut?"

"What was you doing down at his end of the building anyway? You never did give me a good reason."

"Did too! I done told you a dozen times, you turkey head, I thought I heard somebody talking and went to see what was going on. I thought maybe he had some little slut in there. When you ain't here, honey, I guess I'm responsible fer running this place and protecting its good name. Now ain't that right?"

Pollard mumbled something about having to remove everything in the chest tomorrow, muttered several other incoherencies, rattled the chest door, and satisfied that it was secure, turned and pushed Bertha before him out the door, groping her obscenely as they left to her amorous squeals of protest and pleasure.

For a few minutes I lay paralyzed and bathed in the cold sweat of terror over the chilling words I had just heard. What to do? What to do? Oh, Holy Mother of God, I prayed, please rescue me from this horror! A mad panic urged me to drop my tools and run blindly away. But calmer reflection quickly dispelled the notion. This was the safest place in Memphis for the moment, I told myself. Who would ever think of looking for me here, under the very building I now had the greatest reason to shun? I resolved to stay there until sundown, for darkness would increase my options.

Moreover, I had unfinished business, and though terror over my fate continued unabated, now an unrighteous indignation strengthened my resolve and removed any doubts about my right to revenge and Pollard's treasure.

Thus I fell to the task with renewed vigor, and yielding to the hammer and chisel, within the hour a wee opening in the panel widened into a considerable gap. Finally a coin dropped and struck my cheek, then another and another, until a veritable rain of Spanish dollars showered down on me. When the noisy flow abated I shook and rattled the coffer until it surrendered its last reluctant coin. How much money was there I could not calculate in the semi-darkness, but of a certainty it was far more than I had pilfered from Ignatius Downes in New Orleans. My hands fairly trembled with excitement.

Few of the trinkets and garments visible from where I lay caught my eye, though I could not resist lifting a white silk chemise and crimson cravate (as I call them in my language) that reminded me of the ones my purported father wore in my mother's drawing. Pollard had removed them from the cadaver and belongings of an unfortunate youth who died of pneumonia on his way to New Orleans. Pondering these items and spurred by dread, it suddenly occurred to me that were I to dress myself as a woman, I might materially aid my chances of being undetected. Luckily I was newly shaven and had at my disposal all manner of laces, dresses, shoes, gloves, and other finery confiscated from the dead. I extracted a quantity of items greater than I could reasonably employ for this stratagem, unable only to locate a hat amongst Pollard's grisly booty.

Exhausted from my labors and agitated by conflicting emotions of elation, dread, and anger, I lay unmoving as the slow hours ticked by. Once a black hound stuck its head under the building and sensing my presence, barked its astonishment and bared its fangs. But when no one noticed, at last it slunk away, sniffing the ground and pausing now and then to look back and emit a dispirited growl. Exhausted and still, I waited.

Night had fallen when I crawled from under the building, dragging the coins and a bundle of funereal clothing, most of which, on a sudden incriminating whim against Pollard, I strewed wantonly and conspicuously along the street, reserving only the dress I had chosen for myself. I replaced Antoine's tools, hoping that he would not be implicated in my thievery but resigned nevertheless to the likelihood that he and Poulette would suffer because of my escapade. Greatly to my relief, the streets were all but deserted, for everyone, it seemed, had issued forth to see the carnival.

At that moment the same black hound, which must have kept a suspicious eye on me during my time under the building, emerged from the darkness and snarled a challenge at me. Despite my kicks and muffled curses it tore my trousers with its fangs and mayhap had done greater damage if a passerby had not rapped it viciously with his cane. The dog ran away howling in pain as I mumbled a hurried thank-you to the solicitous gentleman and rushed away.

I waited until my benefactor disappeared and then cautiously reentered my room, extracted my few possessions of sentimental or pecuniary value from their concealment, and donning the somber dark dress buttoned to the throat, was soon transformed into the likeness of a youngish and—save for a bosom—perhaps not altogether ill-proportioned woman. To my disappointment, however, the shoes I had taken were far too small and I had no choice to discard them and wear my boots. This setback, I reasoned, posed no great problem, for in the dark it was doubtful that anyone would notice my footwear.

Of much greater concern was my lack of indispensable feminine headdress. This I remedied by forcing access to Bertha's wardrobe where I confiscated a modish black hat given her by Pollard only the week before during their reconciliation ritual. Viewing myself in her mirror, I was astonished by the change and could not but ponder for a moment the advantages it afforded me. Thus transformed into a dubious member of the fairer sex, I emerged from the building to empty streets, yet apprehensive that eyes were watching me.

My plan of escape, only vaguely conceived in its totality and crucial points, was to make my way to the river there to set out northward along the heavily forested roads that offered concealment and head eventually towards St. Louis. But as I contemplated this maneuver, I heard voices. Slinking back into the dense foliage, I recognized Colonel Summerford in the company of a taller man unknown to me.

"Well, it's just what I was sayin', wasn't it?" Colonel Summerford said to the lean man who towered over him. "I told you they'd find out who done it and catch the bastard."

"You still talking 'bout that Thomas girl? Ray, I don't give a royal goddamn who knocked her up or anything about it. I just try to mind my own business. Places I go you learn to keep yer mouth shut, or somebody'll shut it for you—for good."

Colonel Summerford stopped to light his pipe, and in the flaring glow his features were etched with compunction and disapproval. They paused while the Colonel applied the smoking match and sucked to get the tobacco burning.

"Hell, Frank, I was just trying to make talk. Maybe you don't give a rip but folks 'round here do."

"Well, since you're so all fired up to tell me. Who was it?"

"Who was what?"

"Dammit, Ray, the guilty one—or lucky one, depending on how you look at things."

"Well, yeah, it was Petie, that little nigger barber over yonder at Pollard's place. He looks white enough, but we done found out he's part nigger."

"How do you know he done it? The girl tell on him?"

"Naw, not the way I heerd it. Seems Esmer Powell, Pollard's other barber, followed the sonuvbitch once or twice up to the Thomas mansion. He's always hated the little bastard 'cause he's a better barber. When he told the senator, this morning I reckon it was, in hopes of gitting even and gitting the ree-ward, the ole goat liked to bust a blood vessel. His wife big with a nigger kid! This morning he had his men beat the living s--- outta that ole servant of hers. Went over Mr. Thomas's head, he did too, for even though the Thomases are mad enough to chew nails about their girl, they were partial to that ole woman. Been with them a long time, I reckon."

"And?"

"And nothin'. She bellered out ever'thing, how she was in on the whole business fer the money she got paid. Guess anybody'd talk if they laid ye back open with a bullwhip. I reckon she's gonna die anyway. That's what they're sayin'. But she deserves to, don't she?"

"I reckon. But where'd that boy get money in the first place? Stole it? Pollard don't pay his niggers, does he?"

"Naw, I reckon not, sonuvbitch won't hardly pay nobody what he owes 'em. They say he cheated some gamblers down in South Memphis."

"Who, Pollard?"

"No, dammit, Frank, Petie. Petie Prosper, leastways that's what folks call 'im."

"Must be purty sharp if he cheated that bunch o' bloodsuckers."

"Way we heard it, he's 'bout as slick as they come. Learned all them card tricks in New Orleans with the best in the business. But the boys down in South Memphis ain't taking it friendly. Word is, couple, three fellers be a looking fer 'im, and they can do carving magic with a knife. I reckon he won't be studding no more women when they get done with him."

"I thought the senator was after him."

"Is. So's Bascom Harvey and his deputies for fooling around with Pollard's woman. She turned him in, she did. It'll be a matter of who gets to him first. There's a ree-ward, you know. Put up by the senator."

"How much?" Alvis suddenly showed more interest.

"Four hundred dollars, they tell me, dead or alive. The senator don't care which, but maybe dead is better."

"Four hundred," Alvis repeated thoughtfully. "Four hundred. Now that's a right smart o' money, and I would count it most convenient."

"Go a long way to staking our business venture, Frank. We could use that money to git them other wagons and horses we need."

"You got a point. You sure got a point, Ray, no two ways about it."

"Well, somebody'll be collecting it soon enough," the colonel observed as they resumed their walk. "Bascom's deputies got all the roads and the river under close watch. No way the bastard can get outta Memphis alive. They'll be afinding him, and when they do, and if he be still alive, word is the senator's gonna hang him one way or the other. Be a waste of time to have a trial, what with insulting white womenfolk—even if it was Pollard's ole whore—but especially knocking up a white girl."

"I reckon. If I don't put a bullet tween his eyes first."

Alvis removed his pistol from a concealed holster, checked it for ammunition and returned it to its place. "Just in case I get a shot, and one's all I ever need," he remarked to the colonel with a chuckle, "right smart o' money in play."

"Yeah, and we could use it. But let's be gittin on out yonder to the carnival. That boy's as liable to be in one place as another, so we might get lucky and flush him out. Besides, I want to see that there contraption ever'body's been talking about. They call it a 'ball-oon'. They say the ole senator had it brung it over from Paree, France, as a present to his new bride. But I reckon all that lovie-dovie feeling be pretty sour on his stomach right now. Folks say that thing can fly off into the sky, but I'll not be believing it till I see it with my own two eyes. Don't seem reasonable, does it? Folks ain't supposed to fly. Reckon God'd rigged them with feathers and wings, if they was."

"I reckon."

"That's what I allus say, but they's folks that done seen it up in St. Louee or somewhere and they swear it flies and all. Anyway, we'll know for sure tomorrow. That's when they gonna fly it. It's full o' some kinda gas and ready to go out yonder in Henson's pasture, folks be a sayin'."

They disappeared into the night, only the bright glow of Summerford's pipe still visible after they were out of earshot. As their voices receded, the utmost fright came over me. Now indeed all avenues of escape were blocked, and three parties of vengeful men were converging to bring to a violent end my profitless life.

I waited in the foliage for a time as my mind raced to consider and discard options as my demise drew ever closer. Perhaps with luck I could avoid detection for the rest of the night, but with daylight my doom was only a matter of time. Sooner or later people would see through my disguise and my pursuers would be ready to finish me off. Then having exhausted all possible means of escape and the full grip of panic, I was forced into the impossible.

Unable to think of any other possibility of escaping Memphis by the northern route, I bent my steps eastwards toward the carnival grounds, meeting only a few stragglers along the darkened streets. Some of these, well into their cups, offered to escort me to my destination, "tote my heavy bundle," and provide my provocative person with certain other masculine services should I be so inclined. I hurried by without a word, of course, gaze downcast, identifying for perhaps the first time in my life with the inconveniences of the feminine condition.

Imagine my fear, gentle reader, as I saw approaching me a trio of South Memphis cutthroats. But beyond a few leering stares and uncouth offers of companionship, I suffered no material inconvenience from the encounter.

I had progressed but little when I came upon a tense confrontation between Senator McCurtain's men and Bascom Harvey's deputies, each side defending its right to bring "Petie Prosper" to swift justice. The deputies argued for a rapid but due process of the law, whereas the senator's band sneered at this useless legal delay and proclaimed its intention of administering summary justice by bullet if I resisted, by instant hanging if I surrendered. No one paid me heed as I hurried by, head down and averted in a trembling facsimile of maidenly modesty.

Presently, by now the wee hours of the morning, after having skirted with great caution the outlying districts of the city, I came within sight of the balloon as it swayed silvery and ghostly to the gentle caresses of the night breezes. Half way up on its side the name "Caroline" in giant black lettering was inscribed within a red valentine heart, and underneath in smaller dimensions and as a memento of happier moments the inscription "love" and the name of Senator

McCurtain.

I did not muse very much over the ironies confronting me, exhausted as I was from hunger and terror. The coins were an added burden, yet these I clung to with all the force of my being, determined not to yield them even though the resolution might cost me my life. My dress was snagged and stained by the underbrush and dew-moistened cobwebs hung from my hat.

As I drew nearer, I saw that the globe, or "balloon" as the Americans named it in their language, was tethered by two large ropes, one on each side, attached to deeply driven iron stakes. A basket of sorts, large enough to accommodate two or three men hung beneath it some five or six feet above the ground. I saw no one. Evidently, the crowds had repaired to their homes to rest for the stupendous events promised for the morrow.

Because of a fear of knives, several of which had been used against me, I carried on my person only a small penknife with which to sever the heavy ropes. Moreover, I faced the further dilemma of how I might reach them from the basket should I manage to lower it sufficiently so as to clamber aboard.

This uncertainty was remedied by the fortuitous discovery of a long tethering hook used, as I supposed, by the tenders to snare and steady the basket and the dangling ropes. With this instrument, I lowered the basket to a level of easy access, and once aboard with money and belongings, I was able to pull the tethering ropes to within reach of my small knife. As the first gave way, the basket pitched violently toward the other rope and it was some time before balance was reestablished and I was able to sever with trembling hands my remaining tie to earth.

As I was cutting the last remaining strands of the other rope, two men came running towards the balloon, shouting and waving their arms. I redoubled my efforts but before the rope parted one of them grabbed the end of the other one whilst his companion looked about vainly for the tethering hook.

At that instant the last strands parted and instead of a lurch as with the first tether, the basket rose gently, almost imperceptibly, in the still morning air, lifting the clinging, kicking man with it. Although I discerned terror in his face, he clung stubbornly until I rapped his head smartly with the tethering pole. Whereupon, bootlessly flailing his legs and arms, he dropped four or five meters to grassy ground, apparently little worse for his ordeal, for I saw him get to his feet and wobble away. He raised his arms to shield himself as I dropped the tethering pole behind him.

By now the sun was breaking above the tree line on the eastern horizon. Despite my fear and exhaustion, an inexplicable exultation came over me as I mounted skyward. On this virgin course lay my last and best hope for life and freedom.

I was of course, dear reader, at the mere whim and mercy of the elements in my celestial career. Because of the prevailing northeasterly breezes I had assumed that the balloon would ride to the southwest, but no sooner had my fantastic globe risen several hundred meters into the ether than a strong south wind, undetectable at earth level, began to carry it swiftly over the very heart of Memphis and towards the Mississippi River. From my lofty level and above the hissing wind I now seemed to perceive shouts from below, and looking cautiously over the rim of the basket, I spied a throng rushing to the townsquare, waving and shouting in excitement and approval.

Thus I exited Memphis in apparent but fraudulent triumph in Caroline's confiscated balloon with Pollard's money and to misplaced acclaim. As an ironical gesture of acknowledgement, I tossed Bertha's hat down at the cheering townspeople. It spiraled in graceful gyrations toward eager, uplifted hands.

Only the briefest moment passed before I saw puffs of smoke and a long second later felt the impact of a ball in the bottom of the basket followed by the crack of a long rifle. I placed the coins under my feet and squatted as low as I could in the basket, tensely hoping that the money would serve me as a shield. Now indeed I was grateful for the strong wind that carried me swiftly out of range, though not before other bullets, their trajectory almost spent, struck the basket.

No harm came to the basket or my person, but though it was not apparent to me until several hours later, the balloon itself was mortally wounded. Meanwhile, I was carried northward along the course of the giant Mississippi, praying the while to the Virgin, the Savior, the Saints, and the Protestant God alike that the fantastical globe would not fail me and plunge me into its muddy, roiling currents.

The firing and shouting were quickly out of range. Anon Memphis and Caroline were but a vanishing point on the horizon. For now I was flying over swamps and forests at a dizzying velocity. Animal herds bolted in panic at my passing, my head swam, my heart raced, and my imagination invented a thousand perils in the forested vastness over which I was speeding in reckless and uncontrollable flight. But three considerations gave me a measure of consolation: I was alive, I was free, and I was rich.

Translator's Addendum

The highlighted article, apparently clipped from an issue of an early day Memphis newspaper (September 1833), was also inserted in the original manuscript. For reasons similar to those given to justify the first addendum, I offer this information to the reader.

Items

We are saddened to report that in an inebriated state Solomon Lawler fell into a well last Saturday and died. The body could not be retrieved from the collapsing sand. The well was filled and will be his tomb. Let our boys hereabouts take warning and refrain from demonizing drink. It withers the spirit and ruins the body of all who partake of it.

Mr. Hezikiah Turrentyne, of our neighboring town of Sommerville, has had more than an average man's matrimonial experience. He has traipsed happily to the altar four times, and rumor has it that he will soon make a fifth trip. He has married in succession, Misses Martha Jane Hathaway, Viola Mae Thigpen, Hetty Lou McKenzie, and Lizzy Eunice Strawbridge. His prospective blushing fifth bride is Miss Serepth Mahala Hathaway, sister to his first.

With unfeigned sorrow we report that Asa Hardin hung himself last Tuesday, but the world moves on just the same without him.

Clarified at last: the mystery of Melvin Hightower's missing left ear. Jerome Alssobrook swore in Judge Crawford Patterson's courtroom that he witnessed a fight between Hightower and Claudius Jones, both reeling from drink. The latter gentleman finding himself being considerably bested in the fisticuffs, bit off his opponent's ear and broke a bottle of spirits over his head. Hightower lies unable to speak, and Jones has departed Memphis.

We regret to learn that Mr. Darius James, a shining light in our Holiness Church, a bright Mason, and an able statesman for high causes, died lately in a hospital in Murphreesboro where he was under care for insanity. Peace to his dust.

Our pride swells as we report that highminded men of Memphis are bearing beneficent commerce into the extreme west. Colonel Rayford

Summerford, brave quartermaster in the late war, and Mr. Cletis Satterfield, a highly regarded businessman of this community, are preparing a caravan of wagons to transport goods useful for social improvement to the distant Mexican province of Santa Fe. We learn that Mr. Frank Alvis, whose nonparail knowledge of those wild lands is a great convenience, will serve as the party's keen-eyed scout.

In what has to be the first such incident in the annals of recorded human history, the felon known locally as Petie Prosper yesterday confounded local law officials by escaping from Memphis in an imported balloon inflated with helium gas. The balloon, brought to our fair city by the Turner Traveling Carnival through the good offices of the honorable Senator Horace McCurtain, was moored in the area known as Henson's Pasture in readiness for a public demonstration today. Having donned feminine apparel, as it seems, Prosper eluded law enforcement officials, and gaining access to the balloon under cover of darkness, was last seen brazenly soaring away in the ether over the Mississippi River. Shots fired in his direction failed in their intent to bring the evildoer to earth and to justice. To any citizen who should come forth with information about his whereabouts so that his arrest may thereby ensue and accountability for his felonious misdeeds duly proceed, a reward of $400.00 will be forthcoming.

Having been queried about such an unheard of feat and the effects it might wreak on the human body, the learned physician Dr. Thurlow Cheatham opined that the unnatural combination of acceleration and unaccustomed altitude would of a certainty be deleterious, if not fatal, to the human organism.

Prosper, said to be of colored ancestry, was being hunted for several heinous crimes, the most serious being the accusation that he forced his wicked attentions on two white females, and not least, that he robbed Mr. Lucas Pollard, a respected citizen of this fair city and owner of Pollard's Mortuary and Barbershop, of possessions placed above a value of $25.

The younger of the violated ladies in question, whose name we respectfully withhold from public knowledge, stated that governed by sinful lust Prosper must have concealed himself in her room during her parents' absence. Thereupon, having first immobilized her woman servant (lately deceased), he then overcame her desperate but unequal struggle to defend her honor and proceeded to have his wicked way with her. The other lady related a similar attempted assault the lurid details of which cannot be made public.

100

Mr. Lucas Pollard offered his view of these sad events by recounting how he had befriended and protected the fugitive. "I took the Prosper boy into my home and business, fed and clothed him, gave him a roof over his head, taught him a trade—indeed two trades as undertaker and barber—and this is the way he repays me for my Christian generosity. If he does die, as Dr. Cheatham believes he may, it will be God's judgment for his horrendous crimes."

In response to our queries Constable Bascom Harvey made only this brief comment: "This is a very strange case and we are still investigating it. I'd rather not say anymore at this time."

We lay down pen with this observation: our fair community has suffered a series of outrages by this notorious individual and we can only hope that if he survived the flight he will be captured and brought to human justice and that if he did not, then he will surely answer to a Higher Power for his offenses.

Part III: How Peter descended from the heavens and was reunited with Father Branigan; his seminary studies for the priesthood; how He and Lawler Adkins were cleverly relieved of their funds and left holding a braying ass; and how they parted ways.

Far, far from Memphis I flew in fair Caroline's balloon. Hours passed as the south wind moaned and the basket swayed and creaked, carrying me with immeasurable velocity along the serpentine course of the Mississippi. Occasional river craft greeted my passing with their deep-throated horns, and I could make out the ant-like figures of passengers waving their tiny arms at me.

The day finished and night passed as the balloon continued its uncharted celestial trajectory. As morning broke again, I perceived that my curious conveyance had descended alarmingly from its once majestic career. Only then did I espy the bullet hole from which the captured gas was escaping. It was too high for me to reach, and even if by some unlikely maneuver I should attain it, I had no means at my disposal for stanching its wound, nor of knowing whether the bullet had torn another hole opposite the first. A desperate thought crossed my mind that by discarding the coins I might gain time and distance, for a survey of the landscape now revealed only a featureless expanse of swampy desolation. This alternative I rejected out of hand: it was better to fall rich than float poor.

But upon closer inspection of my purloined fortune, it appeared that float or fall, I would not do so as a rich man. The sum was vastly inferior to my expectations, barely exceeding two hundred dollars. Indeed some of the coins—sixty or seventy unless my memory fails— were Spanish milled dollars, but the others—greater in number—were inferior American coins worth much less. I cursed Pollard anew.

By noonday I was riding at treetop level, and before another hour passed the basket touched ground, at first with a mere brush, then with rude bounces and the crashing of branches and slapping of grasses. I was reconciled to ending my flight on this contemptible terrain when a gust of wind lifted me momentarily above the trees and carried me towards what appeared to be a forested creekbed. The balloon swooped into the dark void, made a valiant effort to clear the opposing slope and with a stunning thud slammed into profuse underbrush. The basket was demolished by the impact and I, thrown clear of my craft, rolled several meters towards the water. The chemise and cravate were stained by dirt and grass, and I abandoned them with a momentary sadness.

Like a dying behemoth, the balloon billowed and rippled as it strained to lift itself from the ensnarling branches. But its life was spent, and gradually the valentine heart settled to its death, draped across the scrub. My flight had ended. I had come to earth again, though I knew not where or in what circumstances.

Shedding my dress, I strapped my coins and other possessions around my body, then slid and stumbled my way down to the creek bed. No doubt I exaggerate by giving such a wholesome appellation to the paltry stream I discovered there. For in truth it was but a sliver of water meandering from pool to pool amidst sandy banks. On these I perceived a multitude of animal tracks, but ignorant of nature and lacking the hunter's eye, I could not discern whether they were of beasts placid or predatory. Nor found I any human trace amongst them.

I was ravenously thirsty and hungry. I slaked my thirst in one of the pools, but the prospects for food were so unlikely as to conjure up before me the fearful specter of starvation. I saw fish darting about in the deeper pools, but without hook and line or spear to snare them or fire to cook them, I could fathom no means of converting them into sustenance. Searching further downstream, I discovered a few late-season black-berries that I devoured in frenzied haste.

The berries and water abated my appetite sufficiently for me to consider my options with a clearer head. My earlier aerial survey of the landscape afforded me no clue of human habitation and dispelled any profitless thought of abandoning the creek bed for the forested plain.

As I pondered these dreary possibilities, I thought to perceive human voices, but listening intently for a time, I saw no one and decided with some concern for my health that my mind, weakened by all that beset me, was playing tricks on me. Whereupon, the urge of nature, long delayed, came strongly upon me and I hastened to relieve myself. (Pardon the language, dear reader). Whereupon I clearly heard a chorus of female giggles and espied behind a blackberry cluster three crouching nuns, or so I assumed they were by their habits. Aware that I had spotted them, they emerged from concealment, averting their gaze and crossing themselves but still giggling as I hastily turned away to button my trousers and make myself presentable. The eldest of the three composed herself and scolded the younger sisters in French, who lowered their heads obediently, though not without impish smiles on their faces.

I excused myself profusely in the same language, and, relieved not to have to converse in foreign English, the elder sister explained that they were attached to St. Mary's Church of the Barrens in the town of Perryville.

106

"I am Sister Henriette, and these sisters are Denise and Marie."

I bowed to them in my best manner and commented that I saw no town on my journey, neglecting to explain my improbable aerial mode of travel. Then as courteously as I could, I inquired how it was they were so far from the convent.

"It is there to the north, and we will take you to Father Branigan, rector of the seminary to which St. Mary's is attached. As for our reason for being here, we gather what food nature offers us and to that end came here to pick the last blackberries of the season. We are charged with everyday matters of food and material needs."

"Father Branigan, you say? Could he be the same saintly Father Branigan who taught me letters and Creed as a child in New Orleans?

"That I know not, sir, only that indeed he came here from a former assignment in New Orleans and that he is a man of great learning and even greater virtues, as you shall see when you meet him."

I was stirred by the news, for surely Sister Henriette described my old master. On our way to St. Mary's I mulled the strange providential pathway that seemed to be leading me back to the most beneficial person in my life. Arriving at St. Mary's, Sister Henriette directed me to Father Branigan and then hastily withdrew, scolding the younger sisters for glancing back at me.

It was indeed Father Branigan, heavier and grayer but of the same stern, dear mien that I remembered. Hearing me address him as I bowed to kiss his ring, he was perplexed.

"And who are you, my son? Do I know you?"

"Father Branigan, I am the wayward lad you taught many years ago in New Orleans. I am Peter Prosper."

Recognizing me at last with a shout of joy, he gave me a bearhug that fairly crushed my ribs. Then he stood back and surveyed my person.

"The years have brought you nigh on to manhood, dear lad, as handsome as a stripling as you were as a child, but thin to the point of emaciation. How happens it that you wend your way to St. Mary's? This place is far removed from New Orleans."

"Surely it is the working of Providence, Father. I have traveled here from Memphis and earlier from New Orleans, where you knew me. Life became too hard for endurance in New Orleans, and gave me no better chance in Memphis. So here I am, a wanderer seeking my fortune."

"*Ubi Deus est ibi fortuna tua, Petrus.*"

I looked at him, recognizing the Latin but recalling not its meaning. "I regret to say, Father, that the meaning of your words escapes me. You taught me well many years ago but, dolt that I am, I have forgotten much."

"I said, 'where God is there is your fortune, Peter.' Find Him and let Him find you and you shall have found your fortune."

"I bow to your wisdom."

Perceiving that I was famished, Father Branigan ceased his maxims and arranged food and lodging for me. In the long and crudely constructed log hall—save for a number of sacred icons, St. Mary's Seminary differed little in aspect from the frontier structures I had known in Memphis—I devoured a hearty stew with the seminarians—ten in number—and two priests whose names I shall tell you in due time—presided over by Father Branigan, who served as rector of the seminary. The wine was abominable—a concoction fermented from wild grapes in the region—but the convivial company more than made up for its faults. The young seminarians and seasoned priests alike were so avid to learn about my travels that Father Branigan had to caution them about too great an interest in worldly matters.

"It does not behoove us to be charmed by the world. Peter is here not because the world has favored him but because it has dealt harshly with him. Is that not true, Peter?"

"Indeed, it is, Father, and because of it many parts of my life were better left untold," I said with a double meaning, loath as I was to admit my delinquencies so long as my companions remained in sympathy with me.

That afternoon an excited hunter brought word back to Perryville that he had found an exotic contraption, huge in its dimensions, the likes and uses of which he could not imagine. Queried by Father Branigan, I admitted that it was the flying balloon that had brought me from Memphis and saved me from certain death.

"Peter, you must tell me the circumstance of the thing, and if you have sinned in the doing of it, confess it and receive absolution. You may do so in the confessional if you choose and your secrets will be safe with me."

That evening after our communal meal I did indeed confess to Father Branigan, telling the whole—though not all the parts—of my life and travails in New Orleans and Memphis. Nor did I mention the money I had removed from Pollard's safe. Afterwards he sternly counseled me to change the course of my life lest Providence not spare me again from the consequences of my transgressions against it.

"I taught you Catechism and Creed, Peter, therefore, you cannot excuse your sins with ignorance of the Faith."

I hung my head in compunction, convicted by the truth of his words. "What advice can you give me, Father, for living a better life?"

"You have signaled the way yourself. Did you not say that Providence led you to this place?"

"Yes, Father, but to what purpose I know not."

"It seems clear to me, my son. Peter, God has chosen you for the priesthood."

A chill went up my spine, and my hair seemed to stand on end. Such an idea was the last thing I could imagine. "The priesthood?" I stammered in terror. "Father, I am the least apt to contemplate such a high calling. The priestly life is not for the likes of me, a sinner from my first innocence, but for men of wisdom and learning like you."

Father Branigan chuckled. "Few are born priestly or saintly, Peter. Better you did not know me as a youth in Ireland. God chooses the unlikely, even you and me, to carry out His purposes. You have much to do—studies, discipline, fasting, prayer—and God will mold you to your calling if your spirit is compliant to His will."

Of the four requisites Father Branigan mentioned, only fasting had I practiced with a forced, involuntary regularity. I beheld the others as ghastly prospects alien to my nature and desires. But perceiving no better circumstances and with reverent respect for Father Branigan, I decided to follow his counsel until a more alluring way should open before me. I reasoned, in any case, the seminarians and the fathers ate well and had warm lodging, and with the raw Missouri winter approaching both prospects stood foremost in my thinking.

I was assigned a cell, in truth a crude log cubicle situated along a south wing angling away from the great hall, which as it turned out served us for communion, classes, communal prayers, and meals. The seminary, built on land donated by pious French settler Ferdinand Rozier, Jr., was barely ten years old and still exhibited much of its rough frontier aspect. My fellow seminarians, all but one far more advanced than I in their studies and all, so I perceived, were more resolute in commitment to the priesthood. Searching about in my cell, I discovered a space behind a loose board into which I conveniently deposited my coins, Caroline's odd cross, and certain other appurtenances from my undertaker days.

The exception, one Lawler Adkins, was a gangling Illinois youth of no more years than mine, though in appearance and aspect so different from me as to appear to belong to another category of human physicality. Tall, redheaded, freckled, and blue-eyed, with hands and feet seemingly too large for his thin, elongated body, he was, as I soon discovered, exceptionally astute despite a certain Anglo-Saxon stolidness and want of quick facial expression. He grinned at my fanciful accounts of my former life and out of his own nature easily perceived my carefully crafted falsehoods.

"Pete, you might as well know you can't fool me with your lies. I can read you like an open book, my brother. I've probably done every wrong thing, committed every sin you have, and then maybe some you haven't even thought of. Lying and stealing has been second nature in both of us, a nature we're here to correct supernaturally. So, brother, why don't you just open up and be honest with me? And I'll do the same with you."

Seeing that indeed despite my best efforts I could not deceive Lawler with my fables, nor, for that matter, could he mislead me with his, we proceeded to grow close. For the first time in my life I learned to confide fully—or nearly so—in another person.

For the perfection of our Latin Father Branigan assigned the two of us to the tutelage of Father Xavier Dary, who had studied two years in Rome before asking and receiving permission to work as a missionary on the American frontier. This singular decision and the utter charm of his person went far to persuade us of his saintliness. Of sterner, more demanding character, Fathers Branigan and Jerome divided the rest of our studies—among them Church history and doctrine, moral and natural law, and the rudiments of Scholastic Philosophy—between them.

In Latin I progressed rapidly, aided by the returning memory of my earlier studies and the similarities to the Romance tongues I spoke. For Lawler, however, Latin was an inpenetrable mystery that for weeks resisted his best efforts to understand its structure and meaning. On the other hand, his natural understanding of other subjects was noticeably greater than my own. I spent much time patiently reviewing for him as best I could the cases, declensions, tenses, genders, and meanings of Latin. In turn, he tried to clarify for me the notions of natural and moral law, the headsplitting teachings and debates of the Church fathers, and the subtleties of St. Anselm, St. Thomas Aquinas, and the other medieval doctors. Perhaps his mastery of deponent verbs would be forever deficient, but he seemed to have a wonderful innate understanding of the classic proofs for the existence of God.

Gray winter with its snow and frigid winds had now descended on Missouri, and though Lawler and I occasionally chafed under our restrictive and demanding regimen, we—or at least I—had no wish to venture forth from our crude but warm quarters and nourishing food.

The long winter of our confined contentment eventually passed.

110

Trying to outdo each other in piety, Lawler and I mutually pledged strict devotion to Church doctrine and teaching and obedience to our masters. Spring found us far advanced and near enough to the level of the older seminarians that separate tutoring was no longer needed.

"Young brothers, you have progressed solidly in your studies and preparation and your final vows draw near," Father Branigan told us with a rare smile one day in mid-March. "Nevertheless, you, Lawler, must yet work on your Latin, and, Peter, your mastery of Church doctrine and philosophy, though improved, is still weak."

We thanked him for his conditional praise and pledged anew our devotion, but he waved aside our pious vows with these admonishments: "The priesthood consists not only of studies and mastery of doctrine, though these are both laudable and necessary, but also of service in the lives of men. Now in addition to your studies, which you will continue with due diligence, you must take on additional duties."

Father Branigan explained to us that the pious citizens of Perryville and nearby communities had donated a sum of money for the construction of a bishop's residence and chapel in St. Louis. More was needed, and as additional duties in the following weeks, as the weather permitted Lawler and I would call on key citizens known for their devotion and largesse.

"You, Lawler, with your talent for accounting and eye for detail will keep a careful record of all that is donated and by whom. And you, Peter, with your persuasive rhetorical gifts in several tongues will explain the need and purpose to our parishioners, most of whom are French speakers. Do you understand how I have divided your labors according to your gifts?"

We assured Father Branigan that we did, and not long thereafter, as April waned and May neared, Lawler and I ventured beyond the seminary walls and began our canvassing.

Our efforts prospered though the work was slow. Charmed, as I supposed, by two young seminary students earnestly devoted to the Church and pleased to hear our petition in their own language, they responded generously to our plea. By summer's end we had covered the settlements west of the river within a radius of twenty leagues, amassing a sum approaching five hundred dollars. Father Branigan was delighted with our report and our studies. On a Sunday evening in early September, the entire seminary gathered to offer prayers of thanksgiving for the offerings. We basked in the general praise of our work, but by chance I overheard Father Dary issue words of caution to Father Branigan.

111

"They are both novices in practical money matters, Father. Is it wise to entrust them with the responsibility of delivering the offering to St. Louis, to say nothing of the temptations that may arise from its handling?"

"I am as aware of the risks as you, Father, for human nature is ever weak. Yet we must proceed with faith and trust. We cannot shield these men forever from the world's temptations. That, too, is a part of their training for the priesthood. If they succeed in this mission, I foresee their ordination within two years. They have made remarkable progress and are now nearly abreast of some of the other seminarians who will be ordained next spring. The Church has a pressing need for priests as quickly as we can produce them."

These words disturbed and frightened me. As long as the priesthood lay in the indefinite future, I could abide the prospect, but now that it loomed closer, all my old uncertainties and doubts about my calling came back to trouble me. Doubtless Father Branigan's judgment was weakened by his generous sentimental attachment to us and to his eager desire to see us succeed. But in all events there was still a little time, and for the moment I put the matter out of my mind.

When Lawler and I departed at the end of September for St. Louis with the precious donation—now swollen to more than five hundred dollars with further modest contributions gathered by pious Henriette and the Sisters—no sooner was the seminary behind us than our old animal spirits, piously suppressed for several months, now surged to new life within us.

It felt good to run, jump, and prance in the bright sun. Like the warbling birds, we sang our joy, Lawler with his crude frontier ditties, and I in remembered snatches of French and Spanish melodies. Let me confess, dear reader, that I was somewhat impeded in my youthful exultation by the weight and discomfort of Pollard's coins, which along with my other keepsakes I had strapped snugly around my body. Whether or no I intended to return to the seminary was a truth unknown even to me, one I chose to ignore for the time being.

Withal, we did not forget the theological teachings of recent months, particularly service to mammon on which Father Jerome often discoursed. Although we knew the pious ends to which the money we bore was consigned, yet Lawler was not a little horrified to have on his very person an instrument so often used by the Fiend himself to ensnare mortals. Unloosing the bag, he tossed it to me.

"Here, Pete, you carry it for a spell and give my soul a rest from its wickedness!"

But I no sooner caught the bag than I tossed it back to him. "Think you to lighten your temptation by adding to mine? What kind of Christian brotherhood is that?"

And so we continued along the forest trail, tossing and catching the moneybag, soon forgetting its theological import and converting it to mere sport.

By midday we were exhausted by such play; hunger and thirst now turned our thoughts to food and drink, with which the seminary brothers had amply supplied us. Espying a pristine, pebbled brook meandering through a grove of shady oaks and dark cedars, we spread our victuals on a cloth and, pausing ever so briefly to bless our nourishment, made ready to fall to.

But no sooner had the first morsel touched our lips than a cacophony, much at odds with the harmonious murmurs of the forest about us, conjured visions of demons or savages about to descend on us. The harsh ring and rattle of clashing metals accompanied by a rasping male voice singing in full throat was nearly upon us. Ere long the branches parted and the author of the discordant commotion hove into view between a pair of cedars. We saw a white man of some thirty-odd summers, of slovenly, untrimmed beard and hair, passably clean, untattered shirt and trousers, and boots though muddied that seemed altogether too fine of cut and stitching to match his attire. Trailing behind him, a drooping donkey was loaded beyond measure, indeed beyond belief itself, with every kind of pewtered pot, pan, iron skillet, basin, plate, glass, and cutlery common to the civilization of the American frontier. An elaborate chamber pot encirled with an artistic conceit of yellow flowers and bluebirds and secured by cords passing through the cover handles and under the neck of the beast rested behind its long asinine ears.

Spotting us, the master of this strange assemblage did not modulate his throaty ditty but instead turned its full volume upon us, concluding with these words:

"He-l-l-l-o, the camp! Good Fathers, will you allow this wayward traveler to approach and share your fellowship and a morsel if you can spare it?!"

Flattered that he addressed us as "Fathers," we did not inform him of our true status but rose at once to welcome him and offer him a share of our food. After an exchange of introductions, he allowed the donkey to drink deeply from the brook then tied it to a sapling. There the beast—by name Mildred—drooped to apparent lifelessness, belied only by an occasional futile swish of her tail to ward off molesting flies.

113

Our repast was most convivial. Our stomachs were soon full, topped by generous draughts of the wildgrape seminary wine. Eager for the sight of a new face and news of the outside world, we told Mr. Malcolm Gordon, who struck us both as eminently trustworthy, who we were and incautiously furnished him with enough details of our business in St. Louis that surely he divined the rest. He, in turn, described himself as a wandering merchant and foot pedlar, who with the help of patient Mildred plied both sides of the Mississippi between Cape Girardeau and St. Louis, selling and distributing his merchandise to settlers and businesses.

"Your commerce is therefore sufficiently lucrative, Mr. Gordon," I asked him timidly, "to justify trudging over these barren wastes and swamps in summer heat and winter cold?"

"That it is, Father Prosper, for all hereabouts know me and trust me as the honest merchant that I am. Yet of late there are private matters of a growing and consuming inconvenience to me."

"You did not betray such in your singing, sir," Lawler reminded him.

"Tis true, Father Adkins," he sighed, "yet the most troubled heart often hides behind a song and smiling face."

Puffed up by our untested altruism and convinced that our studies and devotions equipped us to confront any human misfortune or evil, we begged Mr. Gordon to lay his troubles before us in order to receive our sage, healing counsel. At first he demurred, explaining that he did not wish to add his problems to the weighty Church matters with which we were surely charged. Whereupon we insisted all the more, and he, with profuse apologies and great reluctance, commenced to spin a tale of woe that melted our hearts.

The Story of Malcolm Gordon

It is perhaps a detail of little consequence to tell you that I, though born in Maryland, count myself a son of the Kentucky Commonwealth. But with the greatest devotion and pride I confess to you, good Fathers, that since my tenderest years I have followed and obeyed the teachings of the one true Catholic Church. Indeed, that loyalty was to cost me dearly.

When I was but fifteen years of age, my saintly father died at the hands of rebellious Indians, leaving my destitute mother with five starveling children to feed. In desperation, barely six months after my father's passing and urged by extreme necessity, she entered into a second marriage to a rich neighbor, thus assuring us food for our bodies but nothing for the nourishment of our souls.

Our stepfather, whose name I refuse to repeat, was hostile to all religion, alike mocking and scorning Protestants and Catholics. Threatening severe punishment if she disobeyed, he forbade mother all intercourse with the Church, so that we were cut off not only from spiritual comfort but also from those who once were our warmest friends. As the eldest of my siblings—my brother and three sisters—I saw the ravages this cruel edict inflicted on my gentle mother, who was forced to sacrifice faith for food. Defiance grew within me, and not a few times I slipped away to represent my family in the parish church. Word got back to our inhuman master and he proceeded to have his men beat me until I dripped blood like a raw sausage. And as if this were not bad enough, I learned that he also beat mother in the mistaken belief that she had encouraged my disobedience.

Half mad with rage and powerless to defend my mother and family, I ran away from his hated household, swearing I would return only at his death or when I had the means to release my mother and family from his cruel dominion. That resolution I have kept, though in secretive ways I was able to receive news from my loved ones and to assure them that as soon as I had the means to support and defend them I would return to rescue.

* * *

But my orderly plan for a successful overthrow of my stepfather's tyranny has of late taken a more ominous turn.

"How so?" Lawler and I asked in unison.

With some regularity my mother sends letters to Ste. Genevieve to await my monthly visits. In her most recent writing she let it drop that her own health had declined, but her chief concern was for the welfare of my sisters who were under some unnamed but sinister threat from my stepfather. I make my way even today to an inn in Ste. Genevieve, which as you may know, lies hard by the river and is reachable with a good afternoon march. The innkeeper, a loyal, honest man, faithfully guards my letters between visits. He has yet other admirable qualities: his inn is clean and free of lice and fleas and he sets a marvelous table for his guests. There I may learn the latest disposition of conditions in Kentucky, upon which will depend my plans to return there at once to rescue my precious family or to continue my journey to St. Louis.

Lawler looked at me then said to Gordon, "Sir, as we have little knowledge of this region and no accommodations for the night, perhaps we could accompany you to Ste. Genevieve, if our presence does not inconvenience you and may serve you in some way."

I nodded my enthusiastic assent and Gordon voiced his: "Respected Fathers, nothing would give me greater pleasure, and in turn I shall persuade my friend Perrault the innkeeper to secure the best lodging and food for you."

So it was pleasantly agreed. We set off, clanging our way along the trail and startling the birds and forest creatures into silence. At first we all broke intermittently into song, but as the afternoon wore on fatigue silenced us. At last to our relief, Gordon triumphantly pointed to the inn. "Fathers, we have arrived. First, I shall present you to Mr. Jean Perrault, the innkeeper, who will assign you to the best quarters. Then after I have seen to Mildred's feeding, I shall perhaps learn the latest from Kentucky. Thereafter we shall dine at the best table west of the Mississippi."

The inn was indeed as splendid and the innkeeper, though a man of few words, was as gracious in those he said as Gordon described him. And the fare was no less excellent at a later hour. But at table we could not help but notice agitation in Gordon's voice. Inquiring discreetly, we learned that indeed the news from Kentucky was alarming. Affairs there were racing to a climax, perhaps to a calamity for his family, and his mother begged him to return soon before all was lost.

"I have no other choice," he told us with a weariness of voice we had not heard in him before. "At first light, I must in some way suspend my commerce—though I know not how at the moment—and cross by ferry to Illinois and thence on to Kentucky. Two hundred miles separate me from my family, and I fear that even with all deliberate haste I may arrive too late to save them from my stepfather's cruelty. Many things are troubling in this matter, not the least of them my failure to complete my transactions in St. Louis."

"Is there any way, Malcolm," Lawler asked, "that we may serve you in St. Louis? As you know, that city is also our destination."

"How kind of you to offer, reverend Fathers, but I cannot presume on your sweet natures or detract you from your priestly duties to attend to crass matters of commerce."

"Tell us at least the particulars," I insisted.

His face now twisted with compunction, Gordon emitted a weary sigh. "The matter boils down to this, good Fathers. I am—or was—to deliver the pots, pans, and other accroutrements loaded on the back of my faithful Mildred to an inn newly established on Chouteau Avenue in

116

St. Louis. Then I was to present invoices for payment for this and a series of previous transactions to the Missouri Mercantile Bank situated four doors from the inn in question. But alas, circumstances play against me and I shall have to stand in default in both instances. In a choice between business and family, I must incline to family."

"May I ask to what sum these transactions mount?" Lawler asked.

"According to calculations made by banker Georges Duhon in Cape Girardeau, a bit over eight hundred dollars."

The news kindled our excitement.

"Is it possible that we could act as your agents in St. Louis?" I inquired as the vision of so many dollars danced in my imagination. "Then you could hurry on to Kentucky unworried about affairs in St. Louis and recover your money at our seminary in Perryville when next you pass that way."

"Who could fail to trust two Fathers of the Church for whom honesty is an unwavering virtue? But alas that would not resolve my dilemma."

"Then what is the remaining problem?" asked Lawler.

"Father, the gains from these transactions, many months in the making, were to be the money with which to win my family's freedom. But, alas, I fear it has all been for naught."

"Don't yield yet to despair, good Malcolm. God works in mysterious ways. With your permission, Father Prosper and I will confer in private and shortly thereafter make known to you our best thoughts on the matter."

In our room our excitement reached a fevered pitch. "It is surely God's doing," Lawler exulted. "We bear a sum exceeding five hundred dollars in exchange for which we may be able to claim above eight hundred dollars for the needs of the Church. With this transaction we can send Gordon on his way with funds that may be enough to win his family's freedom. We, in turn, like the parable of the talents in the Scriptures, can add to what the Lord gave us in Perryville. Eh, what say you, Peter?"

"I say it is a godsend for all concerned, and since we are agreed on all points, let us lay the proposition before Malcolm!"

Our new companion Malcolm all but wept with joy. "You are truly servants of God, angels sent at my darkest hour to deliver me from my distress. The five hundred dollars will suffice to rescue my dear family, and the rest I willingly donate in gratitude to the Holy Church for this miracle of deliverance. I cannot ask for more, but if you would be so kind, include me in your prayers."

And so the matter was concluded to everybody's satisfaction. Rising early, we found Malcolm awaiting us. He presented us with the notarized letter and invoices that would serve as bona fides in St. Louis. We in turn counted out a sum of five hundred dollars, preserving only a few coins to tide us over until we should collect our funds from the St. Louis bank. We had overlooked Mildred in our arrangement, but Malcolm generously surrendered her to us. Then he added this advice:

"Fathers Adkins and Prosper, the remainder of your journey is long and fatiguing. As a riverboat bound for St. Louis will this very afternoon dock briefly in Ste. Genevieve to lade furs and lumber and take on passengers, might I suggest that you board it and let it do the traveling instead of your legs."

We gladly accepted his advice, exchanged hearty embraces and best wishes, and as he sailed away on the river ferry, settled down with Mildred to await the riverboat.

Eventually it hove into view belching smoke and signaling its arrival with loud horn blasts. We were making ready to board with Mildred when our troubles began. Mildred would not budge. Hitherto the most lethargic of beasts, she turned indocile, kicking her heels and creating a din like a conclave of snorting demons. As Lawler struggled to control her, Mildred bit his hand, drawing blood from the imprint of her teeth. Finally, with the help of four men we all but carried her and her picturesque burden aboard.

But our troubles with Mildred were far from over. No sooner had we secured her reins to one of the substantial timbers just loaded and turned away to attend to Lawler's hand than with an awful asinine braying Mildred jerked loose and proceeded to race about the deck, kicking and snorting amidst a terrible clanging of pots and pans as frightened passengers scurried to escape her wrath. We ran to corner her and thought to have done so. But now at war with all members of the human species, she hesitated for only the briefest instant before launching herself over the railing and into the turbulent waters below. Rushing to look down at the eddy created by her submersion, we waited in suspense for her re-emergence. Anon the chamberpot appeared, though now set at a jaunty angle on her head, then her upper torso and extended tail surfaced and she began a leisurely paddling, pots and all, toward the shoreline. I ran to the captain to ask him to rescue the beast, but he refused.

"With all due respect to you, Father, I'll not have that devilish beast on my vessel!" And with that he dismissed my concerns.

Meanwhile Mildred touched bottom and regally marched out of the water with both her dignity and cargo intact and without a backward look at her erstwhile tormentors.

Lawler and I were consternated and humiliated by this turn of events, but we consoled ourselves with the knowledge that even though this portion of the merchandise was lost, at least we had the notarized letter and invoices to present for payment in St. Louis.

How wrong we were! Arriving in St. Louis and hastening to the addresses inscribed in our documents, we discovered that both inn and bank were fictions and the notarized invoices, the merest forgeries. We, who considered ourselves wise and experienced in the ways of the world, had been hoodwinked by one far more skilled than we in the ancient art of swindle.

To say we were humiliated, angry, embarrassed, and crestfallen is to fall far short of describing our agitated state. Because we now looked on our robes as a mockery and an odious reminder of Gordon's duplicity, by silent agreement we discarded them in an alleyway and for the first time in months emerged as the laymen we had now become. Thereafter, for hours we wandered in a daze about the city, alternately threatening to avenge ourselves on Gordon and castigating ourselves with our residual priestly training for such base thoughts. Finally we fell into a sterile stoicism when it became obvious to us both that there was little we could do in any case.

"What shall we do, Pete?" Lawler asked me, his eyes red with stifled rage and frustration. "And why were we not alerted by his glib tongue and sharp mind, much in excess of what you would expect in a common pedlar? We are duped, disgraced, and all but penniless. We have failed the Church and brought shame upon ourselves. I don't know about you, Pete, but I, for one, could never face our seminary brothers again, much less Father Branigan. It will be a long time before I have the courage to set foot in a church again."

The weight of Pollard's dollars had a comforting effect on my state of mind, though I tried to sound as desperate as Lawler. It now became obvious to me that even without the unhappy episode with Gordon, I had never intended to return to the Seminary. Had I not told Father Branigan that the priesthood was not my calling? It was not in my nature to retrace my steps, but regardless of the next turn in my life, I was not inclined to share Lawler's moodiness or his poverty any longer. Money was strength, and I had a secret supply.

"Lawler, I feel as you do. We could report the loss to the Bishop here in St. Louis, but God knows what burdensome penance and punishments the Church would impose on us. They could very well accuse us of spending the money instead of losing it in a swindle and even charge us with a felony. Neither of us has a history that could stand hard scrutiny. So here is my recommendation: You take most of the remaining dollars we have between us and return to Illinois, where you have kin and the means to reestablish your life. And the sooner the better."

"And you, Pete? Where will you go?" I could see that privately he had already made the decision I recommended, and it offended me that he did not include me in it. Our friendship was disappearing at the first crisis.

"I have heard of Spanish lands far to the west, and since I speak the language, there I intend to go to see what fortune I can make for myself. I have read that in life wisdom consists of deciding which bridges to cross and which to burn. So far I have burned all of mine. Maybe this one will lead to something better."

"But how will you live? And what will you eat? My home is only a few days distant, and I can make it with a few dollars, but Santa Fe is hundreds of miles away, they tell me."

"I have lived hungry before and I can do so again."

Because of the disparity of our journeys, Lawler insisted that I take most of the few remaining dollars. We haggled nobly about the matter, each trying to outdo the other in altruistic generosity, but at length I let myself be persuaded to take the greater sum, whilst he agreed to take the remainder of our food. Then embracing each other, we parted with extravagant pledges of eternal friendship and promises to see that some day our pathways would cross again.

So Lawler, now doubly swindled, turned east and soon his tall frame disappeared in a bend in the street. Eager for worldliness after months of piety, soon I would turn west to seek my fortune, but alone at last, my chief aim of the moment was to spend some of Pollard's dollars on the finest food, wine, and accommodations in St. Louis.

Translator's Addendum

A yellowed newspaper item bearing the date June, 1839, was inserted in Peter's manuscript. It is not certain whether it had any relevance to the events some years earlier described in this section or dealt with matters and persons of later times and circumstances. Since Prosper himself offered no clarification of its significance, the most I shall do is transcribe it without comment for the reader's conjecture.

Item
      Hanged in the public square of St. Louis Wednesday ultimo one Malcolm McQueen, a notorious disturber of public order, agent of uncounted thefts and swindles, and author of many outrages against lawful citizens. Often presenting himself in the guise of a wandering pedlar of household items, notions, medicinal herbs, healing connundrums, and other commodities, McQueen, who was known to use a stock of aliases, was many times lawfully apprehended and as often regained his liberty by his legendary guile and glibness of tongue. But when his final transgression landed him once again in the hands of the law, the good constabulary of our fair city saw to it that justice was not to be again thwarted, and McQueen, gagged and blindfolded, was straightway dispatched to the next world to answer to his Maker for his misdeeds.
      There attended McQueen's hanging an odd display of misguided loyalty. An old donkey said to belong to the condemned culprit broke out of its stable as McQueen was gasping his last and charged into the assembled citizenry with such scandalous brayings, snortings, and kickings that an armed constable was obliged to dispatch the beast with a well-placed bullet to its head. We lay down pen with this moral certainty: Even nature's creatures may be turned to evil purposes by wayward humans. Yet decency and honest dealing are not long mocked; sooner or later the cleverest thief comes to a wretched end and the world marches on.

Part IV: How Peter joined a wagon train and left for Santa Fe; how he was captured by wild Comanches; the strange story of Quaker John and Catholic Miriam; the story of Owl Woman, Young Eagle, and Little Fawn; the ordeal of escape to Santa Fe; his life there and eventual departure for deeper Mexico

Although I saw much to admire and desire in busy St. Louis, I did not long linger there. October was half gone and I had no desire to spend another winter in Missouri. Nevertheless, I enjoyed a few days of comfort and good food in a prime hotel and took the time to purchase new trousers, shirt, drawers, hat, and boots for myself. I discarded their worn and threadbare predecessors as hateful reminders of the recent failed episode of my life. The ease with which Gordon relieved Lawler Adkins and me of our money left a bitter aftertaste in my mouth and I grimaced in shame each time I thought of our gullibility. It was a source of some solace that after I had my locks and beard trimmed in a barbershop hard by my hotel I took satisfaction with my appearance. I promised myself over and again that I would never allow myself such a lamentable lapse of intelligence.

Afterwards, having made inquiries concerning the Santa Fe trail, as it was called, and having learned that the city of Independence at the western extreme of Missouri was the staging area for the wagon trains, I secured passage on the first stagecoach I could find for that destination.

The stage overflowed with well-dressed and—to my discomfort—corpulent travelers who, though in pursuing varied commercial aims were of a single mind, as best I could learn in our four-day journey, were seeking their gain and fortune in Santa Fe. A much hardier and rougher cast of men accompanied our stagecoach on horseback. They were armed with every make of weapon imaginable and gave us of softer complexion and weaker nerve a degree of security, although a pair of Indian scouts caused a certain apprehension in our group. In contrast to the groomed and tailored gentlemen inside the stage, our escorts made a mockery of fashionable dress: wearing buckskins and furs, buffalo skins, coonskin caps, Mexican sombreros, stovepipe hats, crudely stitched boots, leggings, and even Indian footware and blankets, they were, to a man, a statement of barbaric extravagance. Commenting on their bizarre dress, I was cautioned to voice no public statement about their appearance.

"These are half wild men who scorn the disciplines of law and civilization," a St. Louis trader explained to me. "They are easily roused to violence, and I dare say that most of them have killed men, in many cases over the smallest trifles. And they do so without the slightest remorse, unmoved as they are by the moral pangs of civilized folk."

This sharp division of humankind and class failed to include two persons that caught my attention: a handsome young man and an extraordinarily beautiful young woman. The gentlemanly manners of the passengers notwithstanding, I saw that the men could not keep their eyes off her but with pretended indifference slyly let their gaze sweep over her at every opportunity. I was as enthralled as the rest and could barely contain my curiosity about the couple. But to our individual and collective inquiries they offered no substantial information about themselves. Their reluctance excited our curiosity and as surely silenced it. Eventually we spoke of other matters to pass the long, dusty intervals between stops.

The monotony of the journey and the isolation of the occasional inns and stations ended abruptly in the dusty confusion, shouts, curses, grime, and general chaos of Independence. Its streets were a riot of enormous covered wagons, oxen, mules, horsemen, Indians, and drunkards who staggered—and as often were bodily ejected—from the saloons. Hastily erected signs nailed to crude posts and already punctuated by bullet holes announced dry goods, groceries, baths, and other services.

I inquired about lodging of a red-bearded man holding a long rifle and leaning against a corner post. He pointed out three "hotels," in each case a designation that greatly exceeded any rightful claim to the title. I protested the unappealing choices, but the man retorted with a sneer. "There ain't nothing else in this town, mister, unless you want to sleep in one of them whorehouses across the way. You takes yer choice and yer chances. There ain't nothing high-faluting around here, no matter how much money ye got."

"Wait up, friend, if thou wilt," a voice called out as I turned to make my way to what appeared to be the least offensive of the hotels. It was the uncommunicative young man and woman from the stage. "If thou hast by chance information about lodging, wouldst thou allow us to accompany thee? Miriam is exhausted from the trip, and I must find us lodging."

I was pleased to be in their company, and together we entered the establishment, the inner appearance of which was more comforting than its rough exterior. The problem was that there was only one available room, and no amount of wheedling could produce another.

"Friend, thou asked first, so thou hast the right to take the room," the young man told me as he bent down to pick up their two bags.

"Miriam and I will seek lodging elsewhere."

A vague chivalry would not let me accede to my selfish wish and his generous offer. "No, my friend," I replied, "this place is more suitable for the lady, if anything in this town qualifies as such. I can easily accommodate myself elsewhere."

He thanked me profusely in his quaint English, the likes of which I had never heard before, and the gratitude in the lady's eyes was satisfaction aplenty for my gesture. Leaving them, I straightway found inferior lodging in another establishment removed only a few dozen paces from the first. I would meet the couple again in greatly altered circumstances.

In the meantime, though I was impatient to depart for the west, I learned that wagons and travelers were slow in gathering for the next great wagon train to Santa Fe. The wagonmaster refused to set out until he had at least twenty wagons and a sizable escort of frontiersmen and Indian fighters. There was a frightening rumor that the Comanches, most dreaded of the plains savages, were ranging well north of the Comanchería, their traditional hunting grounds, and that only days before they had attacked and destroyed a small train.

Others, impatient to depart for Santa Fe in hopes of completing the journey while the weather was still good, discounted the rumor as the product of hysteria. The trader from St. Louis whom I knew from our stagecoach trip, summed up the feelings of those ready to depart at once.

"We could wait here until winter is upon us for that many wagons to show. How much worse can a pack of half-starved Comanches be than the lawless scum of this town with its daily tally of knifings, shootings, and murders? I tell you, no one is safe here, and I for one favor leaving with or without the full complement of wagons. And the sooner the better. My business will not wait."

Enough people agreed with him to form a train of nine wagons and half a dozen mounted frontiersmen and scouts. There was a heated confrontation with the cautious wagonmaster, insults and even fisticuffs ensued between those arguing the pros and cons, but in the end the impatient dissidents hired their own master and against the counsel of the more experienced wagonmaster made ready to depart the next day.

Eager as I was to make the journey to Santa Fe, which my active imagination magnified into another El Dorado, I intended to wait for the larger train to form. I was honest enough to be cowardly in the face of danger but never sufficiently resolute to run the risk of having to be courageous. There was safety in numbers—and a balm for faint-heartedness.

But my plans changed abruptly that very evening. As I ventured forth from my hotel, I saw a recognizable face whose identity I could not at first recall. The man stared back at me as though puzzled by the same dilemma. Then the chilling truth turned my liver to water and almost caused my heart to leap from my bosom. He was Hezikiah Barton, Bascom Harvey's chief deputy in Memphis, where I was a fugitive under a death sentence and the object of a handsome reward dead or alive. In a panic I turned quickly away from him, and hurriedly rounding a corner, broke into a run to conceal myself amidst a jumble of broken wheels and axles, rotting wagon beds, and ruined harness collected behind a livery. Barton was not far behind me; he came to the corner of the livery and stood for a long moment calmly surveying the wreckage under which I lay in breathless concealment. Mercifully, he did not spot me, and after a time, which seemed to me a small eternity, turned back into the town.

Fearfully I emerged from my hiding place and considered my options. It would not do to linger in Independence and risk arrest or a bullet to the head. Like it or not, I must leave on the morrow with the small wagon train. But as I approached the wagon camp at the edge of town there was Barton talking to the young wagon master. The latter shook his head, which I took as a sign that he knew nothing about me. At length Barton left.

Nevertheless, I took no comfort in this temporary respite. My circumstances were precarious. Barton would surely return in the morning to survey the passengers as the train prepared for departure. Taking this as a certainty, I decided to leave Independence at once on foot and await the train in open country. Looking over my shoulder all the while, I purchased food and a blanket for warmth and set out.

As I slunk fearfully out of Independence, a melancholy despondency darker than the night itself settled over me. I imagined myself as one pursued by the ancient furies from which there was no final saving deliverance. How long before my stratagems would fail and I be captured and killed by those who sought my life? Santa Fe was my last hope, but it was a hope too far, like a barely visible star, and I, a man too frail and flawed to reach it. Still, mechanically I marched on, shedding bitter tears and reciting with melodramatic exaggeration the griefs and failures of my wretched life. I had long since despaired of any fairness in life; now in a defiant gesture of anger, the only semblance of strength and heroism I could summon, I determined to hold off the cruelties of fate as long as I could. Surely I would fall sooner or later but like a cornered fox not before exhausting every trick of cunning I knew.

After walking for several hours, I ate some of the food, then wrapped myself in the blanket against the night chill and slept fitfully under an abandoned wagon some miles west of Independence. By my reckoning, I was well short of Round Grove, which, I had learned, was the first station on the trail.

Morning and more food brightened my mood and dispelled the image of pursuing furies. I yet lived, I crowed to myself, and if fate was my nemesis, lady luck was my fickle companion, and we would see which would win out. My optimism grew not long thereafter as I espied the dust of the wagon train rumbling towards me. I waited by the ruined wagon until it overtook me, then approached the wagon master who eyed me suspiciously.

At first he refused my entreaties to join the train, no doubt thinking me to be a penniless drifter. But seeing my dilemma, the young man I had befriended in Independence appealed on my behalf to the wagon master, and if the latter had any lingering doubts, they vanished forthwith when I produced coins to prove my solvency. He pocketed ten Spanish dollars and assigned me a space in one of the great covered wagons.

We proceeded thence to Round Grove, some twenty-five miles distant, where we made our first stop late in the day. Our pace was slowed by two lumbering teams of oxen that were slower brutes than the teams of horses.

Contemplating ways of adding to my funds, I let it drop that evening that I was a barber by profession and that if scissors and combs could be had, I would willingly trim the hair and beards of those who might desire my services. At first most scoffed at my offer, but seeing the handsome results worked on a couple of willing heads, others came forward. The individual gratuities were meager but the numbers grew such that soon I had replaced the money spent in St. Louis and Independence and recovered a portion of the sum paid the wagon master. The approval of my barbering skills was general, and in no great lapse of days I can say without boasting that I had become a favorite of my fellow travelers.

In the very midst of my improving fortunes, fate again reared its ugly head. By now I had almost forgotten Barton and my old griefs in Memphis, thinking them to be far behind me. But I was wrong; the morning we were to ford the Cimarron River I awoke staring at a large pistol aimed at my head. Behind it stood Barton.

"Rise and shine, Prosper! It took me a while to run you down but I finally caught up with you! Now consider this, my man: I can shoot you on the spot and collect the bounty on you. But if you come willingly,

I'll take you back to Memphis to hang for your crimes. You decide. You're a dead man either way, so it makes me no matter."

I took him at his word and made no resistance at all. Soon I was trussed like a sheep readied for slaughter, and as quickly all the goodwill I had earned in my few days with the wagon train evaporated when Barton told the people of the criminal accusations against me in Memphis. He informed the wagon master that the next day he would take me back to Tennessee to hang for my crimes.

This unwholesome news further disturbed the mood of the train, which became ever more somber as we made our way westward. We were now approaching the Cimarron Crossing where, according to the rumors, not many days agone Comanche marauders had destroyed a wagon train and either slaughtered its occupants or dragged them away to torture or slavery. We were all on high, nervous alert, and even our battle-seasoned horsemen ceased their casual scouting forays and stayed close to the wagons.

Then what we dreaded happened. As we made our way through a dry streambed flanked on the west bank by stunted oaks, one of the scouts saw movement behind the trees. He called to the others, but before the alarm could produce its desired defensive purpose, Comanche warriors swarmed like angry hornets from concealment, firing their rifles or loosing their arrows and emitting heart-stopping screams. The lead team of horses panicked, becoming so entangled in their harness and wagon tongue that in the narrow defile the train could neither advance nor assume a defensive circle. Thereupon, most of our mounted escort wheeled their horses and fled away at full gallop. The others dismounted and rushed to cover behind the wagons. But as the Comanches, above fifty in number, circled the disorganized caravan, the Americans were exposed to attack from the rear.

Within a few minutes the fighting was over and the terrified survivors, fourteen in number, including two women, were dragged and dumped before a cadre of Comanche warriors. The savages unhitched the five surviving horses—for three had died or were in their final agony after the attack—while others slaughtered the oxen and sliced up the dead horses for meat. Others plundered the wagons and yelped in excitement when the young man and woman I had befriended were flushed from their hiding spot under quilts and blankets. She screamed as the warriors seized her, whilst he, striving mightily to protect her, was clubbed down by a rifle butt.

The Comanches then proceeded to strip the older women of dresses and corsets so as to have sport with them. The savages hardly knew what

130

to make of their stout resistance to their play, for amongst the plains Indians it was considered an act of barbarism to deny warriors such pleasurable accommodations. Indeed, I learned that Comanches often share women, believing that the experience strengthens their tribal bonds. Departing from custom, the Comanches did not kill and eviscerate the violated women, for they feared that the caravan escort might yet turn and attack them. The younger woman was spared for greater festivities.

Meanwhile the Comanches appeared puzzled by my condition, and several of them came to touch my ropes and, undoubtedly, to comment about my status in their language. As I struggled to a sitting position I saw that Barton was among the dead. I can say, dear reader, that even though I take no pleasure in the passing of any man, of all the deaths I have witnessed this one pained me the least. For the moment, at least, lady luck had given me a small victory over my fate but at what cost to me I was in no condition to tell.

The Comanches then divided into two bands, one that rode away leading the team horses and slabs of bloody meat and another that took charge of the captives. These they also divided into two groups, one which they tied neck to neck and marched or dragged away on foot, and a smaller group, including me, to be mounted on pack mules. I had hoped that as a prisoner of the Americans I might enjoy a degree of sympathetic clemency from the savages. My hopes seemed about to be fulfilled when one of the Comanches loosened my ropes. But, alas, it was not to be. He freed my arms and legs only to cut away my clothes and dress me in their tribal fashion, which consisted of buckskin leggins that failed to conceal my shameful parts and a fringed shirt of the same material that was secured by leather thongs in front. Unhappily for me he discovered my money and other precious items, which he tossed indifferently on the collected booty. He then bound my arms behind me even more tightly than before.

Having secured me so expertly as to discourage any thought or possibility of escape, the Comanches then commenced to terrorize us in dreadful ways. They rushed at us with uplifted tomahawks as though to strike off our heads, or grasped us by the hair and by their fierce gestures caused us to believe they were about to take our scalps. They responded only with incomprehensible grunts and occasional laughter to my earnest implorations for mercy in every language I could summon.

For the moment, however, and save for the impairment of our sanity, no harm came to us. Their hideous display over, the Comanches covered our heads with deerskins tied tightly with a string about our necks. We had thus suffocated had not one of the savages cut a small hole near the mouth that was barely adequate for breathing. Then two warriors lifted us to the backs of their mules and lashed our legs as close together as possible under the belly of the beasts.

We then set out for an unknown destination, the Indians riding their ponies ahead and the unbridled, untended mules docilely following them at a greater or nearer distance. Given this freedom of movement, the mules wandered erratically, at times straying under tree limbs that struck us unawares, at other times stopping to graze and causing us to lurch painfully forward or, on other uncomfortable occasions, breaking into a trot to regain the ponies and throwing us backward in doing so. The Comanches were greatly amused at our discomfort. Indeed, I learned to judge by their rising laughter that some new aggravation of our condition was about to befall me and did what I could to prepare myself for it.

Since it was late in the day the Comanches paused for the night—a "sleep" as they called it—near a spring. Our blindfolds were removed and our cords unloosed sufficiently to allow us to raise food and water to our mouth. One of the braves had retained a slab of horsemeat—a favorite food of the Comanches—and after grilling the steaks for a short time, fell to satisfying their hunger and slaking their thirst with spring water dipped in buffalo horns.

Offered the sliced morsels, the American prisoners stoutly refused to eat. Indeed, one of them retched and vomited at the very thought of devouring horseflesh. Not so I, for we French consider it to be a delicacy when properly seasoned and marinated. Naturally, the Comanches boasted no such culinary attainments, but my hunger supplemented their crude cuisine and I ate heartily, to the disbelieving stares of my fastidious fellow prisoners.

Early the next morning another band of ten Comanches joined us. They were returning, as I learned later, from a scouting expedition in the north to discover the probable migratory routes of buffalo herds. Not far ahead I discerned a multitude of voices, and when the blindfold was removed, found myself in the midst of buffalo-skin tents numbering close to a score, and of people above sixty as I counted them.

The village, as I was to learn later, was laid out like others of the Comanche nation. Always located close to a water source, its center was a sizeable square, perhaps half a hectare in extent, and in the very middle stood the chief's great lodge. It was surrounded by his wives' humbler tepees and to each stretched a summoning cord attached to a flap. On all four sides avenues led into the square along which were lined the smaller

132

tents of the villagers in order of tribal standing. The largest tents close by the square belonged to important men, the smaller and more distant, to warriors of inferior rank. Since the Comanches take no thought of cleanliness, squalor and stench abounded.

We prisoners, approaching a dozen, including several who preceded us in captivity, spent the chilly night tied to stakes near the chief's lodge. The next morning the survivors of our wagon train stumbled exhausted into the camp. Not long thereafter, six of us were roused from our stupor and marched to an embankment near the stream that supplied water to the tribe. There the savages stripped us and tied hands and feet to stakes a yard or so apart.

Sommer Vaughn, the leader of some of the earlier captives informed me that they were honest horse traders on their way to Santa Fe with twenty-five animals bought in Louisiana when the Comanches ambushed them. Of course I had heard his name before but prudently made no reference to his unsavory past.

"We never had a chance, mister," he pleaded. "The devils slipped past our lookout and right into our camp. Killed two of our fellers right there, good men they were, too, honest horsetraders, just like us. Cut their throats before they could pull their weapons. Kinda wished they'd just finished us off too then and there. That'd be better than what they'll do to us now."

At this the youngest man, Earnest Cobb by name, began to whimper aloud in terror until Sommer told him to shut up and be a man. The other man, whose name I cannot recall—it may have been Delbert Hayes or Haynes—but whose frightened eyes and quivering lips I shall not forget, turned away in silent despair.

Whereupon a cohort of warriors—a few above a dozen—began a slow shuffle, tomahawk in hand, towards us. As the line of warriors approached us, one of the warriors broke from the formation and seizing the youngest prisoner by the hair, scalped him. The wound was by no means mortal, for only a portion of the skin was thus taken, yet the bleeding was profuse and the young American squealed in pain and terror.

The dance or shuffle circled about us, and on the second approach the savages brandished their tomahawks in our faces, putting their hand to their mouth and letting out fierce war whoops. They did me no mayhem, but Vaughn and his men fared not so well. The Comanches grazed the naked flesh of Vaughn next to me and blood ran down his body.

The chanting and circling continued, and on each pass the cutting

133

increased until the bodies of my companions were fairly covered with new and dried blood. I tried to close my eyes to the horror but an Indian jerked my head backwards and obliged me to stare at my suffering companions. Vaughn bore his torture in stoic silence, Delbert prayed for death and deliverance, but young Earnest screamed in terror at the ordeal. This latter behavior seemed especially to please the savages, who halted from time to time to rest, smoke their pipes, and point laughingly at the young prisoner. My own fear was beyond the power of words to convey.

The torture then resumed and continued by my reckoning for more than an hour. Finally the end came for my companions. On the last circling, two Indians broke from the line and now advancing, now retreating, now shuffling left, now right, the while chanting a war song, they approached the helpless men. Then lifting their tomahawks, they smashed the skulls of their victims, beginning with Vaughn, then Delbert H....(?), and finally the squalling youngster Cobb.

I doubted not that my end would soon come in similar fashion. But to my surprise, I was loosed from the stake, forced to take a long look at my dead companions, garbed anew in my Indian attire and with shoves and—as I supposed—threats, returned to the village.

I had not long to contemplate this puzzling turn of events before I was pitched at the feet of the most bizarre human my eyes have ever looked upon. A head taller than other members of his clan, Running Bear, for such I learned later was his name, wore his hair in an untrimmed black mane bound tightly into a pigtail with a crimson ribbon. His arms and chest rippled with corded muscles and unlike the slender, smooth-faced warriors in his company, evidence of sparse black whiskers and chest hair gave him a certain sinister European appearance.

But the most distinguishing feature of his physiognomy, one I shall forever have emblazoned in my memory, was a terrible saber slash across his face and forehead that had reset his right eye below the plane of the other so that his unblinking stare was unnerving in its disparate intensity. Unable to hold both eyes in simultaneous surveillance, as each seemed to mirror different impulses and purposes, one did not know on which to focus or which sentiment to trust.

For a time the gathered clan surveyed me in silence as I wriggled and writhed helplessly at the feet of this human monstrosity. One of the Comanches spoke to Running Bear, who prodded me with the point of his spear, drawing a trace of blood from my side. The warriors broke into peals of laughter at my scream of horror and the women, who hitherto had remained silent in the background, came forward to spit on me and—so I surmised—to insult my manhood. The scavenger cur dogs, with which Comanche villages are always replete, imitated the human contempt by snarling at me with bared fangs and circling to bite me when my attention was called elsewhere. A small, nude boy named White Cloud, Running Bear's son, approached and sprayed my humiliated person with a high arcing stream of urine, to the admiring delight and noisy acclaim of the savages. At this several other boys prepared to befoul me in like manner, but, mercifully, Running Bear waved them aside with his spear.

"*¿Quién tú, hombre, amarrado como vaca?*" (Who you, man, trussed like a cow?), asked Running Bear in broken Spanish, prodding me anew with his spear as his mismatched eyes simultaneously flashed malice, curiosity, and humor.

"*Ay, gran señor y jefe,*" I responded, thankful to hear a Christian language, "*¡por favor, le suplico que tenga piedad de mí! La triste verdad es que me encuentro en circunstancias tan raras y desesperadas*" (Oh, great lord and chief, please I beg you, have pity on me! The sad truth is that I find myself in such strange and desperate circumstances).

Running Bear wrinkled his disfigured brow and spoke in his language to one of the warriors, a handsome, athletic man of lighter skin than the others, who then stood forth to address me in good Spanish.

"Chief Running Bear wants to know who you are, whether you are of the tribe of the vile Americans, and why you were bound as a prisoner?"

"Please, sir, assure your most excellent chief that I am no odious American, but a Frenchman from New Orleans fleeing for his life from their clutches, and that my strange circumstances are matters that I shall most willingly divulge and explain to him."

Young Eagle, for such I learned was his name, so informed Running Bear who seemed curious to hear my story. Despite my pointed hints, the savages offered me no more food or drink but instead gorged themselves on their ample provisions as I looked on with an envious distress I could barely contain. Nor was this deprivation the worst of my cares. For presently, with a satisfied grunt, loud eructation, and a heroic thunder of flatulence, Running Bear instructed Little Fawn, one of his three wives, to deposit my money and possessions in his lodge. I watched this action transpire with forlorn fatalism and only the faintest hope that I should ever see them again. Bereft of my coins, I was certain the next loss would be my very life. And as desolation over my loss mounted, my hope for rescue sank inversely.

The men having completed their repast, the women withdrew into separate conclave to chatter incomprehensibly about their own matters. But their frequent stares in my direction and accompanying giggles left no doubt that I was the object of their sarcastic hilarity. The naked children—the Comanches only attire children above the age of eight or so—whooped and raced in circles about the camp, shouting insults and occasionally hurling debris at me. Even in my dejection and humiliation I could not but notice that despite their unwashed filth some of the younger women exhibited a handsomeness of limb and feature I would not have supposed possible in savages of such harsh and heathenish conditions.

In this puzzling manner—for I knew not why I had been spared—several days passed during which the savages brought me only enough scraps of food and sips of water to keep body and soul together. Running Bear and his select warriors left on a raid, and not until they reappeared did my status change. Barely had the band returned than the warriors gathered in conclave to discuss a matter that appeared to be of some urgency and dissension. Anon the tribal prophet or shaman, one Wise Otter by name, rose with great dignity to address the assembled warriors. The harangue lasted, as I deemed, nearly an hour. Yet in all that time, the Indians sat, heads respectfully bowed, listening in silence to his words, though I could not but notice that Running Bear soon evidenced fidgety impatience. Finally, as Wise Otter had spoken and made his departure, Running Bear stood and pointing his spear first north then east, made a lengthy pronouncement that all accepted with lowered eyes and drooped heads. I learned later that most Comanche clans have both a civil and war chief, yet as best I could determine Running Bear ignored that custom by holding both titles.

The next morning I was dragged before the warriors and instructed by Young Eagle to tell my story, to him in Spanish and to the others through his translation of my account.

I did so willingly, slanting the events entirely to the advantage of my person, extolling my virtues far beyond any respect for truth, minimizing my faults proportionately and making the Americans out to be mere verdugos, hangmen, whose sole and singular reason for hounding me and seeking my arrest was my knowledge of their high and heinous crimes and the enviable and indisputable superiority of my estimable person and generous intentions.

"So you see, great lord and chief, how the favored care and healing I afforded the afflicted earned me the animus of my master, the infamous Luke Pollard, who sought only the death of the ailing so as to profit by their demise. I, on the other hand, did my best to minister to ..."

"You, doctor?" asked Running Bear with sudden interest, not waiting for Young Eagle's translation. "You know White Man medicine?"

"I cannot say, great chief, that I am a doctor by profession, only that—"

"You, doctor, you, liar?" responded Running Bear, his mismatched eyes flashing conflicting emotions, unfathomable cunning in the one, naive simplicity in the other.

I realized at once the trap into which I had fallen, a snare of my own making. But it was too late to retract the lie. I knew nothing of medicine, save the spurious techniques I learned from Thurlow Cheatham, himself a charlatan of the first rank. But there was no turning back. To deny what I had just claimed would place my life in greater jeopardy.

"It is true, great and esteemed chief," I answered with trembling trepidation. "I know about White Man medicine, though because of my youth my experience is less than my study of the medical arts, as you can understand."

Running Bear grunted incomprehensibly, but his narrowed eyes told me of his suspicions about my tale. "When Running Bear return, you go, heal Running Bear mother," he announced in his defective Spanish.

I looked inquisitively at Young Eagle who explained that Running Bear's mother was lingering close to death in Chief White Buffalo's neighboring Comanche camp.

"You heal mother, you live; mother die, you die," added Running Bear with terrifying terseness.

Though exhausted in spirit and body, the anguish I felt over the dreadful alternatives I faced kept me awake far into the night. Furthermore, Running Bear ordered Young Eagle to bind me hand and foot once more. Young Eagle, with whose aid I hoped to ameliorate my captivity, proved to be of no help at all in this cause. He remained deaf to my earnest pleas to leave slack in the painful thongs, muttering only that I must serve the Comanches. When the thongs were again secure, he dumped me unceremoniously near the chief's tent and left me to lie there throughout the night to ruminate over my sad fate.

The camp was astir by first light. With rude pummeling and hateful insults, the women kicked and rolled me away from the fire as they stoked the smoldering embers to new life. Soon the aroma of fresh horsemeat and corn cakes tormented my nostrils. Young Eagle, under whose guard and vigilant supervision I had been placed, came to inspect my condition.

Soon Running Bear emerged from his tent to receive the attention of his wives who scurried to serve him food and stand by at the ready to do his bidding. Nearly fainting from hunger, I begrudged him the corn cakes and strips of horsemeat even as I trembled over my possible fate. No sooner had these dark thoughts overshadowed my mind than he suddenly looked in my direction and calling Young Eagle to his side, gave him instructions concerning me.

I learned that the Comanche male is the most indolent of creatures when not pursuing game or war. He considers it a dishonor and an infringement of his manly condition to exert any sort of manual or menial effort. Women sow and reap their meager crops and do all other chores necessary for the maintenance and welfare of the tribe. Thus on this occasion, delighted to have one of even lower status in their midst, the women asserted their superiority by kicking and pelting me materially with debris and—as I supposed—verbally with insults. To my surprise, I seemed to perceive certain Spanish words interspersed in their taunts. I inquired of Young Eagle but he no more replied to my queries than he responded to my vain pleas for his protection against my tormentors.

The older women took great pleasure in assigning the work of a slave, but ignorant of their language and wishes, I was more often the object of their wrath.

"The women say you are as brainless as dirt and worthless as dung," Young Eagle unexpectedly informed me with a trace of a smile, even though I neither requested nor welcomed his scurrilous translation.

Among other tasks, I was put to stitching sections of buffalo skins with a bone needle and thin deerskin strips. I must admit that at first the women's assessment of my skills was embarrassingly accurate, but after a short time my nimble fingers mastered the technique and at the end there were exclamations of astonishment as I began to outperform even the most skilled older seamstresses. Women and children alike ceased their taunts and crowded about me to witness my skill.

Sensing the tide was turning somewhat in my favor, of a sudden with a flourish of legerdemain I seemed to cause the needle to disappear from my hand. A murmur ran through the assembly and cries of astonishment erupted as the needle, as though by magic, reappeared from behind little White Cloud's ear. A shout went up and Running Bear himself deigned to investigate the cause of the commotion. His disparate eyes widened in surprise as I repeated the trick for his benefit.

The savages were transfixed by what they had witnessed, and sensing my advantage, I informed Running Bear that I could perform greater magic with coins, if such were about. (I had not forgotten my hoard now deposited in his tent.)

Running Bear instructed Little Fawn to fetch me a handful of coins. Thus soon I had again in my possession—if ever so briefly—a few of the precious dollar coins I spirited away from Memphis in Caroline's balloon. These I proceeded to flip and palm and, too fast for human eye to follow, to cause them to vanish and reappear from noses, mouths, ears, and armpits as the savages gasped their astonishment. In the process, several found their way into my pouch where I hoped they might remain unmissed after my performance.

My hopes were dashed, for Young Eagle demanded the dollars when the display was over.

Delighted though my audience was, I was alarmed that Running Bear's disfigured face was now twisted into a scowl of displeasure. Suddenly, he waved away the women and children and took conference with his tribal elders. I waited in breathless apprehension to learn the cause of his melancholy change of mood.

"Chief Running Bear says you lied," Young Eagle explained. "He says you surely possess powerful medicine, else you could not do the things we have seen today. He decrees, therefore, that as his prisoner you must surrender your power to him. Otherwise he will tie you to the stake and take your scalp and your life in the same way we killed the Americans."

A trembling terror possessed me, and I realized to my despair that once again my trickery and mendacity had placed me in the direst jeopardy. In terrified desperation I resorted to the only ruse my befuddled mind could conceive.

"Please say to great chief Running Bear that as his captive I am honor-bound to relinquish to him all such power as I have accrued and collected. This I have willingly done in every particular save one. The power, the medicine as you call it, cannot be easily and readily transferred from one man to another, lest the sky gods take offense and remove it from mortal men forever. With such power surely I shall be able to heal Running Bear's honorable mother, but without it, I fear the malady may take a turn fatal to our hopes and her life. Therefore, I beg the mighty chief to allow me to retain the medicine until this noble purpose be served, for surely it was given to me only for this end. Whereupon, having cured his mother and restored her health, as we most earnestly desire and expect, by its great strength, I shall duly and willingly and according to certain required rituals revealed only to me deposit into his possession and bestow upon his person the power medicine."

Young Eagle translated my message to him as I inwardly cringed, fearful of the savage's response. For a long moment Running Bear squatted motionless, his head hung low and his disfigured brow wrinkled in thought. Then he grunted, rose, and grasped his spear. I quaked with the dread certainty that my hour had come.

He clinched his other fist across his massive chest, pounded his spear twice against the rocky terrain, and uttered his decision.

"The queer French boy," Young Eagle translated, "tires my ears with many words. They buzz about my head like flies after dung. They flow over me like a flooding river. No more words! No more! Now he must keep those he has uttered or he will die as I have spoken. Upon our return he will heal Running Bear's mother with his medicine, then in due ritual he will transfer its power to me so as to increase my strength."

Later that evening, Running Bear retired to his great tent with the strut and arrogance of a petty Asian despot. Although the customary signaling cords ran from their husband's bed to the frontal flap of each wife's lodge, rarely was any summoned save Little Fawn.

I lay awake, fearful and famished under the wheeling stars, again bound hand and foot—and upon his orders to Young Eagle more securely than before—pondering my paltry chances in this forlorn wilderness at the hands of the savage Comanches. Fate had once again gained the upper hand, and escape seemed impossible. Never had my mendacious glibness so ill served me, I wailed. Never had circumstances placed so severe a strain on my customary philosophy of deceit. Truth, which I had always taken to be my enemy, beckoned to me, and for a moment before thinking better of it, almost seduced me into its camp. I resisted the temptation and persisted in my well-rehearsed lying ways, yet I felt that something within me hitherto sure and dependable had suddenly veered towards collapse and betrayal. To my dismay, the violent, vivid terrors represented to me by my awful circumstance now loomed even greater, magnified as they were by a strange rising fear of my own wayward, dangerous, and inexplicable urge to turn to truth and commit honest deeds. (Perhaps I have said all this before, gentle reader. If so, forgive me. These impressions recur and trouble my conscience.)

No sooner it seemed than I had dropped into a nightmarish sleep than Young Eagle roused me to wakefulness with an energetic shake. Although it was still dark, the camp was astir with unusual activity and the tantalizing aroma of cooking horsemeat, venison, and corn cakes, of which he offered me a meager sampling. My gratitude towards him was great, for as the saying goes,

When the need is great, the smallest favor wins us.

Not long thereafter twenty-odd Comanche warriors rode into the square mounted bareback on Spanish ponies with a remuda of ten or twelve spare animals. With their customary agility the savages leaped from their ponies and hurried to Running Bear's tent. But a hush fell over the warriors as Chief Running Bear in full warrior paint and regalia emerged. An incomprehensible dialogue followed, with occasional gestures in my direction, which became clear only when Young Eagle explained the mystery to me.

"Today we ride against the white man who approaches in a large caravan of wagons two days distant toward the rising sun. Warriors from White Buffalo's clan join us for the raid. It has been decided that you will accompany us as a translator for the prisoners we shall take, for none among us speaks fully the American tongue. Serve us well and you may live for a time. Betray us and you will die at once."

Whereupon I made the most servile and profuse protestations of my fealty and devotion to Running Bear and the Comanche nation, pointedly adding, however, that in order to serve, I first must eat. Young Eagle listened impassively as always to my pleas, yet he fetched me not only more corn cakes but—God be praised—a delicious slice of lean horsemeat steak.

Soon thereafter we rode out, some sixty warriors strong, to the excited cries of the children, the subdued concerns of the women, and the melancholy stares of a few old men left to guard the camp. As for me, I was elated, for though my chances for survival on the raid were problematical, they seemed at that moment infinitely preferable to a more certain doom in the Comanche camp once the fraud of my "medicine" should be discovered.

The weapons borne by the Comanche warriors were of the most desultory fashion imaginable. I knew little of arms but I discerned among them American rifles, ancient Spanish pistols. and Mexican daggers and machetes, and in some cases, traditional Comanche bows and spears. Running Bear himself carried two Spanish pistols and a Mexican knife tucked into a broad waistband, and slung on his back an American rifle acquired not many months since in the plunder of a wagon train.

My euphoria over our departure faded as soon as I became aware of the discomforts I should have to suffer. Except for my painful ride on the Comanche pack mule, only once in my life had I mounted a horse and that to a fell outcome. For the beast bolted ere I could secure a grip on his mane, flinging me headfirst into a muddy New Orleans street where I was put to shame by the jeers and jests of onlookers. Thus I knew almost nothing about the raw skin and aching posterior that are the common distresses of the neophyte horseman. To make matters worse, my horse was old and thin and its bones nearly razor sharp.

When it became apparent that neither my nag nor I were of a determination or stamina to keep the swift pace set by the expert Comanche horsemen, Young Eagle took the reins of my horse and forced it to gallop behind his as I bounced, swayed, and clung for dear life to its mane, much to the derisive comments and laughter of the warriors.

By nightfall we reached a forested riverbed far to the east and following an inspection by scouts and a satisfied gesture from Running Bear, the Comanches dismounted and there we took our "sleep." There would be no fire, for, as I was told, we had entered land claimed by a northern Caddo clan, hereditary enemies of the Comanches who would fight a raiding party inside their hunting grounds. The warriors chewed on dried buffalo meat, Charqui, Young Eagle informed me in Spanish as he offered me slices of the shriveled meat, which the Americans renamed "Jerky" in their language. I relished its salty taste.

Much less pleasurable was the wretched state of my tortured, aching body. I could barely straighten my legs and back, whilst the agile Comanches showed no distress whatsoever after our daylong ride. As the night deepened, the chill became an added discomfort, and as my body shivered, Running Bear and the other warriors not only seemed impervious to the lowered temperature but made sport of my unmanly constitution.

Later, somewhat revived by rest and fortified by the leathery jerky, I observed that Running Bear and his warriors were engaged in an animated conversation. I asked Young Eagle to translate for me. He did so only in part.

"The White Man is a woman and will never survive in this land," Running Bear observed contemptuously, staring hatefully at me with his double-planed eyes, "for he can neither stand the cold of winter nor the heat of summer. What have we to fear from him if he cannot even rightly sit a horse? Therefore, we Comanche will hunt him down like a dog and take his possessions, his women, and his life."

"It is said, my chief," offered Red Deer, one of the older warriors, "that the White Man knows cunning tricks to overcome his unmanly nature. The Red Man nations that lie towards the rising sun tell of his great numbers and fearsome weapons and warn us that instead of scorning him for his weakness, we should beware the White Man for his guile and treachery."

"Our brother nations are but cowards and women," snorted Running Bear. "Let the White Man come against us, and he will soon tremble in dread at the great strength of the Comanche warriors. We are not like other tribes who talk as wolves but fight like whelps. Our medicine is stronger than any other. Have we not driven the Apache into the mountains? We are always victorious in war and will drive away the White Man as we would kick a mangy dog and send it howling with its tail between its legs. In time the Great Spirit will destroy the White Man and restore what he has taken."

As he talked Running Bear became more agitated, and I feared that in his rising anger against the White Man he might discharge his wrath against me. But at that moment two scouts emerged silently from darkness. Running Bear and his warriors entered into a long, uneasy conference, but Young Eagle, probably on orders from Running Bear, refused to divulge any information. Only later did I learn the reason for their agitation: The approaching wagon train was larger and better armed than the Comanches had thought. There seemed to be disagreement among them, and I guessed that they were debating whether to attack as planned or begin a prudent withdrawal. Later, to my repeated requests for information, Young Eagle replied laconically: "Tomorrow we attack. Tonight we sleep."

In neither case did Young Eagle's words seem to apply to me. To add to my physical woes, the chill deepened and I shivered uncontrollably. And to make matters worse, the thought of bullets, blood, and possible death, which I could not expel from my overwrought imagination, was a prospect blacker than the stygian, moonless night. Yet sheer fatigue eventually overcame me, and I fell into a nightmarish sleep filled with terrifying scenes of flying bullets and flashing swords. I labored to escape enemies closing from all sides, but though I tried to run away, my steps were agonizingly slow, and I felt death close behind me. Indeed one pursuer overtook me and grabbed my shoulder, but to my great relief I awoke to see that it was Young Eagle shaking me out of my sleep. He handed me two slices of salty buffalo jerky, which I consumed as if it were the finest English beefsteak.

Mounting our ponies at Running Bear's command, we rode quickly out of the riverbed and proceeded eastwards at a fast gallop across the parched plain. After two hours of hard riding that aggravated my aches beyond telling, Running Bear signaled a halt. The reason soon became evident. A few miles to the east a dust cloud swirled and scouts reported a caravan of twenty-odd horse-drawn wagons flanked by two or three

143

dozens of armed escorts. Surveying the terrain, Running Bear positioned his men for an ambush behind a grove of twisted hackberry trees that flanked the south side of the trail. Here wagons had passed not long before, for even my untrained eye was able to espy the deep traces cut by the iron rimmed wheels.

A keen-eyed scout spotted the assembled Comanches, and sounding the alarm with a pistol shot, yelled for the wagons to retreat and form a circle. Only the first three wagons, one of which had broken a wheel trying to execute the sharp turn, were unable to join them in the defensive maneuver. Three of the five occupants leaped out and ran on foot toward the circled wagons. But our warriors now were in close pursuit, and in spite of covering fire from the caravan, easily dispatched them. Seeing that the armed escort made no move to come to their aid, the two remaining Americans surprisingly tossed aside their weapons and raised their hands in surrender.

Thwarted in their main objective and judging the wagon train to be too well positioned to overcome without suffering great loss, the Comanches hurriedly scooped up the contents of the abandoned wagons and the main body quickly retreated in the direction we had come. Paralyzed with stark terror by the bullets that whizzed by, I was left with a few warriors who braved the singing bullets to toss their prisoners like sacks of corn across the backs of the team horses and tie their hands and feet under the belly of the animals. Then we also retreated. One of the horses went down, but without breaking his running stride the agile warrior swung himself behind a companion and all escaped.

At nightfall we found the main Comanche contingent, which had camped for a "sleep." After a time I was brought forth to query the captives. Imagine my surprise when I saw before me the red beard, fat jowls, and quivering belly of Colonel Summerford and the lean frame and sallow face of Cletis Satterfield, both trembling with pain and fear.

Done in by their stupor and fear and misled by my changed appearance—I had grown considerably in both girth and stature since my Memphis days—Summerford and Satterfield did not initially know me. But as the interrogation began, Summerford recognized my voice and let out an oath of recognition.

"Petie, Petie Prosper, is that you? Glory be! Damned and double damned! We thought you was dead! They said you died in that balloon contraption. What are you doing here and how did you end up with these here Indian devils?"

"Petie Prosper? That little nig—, that little barber of ours Petie Prosper?" Cletis echoed in disbelief.

144

Young Eagle, impatient with their chattering, reminded me that the captives were to speak only when spoken to, and that I was to relay all information to him. "Remember, I know some words of the American tongue, enough to punish you if you try to deceive the Comanche," he reminded me with a finger jab to my chest.

"Colonel," I responded, quickly getting down to business, "how I got here is not the issue before us, nor are your questions the concern. Rather, Young Eagle, esteemed warrior of the Comanche nation, will do the asking, and you must, through me, answer him truthfully, if you value your life."

Colonel Summerford paled and promised to answer any and all queries. Cletis blanched and hastened to make the same agreement.

To his questions Summerford and Satterfield answered Young Eagle that the wagon train was headed for Santa Fe but then they became evasive about the details of their business there. Only when Young Eagle threatened to cut off their ears and gouge out their eyes did the colonel's tongue loosen.

"Petie, now you know I was always your friend. So you tell Young Eagle that I promise to tell him ever'thing I know, everything. Understand?"

"Me too," chimed in Satterfield. "And Petie, remember that I never done you no harm. I tried to get all them people to leave you alone, I told them, I did, that you didn't do near all the things you was accused o' doing."

"Your kind sentiments move me deeply," I responded sarcastically. "But if you want to keep your eyes and ears, you had best tell Young Eagle and the Comanches what they want to know."

"And that I surely will, as best I can," answered the profusely sweating Colonel Summerford. "Only problem is I can't say I rightly know everything that coward Alvis had in mind. It was all his doin', you know. He planned the whole thing. Big Indian fighter he claimed to be! Indian fighter, my hiney! Why the first thing he done when the Comanches attacked us was run off like a streakfield lizard. Never fired a shot that I recollect, and after all that talk about protecting us and all. Damn his yaller soul to hell!"

"Yeah, the lying son of a b....!" added Satterfield.

"Cletis here and me put up the money. Alvis said we could double or triple it soon's we got them there guns and whiskey to Santa Fe. Said them Spaniards, or Meshicans, or whatever they be out there would pay off in gold nuggets which they're supposed to have aplenty of. Said we could reach the Dry Run o' the Santa Fe Trail without no trouble. What he didn't tell us was how fer a journey it was, or how dangerous. Now you tell the good chief to just be letting us go and he can keep everything we got."

"He's not the chief. Running Bear over there is the war chief, and he can do with you as he pleases."

"Can't argue with you about that," Summerford answered with a worried grimace. "But maybe we can come to some kind of arrangement. We got money and stuff back in Memphis."

"Young Eagle asks whether you planned to settle and hunt in the Comanchería."

"Lord God no!" protested Summerford, "We ain't never had no idea of settling in this here godforsaken prairie. Only people that'd live here would have to be craz—" he started to add before thinking better of his description.

Young Eagle put several other questions to Summerford and Satterfield and apparently satisfied with the truthfulness of their answers, upon our return to the tribal camp reported the information to Running Bear. The savages appeared to be satisfied that the caravan proved to be no forerunner of others intending to settle in their hunting territory, and Running Bear repeated his boast that the White Man could not stand up to Comanche strength.

"As these captives lie like dogs before me, so shall all the Whites go down in defeat before my strength! Tomorrow we kill these for sport."

The plight and impending doom of captive wretches seemed to alleviate my own lowly condition. After all I considered myself to be in some measure a member of the victorious war party.

Be he chief or meanest man of his tribe, the Comanche never foregoes an opportunity to drink himself into an insensible stupor, and upon our return to the camp there was offered no exception to this sad rule. The captured wagons contained several cases of whiskey. Quickly inebriated, the warriors danced and staggered about the campfire, firing their rifles with dangerous abandon in celebration of their successful defiance of the Americans. Anon the captive women were rousted forth for their nightly ravishment, but no sooner had the merriment begun than White Buffalo's braves disputed with Running Bear's men over who should have the first turn in their despoilment. As for the youngest and fairest of the captives, Running Bear himself claimed her as his fourth wife—his lawful allotment as chief—much to the sullen displeasure of the older spouses and angry mutterings of the disappointed warriors.[5] Thereupon, in a conciliatory gesture to compensate for the loss of such a prize, the other two women, older and less comely in appearance, were allotted to White Buffalo's warriors.

His braves protested the unequal recompense for their clan, and a violent, alcoholic argument ensued that soon led to cocked weapons and dangerous threats. But bloody tragedy was averted when Running Bear agreed also to consign most of the remaining male captives, including her young companion and protector, to White Buffalo for slavery or slaughter even though, he pointedly and vulgarly reminded his tribesmen, the chief himself had stayed behind in his camp, sitting on his fat arse like a woman whilst he, Running Bear, with great courage and daring, had led the Comanche warriors to yet another victory. Nevertheless, for brotherhood and peace amongst the Comanches he would make this concession of his prisoners. On the morrow they would be led away to death or slavery in White Buffalo's camp.

Meanwhile, my fanciful and delusional status as a victorious warrior came to a rude end. I was unceremoniously bound with the other prisoners, by chance next to the young man whose despair over the fate of his lady he vented now in tears of frustration, now in fervent prayers for her salvation. He strained vainly against the cruel leather thongs as blood dripped from his elbow in the earnest but futile efforts to free himself.

On orders from Running Bear the trembling young woman, correctly supposing his intentions and divining her fate, was dragged away by two older women to be fed, dressed, and prepared to receive him on the morrow as her husband. Strengthened by despair over her impending fate, briefly she broke free of their grasp and raced, arms extended, screaming "John! John!" towards the young man who struggled valiantly to receive her. But other women quickly surrounded and subdued her, finding in her dash for freedom the pretext to pummel her maliciously until Running Bear himself, concerned that her beauty might suffer, ordered an end to the maltreatment.

Though numbed by my own fate, yet I felt pity stir in my heart for the unhappy pair, whose unusual handsomeness of feature and noble bearing had excited my sympathy and stirred my curiosity. I presented myself by name to him, related a fanciful version of my own story, including the unjust confiscation of my hard-earned coins, and politely inquired as to their names and provenance and the circumstances that had brought them to this wretched pass. Whereupon, though sunk in despair and grief yet thankful for a kind voice, he responded with well-bred grace and courtesy to my questions in the tale you will hear.

The Story of Quaker John and Catholic Miriam

Friend, thy kindness is a welcome help in this black hour of despair and I thank thee that in thy very misfortune and loss thou showest compassion and friendly concern for mine. My name, sir, is John Greenley, and mortal eyes have never beheld a more sorrowful man. I am a Christian in faith, and in doctrine and heritage a Friend, or as some call us, a Quaker. I hail from the town of Fairdale in the State of Pennsylvania where my father Jonathan Greenley was, and if God wills it, yet remains, a respected, God-fearing man of standing and substance. Indeed, I enjoyed in my childhood and early youth all such material comforts as one could reasonably hope for amongst a people who hold lavishness to be a sin and plainness of life to be a virtue.

I grew up amidst strict but adoring parents, loving grandparents, three precious younger brothers, a beautiful, gentle sister, and many relatives, friends, and admirable townspeople. We were nearly all in my town of the same moral and religious persuasion, so that delinquency and the crimes excited by unbridled passion and unchecked greed were rare amongst us. Oh, kind friend, how wondrous in this present hour of misery doth the memory of those happy years appear to me!

But the Devil never ceases to deceive and lead us astray from the true pathway. As I grew out of childhood into adolescence and came nearer to full manhood, an infernal restlessness invaded and troubled my spirit. Like the Prodigal Son, I wearied of the virtuous but placid life in my father's house and dreamed of adventure in the wider world. I excelled in my studies and was praised for my mastery of letters and eloquence of speech. For Friends esteem learning as much as they cleave to simplicity of life. I read copiously, especially books on travel and geography, and the more I read, the more restless I grew.

Persuaded at length by my importunate requests to wander abroad, my father hit upon the idea of turning my wanderlust to profitable venture. And it happened in this wise. For many years he had sustained profitable commercial intercourse (for he was a merchant by trade) with our Quaker brethren in the State of Virginia and in earlier times journeyed yearly to Richmond and Petersburg for this purpose. Of late, however, though still stout of limb and sound of judgment, the concerns of family and the press of business had prevented such travels. Furthermore, two of his older associates in Virginia had departed this life and the connections that sustained their commerce were weakening. Perchance, reasoned my father, I might serve as his agent, at once satisfying my urge to travel abroad and reversing the troubling decline of his business.

148

I accepted, sir, his proposal with an enthusiasm ill-befitting a sober Quaker and soon made my departure, having been sternly instructed by my father in all procedures of travel and business and abundantly supplied by my anxious mother with clothing, food, and other provisions for my journey. I bore no arms, for Quakers do not traffic in such, nor believe we in their use. Neither stage nor rail conveniently served the greater distance of my trip, and wisely heeding my father's advice, I chose to travel on horseback. With some apprehension he entrusted to me his favorite mount Dan, a black stallion said to have a strain of the Arabian blood in him, fleet-footed indeed and standing nearly sixteen hands high. Our neighbors grumbled that such a horse was an unseemly extravagance for a humble Quaker. But on this singular point my father paid them little heed and for which I would later be extremely grateful.

I departed early on a Monday in high spirits, though saddened at the spectacle of my weeping mother and sister and determined to disguise my inward excitement with a straight face before my somber father and brothers.

By midday my firsthand knowledge of the fields and forests about me was exhausted, so that henceforth I had to rely on my father's instructions as to roads and lodgings. This information proved to be entirely reliable, for my father was meticulous in details, and I had only to follow his indications to make my journey with dispatch and in safety. The roads were good and the inns he had pointed out were clean and the patrons accommodating, particularly when I informed them whose son I was.

In this way I reached the Maryland border without mishap worthy of mention, eventually arriving at the beautiful city of Baltimore. There against my father's advice I lingered to take in its size and wonders and to gawk at its citizens. The handsome teams and carriages of the rich, the crowded, noisy streets, the beautiful ladies and wealthy gentlemen in their stylish finery, the elegant hotels and stately mansions were sights my fevered mind could hardly credit.

My father had instructed me to cross the Potomac at Washington and continue towards my destination along the road skirting the western side of the river in the southerly direction of Richmond. But two companions whom I met during my sojourn in a Baltimore inn told me that the eastern route through St. Charles and lower Maryland was more pleasant and interesting and, further, that their company and conversation would make the journey more amenable. A short distance south of Newburg, they explained, a ferry would transport me across the Potomac to Virginia and thence I could proceed directly to Richmond and thence to Petersburg. This reasoning easily persuaded me and we set off in high spirits, for in all ways my new acquaintances appeared to be fine hail-fellows deserving of trust and friendship.

Oh that I had heeded my wise father! For though we passed the first two days in merry discourse and rode through a pleasant land of spacious tobacco plantations, graceful estates, and friendly people, there were few convenient inns, and none concerning which I had my father's indications, on this less-traveled route. For this reason, as night fell on the third day and we espied no welcoming shelter we were obliged to make our encampment under the stars. This posed no great inconvenience, for the night was warm, our food plentiful, and our spirits exuberant. After seeing to my horse, downing a hearty meal, and reciting my prayers—in which my friends derisively declined to take part—I soon fell into a deep sleep.

Imagine, sir, my chagrin and anger when upon awaking, I discovered myself alone without provisions, purse, or horse. My erstwhile companions had absconded with all my possessions and were nowhere to be seen. After spending a short time taking stock of my unhappy circumstances, I determined to continue on foot southwards to the Virginia border, even though I was uncertain of distances and with only a few coins left to my name. Eventually reaching the village of La Plata, where I purchased provisions sufficient to keep body and soul together, I broadcast a description of my larcenous companions and described their crime against me. One gentleman thought to have seen the pair, but others cast doubts on the reliability of this intelligence. In any case, I was not hopeful of laying eyes on them again, for inasmuch as they were mounted and I was afoot, the natural advantage was entirely theirs. Thus for several days I continued my slow trek toward Virginia, resting in the shade at noonday—for it was July and the climate much hotter than the cool hills and mountains of Pennsylvania.

Night overtook me again yet a few miles from the Potomac ferry, and wearied from walking and in need of shelter and rest, I espied a dilapidated house removed a stone's throw from the road and covered with the wild vines and obtrusive vegetation characteristic of abandoned dwellings. Seeing no signs of human presence on the property, cautiously I sought about for a means of entry into its promising sanctum. To my surprise, the main door, though long since warped and reduced to ruin by sun and damp, opened easily to my touch as though reactivated in recent days. Inside the ruin I found the explanation of the mystery, for newly emptied whiskey bottles and the scraps of food told of recent occupancy. Yet I encountered no further evidence of human presence and surmised that the sojourners had come and gone even as I also intended the next day.

As darkness fell I ate the last of my provisions and whereas hitherto I had felt no apprehension about sleeping under the open sky, this house stirred in me a foreboding that despite all my customary prayers I could not dispel. Troubled by these mysterious sensibilities but fatigued by a long march under the summer sun, I soon fell into a fitful sleep in which I sensed movement, stealth, and a malignant presence.

Nor were these sensations merely the unsubstantial figments of idle dreams, for suddenly I was awakened—I know not how long I had slept—by a piercing scream and the angry growl of voices. Instantly I was awake, though uncertain of what scene I faced and undecided whether to stand or flee. But before I could take action of any sort the door opened and I saw silhouetted against the starry heavens a young woman in the grip of two ruffians. To her pleas for release they responded with threats and curses. Their voices sounded familiar, and thou, my friend, mayest imagine my surprise and indignation upon recognizing the very thieves who had stolen my horse and possessions under the deceptive guise of false friendship.

Now, sir, we Quakers are a peaceful people, much averse to war and violence, yet so strong were my natural feelings at the moment that they overcame my moral restraints, and in an instant I was upon them, snatching the screaming young lady out of their grasp and pummeling them with my bare fists. The feature of surprise in my aggressive assault was favorable at first to my intentions, for though a rank novice in the pugilistic arts, yet I am blessed with considerable natural strength abetted on that occasion not only by the outrage I felt over my own cause but also by my desire to protect and rescue the distressed lady from her tormentors.

But no sooner did the hardened villains realize that I was but the solitary inexperienced man they had robbed than their confidence returned and with wicked skill they nullified my frantic assault. The larger man struck me flush on the chin with his fist, sending me reeling across the room. As I turned to regain my balance, the other ripped a heavy board from the rotting wall and broke it across my head. Stars danced before my eyes, and I swooned into black unconsciousness.

I awoke bewildered in a strange room. Looking about me for a clue to my circumstances, I saw a silver crucifix above the bed and was relieved at least that I was among Christians, though we Friends use no such outward symbols in our worship. At that moment the door opened and a tall, graying gentleman entered, followed upon his approval by a stately lady and the beautiful young woman I had endeavored vainly to rescue.

"Sir, are you in pain? Are you all right?" asked the young lady in a lilting, golden voice that bore a faint trace of the Irish manner of speech.

"I thank thee, kind lady, for thy inquiry. In truth, my pains are considerable but tolerable, for I am certain they will quickly pass."

The tall gentleman spoke with a more pronounced Irish accent: "Be not quick to assume anything just yet, my young friend. You endured a severe beating at the hands of those wretched villains, and the bruises and contusions will take time to heal. Luckily for you, you appear to have no broken bones or disabling injuries, and you have had many hours of healing sleep."

"Sir, where am I? Whose house is this, and how came I here?"

"It is my honor to have you as a guest in my house, the Michael Morrissey estate, and I am the owner, Michael Morrissey, at your service. This lady is my wife Mistress Vivian Morrissey and in a manner of speaking you have met my daughter Miriam. And you, sir, would you be kind enough to tell us your name?"

I complied at once with his request, describing my circumstances and the nature of the business that had brought me south.

"I gather from your manner of speaking that you are a Friend, a Quaker. Am I correct in my assumption, Master Greenley?"

"That is so, sir," I replied. "But I am at a loss in recollecting the events that brought me here. Canst thou tell me what happened and how came I here?"

"Tis easy enough to satisfy that curiosity. My daughter Miriam was abducted by the criminals that assaulted you. She was returning on foot from her cousin's house when they surprised her on a lonely stretch of road between our estates. When she failed to return on time, my men and I set out under my supervision to find her. We saw marks of a struggle, and fearing the worst, followed their tracks as best we could. We were passing by the deserted house just as you bravely took it upon yourself to confront them and rescue Miriam. We might well have missed her altogether had she not screamed when you came at them out of the darkness. We finished what you, sir, so manfully began by capturing the delinquents and freeing my dear daughter from their evil hands. We found you unconscious and, I must confess it, assumed at first that you were one of them. Thanks to Miriam, however, we soon learned the truth, so that instead of taking you to be a criminal we hold you to be a hero. And be assured, Master Greenley, that if your body aches, the two felons are in much worse shape. We saw to that before turning them over to the sheriff."

"Did they, by chance, have with them a black horse, sixteen hands high or so with a saddle notched with the initials JG?"

"Why, yes, so they did," Mr. Morrissey answered with a surprised look. "We thought it strange that they should have three horses when by the looks of them they could ill afford one between them. The sheriff has the animal in his keeping. Know you aught of the horse?"

"Yes sir, it belongs to my father, Jonathan Greenley, and these are the circumstances of its disappearance: A three-day ride from Baltimore these same men, pretending to be traveling companions and gentlemen, stole the horse and robbed me of money and provisions."

That very afternoon Dan was restored to my keeping, along with the remainder of my possessions, though not the money, which the felons had already squandered. Meanwhile, I was served a sumptuous meal and received every form of kind hospitality from Mr. Morrissey and his family.

Several times Miriam and her parents came to assess my state and progress towards full recovery. Miriam's exciting presence, her magical voice, long raven-colored hair, and extraordinarily fair features were like a light in which I pleasurably basked. I do not exaggerate, friend, when I say that no sooner had I gazed upon her beautiful face and looked into her wondrous green eyes than I was deeply and forever in love with this most exquisite and precious of women. Nor do I depart from the truth when I assure thee that as best I could judge in matters concerning the female heart, Miriam's feelings took a similar wonderful turn in my favor. At no time were we alone, yet the looks we exchanged and tender feelings we inspired in each other were secretly and innocently conveyed.

Nor could we long conceal our sentiments from others in the family. Wise in the symptoms of youthful love, Mrs. Morrissey soon curtailed their visits, and although their generous concern for my wounds and attention to my needs never flagged, the Morrisseys soon commenced to show a subtle impatience with my presence.

My agitation grew apace with my recovering health. Soon I was too well in body to remain abed yet too sick with love to depart the mansion. After three days I was again strong enough to stand and ride, and Mr. Morrissey, now seemingly eager for my departure, generously provided me with money and other necessities for the remainder of my journey. I protested his kindness but he kindly assured me that it was but a small favor in comparison to the greater one I had done for Miriam and his family. He then inquired anew—perchance to remind me—about my business in Virginia and pointedly referred to the filial duty I had to comply with my father's instructions.

The prospect of leaving Miriam reduced me to despair, for I now thought it impossible to live without her. Deriving courage from desperation, I made known to Mr. Morrissey the sentiments Miriam inspired in my heart and asked his permission to return, once my mission in Virginia should have been accomplished, so as to call upon her in formal courtship, adding that I believed from certain hints and indications I had perceived in her behavior that she would receive my attentions favorably.

A quick-tempered man, Mr. Morrissey responded indignantly that he would never permit his daughter to consort with an apostate Quaker and that before allowing her to become the wife of a man so remote from God and Church and so close to Hell and damnation, he would see to it that she became a bride of Christ as a nun. Hereabouts was Catholic country, he said forcefully, and Miriam must marry within the Faith, as I must also return to my own kind. Thereupon he regained his composure and thanked me again for my actions but firmly and resolutely ordered me out of his house, off his lands, and away from his daughter forever.

To plead my suit further against such utter rejection would have been to show disrespect for Mr. Morrissey. This I was unwilling to do, though neither was I reconciled to losing Miriam. In the midst of this quandary, Fate—or Providence—afforded us an unsupervised moment alone.

"Meet me day after tomorrow a mile north at the bridge where the road curves to the west," she whispered as she passed me in the hallway.

I made my departure, thanking the Morrissey family anew for their kindness and making no further reference to my feelings for Miriam. For their part, they displayed courteous manners, wishing me Godspeed, health, and prosperity, yet pointedly refraining from inviting me to visit them again should some day I bend my steps that way again.

Inasmuch as Miriam had not indicated the hour of our meeting, I groomed myself as best I could and hastened to the designated spot early on the appointed day, having camped the previous night under the open sky not many miles from her house. Hours passed without any sign of Miriam. In my sentimental agitation I wavered between unchecked expectation and fearful melancholy, but as the afternoon advanced my hopes commenced to decline with the sinking sun. Perhaps the family had prevented her coming, or Miriam herself might have thought better of an unsanctioned meeting with me.

But then as my hopes teetered on the brink of despair, I espied her coming, her fair features protected from the sun by a yellow parasol, and herself a vision of greater beauty amidst the warm colorings and gorgeous flowers of the lovely Maryland countryside at the apex of its summer splendor. Seeing me she ran, arms extended, to meet me, and we embraced for a long moment without a word, so inexpressibly deep and irrevocable was our love become in the brief days of our acquaintance.

Afterwards, we had not long to declare our eternal love and lament our plight before we saw three horsemen racing towards us bent low in their saddles.

"My father and his men!" cried Miriam, wringing her hands. "They will do you great harm, my darling John, perhaps even kill you on the spot! You must ride at once! They are good, honorable men in most matters, as you have seen, but my father is fanatical in religion and greedy in his affairs. He would sooner see me dead than wed to one outside the Church! He has given me two desperate choices: either to prepare myself for a nunnery in Ireland whence my ancestors came or to marry Grady O'Riley, a Catholic neighbor, 'tis true, who has asked my hand but a toad of a man whose wealth and land blind my father."

"I will not leave thee, slay me though they must, for without thee there would be no life for me," I responded.

"Then we will ride away together! For I loathe Grady O'Riley as much as I love you, John, and though I honor Church teachings in all matters of life, yet I have no calling to be a nun! That choice is equally hateful to me."

Had we but had the time to ponder our impetuous decision, perhaps we could have made a wiser determination, but the riders were now bearing dangerously down upon us. Without another word, I helped Miriam into the saddle, and then quickly mounting behind her, I spurred Dan across the bridge and urged him to full gallop along the westward running road. In her haste she dropped her parasol but there was no time to retrieve it.

Happily for us, Dan was rested, well fed, and ready to run like the wind. Even though burdened by two riders, yet with his Arabian heritage and great stamina he was more than a match for the smaller Morrissey mounts. As the miles melted away under his flying hooves, they fell ever further behind us until we could barely make out their dust trail in the distance.

At length we gained a margin over our pursuers great enough to allow the lathered beast a brief rest and a much-needed drink from a bubbling brook, and us a chance to take stock of our predicament. We realized to our consternation that we had embarked on a course from which there was now no turning back. In Miriam's case, she pointed out to me that her father would look upon her decision to elope with me as an unpardonable act of disobedience and betrayal. Should she fall again under his authority, her fate would be summary banishment to the nunnery. As for me, as long as I lived I would stand as an affront to their family honor, and they would not rest until I had repaid in blood the stain I had placed on the Morrissey name.

From this grim realization we turned to the more immediate and pressing problem of our escape route. I knew from the general configuration of the land than not many miles to westward flowed the Potomac River. Could we but negotiate the crossing into Virginia we might breathe easier. But should we fail, we would surely find ourselves, our backs to the river, in danger of being overtaken and captured.

Luck was with us, however, for we found a ferry about to make its last run of the day, and as the long summer afternoon slipped into darkness we set foot at last in Virginia. Now we proceeded at a slower, more cautious pace. My concern for Miriam's welfare was uppermost in my mind, and I knew I soon must find food and lodging for her. Desperate thoughts raced through my mind, and the full weight of my responsibilities now became evident to me.

Inquiring of strangers on the road, I learned that not many miles ahead we should come to an inn. Alas, it was full of travelers, but responding to my pleas, the kind mistress of the establishment took pity on Miriam and made a space for her in her own quarters. As for my horse, she said, there were stables and feed a-plenty and for me a hayloft wherein I could take my rest.

Early the next day after an ample breakfast, I paid our lodging and we took our leave. It was neither in my character nor a feature of my Quaker heritage to lie, but inasmuch as necessity often turns to deceit as its first recourse, I hinted to the inn mistress that Richmond was our destination. In this way, I hoped to mislead the Morrisseys who by now surely would have crossed the Potomac and doubtless were in our close pursuit.

Fearing she might have misgivings after the reality of a harrowing ride, a night spent in the discomfort of strange surroundings, and the general uncertainty of our chances, I asked Miriam to reveal her honest feelings. This she did, leaving no doubt about her resolve or the strength of her impetuous Irish character.

"My darling John, I love you with all my heart and look upon you as my husband, though we are not yet man and wife, and I mean to stand by you for better or worse. Take these words as absolute and final, for you will offend me if you question me again."

Scarcely daring to believe myself to be the happy object of beautiful Miriam's love and devotion, I replied with similar sentiments, swearing to her my eternal love and fidelity—though we Friends believe it sinful to make oaths of any sort. Our resolve thus reaffirmed and our love declared anew, we set our course westward, traveling all that day and the next several across the fair country of Virginia, stopping the night at various inns and taking occasional rests in shaded groves and beside placid streams.

Because Miriam brought no clothes but those she wore, I insisted that we furnish her with a decent wardrobe. She protested my modest funds, but I would hear nothing of it, for I placed her womanly comfort and decorum above all other concerns. Seeing my determination in the matter, she relented and purchased for herself the indispensable feminine articles for a journey of unknown duration and hardship.

Although I wished only to love and honor Miriam, it grieved my spirit when in a calmer state I reflected that by my actions I had brought dishonor to her good name and reputation in the eyes of the world. This I wished to remedy at once and attempted to do so by proposing that we be wed by civil authority at the earliest favorable circumstance. But Miriam firmly rejected my plea, declaring that for her only a church wedding by a priest would be valid in her eyes. Without a resolution to our dilemma, I kept my silence on the matter.

I thought to make our way westward across the mountains and thence north into Ohio. There I knew existed several communities of Friends, including an uncle and other more distant family relations long departed from Pennsylvania but whose location I hoped to find and whose help I intended to solicit. I dared not return to my father's house, for that would place my family in jeopardy of a confrontation with Mr. Morrissey. But thou must understand, sir, that no settlement of Friends would prove to be a permanent refuge for us, because once my fellow Quakers discovered Miriam's religion, I would be expelled from their fellowship, as is our manner of treating those who choose a spouse outside the Faith.

In this intent at the last we were thwarted, however, for Mr. Morrissey, abandoning his personal pursuit and returning to his home in Maryland, then hired expert professional men to hunt us down.

Meanwhile we were making our way by stages and without undue mishap across the wild Virginia mountains, eventually descending through rolling country to Parkersburg on the Ohio River. There to our consternation we saw our names posted with an offer of reward for our detention. Inasmuch as these bore a description of our persons and my horse, it was plain to us that without changes in our dress and mode of travel, our capture would soon occur.

It behooves me to say here, dear friend, that even though often we were obliged by circumstances to call ourselves husband and wife and, indeed, to share quarters at several inns, I bound myself not to take advantage of this intimacy to consummate our union. To this Miriam responded that although our marriage was not yet sanctioned by priest or pastor, in her heart she considered me to be her husband and should I so desire, would surrender herself willingly to my love.

Leaving Miriam over her protests to rest at a comfortable inn in Parkersburg, I proceeded alone into Ohio, for I had reason to believe that a community of Friends lay not more than thirty miles northwest of the Virginia border. This information proved to be true, and I was soon in the welcome company of men of my persuasion, though not of my immediate kin. These, I learned, lived more than fifty miles further north. After prayers and a hearty meal, I came to the reason for my visit.

I explained to the assembled Friends that because I must make the remainder of my journey by riverboat, I had no further use for Dan and indeed had no means to care for him. But rather than sell the noble beast into an uncertain existence as a livery horse, I preferred to leave him with the Friends who would tend him properly as one of God's creatures. Therefore, I continued, if any man should have use for him, then let him make a fair offer and the horse and saddle were his. Only one other condition did I impose: Should my father choose to retrieve him, for I would duly inform him of Dan's whereabouts, then I would accept the buyer's word to agree to the transaction at a price his conscience would set.

Thereupon, a kindly elder, Brother Oliver Cline by name, stepped forth with a fair offer and a promise to deal with my father as I had stated.

"In truth, Brother Greenley, the horse is an extravagance for me, yet I understand thy wish to leave him in caring hands. For thy father's sake, I promise to deal honestly with thee, for he is known by reputation amongst us, though we have not the pleasure of knowing him in person, and 'tis a name respected for honest dealings with men and reverence towards God. It will be as thou requestest, young Greenley."

I was happy indeed with these words, for amongst Friends their word is their bond; they will do whatever they promise to do and refrain from what they have promised not to do.

The transaction thus completed, I said goodbye to faithful Dan with tears in my eyes and soon bent my steps towards the state border. The Friends generously loaded me with food and other provisions and offered me a wagon ride back to the Parkersburg ferryboat. I thanked them for their kindness but declined their offer for farm work was at its summer peak and every man was needed in the fields.

Late the next day I crossed the Ohio and arrived in Parkersburg where I received Miriam's happy embrace and secured our passage on a riverboat. During my absence she had heard talk in the inn of the two young runaways riding a giant black horse. Pretending idle curiosity about the matter, she was frightened to hear rumors of their presence in this region, perhaps in Parkersburg itself, and the expectation of their imminent arrest.

I soothed Miriam's apprehensions as best I could by assuring her that come morning we would sail away from impending danger and thence to the farthest American west, if we must, so as to live freely as man and wife. Indeed the next day we boarded the boat without mishap and sailed down the Ohio River in deceptive tranquility.

But in truth I underestimated both the persistence of our trackers and the evil turn of our fate. For the further we fled, the more doggedly they came after us. We thought to have found a haven in Louisville, Kentucky, but ere long Mr. Morrissey's hired agents appeared to distribute leaflets and send us fleeing anew. Our funds and provisions exhausted, we made our way westwards to St. Louis where word of us had not reached. There I found work as a stable hand in a livery belonging to Mr. Lawrence Barker whilst Miriam, passing herself always as my wife, was accepted into his house as assistant to the housekeeper and tutor to his two children. The Barkers allowed us use of a small room in the servant quarters and gave us leftover food, which we took in the kitchen. Our small but carefully marshaled earnings, though very limited, accumulated to a modest fund, which Miriam insisted should be in my keeping.

But the Devil, who never rests but wanders to and fro like a roaring lion seeking whom he may devour, soon devised an ugly circumstance, which forced our hasty departure from St. Louis. Respectful of Miriam at first and pleased with the delightful way his children Julia and Robert flourished under her charming tutelage, soon Mr. Barker himself was sinfully captivated by her beauty. Thereupon he commenced to trouble her with insinuating conversations and unwelcome attentions. These encounters became more frequent and his solicitous behavior towards her more insistent and disturbing. Miriam said nothing openly to me, yet

I noticed in her behavior a peculiar nervousness and saw occasional tears that I wrongly blamed on a belated homesickness for her father's comfortable mansion. I pressed her about it, but she, shaking me by the shoulders to impress on me her point, sharply dismissed my suppositions and reminded me that I was never again to question her love or her resolve to remain at my side forever.

Then one day the inevitable happened. Mrs. Barker chanced upon one of her husband's furtive encounters with Miriam. Stunned and furious by what she saw and heard, she demanded an explanation. Mr. Barker immediately cast all the blame on Miriam, claiming to have been the innocent object of her coquettish advances and indecent hints. Mortified by what the respected lady must think of her and indignant that her reputation was being thus sullied, Miriam tried to explain the true nature of events. But so stoutly did Mr. Barker insist on his falsehood and so blindly did Mistress Barker trust in her husband's integrity that she believed not a word of what Miriam related.

Upon my return from the livery I found my tearful Miriam awaiting me outside the mansion grounds with our few possessions in tow. I was of a mind to confront Mr. Barker, but Miriam counseled against it and angrily declared that in any case she wished never to set foot in that house again, regretting only that she must abandon her darling young charges.

Thereupon, having exhausted all my stratagems to secure our safety and again facing poverty and arrest, I resolved that we should expend the last of our funds for transportation to the remote west. My hope was to cross the wilderness and leave the American Republic altogether, eventually making our way to Santa Fe or one of the other Catholic cities of Northern Mexico. Alas, my friend, you see the awful result of my wrongheaded decision. For abandoned of God, hunted by men, and now captured by the savage Comanches, in my hare-brained intention I failed wretchedly, and in my failure of a certainty I have brought ruin and shame to Miriam's life and death to mine. Now—

Here I interrupted John's interminable narrative, noting with as much humor as I could muster under our gloomy circumstances that he had given ample lie to the Quakers' fabled reputation for few words and frequent silences. About us the other prisoners snored the sleep of exhaustion, and my own eyelids drooped with fatigue. Thereupon, without smiling at my enfeebled wit, he apologized for the length of his tale, wished me good night, and turning his back to me, commenced his nightly prayers in which I discerned pleading, muffled sobs.

160

The morning dawned crisp and clear, and long before the sluggish warriors roused from their drunken slumber, the Comanche women were already busied with their accustomed tasks. At length Running Bear emerged from his gaudy tent, stretching and yawning so prodigiously that his mismatched eyes seemed about to pop from his disfigured face. We prisoners watched his every move, fearful that upon his signal our lives could suddenly end.

At that moment a Comanche warrior rode into camp and without pausing leapt from his horse and ran to Running Bear. They conversed for a moment in muffled tones as other warriors from our camp, now recovering from their alcoholic stupor, formed a ring about them. Running Bear then signaled for Young Eagle, pointed to me with his spear, and mounted a horse that one of young warriors led forth for him.

"We must ride at once to White Buffalo's village," Young Eagle informed me. "Running Bear's mother's condition worsened during the night, and she nears death. Now you must practice your medicine as you promised, and you know the punishment Running Bear has ordered for you if she dies."

This solicitude surprised me, for I had learned that the Comanches rarely display mercy for the aged and infirm but instead leave them to die if they cannot summon the strength to follow the tribe in its frequent wanderings.

I had not forgotten for a moment the predicament in which I had trapped myself, even though the events of recent days had eclipsed it temporarily. Now it reassumed its horrific priority amongst the various calamities I faced. Yet I had no choice but to put on a brave face and pretend a confidence in my "medicine" that had not the slightest root in reality.

I mounted the same bony nag I had ridden in the raid and the four of us rode in silence, reaching White Buffalo's village before noon. The camp was larger than ours and had the look of a long-established settlement. The Comanches knew the purpose of our visit and were aware of my mysterious "power medicine." They crowded about me with utmost curiosity, some even touching my sleeve, fingers, and face in hopes, so I guessed, of extracting healing "medicine" from me. Young Eagle informed me—with the knowing trace of a smile—that the more foolish tribesmen were telling outlandish stories about how I could cure broken limbs and dying bodies with magic words. With this grand and excited expectation the Comanches escorted me to the dying woman.

I had not the barest notion of a strategy to deceive the savages and save myself, but as I waited outside her tent whilst Running Bear spoke to his mother, it occurred to me that as a minimal requirement I must be alone with her so that the poverty of my skills and resources would be less evident. At length Running Bear emerged, his face betraying no readable emotion at his impending loss. Thereupon I groped my way into a tent so dark that at first that I could barely discern the agonizing woman. The scene so reeked of stale body odors and the putrid aromas of the tribal shaman's vile concoctions that my head swam and I came close to swooning. Green flies, feasting on the filth, added to my discomfort. To my surprise and dismay, Young Eagle wandered away to another part of the village, for I had assumed that he would serve as my translator. Words, after all, were the only thing I had to offer the poor creature before me.

But to my surprise, she roused immediately though in a faint voice when I addressed her in Spanish. "¡Padre, padrecito, *me has venido a mí! ¡El Señor ha escuchado mis rezos! ¡Virgencita, no me has dejado desamparada!"* (Father, dear Father, thou hast come to me! The Lord has heard my prayers. Holy Mother, thou hast not left me defenseless!)

I protested to her that I was not a priest but had come as a doctor, but at that instant she fell into a shuddering paroxysm of coughing and wheezing and did not hear my words. Besides her eyes had about them a demented look so that I deemed it fruitless to insist further. For as the saying goes:

Twere a greater insanity to reason with madmen

Unsure of what to do next, I took her hand in mine as a simple act of compassion. She seized it with both of hers and with an unnatural strength drew it to her fevered lips, murmuring: "*¡Bendito sea Dios! ¡Bendito sea Dios! que me has mandado a este Padrecito! ¡Ten misericordia de mí y perdóname mis pecados!"* (Blessed be God, Blessed be God, for Thou has sent me this dear priest. Have pity on me and forgive me my sins!).

I must tell you, here and now, dear reader, that in all my deceitful past I did not yet count sacrilege and mockery of the Faith among my reprehensible acts, for though it had never gained my full allegiance, at least it had always claimed my reverent respect. Yet as we French say,

Il faut qu'un jour soit la première fois
(one day has to be the first time)

162

For in adversity the urgencies of desperation oft trample the restrictions of law and decorum. Thus with a trepidation that I recall vividly to this latter day, I responded: "Confess thy sins and thou shalt be forgiven them. Be at peace. God is merciful."

At once her breathing grew less labored and gradually the wheezing ceased. A smile spread over her creased face, and she dropped at once into a deep sleep. Not knowing what better thing to do, I sat by her bedside, idly busied in protecting myself from the buzzing flies. Scarcely an hour passed before she opened eyes, which now had about them a look of intelligence.

"You are young, Father, very young, and you wear not the cloth. Nor do I see a crucifix."

"The unusual circumstances that would explain this lack, daughter, are lengthy, and it would tax you to hear them. Take heart only in the fact that I am here to attend you and give you aid and comfort."

She squeezed my hand the tighter and responded: "Then you must first know the reasons for my grief and the request I shall make when you have heard my story. In all my years of living and wandering with the Comanches there was no one to hear my woe or understand my suffering."

I did not know what to make of her admission, but since it was obvious that the end was near for her, I had no other choice or desire in the matter but to hear her out. Young Eagle returned to hear the beginning of her story, but she had not progressed far into her tale when he shook his head, uttered what I took to be a Comanche oath, and to my astonishment exited the tent.

Doña Engracia (Owl Woman)

Padrecito, believe me when I tell you that some of us in this camp were not always the savages you take us to be but which, in truth and in shame, we have become. As a girl I was told that many years ago my ancestors were Spanish settlers who came north from New Spain under the command of Captain Juan de Oñate. The site the captain chose near the Rio Grande was infertile and produced only meager crops. To make matters all the worse, the new settlers suffered harassments by the savages seeking revenge for outrages committed by Spaniards of a much earlier time.

Soon famine broke out, and there was much hardship and many deaths. Defying Captain Oñate, a few settlers tried to return to Monclova in New Spain where they had been recruited. Perhaps they were successful, though some said they perished along the way. Other families,

163

including my ancestors, abandoned the settlement in search of a better and safer location. After much suffering and privation they discovered a fertile, well-watered valley deep within the Sangre de Cristo Mountains beyond the headwaters of Rio Napestle. [6] There they laid out and built the town of Nueva Rosita with its handsome plaza and gleaming white church. (Ah, Padrecito, I can see it now with its high spire and circling white doves that always reminded me of angels!) God smiled on them so that for a long time they lived in peace with the native Utes, cultivating their fields, raising their families, and gradually forgetting the strife and turmoil of the outside world.

Responding to our earnest petitions, for many years the bishops of New Spain sent us priests so that our faith was sustained from generation to generation and we remained faithful to God and Church. But finally, as the depredations of the Apaches and Comanches who were displacing them grew more frequent, both soldiers and priests withdrew to the south and we saw them no more. Many years later we received the unthinkable news that all of New Spain had risen in rebellion and that the Spaniards were overthrown and gone forever. But what I want to tell you happened earlier.

(Here Owl Woman dozed off for a few minutes.)

… I was born in Nueva Rosita. My father was don Benito Valle y Pacheco and my mother, doña Engracia Valle de Valle. You must not be surprised, Padrecito, by the similarity of their names. There were only four family surnames in Nueva Rosita—Valle, Sánchez, Pacheco, and Martínez—so that we were all interrelated many times over. It is probably true that some native blood also flowed in our veins, for there was surely mixing in the days of the Conquistadors, who sometimes took Indian women as wives. Don Juan de Oñate was himself married to the great-granddaughter of Moctezuma. Yet we were mainly Spanish and proud to a fault of our heritage.

I was given the Christian name of Engracia after my mother and grandmother. At fifteen I was married in civil ceremony to don Severino Pacheco, our cousin. He was much older than I yet a man I loved dearly, and until the tragedy I am about to relate overtook me, we lived happily though saddened because God did not bless our union with children.

Alas, Padrecito, one day calamity overtook me and ruined my life. As I was washing clothes alone in the stream—normally a task the women did together—a band of the wild Comanche raiders captured me. I was never again to see my beloved parents and dear husband.

I shall not recount the indignities, Padrecito, I suffered as their slave, for it would not be seemly to speak of such things to a priest.

164

Eventually I was traded to a neighboring band of Comanches and forced to become a wife of White Bear, the tribal chieftain. As much as I loathed him, he treated me with gentleness exceptional amongst the Comanche and exhibited me on every occasion, for it was a matter of great pride that he counted a Spanish white woman among his wives. He took no interest in his other spouses, for which the native women hated me and devised a thousand sly ways to bedevil me and make of my life a hell. (Forgive me for the strong language, Padrecito.)

Always I dreamed of running away, but eventually I discovered myself with child and had no choice but to resign myself to fate. When my son Running Bear was born my maternal sentiments overcame the repugnance I felt for his paternal origins and I did what I could to instruct him in the language and faith of my people.

But Running Bear loved the savage Comanche life and scorned the ways I tried to teach him. When White Bear was killed in a raid on the Jicarilla Apaches my son became the new chieftain. Soon he earned such fame for his strength and ferocity that he was feared and respected by all. I should be thankful, I suppose, Padrecito, for the protection his elevated status afforded me, for without it, surely I would have been killed or left to starve by the tribe. In truth they had never accepted me as one of their own but hated me openly as much as I despised them secretly.

Running Bear loathed not only white ways but also the white blood that ran in his veins. Thus so as to prove himself as a Comanche warrior he determined to become a greater chieftain than his father. He led many raids into Spanish territory and captured or slew many captives. (The saber scar that disfigures his once-handsome face was a stroke by a Spanish captain whom he then slew along with his entire troop.) Against my wishes, he raided Nueva Rosita where he took Young Eagle and Little Fawn, as well as several other children. Doubtless you have spied others in his camp who appear more Spanish than Comanche. Many of them were captured as children and remember only a few words of Spanish and almost nothing at all of their ancestry, which Running Bear forbade me to teach them. Indeed, because my very presence was an unwelcome reminder of the hated Spanish heritage he sent me to live with White Buffalo's people. Thus I was deprived of the pleasure of my grandchildren, though Running Bear was never so perverse a son that he neglected my material welfare. In this one particular alone he differed from the Comanche who customarily abandon their elderly to starvation and death.

And so, Padrecito, now I come to the end of a hard and painful life, and I wish to die in the grace and blessing of the Church from which I was brutally torn so many years ago. I am ashamed to say that I have never been baptized, for at the time of my birth Nueva Rosita no priest had visited us for many years. Padrecito, please baptize me now so that I may die not as a heathen but in reconciliation with my Church and my God! Now…

Forgive me, gentle reader, but here in the high perplexity in which this strange request placed me I must interrupt this story for matters of greater urgency. For at that moment there came to my ears panicked cries and the clatter of hoof beats. I rushed out of the tent to see what the matter was, but the camp was in such bedlam that I was at a loss to understand its cause. Then Young Eagle came running towards me, waving his arms.

"We must ride at once! Word has come that the Americans have attacked our village!"

"Of course, at once! Where will we go?" I asked, assuming we were about to flee and heartily endorsing the option.

At that moment Running Bear mounted on his roan, White Buffalo on his pinto, and a cohort of thirty or forty mounted warriors rushed out to repel the advancing American force.

To my amazement he responded, "To our camp. Little Fawn will need my help!"

"Little Fawn?" I asked in astonishment. "But why must you help her?"

"Once she was to be my wife. She will always be my charge."

Only this intriguing information and nothing else could I elicit from him.

With some difficulty we retrieved our horses, for they had bolted in the general panic of the camp. But barely had we ridden out of the village than we spied the defeated Comanche troop retreating across the plain with the Americans in triumphal pursuit.

"This day Comanche power begins to fail," Young Eagle mused as he watched the debacle, his eyes betraying an odd sadness but his lips forming a bitter smile.

As for me, I did not know whether defeat or victory by either side was the greater peril. For neither the promised death by the Comanches for my failed "medicine" nor legal hanging by the Americans for the outstanding warrants against me in Memphis, New Orleans, and, who knows, perhaps in Missouri as well afforded me hope for life.

"If we ride swiftly," I proposed to Young Eagle, "perhaps we can save ourselves. For now surely all hope and probably all life is lost in the camp."

"I will not leave Little Fawn," Young Eagle replied, "though you may save yourself if you can. I will not stop you if you wish to flee alone, my friend."

I was nonplussed by his unexpected utterance of friendship, for I had neither given him cause to befriend me, nor reason to aid me. For a moment I did indeed savor the exhilarating possibility of saving my life. But then I thought of my minimal chances alone on the barren plains, of John and Miriam and much more poignantly, of my precious dollars residing in Running Bear's buffalo hide tent. Perhaps the hoard was still there, forgotten in the general panic of the moment and overlooked by the barbaric Americans who would hardly expect to find such a treasure in a camp of savage Comanches. Without revealing my true motives but leading him to believe that I was acting on newly found courage, I said to Young Eagle:

"I will ride with you into the jaws of danger, my friend."

Arriving at the camp after a hard ride, we found a desolate scene that made me reconsider the wisdom of my decision: children crying for lost mothers, mothers plaintively calling the names of their lost offspring, warriors, old men, and women bent and twisted with the agony of wounds. John and Miriam were nowhere to be seen, and in response to his inquiries about Little Fawn (as I supposed by their looks and gestures), one old man pointed to the upper slopes. Young Eagle ran at once in the direction he indicated.

Uncertain of aught else to do, I set about—with squeamish reluctance—inspecting and tending the wounded. In the midst of the desolation there occurred a most unexpected and happy event. Miriam emerged from the trees accompanied by a dozen dirty, scratched, but otherwise undamaged children and the two disheveled female prisoners taken in the raid on the wagon train. The youngsters ran to anxious mothers and pointed to the likely hiding places of other children. Over the next hour most of the lost straggled back into camp and when all were counted, the casualties of the attack were fewer than first we feared.

The foremost concern now was the fate of Running Bear and the Comanche warriors, and for the worried Miriam, the whereabouts of John. The children informed us that the Americans had freed the prisoners and taken the red-bearded fat man and several others with them.

I tried to console Miriam with soothing but insincere words, for I was secretly persuaded that unless John had gone with the Americans surely he must have died in the attack. Miriam, however, would have none of my contrived assurances.

"I know he is alive! I feel it in my heart. John is out there and not very far away. Come with me, Mr. Prosper. We're going to find him!"

Concerned about what we might discover should her intuition prove to be unreliable, I protested about the dangers of such a search but then wilted under the disapproving stare in her beautiful green eyes and meekly accompanied her.

We had not gone very far along the bushy slopes when we heard voices ahead of us. Abandoning caution, Miriam ran through the brush, calling John by name, and embracing him tearfully when he rushed to meet her. To my surprise, we found him unharmed save for his previous hurts and a painful contusion on his right foot where a frightened horse trampled him as the Americans were freeing the prisoners.

Unhappily, the same was not true of Little Fawn. She writhed on the ground, as Young Eagle attended her. I inquired of her condition, and John informed me that the Americans had ridden her down as she and the other women were fleeing the camp in terror. Young Eagle added that the Comanche women dragged her to this spot and then abandoned her when they thought the Americans were coming after them.

Luckily her wounds, though serious, proved to be less so than we first feared, consisting of a broken leg and, as best Miriam and Young Eagle could judge, several fractured ribs. Whilst correctly dismissing my supposed medical accomplishments as hyperbolic fictions, the now relieved and smiling Young Eagle displayed remarkable practical skill in devising splints and bandages to comfort Little Fawn and commence the healing process.

Acting on Young Eagle's instructions, John and I devised a crude travois on which to transport Little Fawn back to the camp. It was quite dark when we arrived to find the dispirited clan and former prisoners alike huddled about a small fire, misery having reduced them to a desperate equality of condition. Cur dogs wandered about the camp as addled, it seemed, as their human masters. Three of the warriors returned during our absence, and they dejectedly described the rout, blaming their defeat on the rashness of Running Bear. Of the latter they had no reliable intelligence, but they were certain that White Buffalo had fled to the south, leaving his village at the mercy of the Americans.

Though exhausted, we quickly buried the five casualties of the raid in a shallow, common grave and John spoke biblical words over their final resting place.

After an appraisal of the wounded, Young Eagle informed me—

and I translated to John and Miriam—that despite our hurts and desperate circumstances, with the dawn we must abandon the camp or risk annihilation at the hands of the marauding Americans.

"They will return most likely, now that Running Bear has disappeared, perhaps perished, and White Buffalo has fled south, and this time they will take time utterly to destroy us."

"We will fight again," one of the warriors responded stoutly in the Comanche tongue, certain words of which I was beginning to understand.

Young Eagle sighed and with a faraway look in his eye said to me in Spanish, "Yes, yes, they will fight again, and again, and yet again, until the Comanche blood has run dry and they are no more, and in the end the Americans will conquer their land because of numbers and guns."

"Then what must we do?" I asked in alarm.

"We must travel far to the west, to the mountains beyond the cuartelejo region. There our clan once had friends among the Utes and some of the Jicarilla Apaches. There is a possibility that Nueva Rosita still stands, and thereto we may eventually bend our steps to see if any of our people yet live. It will be a hard thing for those who choose to go, for they have lived here all the years of their life and have seen the rising and setting of the sun for countless days amidst landmarks they know and love. Nevertheless, we must now leave this cherished place or die. It can no longer be our home."

"It will be hard to travel, Young Eagle. Little Fawn has a broken leg, others are wounded, and there seems to be little food left."

"What sayest thou to Young Eagle, friend Peter?" John wanted to know.

"That we are sore beset to begin the journey he speaks of towards a new land where the clan can live in safety."

"Count on my help in the effort, my friends, for Miriam and I must also continue to search for a haven."

"Well, Mr. Quaker or whatever you be, you're not speaking for us," said one of the female captives. "We just want to get away from these blackhearted devils and back to our families and loved ones—if they'll have us. And you must help us."

"And so we shall, madam, of that thou mayest be sure," John assured her.

We spent the night in considerable discomfort and apprehension, but for some in the camp spirits rose with the sun and no sign of the Americans. I was desolate, however, for during the night I had turned

Running Bear's musty tent and furs upside down in a frantic but fruitless search for my money and other possessions. Disappointment must have shown on my countenance, for no sooner had John wished me a good morning than he asked the cause of my unhappiness.

"Ah, friend John," I confided in a restrained but vehement voice, "I am undone by my accursed bad luck! The money and goods that once were in my rightful possession are nowhere to be found in Running Bear's tent. The cursed Americans—pardon the language, it does not apply to you—must have taken my belongings. Thus my damnable poverty continues and my chances in the world miserable as they always have been in my wretched, profitless life!"

"May great Jehovah forgive me for my forgetfulness!" he responded, slapping his forehead. "Thy money and possessions are safe, friend Peter. Knowing their importance to thee, and remembering thy kindness towards me, I took them from the tent and in the confusion hid them yonder in the wood nigh the spot where we found Little Fawn."

At once I went from despondency to elation and urged John to show me the burial plot at once. We hied to the blessed spot and found the money and possessions without mishap. I retrieved the heavy bag and Caroline's cross with a near erotic joy. From the garments tossed in Running Bear's tent we dressed ourselves in as civilized a manner as they afforded. Now my energies were restored, and I was ready to help Young Eagle prepare for our journey.

John and I reinforced the travois and with ropes hitched it to my nag, the slowest and gentlest of our horses. Meanwhile Miriam and the women fed the children with the few scraps of food the dogs had not eaten. The three warriors, rested and able, on orders from Young Eagle whose leadership they now acknowledged, reluctantly helped the seriously infirm to hobble on their way.

Young Eagle determined that—always excepting Little Fawn—the eldest and most sickly members must be left at White Buffalo's village lest they hinder the clan in its migration. Perhaps there they would be cared for and, provided the Americans did not return, might live out the fullness of their lives.

We reached White Buffalo's village and beheld a scene of ugly desolation. The American raiders had inflicted even greater devastation on the larger settlement, burning the tepees, destroying food and provisions, and scattering the Comanches. The more able survivors, including a dozen or so returning warriors, now roamed directionless about the village, kicking dogs away, picking up strewn possessions, and speaking in stunned voices about their ordeal. The Comanches often raided other tribes but until now had little experience at being victims themselves.

The only cheerful news amidst the stark desolation was the report that the Americans had ridden back to the east as swiftly as they had come. We could only conjecture about their sudden departure, but John informed us that during the attack on Running Bear's clan he had heard from his concealment the leader of the raiders refer to much larger Comanche forces not far to the west. John opined that they fled in apprehension of these mythical hordes, and we had no reason to reject his supposition.

To my surprise we found doña Engracia alive in her collapsed tepee though at intervals delirious and ravaged by hunger and thirst. Miriam and the other young women cleaned her and attended to her most intimate needs, but the while she called weakly for the "Padrecito" to administer the baptismal rites and give her absolution so that she might expire in peace.

This prospect disturbed and alarmed me, for as I confessed to you earlier, gentle reader, I was loath to add further sacrilege to my several misdemeanors. It is true, or so Father Brannigan once told me, that any Catholic may perform an emergency baptism, but only a priest can give absolution. This dilemma I confided to John and Young Eagle. The latter turned away with a visible and puzzling display of displeasure, but John offered me a way out of my predicament.

"Friend Peter, fret not thyself about the matter. Within the Quaker fellowship every person, man or woman, is a priest and fully empowered to act as such. It is not our custom to perform water baptism, believing as we do that true baptism is of the Spirit, yet we freely administer it to those who desire to receive it. Therefore, those things that go against thy creed and conscience, I offer to do in thy stead."

Miriam spoke her dismay over such a prospect, as did I, but given the urgency of the case, neither of us could offer a solid reason to deny doña Engracia this final consolation. Young Eagle shook his head disapprovingly and absented himself entirely from our midst.

Thus it was that John performed the rituals of baptism and absolution in his odd fashion and quaint words and not long thereafter doña Engracia expired in peace, believing herself accepted anew into the Catholic faith of her fathers, forgiven and cleansed of her pagan Comanche life, and blessedly unaware that John the Quaker was the instrument of her felicitous restoration. Miriam could not hide her dismay, for though she loved John more than her very life, yet she feared that he had committed a sacrilegious atrocity and was unconvinced by my pious observation that, "Better a godly Quaker should administer the last rites than a false priest." John himself, serene in his own beliefs, remained indifferent to, if not amused by, our theological apprehensions.

We buried doña Engracia and the other victims with becoming solemnity as John spoke memorized Bible verses over their graves. Then we turned our attention to the injured and at Young Eagle's urging, began preparations for our westward trek towards the distant mountains. Before our departure, he extracted from one of the older warriors who had not violated them the most sacred Comanche oath that he would escort the two American women to a location close to one of their outposts.

We departed soon after daybreak, some eighteen souls, including a few from White Buffalo's village, the wounded and weakest mounted on the ten horses we had located, the rest of us afoot. For two days we followed the meandering Napestle, then as it veered northwards, we filled our leather water bags to capacity, abandoned the river, and struck out over the featureless plain. Eventually, so Young Eagle informed, we should intercept the "dry," or southern branch, of the Santa Fe Trail. Young Eagle was acceptably acquainted with that dreary land, having once made a journey to a trade fair in the Cuartelejo region.

Once we thought ourselves to be safely beyond reach of the American raiders—not to mention Running Bear's vengeful retaliation for our desertion should he yet be amongst the living—our concerns centered more on food and Little Fawn's condition than on our possible pursuers.

Ten of our number suffered various degrees of impairment. Little Fawn's wounds were the most grievous, for despite Miriam's best efforts the wound on her broken leg worsened, the pain increased, and she ran a high fever. Young Eagle was constantly beside her, his somber, handsome face reflecting his concern for her welfare.

Inasmuch as our meager food and water were soon perilously nigh to depletion and Little Fawn and several others were spent from the exhausting march, Young Eagle ordered a halt four days into the journey so as to rest the wounded and replenish our provisions. He did this with obvious misgivings for November was a third spent, and the nights were becoming ever colder.

Because he would not leave Little Fawn's side and John and I knew nothing of guns and hunting, the task fell to the three remaining able-bodied warriors in our party, Gray Hawk, White Duck, and Black Wolf. Chafing under the duty of caring for the wounded, they relished this manly task and departed on our best mounts with the promise that soon they would bring us meat in abundance.

To our happy surprise, their boastful prophecy came true. Venturing, as they proudly recounted upon their return, upon a small herd of the misshapen cows the Americans call "buffaloes," they managed to bring down two of the shaggy brutes with their confiscated American rifles. The meat proved to be exceptionally lean and delicious, surpassing the best beef in succulence, and the fresh water that bubbled from a small ojo de agua, or spring, in the rocks above our camp satisfied our thirst for fresh water.

At first Little Fawn shook her head at the proffered food, refusing all sustenance with an adamancy that dismayed us and caused us to fear for her very life; but at Miriam's persistent urging, reluctantly she accepted a small serving of buffalo steak. Apparently this aroused her dormant appetite, for not long thereafter she requested a larger serving and drank copiously from a calabash gourd Miriam held to her fevered lips. Thereafter she stared searchingly at Young Eagle and, though still running a high temperature, anon fell into a sleep that mirrored death itself.

Now believing ourselves to be remote from danger, our stomachs full, warmed against the chill by a crackling fire, and with my curiosity similarly ablaze, I queried Young Eagle about the strange events I had witnessed in recent days, in particular his odd behavior toward doña Engracia. He stared at me for a moment as though pondering matters in his judgement and then related the events that follow in the translation I rendered for John and Miriam:

Doña Engracia (suite)

Know, my friends, that I was not born a Comanche. Even though it now sounds strange to say it, my Christian name is Diego Valle y Martínez, and if I choose to speak of these matters at all it is to correct the distorted account that doña Engracia—may God have mercy on her soul—related to Peter and any other who would listen. Hers was a lie that from so many tellings perhaps she had come to believe herself. For she repeated the story many times, always with a different turn to it, but they were lies, all lies, my friends! She was not the victim of circum-stantial fate as she pretended but the agent and instigator of great sufferings, as you will hear.

It is true that she was born in Nueva Rosita, the daughter of don Benito Valle y Pacheco and doña Engracia Valle de Valle. But beyond that fact the truth is a far different story, and though it troubles me to say so and may seem to you a cowardly act to speak disrespectfully of the dead, yet, my friends, the truth, though not favorable to her, must out. May God forgive me for the harsh sentiments that now and perhaps forever I hold against her for her wickedness!

Headstrong and disobedient as a daughter, against her will she was married at fifteen to don Severino Pacheco, her father's aged cousin. You must understand that when I say "married," it was not by the Church, for no priest had attended our town and people for more than a generation—Yes, friend Peter, I will explain my part in the story if you will be patient—nevertheless, it was a wedding fully recognized as such by all in Nueva Rosita.

From the start doña Engracia was, I repeat, a rebellious girl, and so anxious were her parents to affix her in a stable marriage that they were persuaded against their better judgment to give her hand to the decrepit and avaricious old Severino. Oh that they had heeded a better counsel, for great evil and pain flowed from their unwise decision! All these matters were items of common gossip that as an adolescent I heard repeated by my parents and the townspeople.

It was, as they say, a marriage forged in hell, for it mismatched the headstrong and lusty Engracia with the greedy and shriveled Severino. (Here I—Peter—was obliged to pause as the corresponding English words eluded me for a moment.) Had there been more young men in Nueva Rosita mayhap events had taken a different turn. But most of our youth were wont to leave our town for better chances in the world beyond our valley. Few of them ever returned; fewer still remained. Thus Nueva Rosita became in time a dwindling population of widows, maidens, and old men.

It was even rumored that Engracia withheld herself intact from don Severino while enticing and seducing the men of our town. Perhaps that part is untrue, but there is no doubt—for my parents heard them with their own ears—that angry screams and terrible cursings issued almost nightly from don Severino's house. By day in order to avoid her husband's unwanted attentions, she took to wandering in the fields and mountain slopes where, or so it was rumored, she held rendezvous with certain married lovers. On one such foray she was seen with an Indian warrior—or so a jilted lover told, claiming to have seen them together. The savage was reported to be not one of the Apaches who plagued our region but instead a chieftain of the shorter, darker Comanches who had recently migrated to the region from the land of the Shoshones in the far north whose kinsmen they were.

I cannot say of a certainty what happened thereafter—for you must remember that I was too young to have direct intelligence of these early

174

events—but within a few days or weeks doña Engracia suddenly disappeared from our midst, leaving her parents unconsolable and don Severino so humiliated in spirit that shortly thereafter it departed his mortal body. Her family spoke of abduction but privately it was rumored that she had gone willingly with her savage lover. Be that as it may, Nueva Rosita heard nothing else of her until several years had passed.

When next we had word of the terrible doña Engracia I had grown to adolescence and had no other ambition than to marry my cousin Pilar Pacheco y Valle, known to you as Little Fawn lying yonder in her injured state. We had grown up together, never knowing a time when we were not in love with each other, and finding no opposition to our union but rather consent and approval in every quarter, from our tenderest years we confidently looked forward to the day when we should become man and wife.

Alas, at that happy moment the evil shadow of doña Engracia fell over us, bringing unspeakable tragedy to our life and love. Much of what happened was not clear to me until long after I was abducted. Only then was I able to piece together her evil career.

White Bear, her lover and abductor, probably intended to add Engracia to his harem as a token of his power and ascendancy in the Comanche nation. But if so, then he reckoned poorly, for in reality he had put a venomous serpent in his bed. For no sooner did Engracia begin her liaison than she gained dominion over him. Upon her arrival in the camp she ordered him to dismiss his concubines and their children and within a short time established herself as the true power in the clan.

Eventually she gave birth to Running Bear. By this time she had renounced utterly her Catholic and Spanish heritage and was a fiercer savage than those under her sway. Burning with an insatiable lust for power and having utterly mastered White Bear, she sent him ranging far and wide with his marauders, upsetting old alliances and ancient friendships and making enemies of the Apaches, Navajos, Utes, and many other tribes, to say nothing of the Spanish civil authorities.

But as White Bear aged he took to drink, and within a few years his desire for war ebbed and his physical prowess declined. Like many of the Comanches, he was hardy without being healthy. It became evident to Engracia that if she were to expand her evil ambitions she would have to ally herself with a stronger man than White Bear. She considered many men as her chosen lover and leader but all failed under her insatiable passion and hunger for sway and power.

Running Bear then proved to be the willing minion of his mother. Whether or not it was he—perhaps acting on his mother's suggestion—

who murdered his father during a raid, neither I nor anyone else can say for sure, though such was rumored and is whispered to this day amongst the older Comanches.

Engracia, or Owl Woman as she renamed herself, found in her son the better instrument of her ambitions, and for a time they schemed to forge the Indian tribes into a grand alliance dominated by the Comanches under Running Bear but ruled over by Engracia.

Even though she had renounced her heritage and spat on the memory of her people, Engracia neither forgot nor forgave the humiliations and malicious gossip she had suffered in her loveless marriage to don Severino, and as time passed and her power grew so did her insane rage for revenge against our townspeople.

One day we awoke to shots and screams in the plaza. The Comanches were upon us without warning or pity, burning, pillaging, and slaughtering men and women alike. My parents were amongst the first to perish. I do not know how many, if any, were left alive. The Comanches slaughtered the infants and most of the children but some of the youths were spared for later sacrifice or slavery and the girls as concubines of the warriors. I was made the menial of sub-chief Strong Buffalo.

My grief knew no bounds, for my family, of course, but even more so for my darling Pilar to whom I could offer no aid or comfort. Apprised of our mutual devotion, Engracia took cruel delight in taunting us as she gave Pilar to Running Bear for his pleasure. She ripped away our crucifixes, cursed our faith, and forbade the use of Spanish. How I restrained myself I know not. At that moment I made a silent vow, to this day never broken, that I would persevere and gain whatever power and freedom possible for one in my situation so as to stand ready if ever the chance came to serve and to save Little Fawn, as she was renamed as Running Bear's favorite wife. In this determination I fared better than I dared hope. Unlike the other boys taken from Nueva Rosita who were either scalped and then murdered or succumbed to the rigors of Comanche life, I lived only for Pilar and a day of vengeful reckoning.

Soon I mastered the Comanche language without forgetting my own, and the Comanches utilized my abilities in trade and the bartering of captives. After a time Strong Buffalo died and I became the property of his nephew Running Bear. This proximity allowed me occasional chances to speak to Pilar-Little Fawn and to tell her of my unwavering love and my dreams of our eventual rescue. These admissions but terrified her the more, for she lived in mortal fear of Running Bear, who was not above murdering women who displeased him. She begged me to forget her and to save myself if ever the chance should come. She whispered that even though her love for me would last forever, she could never be my wife for her womanhood was sullied as the unwilling spouse of Running Bear. I would hear none of her arguments. Nothing she or anyone else could say would shake my conviction that she was, and forever shall be, the one true love of my life.

With my undying love for Pilar as my North Star, I learned the Comanche ways and earned respect for my steady hand and fighting skill. I plucked and singed my beard and became nearly as bronzed as the Comanches. Indeed were it not for my blue eyes and lighter skin, one would hardly distinguish me from a blood Comanche. As time passed they began to forget my origins and to relax their vigilance over me. And as I proved my valor and strength in battle and my steadfastness in all duties that fell to me, their trust grew until finally Running Bear released me from slavery and the clan accepted me as a full warrior.

So strong was my love for Pilar that I took no wife, nor sought I the intimacy of other women. She urged me to seek the companionship of a mate, pointing out that although her heart would ever be loyal to me, against her will she now belonged to another man. Yet I remained true to my love.

I alone remain of the young men abducted from Nueva Rosita. The two young women you see yonder by the fire are also survivors, but so young were they at the time of their abduction that with the passing years they forgot all but a few words of Spanish and now preserve only the faintest memory of their former life. Confused by these early recollections and later ties, they accompany us on our journey with great misgivings. I suspect they would turn back at once if their owners and husbands were to appear to claim them. Nevertheless, I cannot judge them harshly for they know no other life and their families and children now bind them to the Comanche ways.

In time the similarity of their character and mad ambitions created a rift between Running Bear and Owl Woman. Running Bear came to resent his mother's imperious oversight, and she, to distrust his rashness and haughty insubordination. She sought to ally herself with other factions amongst the Comanches so that by shifting and dividing power she might in the end preserve it for herself. Running Bear learned of her intrigues, and after winning a long struggle with her for tribal supremacy, banished her altogether from the clan, sending her to live with White Buffalo's people. Yet his punishment was limited to her exile, for even though it is probably true that he assassinated his own savage father, he had not the heart to deal in like manner with his more treacherous mother. Thus in a twinkling Owl Woman passed from exalted power in our clan to a humiliating life as an unwelcome exile amongst our neighbors.

Nor did Running Bear himself fare much better in the end, for whilst the Comanches were awed by his great strength and admired his skill as their war chief, most found in him few of the higher qualities of reason required of a true leader of men. For this reason many of the warriors slipped away from his camp and aligned themselves with White Buffalo's people or one of the more distant Comanche villages. Our tribe, once numerous, dwindled to a mere clan.

My chief regret is that I had not the chance—and perhaps for a long time not the daring—to drive a spear through Running Bear's despotic heart or to take my revenge on Owl Woman for my parents' death and Pilar's fate. I have lived with these twin obsessions these many years, yet I will now forego vengeance for the greater gift of Pilar's life.

For know, my friends, that from this moment henceforth she is no longer to be called Little Fawn, nor I, Young Eagle. She is once again Pilar Pacheco y Valle and I, Diego Valle y Martínez. And in her true name and mine, I do here before you foreswear the false gods, wicked incantations, and evil customs of the Comanches and intend with God's guidance to return to our own faith and, if any of them yet live by God's grace, to the remnant of our families and people.

Whilst I sat momentarily astonished at the words we had just heard fall from Young Eagle's—pardon me, Diego's—lips concerning his true character and provenance, John and Miriam rushed to his side with words surely incomprehensible to him in meaning but unmistakable in tones of comfort and compassion. Roused from my staring stupor by their pleading looks, I hastened to translate their noble and generous intentions. Diego responded with similar sentiments, and from that moment their friendship, already deep, was sealed forever.

Pilar, as we also remembered to call her, awoke much improved, and Diego was visibly overjoyed. He roused us to the day's march with renewed enthusiasm, though I saw no such animation in Gray Hawk, White Duck, and Black Wolf, who, as I now suppose, sensed the curious, alienating transformation in Young Eagle-Diego. Indeed, the farther we journeyed from their camp and clan the more dispirited they appeared to grow. From time to time I saw them conversing in low tones.

After a prodigious daylong march we saw the first low mountains rising along the western horizon. Diego halted our procession as he verified certain landmarks known only to him and having made the needed adjustments, led us to a sheltered campsite as night closed in. The horses were badly in need of water and fodder, and after we had set up our camp Diego directed Gray Hawk to let the animals graze on the rich grasses that flanked a small stream in a dale below our campsite.

Gray Hawk failed to return from his watch, and after a hurried inspection, we discovered that White Duck and Black Wolf had disappeared as well, along with six of our horses and most of our food.

"So be it," pronounced Diego. "Their heart was never in the journey to start with, and what the Comanche does not embrace or understand he soon betrays. We are better off—and safer—without them."

Despite Diego's brave words, their desertion turned the euphoria of the morning into a dark foreboding by night. The next day our pace slowed to a lamentable crawl; only the most impaired could ride our four remaining horses. The others limped along as best they could but needed frequent rests. By nightfall we had barely progressed a dozen miles. Diego was plainly worried about our chances, though his words were encouraging.

Withal, Pilar's resurgence was a like a ray of sunshine in our general gloom. Her appetite had rebounded to normal, but Diego plied her with so much food and drink that at length she pushed his offerings away, gently protesting with a sweet smile, the first I had seen from her. She and Diego yet conversed in Comanche, and when I addressed her in Spanish she responded haltingly, often groping for words in her half-forgotten ancestral tongue.

We made no swifter progress the following day, or the next two. On the morning of the fourth day after the desertion, Diego took counsel with John and me concerning our plight.

"Our food is running low, my friends, and the signs are that a winter storm is about to descend on us."

"Storm? But, friend Diego, the weather is fair and warm indeed, almost summery. What signs do you heed?" I wanted to know.

"Peter, it would be hard to explain—the altered flight of an eagle, the shape of a cloud, the spin of a falling leaf, things too faint and subtle for a white man to see—but the Comanches know of such things. You must trust me, and we must take the needed precautions."

"Then tell us what we must do, friend Diego," John responded as I translated Diego's alarming words.

"First, we must seek shelter against the approaching winter blast, then the task is to find more food. We are yet a four-day march, perhaps

179

five until we leave the Comanchería and enter Spanish—now Mexican—lands in the eastern sector of the Cuartelejo. Our disabled and wounded members will perish if we are caught in the open."

"Then instruct us as to our tasks, I pray thee, friend Diego," responded John, rising to his feet in readiness.

"With luck, my friends, and a supreme effort, by nightfall we may be able to reach the Mesa Negra where there are certain sheltered canyons and, if we can find them, abandoned Spanish mines. There we can ride out the storm. Meanwhile, aid the wounded and infirm and keep them moving."

We departed at once, saying nothing to Miriam, Pilar, and the others of our concerns, though they sensed our worry and willingly did their best. We halted to rest only when the wounded could go no further. By mid afternoon Diego's face suddenly brightened as he recognized a line of dark mountains looming in the west.

"That, my friends, is the Black Mesa," he pointed, then sweeping his arm towards the north, he added, "and there comes the ventisca!"

John looked at me in puzzlement.

"I have heard of something called a blizzard. I believe that is the word in English."

The sky had taken on a pale, pasty appearance, and in the distance a yellow dust cloud bore towards us across the undulating plain whilst a black counterpart overspread the sky like a shroud. Mere moments later the first winds swirled about us, sand mixed with snow stung our faces, and the temperature commenced a frightening drop. Within the hour the winds lashed us with such ferocity that we could barely hear voices or stand erect.

"We must not stop now!" shouted Diego over the moaning winds. "Not far ahead at the foot of Mesa Negra there runs the Cimarron nearly dry and easily fordable in this season. There we shall find shelter! Come! ¡Ánimo! ¡Ánimo!"

John and Miriam needed no translation from me to understand the urgency in his voice. Bent nearly double against the wind, we pressed on as Diego ran ahead to find us shelter. We called to him, but so fierce were the winds and so blinding the snow and dust that we could discern no response or distinguish any forms but our own.

It was either the favor of Providence or the vagaries of mere chance that ere long we found ourselves on the banks of the Cimarron and standing on the yonder bank, shouting and waving frantically, was Diego, urging us towards a dark five-meter wide opening between matching boulders cleft in twain in the infancy of time. Fifteen meters or so beyond the entrance accumulated debris from the mountain slope behind the boulders all but sealed the rear opening and vines and roots interlaced above to form a partial covering.

We forded the still warm and shallow stream, and no sooner entered we the cleft than the roaring winds subsided and we could stand erect and make ourselves heard. Two of the children were crying in terror but their mothers soothed them with reassuring words. The horses were not so easily calmed. They stamped and snorted at the dust and snow, and in their panic were about to trample some of our people ere John perceived the danger and hastened to restrain them with a firm hand and soothing words.

We fetched plentiful wood and in some wondrous fashion unknown to me Diego and one of the women managed to ignite a blaze that soon leapt to heroic dimensions. We were able to dry our garments and though food was sparse indeed, to accommodate ourselves for much needed sleep. After completing my assigned watch and relinquishing my duties to John, I wrapped myself in a tattered blanket and fell asleep, dreaming of hoar-frosted windows in the Vieux Carré and thinking myself transformed again into a barefoot urchin in the damp, New Orleans winter.

Morning dawned in winter splendor. Peering out from the boulders we saw a wonderland of snow and ice. The clouds were yet thick and snowflakes floated down intermittently. The winds had died away but our breath steamed in the intense cold. Venturing outside we were astonished at our good fortune, for we discerned no other natural shelter, and Diego assured us that he had only the most general intelligence of this land and its features.

Notwithstanding our passing good fortune, I was altogether miserable, having discovered long ago that cold was my most repulsive natural enemy. My mind wandered to warm climes and gentle tropical breezes.

My melancholy musings came to an abrupt end when Diego, returning from reconnoitering the area, summoned me to translate to John and Miriam what he had already told our Comanche comrades.

"Friends, we were indeed fortunate to find this shelter in time to save ourselves, but our food supply is critically short and will not last until the weather improves enough for us to resume our journey."

"Tell us, friend Diego," John responded at once, "what we must do and with God's help, we shall obey thy orders."

"Food is not our only problem. I believe we are being followed by several riders, and the clan is nearly defenseless. We are only six men, two of whom are old and lame and two—you will pardon me for saying so to your face—who lack any familiarity with the few weapons we possess or the will to use them."

Stunned by the revelation of unknown pursuers, quickly we all turned to peer out over the snowy plain beyond the Cimarron.

"But friend Diego," I protested, "we have seen no human trace in these many days of travel. What signs have you observed? Who approaches us in stealth and why?"

"I cannot put into words the reasons for my warning. But you must trust me, for your life may depend on it. The riders are near and coming closer."

"We are ready and willing to do as thou sayest, Diego," said John, resolutely speaking for us all, though my heart was now fairly bursting with fear.

"You must guard the horses at all costs," Diego added. "Without them we are doomed in this wilderness. If these are Comanche raiders, as the signs indicate, they can steal the horses from under the very noses of white men and slit a throat before the victim feels the knife. And with equal vigilance you must keep watch over the women and children."

"But what of thee, friend Diego?" wondered John. "Thou speakest as though absent from our defense."

"I will not be far from you. But Tall Bear and I must hunt for game, else we shall starve. The storm is only at a lull; tomorrow it will snow again, and days may pass before we can venture from this shelter. I have no choice but to leave the camp, the families, and my beloved Pilar in your hands."

Without waiting for my translation or our response, he quickly rose to his feet, spoke a few words to Pilar, unhobbled his pony, and, motioning for Tall Bear to follow him, rode out of the camp.

The intelligence Diego had just revealed cast us in a nervous, fearful mood. We now imagined a savage behind each mound of snow. Each darting shadow and raucous cry of a troop of crows whose territory we had invaded filled us with shivering dread. But as the hours passed and we spotted no movement beyond the opening of our sheltering boulders we decided that surely Diego was mistaken in his apprehensions.

How misguided we were! For as we clustered at the entrance to survey the landscape before us for any hint of human presence the wily Comanches silently breached our shelter from the rear. Turning to cries from the children, we encountered four Comanche warriors, including the husbands of the two Spanish women, two with guns and two with iron-tipped arrows aimed at us.

One of the warriors emitted a piercing scream exactly replicating the cry of a raven and shortly thereafter Running Bear and five warriors, including the three who had deserted us, appeared at the entrance. The spouses ran quickly to the side of their mates whilst their children clapped and chattered happily at the sight of their fathers given up for dead.

Running Bear strode through our midst, his misshapen eyes glaring silently at our frightened group. Then spotting Pilar and Miriam he approached and gave each a terrific slap. I reacted only with a silent grimace, but John rushed forward to protect them. Whereupon one of the Comanches struck him flush with the butt of his rifle and John staggered and fell in an unconscious heap. Miriam screamed his name and would have rushed to his side but for Running Bear's cruel grasp.

Pointing to John and me, Running Bear spoke to his warriors, and from the few words I could understand I knew he had ordered our death. I sank to my knees in supplication for my life, but John, now conscious again, made no whimper of protest.

So terrified was I that my legs failed me so that the warriors had to drag me from the shelter. John, though groggy and bloodied, walked by his own strength, head held erect. Escorting the hysterical Miriam to witness the execution, Running Bear came behind us.

A dozen paces from the exit Running Bear barked a command. One of the Comanches drew his tomahawk and was about to dispatch John when a shot rang out high on the slopes above us. Running Bear turned his awful eyes upwards in an odd combination of rage and astonishment, clutched his heart, and, releasing Miriam, slowly wilted into the snow as his blood stained it red. He twitched and lay still, one eye closed, the other open and vacant. Running Bear would run no more in this world. Summoning my utmost courage, I waxed so bold as to give his corpse a timid kick.

The warrior with the raised tomahawk made as though to strike, whereupon another bullet whined past him and thudded into the snow. He quickly sheathed the weapon and ran with the other Comanches for the protection of the shelter.

Soon Diego and Tall Bear appeared and protecting themselves behind a small boulder, called out to their erstwhile companions. I cannot transcribe the words they exchanged, but Diego's words sounded decisively spoken. I deduced that he offered the hungry men food and freedom—for he and Tall Bear had slaughtered a mule deer—on the condition of Pilar's safety and their assurance that the Comanches who

183

wished would be allowed to continue the journey unmolested.

Without Running Bear to goad them and perhaps uncharacteristically heeding the pleas of their women, the leaderless warriors relented and cautiously emerged from the bouldered recess. There followed a long council with much gesticulating and designs traced in the snow. Finally, Diego reported to us their decision, which I translated to John and Miriam.

"The Comanches will go their way, likely to return to the Comanchería, taking their wives, children, and all others who wish to accompany them. Because they are entirely without provisions we will share with them the meat we have taken today. They have sworn an oath not to molest us further, yet for all their swearing it will be unsafe for us to remain in their presence for even one night. They must return to a campsite they have some leagues distant, bearing with them the body of Running Bear. We shall be reduced to nine souls but keep our four horses."

"Are they men of their word, friend Diego?" asked John, "or will they work treachery on us?"

"With their Comanche kinsmen their word is unbreakable, but in late years with white men it is but a prelude to betrayal. At the moment they are puzzled and do not yet know whether to look on me as Comanche or white. Eventually they will realize that I have reverted to the ways of my Spanish ancestors, and then we shall be in peril. For this reason we must remain alert and strike out for the Cuartelejo as soon as the storm permits."

Without further words the Comanches and their families filed out of the shelter and departed for their camp with the bloodied corpse of Running Bear draped across a skittish, wild-eyed horse. Diego stood outside in the snow and watched them go in imponderable silence, but Pilar commenced to sob and shake uncontrollably as soon as they were out of sight. Miriam rushed to her side and took her hand in hers. To our puzzled looks she responded simply: "Be patient and let her weep as much as she can; it is her way of cleansing herself of the degradation in which she has lived these many years."

Two days later the storm abated, and temperatures rose quickly. Water from the melting snow commenced to drip, rising as miniscule puffs of steam as it struck our campfire. At noon Diego ordered us out of the shelter and on our way. We responded with enthusiasm, anxious to leave behind the unhappy memories of the place.

Our reduced numbers did not help our progress, for either by choice or rejection by the Comanches the ill and infirm had remained with us. Dusk found us advanced only a few miles, but far enough, or so Diego assured us, to have intersected the Dry Fork of the Santa Fe Trail. Indeed, we discerned wagon and cattle tracks in the melting snow, and not far ahead we came upon a campsite, abandoned at the moment but with evidence of recent travelers. A crude lean-to afforded us shelter against the icy mountain winds, and there was firewood aplenty for us to warm ourselves and cook our venison. For the first time in several days our tenuous hopes for survival grew stronger.

The weather held fair, and we progressed without further misfortune during subsequent days. We passed a location that Diego recognized as Ojo de Bernal, and not distant from it we came upon the village of San Miguel, home to two dozen souls who peered fearfully at us from draped windows.

"We shall soon be within sight of Santa Fe," he announced happily.

Emerging from a mountain pass on the fourth morning we were elated to espy the church spire of Santa Fe not more than three leagues distant. In mid-afternoon as we entered the central plaza, townspeople clustered about our bedraggled troop with suspicion and curiosity, eyeing our Indian dress and especially our Comanche companions with murmurings and misgivings. Assuring them that despite his savage dress and bronzed skin he was Spanish and not Comanche, Diego explained our origins and intentions to town officials. Whereupon one of the latter, Enrique Sánchez by name, emitted a gladsome cry of recognition and rushed forward to embrace him. Born in Nueva Rosita he was perforce cousin to both Diego and Pilar. With this happy bond established the public mood changed from wary suspicion of our motives to felicitous celebration of our survival. The only somber note in this happy meeting was the sad news that Nueva Rosita was no more. Not only had the Comanches killed or enslaved most of its citizens but had also burned its buildings.

Noting our weariness and particularly Pilar's distress, the stout and merry Enrique insisted that we lodge at his house where, he heartily assured us, there were servants aplenty to arrange for our comfort, care for Pilar, and ply us with more food and drink than we could consume in a score of weeks. We soon confirmed what we suspected from the start: that Pilar and Diego's kinsman was in all things hyperbolic, yet his were not mere lies of the sort that I, it pains me now to confess, might invent under pressure of need or temptation of convenience, but rather exaggerations of solid truths. For indeed his house was nearly all he claimed and his hospitality more than we dreamed.

Only when it came to our Comanche companions did Enrique waver. For most of his family had also perished in the attack on Nueva Rosita many years earlier, and for him now to gather round his hearth the kinsmen of their murderers seemed a greater accommodation than the rules of hospitality could permit.

The tense impasse was resolved when a chief of the Jicarilla Apaches, encamped for the winter on the banks of the nearby Santa Fe River, stepped forth and in sign and trader language offered shelter to our Comanche friends. "In the days before the power of Running Bear and his evil mother," he explained to Tall Bear, "your people and mine were friends and often shared meat and campfire. Now we hear that Running Bear and his mother are no more. If this is so, then let us live again in friendship."

Tall Bear and his Comanche companions were happy with the chief's words and nothing loath to accept his hospitality. Indeed, they accepted the offer with what seemed to us to be visible relief. But to dispel our puzzlement Diego pointed out that so greatly despised the Comanche the confinement of walls and houses that what the White Man relished as comfort they suffered as prison.

And relish we did in the days that followed. Food, drink, and abundant comforts were ours without the asking. We marveled at Enrique's largesse, not reduced in the slightest by his wife Leonor and daughters Alicia and Elena but rather enhanced by their own generous and genial spirits. Amidst these happy circumstances the rigors of our recent ordeals commenced to fade from our recollection and we regained our confidence and hope for a better tomorrow.

Although as yet uncertain of their livelihood but shed of the nightmarish terrors of unhappy memory, John and Miriam expressed their ardent desire to solemnize their union. This news cheered us all for we could not but love their noble spirit, handsome bearing, and purity of motive. The local priest, Padre Juan, at first was as pleased as we, but upon learning of the prospective groom's religion he explained with considerable consternation that the Church would not sanction the union of Quaker John and Catholic Miriam. The news was heartbreaking to us all, but try as we might we could not avail ourselves of a practical solution. Not even a civil ceremony proved to be an alternative, for in Catholic Santa Fe the civil authorities interdicted any and all such actions as might be contrary to Church doctrine and custom.

After several days John summoned us to announce a decision.

"My good friends, in heart and soul I am already wedded to this dear woman, for she is, and ever shall be, the love of my life. In lengthy

186

prayer and meditation I have considered this matter and now wish to reveal to you my decision. I am a Christian first and a Friend, a Quaker, second, as indeed I have ever believed ought to be the proper order of all faithful Christians in their several sects and denominations, and I will not be separated from my darling Miriam by a dogma that, though much different from mine and unclear to my poor understanding on many points, for all its mystery yet teaches men to love God and to come to Him through Christ His Son and our Savior. Since this is also the foundation of my creed and the core of my life I doubt not that I shall be able to reconcile myself to all other points. For I am persuaded, dear friends, that in our recent ordeals God has not spared me merely to return and persist in my old ways but to begin a new and better life in these circumstances into which He has brought us. In short, dear friends, I am prepared to make my confession to Father Juan and with his help and by God's grace, to become the Catholic husband of my beloved Miriam."

As he ended these momentous and stirring words, the lovely Miriam could not restrain herself but with a cry of delight flew to John with outstretched arms, embracing and kissing him with such joyous abandon and wonderful affection that all present cheered and applauded, even though most did not understand what he had uttered until I translated for them. Even the benign Father Juan indicated his indulgence of Miriam's behavior with a smile and his pleasure over John's decision—once he had the chance—with a hearty abrazo.

Whereupon Diego stepped forth, hugged his friend John, and asked us to listen to his words, which duly translated, you, dear reader, will now hear also.

"Words cannot express, John, the happiness I feel for you and dear Miriam. I want you to know that in me you have a friend for life, and if ever I can do anything on your behalf you have only to ask me, and if it is within my power, it shall be done. Now to this pledge I wish to add another. You see before you Pilar still hobbling on her crutches, yet nearly healed of her wounds, thanks to the loving care that my cousin Enrique, his dear wife Leonor, daughters Alicia and Elena, and others of this household have given her. A thousand thanks to you in Pilar's name, and if I speak proprietarily in her regard it is because my affections so direct and obligate me. I have loved Pilar since earliest childhood, as you know, and now that God has freed us from the evil that bound us for so many years, I do pledge her my love and ask her before these assembled friends and family—ask you, Pilar—to be my wife."

All eyes now turned to Pilar who paled and perhaps would have fallen if at that moment Enrique had not steadied her and helped her to a chair. With great, halting efforts and tears in her eyes she responded to him in her still deficient but improving Spanish.

"Dearest Diego, you ... do me honor with your ... request, an honor I cannot accept. You ... deserve ... a better wife. For although you know that I did not ... willingly ... become Running B—that man's wife, still I was ... forced ... to become so against my will. Dear Diego, you cannot know, can never know, how ... sorry ... I am that I cannot come to you in the ... purity and ... innocence ... of a new bride, as we hoped and dreamed so many moons ... years ... in the past."

"All this I know, dearest Pilar," responded Diego, "but those were matters beyond our power to prevent or remedy. There is no blame or shame for things that we cannot control. One thing only could cause me to accept your refusal."

Overwrought with emotion, Pilar could not find the words to ask what that cause might be.

"Only if your love for me has withered and died, Pilar," Diego continued. "Only then would I accept 'no' for your answer."

Half rising from her chair, Pilar responded in a Spanish rendered eloquent by desperation, "Never, never, dearest Diego! You know I love you, have always loved you, and will love you until I breathe my last!"

"Then, Pilar, you have answered me," Diego smiled, taking her hand in his. In a softer voice, he repeated, "Yes, you have answered me, Pilar, and you have answered for us. Finally, after all the bitter years and all the sufferings and evils of our captive life, you have answered 'yes' for us both. And before our assembled family and friends I accept your answer and ask Father Juan to instruct us in the proper rites and to bring us into the fold of the Church as man and wife. Is this your will and wish, Pilar, as it is mine?"

"Yes," she said timidly. Then as happy tears flooded her eyes and ran down her face, she enfolded Diego in her arms and repeated so loud than none could mistake her answer, "Yes! Yes! YES!"

Again we cheered and applauded this felicitous triumph of faithful love over treacherous circumstance.

You can scarcely imagine, dear reader, the happy days and weeks that followed as the two couples prepared to take their marriage vows in a twin ceremony. Dresses were sewn, adornments prepared, foodstuffs replenished, protocols established, invitations distributed, and parties planned. The Sánchez household became a veritable factory of humming matrimonial industry.

The only dark cloud on this blissful horizon was the precarious economic status of the two future husbands. With the example of his father before him, John naturally turned his thoughts to trade and commerce. Indeed, as fate would have it, one of Santa Fe's established merchants, enfeebled by age and without family, wished to divest himself of his store and merchandise. John proposed a business partnership with Diego, who had progressed so rapidly in his mastery of English, and John in his Spanish, that they no longer needed me as their translator. Together the two of them approached Enrique in hopes of securing a capital loan. Alas, for all his genuine generosity and blustery pretense of unlimited wealth, Enrique was obliged to confess that most of his money was committed to land, cattle, teams and wagons and therefore not easily redeemable in immediate cash. At the moment he could help them but little, and unable to raise more than a third of the needed amount, the would-be partners sadly resigned themselves to seeing opportunity pass them by.

Thereupon I entered into a fierce and hateful contest with my conscience. You do recall, do you not, my all but erotic attachment to my lucre? Imagine, then, the distaste, the displeasure, the outright horror I felt at the mere thought of parting with my beloved money to aid my friends. I assure you, for you may doubt it, that I was truly fond of John, Diego, and their respective brides-to-be, and I would have done anything for them short of expending my cash or inconveniencing my person.

The old storekeeper, don Humberto Toledo by name, had taken a liking to the two young men and sincerely wished to sell his business to them. But another had tendered an offer in the meantime and unless they could come up with half of the money by Friday next, the old man could not with good reason forestall the transaction any longer. Gloom settled on the handsome features of my friends.

That afternoon, the Thursday before the fateful Friday, I could stand it no longer. With bitter tears in my eyes, anger in my heart, and a churning in my stomach, I counted out my precious coins, gripping them so tightly that they fell with the greatest reluctance from my fingers to the mounting heap on my table. I counted them twice, wondering whether even at this late hour I might through some clever manipulation save at least some of them. Finally, when I could delay no longer, I sighed in despair, tied the coins in a handkerchief and went downstairs where my friends were engaged in earnest but fruitless conversation. Without a word I tossed the coins on the table where they sat, glared at them, and hurried out of the room without a backward look.

The amount was sufficient to save the opportunity. Thus the transaction was completed, and both John and Diego were able to establish themselves in their common business and individual residences.

189

My friends, old and new, lauded my generosity, little knowing the true sentiments that seethed in my heart. Nor did their earnest promises to repay me with interest soothe the agitation of my spirit. From that day forward I commenced to think on my departure from Santa Fe, awaiting only the celebration of the twin weddings to bid my friends adieu.

In the meantime, however, I was able to render yet another service to my friends, but unlike the painful separation from my precious coins this second favor I did with pleasure. The town's elderly barber, don Ricardo Gómez, had become so palsyied in late years that the townsmen feared his shaking razor. This circumstance placed John and Diego in a quandary, for it would not do for them to present themselves on this happiest of days with nicked ears, cuts, and poorly trimmed beards and moustaches. I reminded them of my barbering experience and offered my services if they could procure for me the proper instruments. This they did with Enrique's help, and on the morning of the joyous day I carefully applied all my skill to the task. I do not boast when I say that my friends were delighted and I, pleased that my skills had not diminished. The task was unequal: harder in John's case with his heavy beard, easier with Diego who during his years amongst the Comanches had singed and plucked away most of his facial hair. That afternoon the ceremony commenced. Having shed all vestiges of his Comanche past, Diego was now transformed into the very essence of a handsome Spanish caballero, whilst it would have been nigh on impossible to find a finer specimen of Anglo-Saxon manhood than John. Under Father Juan's instructive guidance, both were now in harmony with the Church and duly rehearsed in the proper rites they must observe on this happiest of days. And whilst the skilled Diego progressed rapidly in his English, John struggled manfully to shed the archaic vestiges in his. Occasionally a "thou" or "thee" still slipped out.

As for the respective brides, on her wedding day Miriam astonished and delighted all with her exceptional beauty. There were admiring comments as she glided down the aisle in her white dress and veil and long train. I had to admit that even my beloved Caroline— whom I missed with a renewed poignancy that day—could not have outshone her in feminine splendor. Never in the history of Santa Fe, all agreed, had a more beautiful bride walked down the aisle. There were, I am almost certain, several tears when she thought of her parents and wished she could have approached the altar on her father's arm instead of don Humberto's. Yet this sadness but enhanced her love for John, which she radiated as a deeper happiness that captivated all in attendance.

Then it was Pilar's turn. Dressed in a becoming maroon dress, matching corsage, and dark veil and completely recovered from her physical injuries—though perhaps not fully from her spiritual scarring—she marched belatedly towards her happiness in stately dignity on Enrique's arm. Apprised of her tragic history and in keeping with the nobility or baseness of their individual condition, the congregants stared at her with benign or malevolent intensity. But whereas Miriam smiled at the guests in the friendly American manner, Pilar looked straight ahead with a sterner Spanish demeanor, her dark eyes a mystery of emotions too deep for us to fathom.

If in her youthful freshness and splendid physical beauty Miriam was the fairer of the two, Pilar in her mature and wounded womanhood was the more intriguing and in her imponderable, mysterious way more memorable. It can be said without possible contradiction that Santa Fe had never seen, and perhaps would never see again, brides more appealing and unforgettable, or grooms more eagerly and amorously captivated by their beauty. Gentle reader, I confess to you that I have failed to do justice to the exquisite details of their dress and personal luster. I am limited in superlatives suitable to that purpose and, therefore, deem it better to give mere hints of their bridal beauty than to distort their lovely description with inadequate language.

To the delight of all present the marriage vows were exchanged without further notable details that I can recall for you at the moment, except to report that at Diego's urging and with Father Juan's reluctant permission, our Comanche friends stoically witnessed the wedding from the very back pews. After the customary congratulations and tossing of rice at Church door the respective parties, including Father Juan, bent their steps to Enrique's house wherein music, meals, and festivities began that would last nearly a week. The Comanches solemnly declined to take part, and as they filed out silently to return to their river encampment, we wondered whether Diego and Pilar, or indeed any of us, should ever again cross paths with them.

At the urging of my friends and with the complicity of don Ricardo's family who wished to retire him from strop and razor, I agreed to rent his shop, tools, and an adjacent room for my residence. Thus I resumed for the space of nearly two years my old profession as a barber.

Of those years I have little to say. You may think it strange, dear reader, but life has its silent stretches that have no telling. The truth be told, most of us cannot abide the placid life. Peace, which all claim to cherish, is no sooner won than it begins to cloy and weary the soul.

Within a short time my barbering skills, nothing worse despite my absence from their exercise, won back don Ricardo's old customers and earned me new ones. I accepted a young apprentice, Luisito Moreno, for the business soon grew beyond my personal capabilities. I paid him a mere pittance and overlooked his small pilferings, responding to his frequent complaints that I had worked for less during my apprenticeship. Feeding on such stringent economies and without other dispensations to speak of, my depleted treasure recovered some of its earlier volume.

I was weary of virtue. The continual nobility of spirit I was obliged to exhibit with my friends was beginning to annoy me, and as a barber I was daily reminded of my old love and heartbreak in Memphis. With some regularity I sought to relieve the ennui of my circumstances by gambling with the riff-raff in El Puchero tavern behind the plaza. But even though my winnings were considerable, the frequent rowdiness of the inebriated Americans frightened and repulsed me. For as summer arrived and traffic on the Santa Fe Trail increased, daily the violence grew as more Americans poured into the city. In one spectacularly dangerous incident, for instance, the alguaziles clubbed down a drunken group of young cattlemen. But instead of lessening the violence, the incident provoked the sizeable American community to other confrontations. Indeed, so dangerous became the situation that I thought it more prudent to suspend my visits to El Puchero and seek more tranquil taverns for my entertainment.

Here, dear reader, I should add that my twenty-fourth or twenty-fifth birthday had now passed. I had grown measurably taller and stronger than in my previous sojourns in Memphis and Perryville, and my beard was beginning to take on the luster of manhood. I even dared imagine that I could defend myself against Henri should I ever have the misfortune to cross his path again.

For some time a plan had been forming in my mind to leave the northern frontier for more southerly climes where my assorted skills might win me a fortune at the expense of the gullible. Mexico, so I learned from certain travelers, with its gold and superstitious masses might prove ripe for one of my talents. Even though I had recouped a sizable portion of the money gifted to John and Diego, I promised myself that never again would I allow insipid sentimentality to drain hard coin from my purse. And I had not forgotten the bitter lesson learned at the hands of Malcolm Gordon.

Not many months passed before I announced my intention to leave Santa Fe, but such were the outcries and pleadings from my friends that I was obliged to delay my journey for a few more weeks as they plied me with parties and petitions to remain. There were pointed insinuations that Enrique's older daughter Alicia would be receptive to my courtship, but although her father's property and prospects for fortune were indeed appealing, her dark brunette coloring and plump figure were not to my liking. For I confess that I could not cast blonde Caroline from my thoughts.

Both Miriam and Pilar were now expecting the birth of their first child and they pleaded with me to remain until the happy events should be consummated. I was of such a mind to leave that not even John and Diego could have persuaded me to stay, but I had not the heart to refuse the earnest requests of their dear spouses.

Miriam gave birth first, in early October, to a beautiful green-eyed daughter whom they named Vivian after her mother. John was beside himself with joy and overflowing pride and could not refrain from proclaiming to everyone how his daughter had inherited her mother's great beauty. Indeed, he asserted to the smiling assent of all that, objectively speaking, he had never seen a more beautiful baby.

Two weeks later Pilar gave birth to Diego, hijo (jr.), a healthy, hungry infant whose happy arrival seemed to erase like a vanishing nightmare the last of Pilar's bitter memories. I fear I have failed to tell you, dear reader, that both in physical traits and spiritual affinities Diego and Pilar much resembled each other. No wonder, then, that Dieguito, as he was promptly nicknamed, was the very image of both ecstatic parents.

Both sets of parents would have willingly named me godfather to their offspring, but I refused them gratefully and gently by explaining that I knew not where my pathway might lead me, perhaps never again to Santa Fe.

After the happy christenings, gifts, and congratulatory visits to both families, it was time for me to go. I had relinquished the shop to don Ricardo's family and despite his small perfidies recommended Luisito to them. At last all was in readiness, my friends had bidden me adieu with tears and embraces—Alicia was sobbing—and loaded me with gifts and provisions. I was about to mount the best horse brought from Comanche country when John and Diego called me aside to hand me a heavy bag. It was the money repaid with generous interest. I thanked them with tears of joy, feeling like the patriarch of old whose prodigal son had returned home. And although I saw no need of the document, John insisted that I take along a letter identifying me as Peter Prosper and requesting of all who should have dealings with me that I be accorded all the courtesy, credit, and respect due a gentleman of honor. I deposited it in a pocket, and because I could imagine no profit from its possession, gave it no more than passing thoughts. Then I repacked my money about my waist so as to accommodate the unexpected influx of

193

new coins, mounted my horse, waved goodbye to my friends, and rode south.

During the first stage of my journey, as yet only vaguely conceived in its trajectory and destination, I was accompanied by a half dozen fellow travelers banded together for companionship and protection from marauding Indians and bandits. We followed the road that snaked southwards crisscrossing the shallow Santa Fe River and following to its conflux with the Rio Grande. Not many hours thence I spurred my mount to the summit of a low mountain so as to take a final look at Santa Fe, wondering if I should ever again enjoy such friendships as I had forged during my ordeal amongst the Comanches. Then I wheeled my horse like the expert horseman I had become and casting maudlin thoughts from my mind, spurred him to a gallop back towards the road, buoyed in spirit by visions of fabulous fortune awaiting me in warm lands beyond the southern horizon.

Translator's Addendum
[This fragment of a longer correspondence between Peter and John Greenley, apparently written some time after 1850, was inserted in the materials.]

... Miriam was saddened beyond telling by the news of her father's death. For all his flaws, and he had fewer than most men, Mr. Morrissey was an honorable man, true to his word and his God. It always weighed heavily on my conscience that I was the cause of their estrangement, but Miriam always assured me that under the circumstances of that time we did the only thing we could, short of renouncing our love and going our sad and separate ways. Nevertheless, I always hoped that in time and in God's benign providence our differences would be settled. Alas, it was not to be in this life, even though to that end I wrote several conciliatory letters to Mr. Morrissey but received no response from him. Miriam sent them portraits of the children, and if Mr. Morrissey remained rigid in his vow never to receive his daughter again, Mrs. Morrissey happily yielded to her love for Miriam and her grandchildren.

You may imagine how torn we were when Mrs. Morrissey pleaded with us to return to Maryland and assume oversight of the plantation. We had lived in Santa Fe for nigh on fifteen years, our business was flourishing, I was respected in the city, and our family was happy with the many strong friendships we built, chief among them our unbreakable

194

bond with Diego, Pilar, and their children.

Even though Miriam left the decision to me, I knew in her heart she longed for her mother and Maryland. So we returned, and here you have me supervising a score of workers on the Morrissey plantation.

It will not surprise you, dear friend, to learn that I am attempting to reconnect with my family in Pennsylvania. My blessed mother has written, praising God that I am yet among the living, but my father is so far unbending. May God guide us to reunion.

Part V: How Peter fulfilled an ancient prophecy and became a holy man of miracles; the miracle of the Reluctant Virgin and the Fray Domingo Prophecies; the murderer's confession; how Peter fell from grace and was imprisoned; The humorous manner of his rescue and his time with Bernardo and the bandits; Raquelita's tale of revenge; how Peter delivered his own funeral eulogy; and how thereafter he received his just reward in an unusual manner and began a hurried journey towards his after-life a step ahead of the authorities.

For the better part of four days we rode uneventfully southward through a melancholy, parched land quickened only by groves of cottonwood and greenery hugging the Rio Grande. So anxious were my companions to push onward towards El Paso del Norte that we paused only briefly in the Plaza de Albuquerque to find repast for ourselves and fodder for our horses. There three more travelers joined us. Soon my senses were again indifferent to the circumstantial dreariness about me as we resumed our journey, and rapt in happy thoughts of fortune leagues removed from the serious meditations you have just read, dear reader, I was startled from my reveries by a freckled, grinning face thrust close to mine. It was one of our new companions, a lanky young American who, though somewhat taller and heavier than I, was near me in age. He had a familiar look about him though I could not remember an earlier encounter between us.

"Been wanting to talk to you, good buddy. Where you heading to?" he inquired as he leaned out of his saddle to study my features and peer into my eyes.

"Well, sir, I—er—am not yet sure of my destination, just south, I suppose," I hedged evasively, bothered by his meddlesome intrusiveness, "I can only say that I am more anxious to leave Santa Fe than to arrive anywhere else."

"That makes two of us," my intrusive comrade laughed. "Santa Fee ain't been real friendly to me neither."

He stared at me unrelentingly, awaiting my reaction.

"Oh?…s that right?" I said after an awkward pause.

I could see he was desirous of telling someone his story after others in our company had rebuffed him. For of a certainty they must have known better than I the truth of the ancient adage,

Those who fear solitude make the worst company.

I sighed inwardly at the prospect, knowing that any response from me would be a pretext for him to launch into a tale that at the moment I had no wish to hear.

"No mister, it ain't right," he replied, misunderstanding my comment. "But that's the way my luck's been running lately. Name's Wells, Billy Wells. And I tell you, friend—. Er, I guess you didn't toss me your name, or if you did, I didn't catch it," he said, laughing heartily at his banal cleverness.

"Peter Prosper, at your service, Mr. Wells."

"Well now, I'm pleased to make your acquaintance, Pete. And none of that 'mister' stuff. Makes me sound like I'm a hundred years old," he responded, giving me a smug smile as if he had just uttered the profoundest of insights and extending a large hand to shake mine with prolonged, pumping vigor that fairly threatened to disconnect my arm from its socket. I disliked his company immediately, for he was one of those unfortunate beings whose anxious eagerness for acceptance caused others to shun him.

"Then Billy it is," I said, trying to retrieve my numbed hand. "Since I don't know where I'm going, why not tell me about you? What kind of trouble did you get into in Santa Fe?"

"Well, sure, Pete, I don't misdoubt that you got reasons fer not telling folks your business. But I don't mind telling you mine. I ain't done nothing to hide and so I ain't got no bad secrets. And I mean to tell everybody I see how them low-down Meshicans in Santa Fee done robbed me and left me in a mess o' trouble."

His beardless face took on an angry scowl as he remembered. Seeing that I was in the company of an obsessed simpleton, I decided to humor him.

"How so? What did they do to you?"

He cleared his throat, spat out a wad of tobacco, and eagerly began his story.

Billy Wells's Story

Well, Pete, it all started way back yonder in Missouri country. That's where I come from, and sometimes I wish I'd never left. But I did and now, as the man said, there ain't no going back, specially not with the trouble I got myself into here lately. When I was fourteen—nigh on eight years back, it was—I ran away from my poppa's homestead and the whuppin's he used to give me and hired on to work for Baldy Varner. His real name's Theodore but everybody calls him Baldy 'cause his head's as slick as one of them billiard balls. One day I just decided that Poppa wasn't gonna whup me no more. Because you see, Pete, by then I already stood as tall and stout as most full-grown men, and a better rider you couldn't find in hell and three counties. Why, I could ride bareback better'n most could sit the finest saddle in St. Louis. Well, so

Baldy hired me on at man's wages, don't you see, to be one of his cattle drovers. Out here the Meshicans call 'em vaqueros. That's a Meshican word, don't you see? I can talk considerable Meshican, and if you need my help dealing with them you just let me know, you hear?

(I thanked him for the offer, which he acknowledged with the comically grave seriousness that fools assume when advantaged by an imagined superiority. He stared at me to impress the importance of his knowledge and then continued his tale.)

Baldy was grazing his cattle on open range up and down the Missouri River Valley. Had been for years. But then t'wasn't long before things started getting crowded. Them clodhopper farmers from over in Illinois kept amoving in, and first thing you know they was aputting up fences and plowing under the natural grass. Old Baldy popped a couple of 'em with his ole sawed-off when they started smarting off about their land titles and rights and all that legal stuff. Well, Pete, word got out that federal marshals were acomin', and so old Baldy, Dorothie his wife, and two boys lit out west to the Republican River valley. Most of his drovers went with him, ten of us I reckon. You see, Pete, he was always square with us and we was not about to leave him just because he put a load o' buckshot in some smartass farmer's behind.

We lost some of the herd on the drive to what folks call Kansas territory, but it turned out to be good cattle country even if the Indians slaughtered some of them and rustlers stole some more. Afore long Baldy made up his losses and had a bigger herd than before. That's when he sold a couple hundred head to a Meshican in Santa Fe by the name of Henrickee Sanchcz (that's Meshican for 'Henry', don't you see?). He's got a lotta land and wants to build up a better herd than them scrawny ole Spanish range cows you see out here. Baldy made me foreman and give me four men for the drive. Not many twenty-two-year old men get to be boss. I bet you can't name one, can you?

Now I'm here to tell you, Pete, that drive was the hardest and nastiest work I ever done in all my born days. We had rain and wind, wolves, cold, snow, and a run-in with old Gray Owl's Comanches just about the time we got caught in a blizzard a few months back. Lost a few head and like to a froze to death saving the others. I don't guess you ever was in a blizzard, was you, Pete? Naw, I'm sure you ain't been, or you'd know what I'm talking about.

Well, we got to Santa Fe with a hundred and eighty head, which was mighty good numbers considering all we had to put up with on the trail. We was all just sick of cows and dust and we ain't slept in a bed for nearly three months. Now, I'm not a drinking man, Pete, but after all we'd been through we went on a spree to get the dust outta our throats. I had Baldy's money put away in a special moneybelt, and he had told me how much to count out for myself and the other drovers.

Well, Pete, there we was, raising hell, gambling and drinking in one of them taverns over there back of the main plaza, El Puchero, I think it was, when a couple of them little Meshican señoritas start to dance and sing a little. The boys was liquored up by then and I guess one of them tried to git a little something going with one of 'em. Well, she screamed her head off and called him all kinds of dirty things in Meshican. The owner runs out for the alguazil—something like one of our constables. Pretty soon he shows up with a whole drove of deputies to arrest us. We tried to explain that we meant no harm to the girls, maybe just had a tad too much to drink. They played like they didn't understand us, even though we spoke out loud enough for anybody to know what we meant. The captain grabbed me by the arm, for I had done the talkin', and started to haul me off. The boys come to my defense, and we just about tore that old tavern apart. But they was just too many fer us, and when it was over we was bruised, drunk, and in the calaboose. Wonder they didn't shoot us.

Worst thing was they took our money and belongin's, including my moneybelt with Baldy Varner's money. Next day the head alguazil shows up with these here two fellers he ran across in the plaza, an American feller named John Greenley and a Meshican man by the name of Diego somebody. They helped get us outta jail, but when we went to get our things the moneybelt was empty. I swore and cussed so much the alguazil was about to throw me back in jail. I accused him of being a thief—'cause he was—him and that whole sorry bunch of Meshicans in Santa Fe! He told Greenley and that other feller that I musta gambled and drunk up all the money, and maybe had give some of it to one o' the little señoritas at a house down the street. Now, Pete, that's a damn lie! I might waste my own money, but I would never touch old Baldy's. No sir, Baldy Varner trusted me, and I'm not one to let a man down when he's done fer me what Baldy has.

When it was all over, the alguazil told us to get outta town and not to come back. Claimed we had slandered his good name and the name of Santa Fe. Said we had behaved like barbarians or something like that. Well, Pete, here I am as innocent as any man can be, and yet I couldn't prove nothing against them thieves.

The other drovers can go on back up to Kansas, I reckon, but I can't. Baldy'd skin me alive, might even shoot me if I showed up without his money. So all's I can do is just drift on to some other place.

202

I thought I might head on down the river to a town they call El Paso. I hear tell it's a wide open place, lotta gambling and women, and money to be made down that way. But there's a bunch more things I want to tell you first about what happened to me in Santa Fe. I'm here to tell you, Pete, that I ain't finished with them crooks. If it's the last thing I do …

Forgive me, dear reader, for breaking off Billy's tale well before he had ended it. The remainder was drivel and blather fit only to waste your time, and I should be pained to subject you to it. Everyone has a story, as they say, and maybe after all is said and done we are nothing but the tale of life we weave. Father Branigan often cited a Scripture that vouchsafes my claim:

We spend our years as a tale that is told.

But the point to be made, gentle reader, is that not all stories are equally interesting, for men are not equal. Some, rarely, create a life of high drama; others, commonly, scofflaws like Billy or yours truly, compose lives of low farce.

As Billy droned on and I drifted off into my unfocused meditations, the skies darkened and lightning commenced to flash in the southwest. We were in the shallows of the river, crossing to the west bank when Billy roused me out of my daydreaming with a curse and a warning.

"Dammit to hell, Pete, we better get outta here and catch up with the others! Looka yonder! There's a bad storm atoppin that mountain! Man alive, just look at that lightnin, would you!"

Alas, his warning came too late for me. For as we spurred our mounts to overtake our companions, a fearsome bolt of lightning and ground-shaking peal of thunder caused my steed to bolt in wild-eyed panic towards a thick grove of cottonwoods. Before I could rein him in he ran under a low-hanging branch that struck me on the temple, nearly knocking me out of the saddle. I remember only swaying in semi-consciousness and trying to get the runaway horse under control before blackness closed in on me and I fell from the saddle.

At least that was my later and calmer surmise of my misfortune, for when I regained my senses I remembered only the horse's panicky career and nothing of the impact and fall. Both my mount and Billy— and later I discovered, Caroline's cross, and my letter of identification— had vanished and in the stygian darkness, punctuated at short intervals by luciferian lightning flashes, I was unable to determine an intelligible sense of direction. Only a single hastily confirmed fact consoled me: Although my extra clothes and provisions were gone, but oddly enough, my precious gold was still safely strapped tightly in a pouch about my waist where Billy, as I supposed the thief to be, had not searched.

This favorable fact notwithstanding, my circumstances appeared to be grim indeed. My horse was nowhere to be found, I was drenched to the bone, and the rain pelted me in blowing, horizontal sheets. My teeth chattered, exacerbating the unrelenting dolour in my temple as though at any second my head might explode. To tarry where I had fallen was impossible and to find shelter of any sort in this unfathomable wilderness, as improbable as it was urgent.

As I thrashed about in the undergrowth a radiant bolt of lightning that held for an uncommonly long moment revealed an ancient roadway. I followed it as best I could, hoping my horse had taken the same path and might be awaiting me ahead. Several times I went astray in the darkness into slapping branches and tripping underbrush and was obliged to await the lightning flashes to retrieve my way.

Eventually the road led me up and over the summit of a low line of hills that rose from the western side of the river valley. The storm was receding towards the northeast and the lightning waning, though the rain continued to pelt me and I was cold, wet, and exhausted beyond description. My horse had vanished for good it seemed, and after trudging for several leagues I was about to sink down in utter weariness when I thought to espy a light flickering through the dripping leaves. Excitement spurred my flagging strength, and I hurried to a better vantage. There I saw not one light but several not more than a league ahead.

I stumbled my way into a small town the general configuration of which I could not discern, for the lightning had retreated far to the northeast and the lights I had seen were now extinguished. Nearby a dog commenced to bark at my intrusion, but I detected no human presence. Feeling my way along the west wall of one of the adobe buildings I came to a small portal. Alas, it was locked. I groped elsewhere but finding no entry, returned and in desperation began to pull and tug on its rusted handle. Abruptly, the eroded metal snapped and the door opened with a screech. So anxious was I for shelter of any sort that I rushed in, heedless of any peril I should encounter.

Feeling about in these unacquainted surroundings, I seized upon what felt to be a sarape or poncho. I doffed my soggy garments, taking care to deposit my gold on what felt to be a small table, and snuggled into the warm, woolen cover. Despite the pain of my wound, no sooner did I stretch out on the floor than I fell into a deep and dreamless asleep.

I awoke to voices and the glare of sunlight flooding through a collapsed section of the east wall. What I had mistaken in the dark for a sarape turned out to be in the light a frayed Franciscan habit. But a greater surprise followed. Looking cautiously about me and fearing the worst, I was amazed to find myself surrounded by a score or so of humbly dressed persons of both sexes, though predominantly of the distaff, all engaged in fervent, rapturous prayer. What I had mistaken for a table was, as I saw in the light, the remains of a ruined altar. As I stirred, the prayers ceased and villagers fell silent. Then a tiny girl's voice broke the silence with these excited words in Spanish:

"¡Mira, mamá, el ángel está despierto! (Look, Momma, the angel is awake!).

Whereupon the villagers crossed themselves and with beatific faces lifted heavenwards began a joyous chorus of thanksgiving to the Virgin. I turned immediately to my precious money. To my utter dismay it was gone and in its stead was a large silver crucifix. I liked not the look of things.

"Where am I?" I inquired.

The assembly seemed stupefied by my question and then some amongst the congregation began to laugh nervously. One of them, a lean dark man—don Jerónimo, I learned a moment later—with blue eyes made more intense by his swarthy coloring and dark mustachios, stepped forward, nervously twisting the brim of his wide sombrero with his sinewy hands.

"Vaya, señor (come now, sir), as if you did not know that you are in the town of San Cristóbal de los Frailes and what remains of the Shrine of Our Lady of Guadalupe," he responded with lowered eyes and a knowing smile. "We have awaited your arrival for these many years, assembling ourselves for prayer and happy expectation each year on the anniversary of Fray Marcos' passing. And though the count of years had grown long, our faith was not diminished. We knew that in time our vigil would be rewarded. Now we give thanks anew to the Virgin that our prayers at long last have been answered. For before our very eyes the prophecy has been fulfilled by your divinely ordained visit and the gold to restore our shrine delivered to us, even as Fray Domingo predicted."

Curious and perplexed over this bizarre turn of events, I summoned all the wits I could muster so that I might turn these strange circumstances to my advantage or at least not suffer loss. Evidently they mistook me for a personage of considerable importance to them. Perhaps, I reasoned, there was profit for me if I could but discover the need that gave rise to their earnest prayers. Armed with such knowledge I might then manipulate these naïve souls to my advantage. But I knew that in matters so close to men's hearts one must proceed with all deliberate caution, lest a clumsy word or inexpert move turn their reverent expectation into vengeful retribution.

"You presume too much, good people. I am but a man like you, and even though I have been sent to you on a mission of great importance, I was not told of its urgency and, therefore, my understanding is limited."

"Forgive us if in our ignorance we have offended you, Father," said don Jerónimo. "We know only that you have been sent in answer to our prayers and in fulfillment of the ancient prophecy of Fray Domingo. In our eagerness we took you for an angel."

"The first part I surmised, good Jerómino (for my sharp ears had heard another whisper his name), but of the prophecies you speak of I am ignorant. For I am no angel but, I repeat, a man, and a young one as you see. My superiors informed me only that I should be told upon my arrival what was needful for me to know. But first, good people of San Cristóbal, since I am a man of ordinary flesh and bone you must let me arise and refresh myself. If you will be so good as to provide me with food and drink so that I may replenish my strength, then I will hear your story, as you shall hear mine if you desire. Later I shall help you as best I can. For to that end I was sent."

There was a gasp of astonishment as I said Jerónimo's name. "It is a miracle," said one. "Yes, for how else could he know the name of a man he has never met before?" answered another. "Angels are wont to disguise themselves so as to test our faith with simple appearances," yet another whispered. Others murmured their agreement, and I heard the word "angel" repeated as they respectfully departed.

Not all were convinced, however, and I heard several muttering skeptically amongst themselves as they exited, pointing to my discarded garments as the reason for their doubts. I knew I must concoct a convincing story before I next met with them.

A pug-nosed woman appropriately called Chata [pugnose] set before me a pitcher of water and a steaming soup so richly spiced with fiery condiments that it burned my tongue and brought tears to my eyes. Withal, so substantial it proved to be in beans, onions, and cabrito that anon I felt my strength returning, and although the subsiding pain in my temple yet troubled me, I was not physically worse for my ordeal in the storm. In any case, there is much truth in the Spanish saying:

Barriga llena, corazón contento
(Full belly, happy heart)

Within the hour the curious and eager villagers crowded about me anew. As I suspected, the skeptics amongst them demanded to know why I, a cleric and not an angel as they first presumed, arrived attired as a layman. I was ready with my explanation.

"Perhaps you are unaware, my children, that a fierce rivalry between the Jesuits and our noble Franciscan Order, thought settled many years ago on express orders from the Holy See itself, has flared again after the lamented passing of the former Holy Father and the advent of a new regime in Rome which, unhappily, has lent an ear to their nefarious cause. The zealous Jesuits, long ago expelled from these lands by order of the Spanish king, now under the new Mexican regime, seek to insinuate themselves anew at the expense of the Franciscans. Daily they slander and insult our noble order. So fierce has the rivalry become in the southern provinces of the Republic that, as scandalous and incredible as it may sound to you, good people of San Cristóbal, physical assaults on our members are not unheard of. For reasons of personal safety, therefore, of late our superiors permit us to travel in secular clothing. This is why I came disguised in lay garments as you saw."

This information, outwardly reasonable in form but naturally remote from the truth in substance, perplexed the ignorant villagers but seemed to quell their doubts about me. Don Jerónimo then stepped forth timidly to speak for the assembly. "We give thanks anew for your arrival in San Cristóbal, Father. Tell us your name, we beg you, that we may address you with due respect and honor. For even though you appear to be very young, surely you are the answer to our prayers so long repeated to the Virgin. Ask of us what you will and you shall have it, if it be within our power to grant. And forgive us our curiosity, Father, but pray tell us whence you come, for your Castilian is rapid and strange to our poor ears, as of one not from these lands."

I responded, as I recall, with these or similar words: "I am called Padre Pedro, though my birth name was Pierre de Tourmoulin and my mother tongue French. I was born in the French Antilles, the son of Count Antoine de Tourmoulin, who perished heroically in one of the revolutionary disturbances in those islands, and a Spanish lady of the noble Montes family. As war and rebellion spread in the French islands my saintly widowed mother departed with us—my brother and sister—for Cuba, where I learned the Spanish tongue, and thence to New Orleans where under Father Branigan's influence and tutelage I renounced all my noble titles and secular ambitions and dedicated my life to study and the Church. Then for a time I was sent among the apostate Protestants to impregnate their hearts with the seeds of the true creed. As for petitions, I have none save a request for modest board during my stay in San Cristóbal and a desire to acquaint myself with the famous prophecies of Fray Domingo, if, as you say, they have a bearing on my mission."

"*Pierda cuidado, Padre Pedro* (Put aside your concern, Father Peter)," answered don Jerónimo, "We know little of the places you mention, but we shall attend to your material needs. The good Chata will cook and clean for you, and although we are pained that in our poverty we have no better lodging to offer you than these ruined quarters where Father Domingo himself resided many, many years ago, our carpenters will do what they can for your comfort."

I looked at the gaping hole in the collapsed wall and wondered by what makeshift strategy they might make my surroundings bearable. Not that my doubts raised any deep concerns, for I intended to depart—probably by night and, God willing, with my money—as soon as I should be sufficiently recovered from my head wound. Furthermore, upon inspecting the town, I could discern no natural or lucrative features in its favor. It lay close to no ample source of water, and as far as I could tell, lacked defensive perimeters and fertile farmland. I put the question to don Jerónimo.

"How is it, don Jerónimo, that your ancestors chose to make their settlement here? You will forgive me for saying it, but it does not appear to offer many attractive features."

"Unless you know the story, you cannot understand how our town came to be exactly where it is."

"There is a story?"

"Yes, Padre, and a miraculous one, if you would care to hear it."

"I would indeed," I replied. "There appear to be more things about this place than meet the eye."

With that don Jerónimo laid aside his hat and respectfully bade me sit. After a moment to gather his thoughts he commenced to tell me a story too fantastical to be true yet too compelling to be false.

The Reluctant Virgin

In olden times when the Spanish first came to these lands there was a pious caballero, a certain don Juan de Aranda by name, who was among the first to take lands in the extreme north. In this he was encouraged by Spanish officials who, aware of don Juan's prowess as a youthful military leader in both Spain and New Spain and pleased by the considerable number of able men who served him, believed he could be a stabilizing force against marauding Apaches and other savage tribes. Lately, these, having stolen Spanish horses and arms, were threatening to drive the Spanish from the entire northern frontier and return the region to the heathen ways of their ancestors.

A man of great faith with a particular devotion to our Lady of Guadalupe, don Juan commissioned artisans in Mexico City to create an icon of the Virgin, which duly blessed and consecrated by the Bishop began its long journey to don Juan's estate. The caravan of coaches progressed without incident until it camped at the very spot where San Cristóbal stands today.

The next morning, Padre, a miracle of God happened: The coach conveying the holy icon would not move from its spot, not even when the muleteers fairly skinned the team with their whips. Fear and confusion then descended on the camp, for some believed they had strayed beyond the bounds of Godly grace and wandered into the realm of the Devil himself.

It was at this moment of panic that a certain Fray Cristóbal, who had aided in the creation of the holy icon and was escorting it to its final restingplace, received an illumination.

"The Holy Mother is reluctant to go further. Here in this remote place she has willed to stay, and surely here a shrine must be constructed for her."

Others scoffed at Fray Cristóbal and looked for natural reasons to explain the matter. But they could find none, for when the icon of the Holy Mother was removed from the coach, it rolled easily forward, but no human or animal force could budge it when it was loaded again. In the end all acknowledged the divine miracle. Word was then sent to the pious don Juan de Aranda, who came to worship at the site and to authorize the construction of a shrine. It stands on the very site of the miracle.

Fray Cristóbal dedicated his life to the shrine. For many years he welcomed travelers and pilgrims and did what he could to instruct them and to see to their comfort with the few resources at his disposal. But then as he grew old, others came to construct buildings. Thus our modest town came into being, bearing the name of the saintly Fray Cristóbal, who though not a saint of the Church as is his namesake, was fully so to us.

For as long as they could, our ancestors maintained the Shrine of Our Lady. But in time their resources dwindled and the miracle of the

Reluctant Virgin was all but forgotten. Newer roads bypassed San Cristóbal, and pilgrims no longer came here. Indeed, San Cristóbal itself has nearly ceased to exist. We are but a few dozen souls, and yearly our numbers dwindle. Our only hope resides now in the prophecies of Fray Domingo."

"And what of the icon itself? Does it still exist?"

"Alas, I cannot say, Father. When the descendants of don Juan Aranda learned of the decline of San Cristóbal they came and took the Virgin away by night, some say to the Aranda hacienda, but others claim she was carried to the great cathedral in Mexico City. No one knows of a certainty."

"But how could they remove the Virgin if she had determined that this was her place?"

"We have also pondered the mystery, but we have no answer for you."

"What of the prophecies of Fray Domingo you speak of? Are they of a form that you can read them to me?"

Don Jerónimo appeared pained, as did his companions, and a long silence ensued before he spoke. "Alas, Father Pedro, we are ashamed to confess that we are all analfabetos, illiterates. San Cristóbal long ago became too poor to afford schools or teachers, and since the passing of don Felipe Treviño—may he rest in peace—we count no truly educated persons amongst us, though with great effort a few of us can read simple words, and your humble servant can scribble a signature. For that reason the people think of me as their mayor."

"Then the prophecies are written that I may examine them myself?"

"Indeed, they are, Father Pedro, and penned nearly a century and a half ago by the learned and saintly Fray Domingo himself, but because so many years have passed the lettering has faded badly, and parts of it are nearly invisible. I confess that I have tried to read them but they are beyond my knowledge and understanding. In the main we know only the stories that our fathers passed down to us about his saintly work and inspired writings. They tell how after many years had passed and we were at our darkest hour one should arrive bearing gold to restore the Shrine of our Lady and bring healing to our village. The prophecies even gave the day—yesterday—when the appointed one should arrive, the very day, Father, that you appeared to us. They speak of many wondrous things to befall in ages to come, but these are strange matters that our poor minds cannot grasp."

I shuddered at what I heard, for the villagers' long-cherished expectation of a miraculous gift of my money was hardly in harmony with my customary hope to disencumber their wretched town of what little coin might yet circulate within it. Withal, even though my own ability to read Spanish was more limited than ever I should confess to these simpletons, my partial knowledge gave me a great advantage over their total ignorance. For as the Spanish aptly say:

En el reino de los ciegos el tuerto es rey
(In the kingdom of the blind, the one-eyed man is king)

Whereupon don Jerónimo dispatched a townsman to fetch the slender manuscript wrapped in oilcloth and meticulously tied with two yellow ribbons. I requested time to read it, to which don Jerónimo and villagers politely agreed. After the townspeople had filed out, only Chata remained, lingering close by despite my sharply stated desire for privacy. I suspected she was acting on instructions from don Jerónimo to keep an eye on me and to report my doings to him. As best I could understand and transcribe them—for the Spanish was written in ancient lettering and many words and idioms were unknown to me—the prophecies were as you, dear reader, shall now hear for yourself:

The Prophecies of Fray Domingo
In the month of June of the Year of Grace one thousand six hundred and thirty, being the thirty-first year of my mortal life and ninth in the reign of his majesty Felipe IV, King by the grace of God of Spain and Portugal, and Emperor of the Spains beyond the Ocean Sea, I was instructed by the superiors of my Franciscan order to leave Burgos for Cádiz and thence for New Spain aboard the vessel Nuestra Señora de Atocha.[7]
The ocean voyage was arduous beyond description, and I, a mere novice at sea, suffered unbelievably from seasickness. Indeed, from moment to moment I thought to expire amidst the tossing and heaving of the ship in the fearful storms we encountered in the great crossing. Yet by the grace of God I survived the six-week ordeal and after stops in Santo Domingo and Havana disembarked at last in Vera Cruz of New Spain where my fellow Franciscans awaited my arrival. Their cheerful and pious companionship, the feel of solid ground under my shaky feet, and the replenishment of my spent physical strength with wholesome food and drink soon restored my spirits as well, and four days later we set off on foot for Puebla and thence to the great city of Mexico.
There we received new assignments. With two of my new

211

companions, Fray Marcos and Fray Benito, I was ordered to journey into the far northern territories to a newly established town called San Cristóbal, said to be the site of a miracle. We three were to be the vanguard of a larger company to follow. For in that remote mountain wilderness my superiors thought to establish a monastery and by the grace of God to convert the heathens of that untamed frontier to the true faith.

From the moment we set out, however, hardship dogged our steps. Our wise and gentle companion Fray Benito fell ill in Querétaro and despite our fervent prayers and earnest ministrations, he departed this life the tenth day of March 1631.

Fray Marcos and I were plunged into great sadness and perplexity. Ought we to continue our journey or return to Mexico City so as to receive fresh instructions and perhaps additional companions? I favored the latter option, Fray Marcos, the former, and because he had the stronger will and greater force of character, we prevailed on the authorities of Querétaro to relay the sad news of Fray Benito to our order in Mexico City and then resumed our northward journey along the Camino Real. After several weeks and much privation we reached a river of a volume of water similar to the Tajo which they call El Grande and a village named El Paso del Río. There Providence favored us with a stout company of soldiers and several families of settlers bound for San Juan de los Caballeros. After a delay of some weeks we resumed our northward march.

Only a few days had elapsed in October when we reached a crossroads called Doña Ana. There we took our leave of the settlers and most of the soldiers whose destination would take them many leagues further north. There we rested from our travels for two days. Then in the company of five stalwart soldiers who volunteered to escort us, we proceeded along an Indian trail through the Mimbres Mountains towards San Cristóbal. We arrived after an eight-day march across sere, inhospitable plains and densely forested mountains wherein resided strange birds and beasts, the likes of which I had never seen in Spain. I shall not soon forget the terror we felt upon encountering a whitish bear exceeding a large donkey in size. Mayhap we had all perished had not the brave Fray Marcos boldly advanced towards the creature with crucifix extended. Unable to stand before this symbol of divine power the great beast turned and with a horrendous roar fled into the forest.[8] Deaf to our earnest pleas that they remain with us until we should be better oriented and able to determine the conditions and needs of the people, no sooner had the soldiers witnessed the devastation of San Cristóbal than they resolved to hasten towards the town of Socorro in the hopes of intercepting their comrades and the settlers. They justified their desertion by explaining that they must inform Commander Chacón y Salazar of Apache depredations in this sector.

For we found San Cristóbal in a state of total calamity. Not long before our coming, marauding savages thought to be invading Comanche clans or perhaps Apaches had burned the town and Shrine, destroyed or stolen its food, and slain or taken captive fully a third of its two hundred souls. Their beloved priest Father José was among the dead. Most of the young men and women were counted among those taken captive, and the ablest men lost their lives striving vainly to save them. Since that dreadful day San Cristóbal was reduced to a joyless, fearful village of elders and children who huddled hungry in the ruins. Weakened by famine, age, and grief, many of the survivors had taken ill, and weekly the count of burials increased.

The decimated population welcomed us with tears of joy and thanksgiving, and were heartily persuaded that we were come in divine answer to their supplications for the salvation of their colony. It was truly heartrending to see them vainly imploring the cowardly soldiers to remain. Nevertheless, under Fray Marcos's manly leadership and saintly altruism we did what we could to save them. He organized the remaining able-bodied men and instructed the majority to begin the repair or salvage of standing structures, giving priority to the burned-out Shrine of Our Lady. For, as he steadfastly proclaimed, the house of God must come first. The others he sent to gather wood and to hunt, fish, and scavenge for additional provender. For winter was upon us and without more nourishment the townfolk surely would not live to see the spring. With the help of the women he gathered, inventoried, and rationed all available food, bedding, and clothing.

Inasmuch as I had some acquaintance with medicine and nursing—having attended the sick in a cholera outbreak in Burgos of Old Castile in 1624—my main task was to minister to the ill and dying. I did so as best I could, and when many of the afflicted passed from this life I explained to the men the importance of deep burials, lest the town be infested with cholera and plague.

Fray Marcos labored as one obsessed, foregoing sleep and food in his determination to save the people of San Cristóbal. I shared his fervor but, alas, not his strength. Often as he worked far into the night I was forced to lay head on pillow in complete exhaustion.

With late March came warmer days and the first greening of trees. The worst was over for the hundred fifteen survivors, and not long thereafter a company of soldiers struggled over the snowy mountain passes bringing precious supplies and medicines and the welcome news that twenty new families would arrive as soon as the snows melted.

Yet even as springtime lifted our spirits we were dismayed and saddened by the unexpected illness of Fray Marcos. For months he had demonstrated strength and perseverance far above the ordinary powers of men—gifts I doubt not that were granted him in answer to his impassioned prayers—and when the worst had passed for San Cristóbal he settled again to the level of common mortality, now greatly overspent from his mighty labors.

I wept many tears over my beloved brother Marcos and importuned Heaven with fervent prayers that he might be spared to the town's great need and that I be taken in substitution. As for Fray Marcos himself he lived out his final hours in serenest peace, bestowing blessings on the weeping town folk. When in anguish and despair I dared question the divine power for taking him before his time, he gently reminded me that our lives are not our own and that the will of God plays out too high for us to understand his workings. But he reassured me the purposes of the Almighty are good and more than worthy of our faith and trust. Then as the end neared he whispered these words that are burned forever in my very soul: "Do not despair, Brother Domingo. There is a further purpose for you here. It will be revealed to you soon." Then he closed his eyes and departed this vale of tears for a sure and certain reward. Though I protested any consideration for myself, in order to honor us the towns-people renamed their city San Cristóbal de los Frailes [Saint Christopher of the Friars].

Deeply we mourned his death and strove to continue as best we could the work he had begun. With his passing the duties he had so ably assumed fell to me, and the weight of them was intolerable to one so frail of frame and timid of temperament. For this reason I spent many long hours in fervent prayer that I might be strengthened for the task.

One night as I was kneeling by my bed an illumination appeared in the darkened room and grew in intensity until it was too bright to look upon. I shrank back in reverent awe and intimate terror. Then a shape commenced to form and a being whose face shone brighter than the supernaturally white luminescence about it towered over me. It was much larger than my small room yet seemed not to be in any fashion hampered by its material confines.

No words were spoken, at least none I heard, but the being, which was surely the Blessed Mother, extended its hands towards me. It was then I saw that she was holding a quill and a scroll of paper and seemed to desire that I take them. But as I reached for them, the image commenced to recede and fade and soon the room was dark again.

Long I pondered the vision until at last I drifted into sleep. Then the mighty things I had witnessed were converted into a long, agitated dream. The next day I awoke with a vivid recollection of the experience, but within the hour it began to dissipate. Soon I was busied the urgent tasks at hand and thought about the apparition only sporadically.

A week passed without repetition of the vision, and I decided that it was but a dream rendered particularly vivid by my grieving state. Then without warning, the being reappeared three nights later, again proffering scroll and quill but again disappearing as soon as I reached for them.

These luminous visitations, sit venia verbis (if I may use the words), continued off and on for nearly a month. I knew not what they portended, but feared instead for my very sanity.

Nor were my concerns without foundation. Word came from the south and eventually soldiers brought the news to San Cristóbal de los Frailes that due to the growing turbulence on the northern frontier, the Order had abandoned plans to establish the monastery. Furthermore, so as to complete their records my superiors in Mexico City desired information from Commander Chacón y Salazar about the manner in which the friars Marcos and Domingo had perished. Thus, in the eyes of my superiors I was accounted as deceased and my name erased from the roll of the living. And Heaven alone knew when, if ever, the error should be corrected so that my name might be counted again in the world of flesh and blood. For as the Spanish say:

Las cosas de palacio andan despacio
(Palace affairs go exceedingly slow)

By then, however, having become resigned to my fate, I reasoned that if God had brought me to San Cristóbal, then here I would serve as best I could. Moreover, daily our material circumstances improved, and as the weeks passed without further nocturnal visions to disturb my sleep, my disposition grew ever more hopeful and resilient.

Then, without warning, the luminous being returned, and although I cannot say in truth that I understood its intentions with my mortal senses, yet I was made aware of its displeasure with my obtuseness. For once again as I reached for the proffered quill and paper, the luminosity faded and the earthly darkness of my room returned.

Greatly disturbed by this mysterious apparition and overburdened by the fear of disobeying Divine Providence, I could not but confess my apprehensions to the village elders, for the burden of them was intolerable. These, however, simple souls that they are, signed themselves and offered no worthwhile advice but shared only my perplexity.

But God in His wondrously inscrutable ways often chooses to put the greatest wisdom in the mouth of the most unassuming persons. For having eavesdropped—as was her infernal custom—on my conversations with the village elders, the good but unlettered Dolores, busied as always with her cooking and cleaning, approached me timidly after their departure with these words:

"Pardon my boldness, Father Domingo, but it is plain that the Holy Mother is displeased because you have not done as she desires."

"And pray, good woman, what is that?" I asked in astonishment at her words.

"Why, Padre Domingo," she answered in surprise, "your very words—which by happenstance I overheard—tell plainly what the Blessed Mother desires. You are to obtain quill and paper to write down her message."

Somewhat wounded in my petty vanity, my first impulse was to ignore Dolores, who often irritated me with her gossip and meddlesome curiosity. But upon thinking better of the peculiar circumstance, I was struck by the simple reasonableness of her words. That night I placed quill and parchment at my bedside and accounted myself prepared to receive the supernatural apparition. For two nights nothing happened, then on the third, the now familiar luminosity flooded the room as I prayed, this time pointing to the implements I had procured.

I heard no voice, as men hear voices, yet the words that now you will hear came to me plainer than any ever formed on human tongue. I therefore wrote them as they were made known to me:

Of Things Present

Know, Domingo, that you stand on consecrated ground. This place was ever my preference, and from here I shall not be removed. Here I shall again abide when the time and season are right for it.

Domingo, the powers that now hold sway over this land are unsubstantial and unblessed and will soon be overthrown. Here kingdom shall follow kingdom in the passing way of this world. Yet San Cristóbal de los Frailes shall survive to serve a greater purpose.

Do thou, Domingo, the best and purest works according to the sacred truths thou hast been taught since thy youth. For these only abide, as those works endure in eternal favor that partake of them.

Here the message ended, the illumination faded, and I was alone again in my room. The next morning, upon reading what I had written, I found it to be so different a hand and so alien to my comprehension of things that almost nothing registered in my poor understanding. Three nights later, however, these initial perplexties paled before the much greater ones I penned in the second message:

Of Things to Come

Know, Domingo, that in ages to come lawless and cunning men, slaves of the Evil One, will devise many wondrous artifices. But think not that these creations surpass the will and plan of the Almighty who bendeth all things to his purpose. Thus it is that those acts conceived in lawless estrangement from His righteous will yet serve his greater glory.

Know of a certainty that in a time to come when there shall be great need and decline of true faith in the world, one will come to San Cristóbal bringing gold for the rebuilding of my shrine, though that purpose be not revealed to him and his thoughts be fixed on unholy intentions. Expect him the day that Marcos departed. This is a promise made for thy faithfulness and for the intercessory love of Marcos: As long as the age lasts, the shrine shall stand as a sign of favor and an example for generations yet unborn. Consecrate holy things in this shrine, and let those truly repentant and pure of heart pray within it and in their reverence many shall be healed of their infirmities.

Know also, Domingo, that in an age to come men shall no longer ride on breathing beasts, nor harness living creatures for draft but will mount on winged metal instruments and speed across the land or fly through the skies quicker and higher than the soaring eagle. Whining machines faster than the swiftest horse will race over great highways and still larger conveyances will roar over metal roadways. Noise shall greatly increase, for loudness and rushing about are the companions of sinfulness. Structures as tall as mountains shall spring up. Men shall speak to one another over vast distances and their very voices and images shall be sent and received far beyond their physical sight and hearing. Yet for all his cunning, man will live in fear as famine and epidemics prove to be too great for human remedy.

Know also that in ages far ahead San Cristóbal de los Frailes shall grow into a great city. For the Almighty has selected this site on which to manifest glorious and miraculous works.

Yet the Evil One resteth not. In years that shall witness the splendor of San Cristóbal de los Frailes there shall descend suddenly from the heavens a great abomination—

Here I must say to you, gentle reader, I left off translating the prophecies, and you will understand why I did so when I tell what I found in them. It was plain to me that his many sufferings and travails had demolished poor Fray Domingo's reason, and therefore I judged it to be the greater favor to his honor rather to silence his overwrought ravings than to reveal them in dishonor to his revered memory. For as my eye raced in horrified fascination over several succeeding pages I saw mention of things impossible save in the maddest delirium. In his insanity he wrote of devices far too wondrous and powerful for the finite mind of man to create, of arms and weapons too horrendous to conceive, of luminous cities vast beyond imagining, of the harnessing of powers more subtle than lightning, of travel faster than a beam of light or an evil thought, of the fell commingling of man and beast, of dangerous inversions and journeys to and fro within the river of time itself, of the creation of a race of beings remote from kinship to living men, of the duplication of life, of the discovery of dread immortal secrets hidden from human knowledge since the foundation and fall of the world, of prodigies, in sum, which if true should seem to call into question the very sovereignty of God over the world.

What other fantastical prophecies were contained in the final pages of the strange document I cannot say, for my courage left me and I could not bring myself to read further than I have said, lest my reason also fail even as his abandoned the good Fray Domingo. (And would to God that I had never set eyes at all on these prophecies! For oft at night as I look at the stars and ponder the meaning and destiny of things those unwholesome prophecies intrude upon my thoughts, and though I am consoled by knowing them to be false, yet I confess that I have never rested as easy since I gained intelligence of them. There are things it were better not to know. Often I yearn for my first ignorance.)

I doubt not that the good Fray Domingo believed the Holy Mother revealed to him these monstrous things, yet rather than lend them credence, it were more reasonable to suppose that surely the Fiend himself took on her guise to seed his overwrought mind with deceptive lies. For is it not written in the Holy Scriptures that Evil One oft assumes an angelical appearance thereby seducing even the devout? At least that is what Father Branigan taught me. And Jett Hale, the Memphis preacher, also warned of the Devil's clever wiles.

But these doubts and queries were destined to remain forever suspended by what happened a few days later. Under circumstances that none could explain, don Jerónimo found the charred and still smoldering

218

remains of the prophecies on the floor of his office. Someone had opened and removed them from the locked strongbox wherein they customarily resided. Yet don Jerónimo had the only key, and he was above suspicion. On this puzzling matter, dear reader, I shall not speculate further.

Hoping to discredit the vanished prophecies and thus rescue my treasure from the sanctimonious intentions of the parishioners, not without considerable trepidation and circumspection I expressed my reservations to don Jerónimo and the curious townspeople.

"But, Father Pedro," objected don Jerónimo, "what you say may be so, and indeed our fathers and forefathers always warned us not to delve deeper into the prophecies than those concerning our time and place, for the others spoke of ages yet to come. But to the point: Is it not true that you appeared to us on the appointed day, bringing with you coinage to rebuild our shrine to the Virgin of San Cristóbal just as Fray Domingo foretold?"

"But the money is mine!" I blurted out angrily, not weighing the dangerous effect of my words.

An unpleasant murmur ran through the assemblage, and on don Jerónimo's dark features I saw indignant anger flash.

"No, Father Pedro," he rebuked me, "the money is not yours, but is now become the property of the Shrine of Our Lady of Guadalupe, money promised to this parish long ago in the prophecies and for which we have waited these many years. No, Father, we like not that you speak of deception at all in the prophecies now lamentably lost forever, but the deceiver were you should you try to keep for yourself what the Virgin promised for a better cause."

Mindful of the peril in which I had placed myself, I sought for soothing words to extricate myself.

"Forgive me, don Jerónimo and good people of San Cristóbal. I misspoke myself, as I sometimes do in the Castilian tongue, which as you know is not my first language. Of course the money does not belong to my person. How could it? I have renounced all such material claims. I meant to say, but regretfully said poorly, that I must have a voice in the use and dispensation of the money. For all that my coming was foretold in the prophecies, there is yet a mundane dimension to this matter. My superiors are men as reverent in faith as they are practical in material affairs, and having entrusted me with this mission, they will require of me a careful accounting of my actions here."

"It will much please us to have your help and advice, Father Pedro," answered don Jerónimo in a conciliatory voice, even though I yet read uncertainty and suspicion in his eyes.

From that time forth the reverential esteem in which the people of San Cristóbal had formerly held me commenced to diminish, and I believe some hinted darkly that perhaps I had to do with the destruction of the prophecies. I deny it. In any case I was certain that much speculative gossip about me was afoot. I knew that my days amongst them were in few numbered and I began to think on a suitable opportunity to retrieve the former high esteem I enjoyed so briefly or, failing to do so, to make a discreet if not profitable departure.

An unexpected opportunity soon presented itself. One day as I was inspecting how work on the Shrine was progressing and calculating how well and far the gains I had made would serve me, I felt a tug on my sleeve as a gravelly voice implored me, "Attend me, Father, for I am sorely in need."

I turned and regarded the most wretched living man that ever my eyes had beheld. He was dressed in rags and rested his weight on a pair of worn crutches. His graying, untrimmed beard reached nearly to his waist. Of shoes he had none, and by the look of his gnarled, callused feet had limped unshod over many a rough road. A filthy, tattered sarape covered the rest of his drawn, palsied frame.

"What would you ask of me, my son?" I asked, involuntarily withdrawing my robe from his vile touch.

"Alms, Father, alms, that I may eat and retain mortal life in this ruined frame, for I famish to the edge of death," he responded, holding out a claw-like hand for aid.

"It is not the practice here to give alms, but to receive them," I responded haughtily. "Take your begging to the streets. There you will find pilgrims who seek to do good by helping those less fortunate than themselves."

"Perhaps there is some service I could render you, Father?" he answered with a glint of sly cunning in his eyes.

"And pray, what might you in your lowly condition do for me in mine?"

"Father," he responded gravely, settling his lean frame into a nearby pew, "I have been known to cause healing miracles."

I laughed at his absurd assertion. "I would say that you are poor proof of your claims."

"What you say is true, Father, for I have suffered evil reverses of late. Yet there is talk in the streets that your fortunes have also declined. Could we not, therefore, both profit from a miraculous intervention in our affairs?"

His words and brazen manner piqued my curiosity, and with

misgivings I escorted the limping derelict into my chamber. No sooner began we to talk without pretense than we understood each other through that mysterious affinity whereby thieves unfailingly recognize those of their brotherhood. Whereupon he set his crutches by, straightened his shoulders, and in an instant was transformed from a picture of abject decrepitude into the image of a stalwart brigand, by the look of him not much above forty years in age. He knew my situation as well as I and offered me a means of remedying my deteriorated standing in San Cristóbal. I was, in fine, in need of a redeeming miracle, as he put it, and he in want of bare essentials. I was to leave the "miracle" to him and he would rescue us both.

By happenstance it fell to me to say a mass the following day in rededication of the Shrine. I viewed the sacrilege with extreme agitation. For I have explained to you before, gentle reader, that despite my misdeeds it was never my intention to show disrespect for holy things. Yet my desire to reverse my fortunes overruled this trepidation, for to refuse the request would but confirm the doubts already circulating abroad about me. Furthermore, I was doubly nervous, wondering what "miracle" Sigifredo Baca—for so the derelict was named—would perform for our alleged mutual benefit.

Years had passed since Father Olmos, the last and long departed priest, said his final mass in the Shrine of Our Lady of Guadalupe. Now there was a grand expectancy as almost the entire population of San Cristóbal crowded into the newly restored structure. Thus it was that before the altar I had no choice but to bless the elements and say Latin words remembered from my studies with Father Branigan, silently thanking Providence for the saving ignorance of my parishioners. For as it is said:

> The charlatan rules
> In a kingdom of fools

I was concluding the mass and thinking with much relief of spirit that I was but minutes away from the welcome end of my charade when Sigifredo Baca made his appearance. He had outdone himself in wretchedness: His clothes were even more tattered, his person more drawn than when he first presented himself to me. With grotesque lurching and swaying he limped forward noisily on his crutches, his face uplifted as though in a mystical trance. Reaching the altar to the awed silence of the congregation, he abandoned his crutches and fell prostrate, stretching forth a bony hand to touch the hem of my garment. Seizing it, he brought it to his lips, kissed it reverently and fell back limply at altar's edge as though mortal life had departed his body.

But then he stirred, opened his eyes, sat up, and slowly got to his feet, his former bent frame erect and his legs now firm and strong and his face aglow with joy. The assembly murmured its astonishment.

Before the congregation could react to Sigifredo's miracle, however, a drawn, elderly woman, the last of the parishioners to partake of the bread, cried out and fell limply to the stone floor. Her family and friends rushed to her aid, but after a moment she arose no worse for the fall. On the contrary, ecstatically she proclaimed herself healed of a deformity that had bent her nearly double since girlhood. And she stood erect to prove her claim.

"Healed! Healed!" shouted the congregation. "The lame beggar has cast away his crutches, and doña Mercedes is cured of her hump! These are miracles!" The cry went round and round the Shrine, and a chorus of voices raised praises to the Virgin. Without waiting for me to give a facsimile of a nunc dimittis, the congregation began streaming out into the plaza, proclaiming the miracles to one and all.

Nor subsided the excitement over these extraordinary happenings but instead soon spread abroad through the countryside to other towns and villages. Not many days elapsed before lame, diseased, and curious pilgrims began arriving to see these prodigies, make vows, and seek healing for themselves or their loved ones. The walls of the Shrine were soon festooned with dijes attesting to other miraculous cures. It is true that after a few days doña Mercedes no longer stood quite erect and some of her ancient hump returned, but not to the same degree and in any case not nearly enough to check the holy hysteria. The townspeople were fiercely proud of their miracles and were not about to explain them away. As for Sigifredo, he was anxious to leave San Cristóbal at once for fear that he might be recognized and held accountable for his many chicaneries elsewhere.

"You promised me one miracle but generously gave me two," I laughed as I counted out the agreed-on sum of money for Sigifredo.

"Father, I must confess something to you," he replied in a grave tone I had not heard from him earlier. "The miracle of doña Mercedes was not my doing. Beware, Father, there is a power at work here greater than human cleverness. Be careful, lest it bring you down and consume you."

I little heeded and soon forgot Sigifredo's warning as I urged his early departure from San Cristóbal. All doubts about me were forgotten in the frenzy, and again I was a revered and respected personage. People

222

bowed to me and kissed my hand, and old men and women fell to their knees before me, imploring my blessing and comparing me favorably to the legendary friars Marcos and Domingo. Meanwhile, work on the Shrine of the Virgin of San Cristóbal continued, and within a fortnight the carpenters and masons had completed their labors. Rumors circulated of other miraculous cures, and even though I witnessed none of them and could not reliably testify to their authenticity, yet in the end the public apotheosis of these events, real or merely wishful, worked its effect on me also. I waxed almost as credulous as the rest of San Cristóbal de los Frailes. For the ancient rule held true: The liar becomes the substance of his lies.

Nevertheless, despite this heady excitement my customary acquisitive instincts did not abandon me. My earlier intention to leave San Cristóbal at the first opportunity now gave way on second thought to a consideration of the happy advantages I enjoyed and others that were within my grasp. For one thing, the carpenters outfitted my quarters with considerable comforts, and I was everywhere welcomed and fed. My opinions were heeded as though they were the very oracles of the Most High. Contributions commenced to pour into the church, and pilgrims plied me with private donations because of my newly elevated status. I accepted their presents, especially those of a pecuniary nature, in the name of the Virgin and the parish and promised to apply them faithfully to holy purposes. Naturally, as a man of the cloth, I considered myself numbered amongst the most holy. Soon I was become all but a living icon, as it were, in the town and surrounding country such that no one would have dared question my ecclesiastical stature. Having risen above scrutiny—or so I thought—in no long lapse of days I amassed a respectable replacement for my lost treasure, and my hoard was growing apace.

Certain other privileges, I hesitate to confess for fear of embarrassing my loved ones, also presented themselves for my plucking. Plentiful food soon fleshed out my frame, and public adulation engendered in me an unaccustomed sense of power and invincibility. With careful grooming of my beard and hair my appearance experienced an appealing renaissance. In short, I was soon acclaimed to be not only saintly in spirit but by some admirers, I am vain to say, angelic in physical appearance as well.

These opinions, innocently spoken by most, were insinuated with less pious intentions by some of my worshipful female visitors, for it has ever been true that power and position attract the fair sex as surely as nectar lures honeybees. Insofar as I was able, I scolded these wayward daughters—especially the less comely—with righteous severity and bade them forego earthly lusts for a greater reward in the next life. But in a few other instances, dear reader, it did not seem meet of me to reject the fairest creations that Heaven itself had placed at my disposal and thereby risk committing the sin of supererogation by pretending a piety greater than that of the very patriarchs of old. Convinced, therefore, by this evangelical logic and impelled by lusty urges, I allowed myself occasional romps in Eden with the fairest of Mother Eve's daughters.

Within weeks San Cristóbal was prospering and growing as never before. Posadas sprang up to provide food and lodging for the throngs of pilgrims, and shops, stables, and stalls were erected to cater to their needs. Whereas the Shrine of our Lady of Guadalupe had languished for generations, now proudly refurbished it gleamed alabaster white, its pews and altars restored and its broken, porous walls and roof repaired and rebuilt. Vendors hawked images of the new shrine in the congested plaza, and women filled the air with pungent smoke and aroma of tamales and tacos. Wagons and carts arrived daily with merchandise and provisions, and local farmers now sold their produce at prices unthinkable only a few weeks earlier.

Rising apace in esteem with the new fortunes of San Cristóbal, I soon reached the very apogee of my power and influence. Gorgeously garbed in the handsomest robes, I said mass in a Latin characterized by sensational intonations and dramatic pauses that were all the more admired the less the words were understood. But I do not boast when I say that a truer eloquence enlivened my sermons and homilies, the which I laced with apocalyptical imagery and delivered in a mode remembered from Jett Hale's sermons in Memphis. In other words, I was now a Catholic clergyman by office and a Protestant preacher by style. Time and again I heard it said admiringly: "Not in vain do they say that the Franciscans are the best preachers." Warming to the office, I performed weddings, conducted funerals, and heard dozens of tawdry confessions. For the most part I resisted the temptations learned during my days as an undertaker, yet I was not above confiscating from the dead a handsome trinket here or there, reasoning that they would more usefully serve the needy living than the indifferent deceased.

Then occurred the crowning wonder. As workmen prepared foundations for the new buildings one of them struck an object with his shovel. Digging around it, a stone arm and torso appeared. Excitement grew as the figure was retrieved and cleaned. Then a cry went up and a chorus of voices repeated it the length and breadth of San Cristóbal: "It is Our Lady of Guadalupe! She is restored to us! She never left us, and evil men could not remove her, for her power is greater than theirs!"

For days thereafter the town lived in a continual euphoria. And if the rebirth of San Cristóbal de los Frailes was lively before, with the discovery of the buried Virgin the townspeople became evangelical in their pace and zeal.

I rose to the pinnacle of power and influence, but my standing was not without its private inconveniences. I was busier than ever with confessions, homilies, absolutions, weddings, and a thousand other things that demanded my precious time.

The mention of confessions brings to memory again a singular admission made to me that was so different from the usual banalities of the confessional that never in all the many years since have I forgotten it. I had spent—or wasted—a glorious April afternoon dispensing my usual false absolutions to repentant old women for their malicious gossip and vulgar disputes. Because so few men confessed and then only for more interesting and lascivious reasons, I took more than usual notice when a man who looked to be about forty-five years old began his confession with these words:

"Father, forgive me for I have killed a man, and I would tell you the why and how of the deed, if you would hear me."

His words produced a nervous shock in me, and I sat bolt upright. There, not more than a few centimeters away, were the lean, rough hands of a murderer. From the confessional I stared at the side of his face visible in the shadows, trying to discover in his features some revealing trait that separated him from common men. The practiced words dropped mechanically from my lips:

"Confess your sins, my son, for God forgives those who truly repent of their errors. Ave María Purísima" (Hail, Mary most pure).

"Sin pecado concebida (Conceived without sin). Willingly I confess them, Father, though repentance is a harder matter, as you will understand if you hear my story."

I bade him continue and in a tone that betrayed a soul much acquainted with suffering he told me the following tale:

The Murderer's Confession

My name, Father, is Mariano Otero. I was born and lived my early life on the prosperous hacienda of don Cayetano Aranda that spread for several leagues along both banks of the Nazas River as it flows west from Torreón. For many generations my family had served the Arandas loyally as charros (ranch hands) and capataces (foremen). Father replaced grandfather, and son succeeded father in a proud, unbroken line.

225

The Arandas repaid the loyalty of all their workers with Christian charity and affection, ministering to them during illness, providing a school for their children, and giving gifts for saints days and first communions. In truth we loved and respected them with a devotion that rose above our differences of class and station in the world.

Nowhere was this hereditary bond between our families warmer or more evident than in the friendship that united me to Alvaro Luis Aranda y Figueroa, the only son of don Cayetano and his wife doña Catalina. As we grew up together, I was fiercely proud to walk and ride beside him and hear him tell others of our friendship. Willingly I would have put my hands in the fire for him, so great was my devotion and gratitude. For in truth our gifts were greatly unequal. He was taller and stronger than I, though we were near in age to each other, and as a horseman and marksman he had no peer in all the haciendas of that country, nor could any youth match him in demonstrations of strength and daring. In contrast to the stern and morally correct don Cayetano, Alvaro, who was as handsome as his mother doña Catalina was beautiful, soon gained further fame as an irresistible seducer, and many stories were told of his conquests of maidens and married women alike.

I, on the other hand, was only passably adequate in the skills expected of a capataz and charro and entirely wanting in the qualities for winning the fair sex. Yet my father taught me the former with patience such that in time I overcame my awkwardness and achieved a level of competence that don Cayetano himself saw fit to praise. It was a matter of great pride for our family to hear him acclaim me as the worthy successor to my ancestors and future foreman of the hacienda. But as to the latter qualities I spoke of, they were beyond my father's ability to teach, and I remained as timid and tongue-tied as ever when it came to señoritas.

Disturbed by Alvaro's many amorous scandals and dangerous escapades and seeking to curb and discipline his reckless nature, in 1806 don Cayetano sent his eighteen-year-old son to study in Mexico City and thence abroad to complete his education and acquaint him with the civilizing cultures of Europe. For nearly six years I barely saw Alvaro at all. From time to time in response to our inquiries, don Cayetano would relay news of him from Madrid, Paris, or Rome.

Meanwhile, despite my clumsiness with women, I met and fell in love with Lupita Mendoza, the shy, pretty seventeen-year-old daughter of don Marcelino Mendoza, a retired and widowed Torreón magistrate who shared a passion for the chase with don Cayetano and often came to the hacienda for hunting trips to the sierra. Because doña Catalina had no daughters of her own, she persuaded don Marcelino to leave her goddaughter Lupita in her care on these occasions so that she might spoil her with gifts, dresses, and the maternal affection that only a woman could offer.

Having led a cloistered life in a convent school in Torreón in complete innocence of the outer world, Lupita thrilled to the newly discovered beauties of nature and often asked permission to take long carriage rides through the hacienda and surrounding countryside. Although doña Catalina was always ready to indulge her goddaughter, household responsibilities often did not leave time for her to accompany her charge. On these occasions doña Catalina would ask me to escort Lupita.

It is unnecessary, Father, to describe to you the profound impress that Lupita's innocent charms and joyous nature made on my heart. She was able with a look or a word to dispel my grave disposition and bring an unused smile to my lips. Suffice it to say that I fell so completely in love with her that no other woman would ever hold any appeal for me. So strong, indeed, was my love that eventually it overcame my customary shyness and our differences of class, and I confessed my feelings to her and my earnest desire to be her husband.

She reacted with surprise, nay, more, with astonishment, Father, for such sentiments were as yet unknown to her. Withal, she responded nobly and sincerely, as was her wont, that although she esteemed and trusted me as a dear friend, she did not feel the love for me that she had read of in books or heard as gossip from other girls. She protested that class differences meant nothing to her and that her respect for me was limitless.

I was not discouraged by her rejection of my proposal but instead deemed myself highly favored to be counted as her friend. I did not again mention my amorous feelings but rather redoubled my courteous and respectful attentions and sought in every way to merit her high regard. As time passed and our friendship deepened she confided her feelings, especially concerns for her father's health.

These worries were not unfounded. As her eighteenth birthday approached, the venerable don Marcelino took to his deathbed. His one remaining worldly concern was for Lupita's welfare, and he regretted to leave her alone without the affection and protection of a good husband. Thereupon she dutifully made known to him my feelings for her. At first don Marcelino expressed misgivings about my inferior standing, but upon receiving reassurances from don Cayetano concerning my Christian character, loyalty, and my family's modest but solid material holdings, forthwith he became my advocate and gave his blessing to our union. To our great sorrow, only days thereafter he expired with full rites of the Church and comforting reassurances from the weeping don Cayetano and doña Catalina that henceforth Lupita would live at the hacienda where she would be loved and wedded to me as their own daughter.

Alas, Father, what man proposes to his happiness oft goes awry to his misery. At that fateful moment in 1812 the long absent Alvaro returned from his travels. Taller and handsomer than we remembered him, to his native charm he added Old World sophistication and flourish. His parents were delighted, and don Cayetano, himself rapidly declining in strength and health, thought only of turning over the affairs of the hacienda to his prodigal son. As for doña Catalina, she hoped to see him promptly married and dreamed optimistically of numerous grand-children.

As fate would have it, therefore, Alvaro and Lupita coincided in their arrival at the hacienda, and no sooner had they met than Alvaro, indifferent to my prior claims to her heart and more polished and pro-ficient than ever in the seductive arts, at once commenced to bedazzle her. Within days she became distant and distracted in our conversations. I pressed her as to the reason for her change of mood, and unable to dissemble, she tearfully confessed her love for Alvaro, though out of loyalty to me and in obedience to her late father's instructions she intended to honor her promise to marry me.

With a broken heart I offered to stand aside. At first Lupita was unwilling to see me suffer. In her distraught state she sought the counsel of doña Catalina, who in her anxiety to see her volatile son settled in marriage ignored my plight and advised Lupita to accept Alvaro instead. Returning to me with this advice, she asked permission to end her betrothal. I granted her wish, pledging my friendship and help, if ever she should have need of them.

They were wed and less than a year later Lupita gave birth to a daughter, Raquel, as beautiful as herself. They honored me with a request to be her godfather.

At first Alvaro was devoted to Lupita, and despite my personal pain I took pleasure in witnessing their happiness from afar. But soon Alvaro began to slip back into his old vices now made worse by his scorn of our provincial ways. Before many months had passed he tired of Lupita and his daughter and began drinking and gambling in the local taverns. Gossip commenced to circulate of new mistresses.

This unhappy news and Alvaro's wanton behavior, which in every respect was so alien to his own high code of conduct, accelerated don

Cayetano's rapid decline, and before two more years had passed we mourned his death as the loyal friend and generous patriarch he had always been. Nor did doña Catalina long survive him. Distressed by the loss of her husband and driven to near insanity by the scandalous behavior of her son, she soon took her place beside don Cayetano in the cemetery.

Thereupon Alvaro dropped all pretense of responsibility and began an orgy of drinking and dissipation. The hacienda was soon mortgaged and jeopardized, for though my father and I tried our best to maintain it, we could not stanch the financial drain caused by Alvaro's excesses. To worsen matters, wily bankers took advantage of us, and we lost most of our own money in the futile effort.

Lupita was mortified and humiliated by her husband's brutal, abusive behavior and cynical disregard of the family's welfare. Determined to be true to my promise, I befriended her in every decent way I could and lavished attention on the shy and reserved Raquelita as though she were my own daughter. In truth, I looked on her as such, for she was the daughter I would never have and Lupita, the wife I would never call my own.

Despite our efforts, not many years passed before the hacienda came to utter ruin and creditors came forth to seize it from the drunken Alvaro. The neighboring haciendas could offer me no work, for the war against Spain had devastated our region. Thus it was with great sadness that I announced to Lupita that I must leave Torreón to seek my livelihood elsewhere. My own father was now in decline and too broken in body and spirit to accompany me. I made provisions for him to live near my married sister Francisca in Chihuahua and with a heavy heart left the high country of Torreón and drifted to the tropical land of Chiapas where I worked for many years on a coffee plantation. After a few years I received word from Francisca that my father had died. I wrote often to Lupita and Raquelita and treasured their infrequent responses, though unlike her mother shy Raquelita wrote but sparingly. Then after a few years their letters ceased altogether, and I had no more news of them.

Twelve years passed before I was able by hard work and frugal hoarding of my earnings to leave Chiapas and return to my ancestral Torreón. What I found there, Father, was a thing unbelievable though on my mother's honor I swear to its truthfulness.

The hacienda was vastly changed, and its present owner did not welcome my inquiries. To my questions about Alvaro Aranda he sneered that I should seek him in the streets and taverns of Torreón. There indeed

I found him, but in the most wretched state imaginable. The once princely Alvaro, now consumed by alcohol, shuffled and shook as he begged abjectly for money on the street. He seemed not to recognize me when I spoke to him, but his once handsome face twisted into a travesty of his brilliant smile when I deposited coins in his proffered cup, for his teeth were gone and his jaws shrunken.

"Mariano?" he lisped blankly, "Mariano Otero, you say? That is a name I know. I have known you somewhere, friend, long ago perhaps. Invite me to a drink and surely my memory will return. My memory revives after a drink."

We sat and he drank, and indeed he seemed to remember me after a time. But though he recalled a few of our boyhood adventures, he turned evasive when I asked him about Lupita and Raquelita. Abruptly he cursed me for meddling in his affairs and staggered out of the tavern. I turned in bewilderment to the tavern owner, who rolled his eyes in disgust.

"I overheard your name and remember your father, señor Otero, and it is a name still respected in Torreón. Only out of respect for you, señor, have I allowed Alvaro Aranda to drink in my establishment at all. For he is man who deserves no consideration, or for that matter, does not deserve to live!"

"That is a harsh thing to say, my friend. It seems odd that you, a taverner, should so condemn one whom the bottle has destroyed."

"I do not say the thing for his vice but for the much greater guilt he bears."

"And what is that?"

"You have indeed been long absent from this city not to have heard what he did to his wife and daughter."

I rose from my chair and confronted the man, who mistook my anxiety for anger.

"Do not be angry with me, señor. I am merely repeating what is common knowledge in Torreón. Ask anybody and they will tell you the same."

"The same 'what'? What did he do to his family?"

"Ah, señor, it is the saddest of stories. When Alvaro lost the hacienda, the family began a life of poverty. They took a dilapidated room in Torreón, and the lady Lupita and her daughter lived for a time on the charity of the Sisters and a few loyal friends. But Alvaro seized all they were given and used it to continue his drinking and gambling. Soon the friends tired of Lupita and Raquelita, and the Sisters of Charity refused to give them more aid for Alvaro to squander. Now indeed they were reduced to utter misery.

"It was then that Alvaro ordered them into the streets to beg. At long last the meek doña Lupita refused. But in his insane rage Alvaro gave his wife a savage beating, as he often did, and then, if the rumors be true, sold the fifteen-year-old Raquelita to a house of prostitution. There, I was told, she was auctioned to wealthy bidders, the winner paying a handsome sum for the privilege of deflowering her. Within weeks they say she was taken to Mexico City, and no one has seen or heard of her since.

"The pain and shame of it drove doña Lupita mad. For years she wandered the streets of Torreón calling for Raquelita. Malicious children tormented her in the street, and people threw her scraps to eat and rags to cover her back, but Alvaro himself made sport of her madness. Finally, they found her body in an alley and buried it in a pauper's grave. And as surely as my name is Jorge Castellano, señor, that is the reason why I will not permit Alvaro Aranda to enter my establishment, not if he had all the money in Torreón."

I left the tavern in a red, trembling rage, determined to find Alvaro and avenge Lupita and Raquelita. But as I walked the streets in search of the monster, I thought better of my unpremeditated plan to strangle him on the spot. For why should I go to prison or perhaps to my death for killing a man who, it was commonly agreed, did not deserve to live? Instead I purchased a bottle of cheap wine, opened it, poured in a generous quantity of arsenic, and replaced the cork. Then I searched the streets until I found Alvaro begging at one of his accustomed spots. He eyed me warily until I offered him the bottle with this warning:

"Alvaro, you may have this wine if you wish, but I warn you it contains poison and you will die if you drink it."

With a curse he grabbed the bottle, glared at me for a moment with a malicious hint of his former intelligence, and muttered as he fumbled to pop the cork: "I have been dead for a long time anyway, Mariano."

With that he flipped the cork aside and took a long gurgling draught, his throat pumping rhythmically as he drank. Shortly thereafter he fell to the ground and began to twitch and convulse as curious onlookers gathered to watch him die. So ended Alvaro and with him the proud, illustrious Aranda line.

The authorities conducted only the briefest of inquiries into the cause of death. Had not doctors warned him many times that drink would kill him? But, Father, they never knew the truth I tell you now, for if there was gossip that I had a hand in his death, it did not reach their ears.

I paid for his funeral out of respect for his parents and the early memories I had of him. Lupita's gravesite was unknown, so I could only have a mass said for the eternal rest of her soul. Despite my efforts, I have been unable to find my goddaugher Raquelita, yet I continue to search for her, pursuing one phantom rumor after another. For I love her like a father, and for my beloved Lupita's sake would give my life for her.

And that, Father, is why and how I killed a man.

For a moment I sat in stunned silence at the revelation I had just heard. Then remembering my expected response, I gave him absolution, lecturing him on the gravity of his crime and counseling him to confess his guilt to the civil authorities. But I required as penance for the deed that he surrender something of value. He offered a solid gold cross, which I accepted in the name of the Church and, naturally, kept for myself.

Daily my reputation for sagacity grew as the townspeople mistook my fiery rhetorical skills for wisdom. Don Jerónimo and the elders now sought my advice on other matters, for the burden of administering a municipality growing by the day was rapidly exceeding their modest talents.

Thus, dear reader, instead of slinking off in disgrace in the dead of night, as my earlier intention had been, I now thought to remain indefinitely in San Cristóbal, the better to serve God and man, most particularly the man Prosper. For never had I eaten better or resided in more comfortable quarters. Furthermore, for the first time in my life I found myself honored and respected, and that sweet, unaccustomed sensation was one I dreamed vainly of enjoying forever.

Vainly, I say again, gentle reader, for my vaporous hopes arose from so false and flimsy a foundation that I marvel at my own blindness and inability to foresee that it was doomed to collapse into ruin. Hear now how, sadly for me, my days of glory were soon ended.

One of the young women I alluded to earlier, angered by my rebuke and rejection of her unwanted attentions, spread the lie that I, taking advantage of her youth and inexperience, had made a proposal to her lewd and indecorous in its intent. Even though most of the townspeople rejected the gossip as vicious—so high was the esteem in which I was now held—nonetheless eventually it reached the ears of her cousin don Tomás Fonseca, a nephew of the Bishop. Don Tomás informed his uncle of the matter, and although the latter took little note of a peccadillo not uncommon with younger clergy, he was greatly interested in the young Franciscan whose reputation and pious commotion on the northern frontier had recently come to his attention. Learning to his dismay that no Franciscan by my name could be found in the order and with his suspicions now duly aroused, the Bishop dispatched trusted men to investigate. These, who arrived not long thereafter as unannounced pilgrims, heard my travesty of a mass and immediately took measures to put a halt to my charade.

Barely had I concluded the morning mass and the pews emptied when the Bishop's outraged agents and civil authorities from San Juan confronted me on the church steps. For a few minutes I bellowed a stentorian denial and defense as a crowd of curious onlookers gathered, but in the end I was arrested, stripped of my gaudy robe, manacled, and led away to jail, to the great consternation of the faithful and evil glee of the town gossips.

Once solidly in my favor, public opinion hastily turned against me as word of my duplicity and incarceration spread, and just as rapidly many claimed to have harbored doubts about me from the start. Some pilgrims from the north recalled how much I resembled a gambler they had seen in Santa Fe, a man by the name of Petie something or another. My fall into disgrace was as sudden as my rise to favor.

For many years dormant little San Cristóbal de los Frailes neither had detention facilities nor need of them. But when pickpockets and thieves began to infiltrate and swindle the gullible pilgrims, don Jerónimo authorized the construction of a small holding cell next to the adobe building that housed his office. No sooner was I jailed than for several days the cell rivaled the Shrine in the agitated throngs it attracted. Angered no doubt by their former gullibility, my erstwhile admirers gathered about the small window and barred door of my cell to taunt and threaten me for my chicanery. Fathers vowed to murder me upon discovering that their hysterical—and already pregnant—daughters were not truly wedded; bereaved families were outraged to learn that deceased relatives were dispatched from this world without the proper rites for entry into the next; and individuals, wed or no, worried nervously over shameful, dangerous confidences whispered in the ear of a false priest.

Don Jerónimo decided not to remand me to San Juan for trial for fear of my assassination en route, but instead sent a request to Santa Fe for a magistrate to try my case in San Cristóbal. But that would take time, if indeed the authorities honored his petition at all, and I was fearful that in the meantime the angry townsmen might execute a swifter justice before a trial. For as the old saying goes:

Quickly hanged and quickly buried,
Then villain's guilt we try unhurried.

      Thus in my wee cell I lay in this morbid apprehension as the long days of my disgrace dragged on into dreary weeks and months.

      Meanwhile, Bishop Fonseca y Pardo, who supervised my downfall and whose distaste for spontaneous outbursts of religious fervor was no secret, thought it prudent to dispatch to San Cristóbal an elderly priest of his entire confidence and trust as my replacement, lest the popular hysteria degenerate into uncontrolled pagan superstition. Father Valladares, as the venerable priest was named, soon corrected the chaos I had caused and restored order with a kindly demeanor but a firm hand.

      As weeks passed and wondrous tales circulated about miraculous cures at the newly dedicated shrine, my own epiphany in supposed fulfillment of the Fray Domingo prophecy was all but forgotten and, thankfully, even though reviled as a false priest, I was also ignored as a matter of little future consequence. Thus I languished for several months awaiting magistrate and trial, eventually even losing count of the days. To show their contempt the authorities made me subsist on coarse bread, water, and thin soups made from bone, gristle and scraps from the kitchen of the Sánchez posada. I was deprived of comb and mirror and denied the means to trim my beard and moustache. Worst of all, I was not allowed to bathe or relieve the stench of dirty, rotting clothes and accumulated filth. Water ran across the floor during infrequent rains spreading the stench from the corner where I attempted to confine it. From time to time don Jerónimo had his men dump fresh straw that served me as a bed. As the days and weeks passed, of a certainty I took on the aspect of the basest primitive, in appearance more like a beast than a man.

      At length so had my early dreads diminished to a gloomy stoicism concerning my plight and circumstance that at first I paid no heed to a great commotion in the plaza but instead dismissed the shouts as the arrival of an exceptionally large company of miracle-seeking pilgrims. It was not until I heard gunshots and terrified screams that I roused myself to take notice.

      The screams and shots were directed at a half dozen horsemen charging wildly back and forth across the plaza, trampling plants and flowers and knocking over a large statue of St. Christopher and two smaller ones of the town's legendary friars Marcos and Domingo. Concentrated in irregular, sheltered formation behind the municipal offices on one side and one of the newly erected posadas on the other, a

234

company of recently arrived soldiers and newly appointed alguaziles were trying to contain the riders in a shifting but tightening perimeter. Two riders were down from their volleys when the leader rallied them for yet another charge. So reckless and desperate was their thrust that they broke through the line of tormentors and were all but free from their peril when the leader's wounded roan stumbled, pitching its rider head-long onto the granite paving stones. The remaining riders wavered then, perceiving that he was beyond their help, galloped away to freedom.

Immediately the soldiers rushed to the street firing a few parting shots at the fleeing bandidos, then on orders from their captain they turned from that futile waste of ball and powder to examine the bodies of the downed trio. It was soon plain that the first two had expired, but the leader yet breathed. Shortly thereafter, I heard excited, angry voices. The door of my cell, closed for weeks, abruptly opened, and with rude pummelings and abundant curses the dazed and bloodied outlaw was shoved headfirst at my feet. By the look of him I judged his age to be above thirty.

As the door slammed shut again, the man groaned, rolled over, got to one knee, and bracing himself unsteadily against the wall, stood erect, towering several inches over me. Relieved that his hurts were of a superficial and easily curable kind, he then turned and looked me up and down with such unnerving intensity that I had to lower my eyes to avert his gaze.

"I have seen few men in my time in a sorrier state, hermano," he said with a handsome smile. "In truth you have the look—and smell, let me say without intending offense to your person—of one abandoned by God, man, and bath alike."

"Your surmise of my state, sir, is unhappily exact," I answered. "For I am so low fallen in the world that all I have left is my name, Pierre de Tourmoulin, and a willingness to be at your service if in any way I could."

"Your words much excel over your smell and appearance, amigo, but their tone and your name sound foreign to my ears."

I responded, giving him false details of my origin, naturally embellished with further fabrications so as to show myself in a better light.

"I have heard of you, Pierre, or Padre Pedro," he said, eying me with cynical respect, "for your exploits as the false priest of San Cristóbal de los Frailes are the talk and envy of every knave and thief in Coahuila. Indeed, you, my friend, are the principal reason we rode north."

"I? How so?" I asked in astonishment.

"Your fame and word of the miracles of San Cristóbal have spread far and wide, attracting pilgrims and their gold from the far corners of the Mexican Republic. And where the gold is, thither we come to take it."

"Then, sir, am I to assume," I asked hesitantly, "that by trade you are ... a thief?"

"Come, come, my friend, do not be afraid to speak the truth! I am not just any thief," he replied, laughing at my timidity, "but the master and prince and king of thieves. I am Bernardo Aguirre. Perhaps you have heard of me even in this remote place?"

"Who has not heard of the legendary exploits of the famous bandit don Bernardo Aguirre! A thousand tales are told of you, Señor Aguirre, many of them surely exaggerated, yet as the Americans say:

Where there's smoke there's fire."

"I do not speak much the English," responded Bernardo laughingly in that tongue, "though I know enough words to rob and to make my wants known. But you, padrecito, speak several languages and are otherwise skilled for even greater swindles than mine. For I rob with pistol and blade, but you with tongue and guile. Together we could do much mischief."

"Alas, my friend, I fear we shall not have that interesting opportunity. I have lain for months locked in this squalor, and now you, a famous bandido, will be tightly guarded until the day of your trial. Furthermore, I looked until I wearied at the locks, and even though I am an experienced pick, I could conceive no way to reach them. As you can see, they are more than arm's length below our window."

"You are dispirited by your imprisonment, my friend," responded Bernardo, shaking me gently by the shoulder. "Take heart! There will be no trial, and we shall soon be free of this wonderfully aromatic place!"

I sat up alert at his words. "Free? How so, Bernardo? There can be no acquittal for my misdeeds, and you will forgive me for saying so, but surely your crimes are sufficient to hang a dozen men."

"Have you never heard the saying, Padre Pedro,

Sólo ahorcan a los pequeños ladrones;
los grandes siempre se salvan?"
(They only hang small thieves;
The great ones always are saved)

236

"Until now, Bernardo, only in French:

Seulement les petits larrons son pendus,
Pas les grands qui se sauvent toujours.

"But I cannot see how these sayings apply to us in this dilemma."

"In this you must trust me. I have been in worse circumstances, and luck has never deserted me. Bernardo Aguirre was not destined to perish in this wretched place. I still have many roads to ride, many men to rob, many women to love before I bid this world farewell."

"There is always a first time, that is to say, a last time for every man to be executed."

"Friend, friend," he admonished me, "have done with such morbid talk! You will soon see the world differently with a full purse and a swift horse under you, and perhaps the favors of a shapely señorita."

My adopted stoicism and mournful mood soon evaporated in the presence of Bernardo's ebullient spirits, and before long we joined our voices in several lively songs and poetic recitals. Meanwhile, without our cell admiring crowds gathered anew to comment in proud, hushed voices the presence of so famous a bandido in San Cristóbal. Bernardo obliged the crowd with entertaining stories and lively jests and to the women he directed extravagant but courteous comments about their beauty and grace.

"I have known many women, Pedro," he explained, "in every sense that you may wish to understand the words, and I am proud to say that never have I shown disrespect to any. It is one of the few lessons I remember from my honored father's teachings. It is said, and well said, that Heaven laughs at lovers' perjuries, but though women are ever ripe for deceit in matters of the heart and bedchamber, yet they must also be respected because they are women, even when life has been so woeful to them that they do not respect themselves. Besides, more than one has repaid my courtesy by alerting me to danger and thus saving my life. Indeed, unless I am mistaken, such will prove to be the case now as well."

I queried him for his meaning, but he would offer no other explanation.

"Wait and you will see. Do not be agitated over the matter. Now that darkness has fallen and the crowd has departed for the day, let us sleep. My body is sore in every joint and we shall need our strength for what lies ahead of us in days to come."

With that he stretched out on the straw, folded his muscular arms across his huge chest, closed his eyes, and seemed to fall immediately asleep. But I, on the other hand, was left wide-awake to ponder the mysterious but promising portent of his words.

Two days later, around midnight as I recollect, gentle reader, I was roused from a light, dream-filled sleep by a commotion near the shrine. A crowd was quickly gathering, obscuring my direct view in the bright moonlight, but from what I could make out and deduce two men were engaged in a knife duel. Back and forth across the plaza the growing, shouting crowd surged as the fortunes of the dueling combatants rose and fell, first in favor of one, then the other. Soon the disheveled don Jerónimo, a dozen or so half-dressed soldiers, and a few bewildered alguaziles, came running to investigate and quell the disturbance.

Suddenly, our cell gave a sensible lurch, and above the din of the crowd I heard the wrenching of metal. The door opened with a screech of unused hinges, and a female voice whispered in the gloom:

"We have come, Bernardo. You are free!"

"My friend Pedro here goes with me. Have you enough horses?"

"More than enough with the extra mounts we borrowed from the alguaziles for our next diversion!"

"Then, quick, Raquelita, get on with it!" ordered Bernardo.

Using several ropes lashed to the saddles of the rearing, wild-eyed horses, the bandits tied them expertly to the reinforced cell door. Then as one of the bandits laid whiplashes across their rumps the horses bolted for the street. For an instant they were checked as the ropes tightened. The whip cracked again, and in a disorganized, neighing panic they lunged anew with greater fury. With this the cell twisted free from its foundation and was dragged tumbling and bouncing as the runaway horses raced past a posada towards the north end of San Cristóbal.

Meanwhile we had mounted and circled our horses unseen behind the municipal office. Having abandoned the duelers in the greater excitement of the runaway jail, the officials and onlookers ran screaming for its recapture. With that, the suddenly peaceful combatants sheathed their knives and ran for their waiting mounts and laughing companions. Only a few bewildered townspeople witnessed our drumming exodus via the southwest road. It would take time for don Jerónimo and the alguaziles to sort out the double deception. And time enough it proved to be for us to make good our escape.

I cannot now reckon how many hours we rode swiftly southwards, but as morning light began to break over the eastern peaks, we left the road and following a twisting, narrow trail, rode in single file westward into the higher Mimbres Mountains. After some hours we paused for an exchange of mirror signals with a scout perched halfway up a steep peak. Then satisfied that all was well, Bernardo led us forward to a stream in a dead-end canyon with sheer granite walls. I supposed that we had lost our way, and said as much to Bernardo.

"You worry too much, my friend," he laughed. "These mountains are as the palm of our hand to us. But we have a small chore to do before we end our journey and take our ease."

"And what is—?" I started to ask before two of the bandits roughly dragged me from my horse and stripped me of my rags. Instead of turning away, the woman laughed heartily and urged her horse forward to get a better look. I was mortified by her presence but helpless in their grip.

"He is indeed as filthy as you say, Bernardo," she observed. "I would not have believed the grime that covers him had not my own two eyes seen it and my nose told me. And, Patrón, with all the respect due you, after we get the horses and men inside, maybe you should return here to take your bath, also. For some of his perfume floats about you, too."

Thereupon the two ruffians dragged me into the stream and proceeded to scrub and dunk me unmercifully to the grand hilarity of the onlookers. The water was icy from the melting snows of the peaks, but when I realized their purpose my indignation vanished and I joined in the fun-making. In truth it felt good to shed months of accumulated filth. As I emerged, hair and beard dripping and my body aquiver with cold, one of the bandits tossed me new trousers and shirt. "We will get you better boots and hat later," he promised. Then looking up at Bernardo, he added with an impish sigh: "Patrón, do you think all the fish downstream will die after this?"

"It could be," laughed Bernardo, "it could be, especially when I take my bath. But better the fish die than we! Would you not agree?"

The men celebrated the humor, and Bernardo signaled us to move forward. I was puzzled. Where were we going? We had not ridden far when the trail disappeared and we dismounted at the very edge of the sheer north wall of the canyon. One of the bandits ran to a pile of dead shrub and, flinging it aside, revealed the entrance to an ancient mine. We led the horses inside, and as the man cunningly replaced the concealing shrubs, another lit a torch and led the way through the dark tunnel. A hundred meters or so deep in the mountain I saw another light ahead of us and heard echoing voices. Three bobbing torches approached us in the blackness.

"*¡Patrón! ¡Patrón!* Is it really you? My God, it's good to see you again! We thought we had lost you!" shouted a short bowlegged man, almost a dwarf, who handed his torch to a companion and ran to embrace Bernardo.

"Tacho, faithful Tacho," Bernardo answered softly, wrapping his mighty arms around the shorter man. "I have missed your companionship, old friend!"

"My heart sank within me, Patrón, when they told me you had fallen into the hands of the soldiers and alguaziles, for I feared they would celebrate the capture of Bernardo Aguirre by hanging you as a trophy from the nearest tree!"

"That tree, Tacho, wherever it be, is yet a mere seedling and uncounted years must pass ere it takes the measure of my neck! It the meantime let us live and make the most of our time! Tomorrow will take care of itself, whatever it may chance to bring us."

"Ah, Patrón, what am I to do with you? You ignore my warnings and mock my worries. But come, we have food and drink and rest for you and our friends."

Spotting me for the first time still shivering from the cold water, Tacho came over to eye me up and down. "Your friend, Patrón," he said in a rare jest, "looks as careworn as a man who has walked all day with large corns and tight boots."

Two of the younger men led the horses away into a side shaft that veered to the right whilst we continued along the main one. Eventually the dark tunnel lightened from a reflected glow far ahead, and in the distance I heard the echo of more voices. Then we emerged into a spacious semi-circular chamber with a high-vaulted ceiling. A roaring cooking fire illuminated the place and dispelled the chill of the granite. The smoke rose, swirled in a mysterious cross draft, and disappeared through a fissure in the dome. The smell of meat excited my nostrils and tantalized my empty stomach. Soon we ate delicious steak and washed it down with coarse red wine to the contentment of our hearts and the entire satisfaction of our bellies.

For two days the outlaw band ate, drank, and sang to the accompaniment of guitars. They were pleased with my skill and voice and requested so many songs of Padre Pedro, as the bandidos sarcastically called me now, that eventually my repertoire and voice were alike exhausted. Whereupon they began the boastful telling of adventures and exploits, and to believe what was said would have been to convince oneself without a doubt that never in the history of mankind had so many brave and ferocious men convened in one spot. Yet among the countless exaggerations and lies boasted by my new companions, what Raquel related when her turn came captured my keenest interest, though I did not reveal to her or the other bandidos the reason for my fascination. But you, dear reader, will understand as I relate her tale to you. I call it

Raquelita's Revenge
I was born in Torreón and spent my earliest years on our spacious and prosperous hacienda inherited from my paternal grandfather don Cayetano Aranda. My father Alvaro was his only son and my mother Guadalupe Mendoza, the only child of Magistrate Marcelino Mendoza. My grandparents died before I had memory of them, but the many stories told of their noble character and admirable generosity filled me with a posthumous love for them and a fierce pride in my ancestry. Descended on both sides from ancient Spanish nobility, since the earliest days of New Spain they were one of its foremost families.

My handsome father was acclaimed the most desirable young bachelor in the whole region of Torreón. Upon his return in 1812 after five years of study and travel in Europe, he stirred the hearts and raised the hopes of every marriageable señorita for many leagues around. But from the moment he cast eyes on my mother his heart was captivated by her beauty, and they were soon wed.

But now I must introduce into these happy circumstances the despicable Mariano Otero, a vile monster of a man who was to inflict fatal evil on my family. Not long before my father returned from his years abroad, Otero had dared to propose matrimony to my mother, even though as a mere worker and charro on our hacienda he was in every way inferior to her in class and standing. Her father had given his deathbed blessing to the union, but her godmother, my grandmother doña Catalina, dismissed his approval as evidence of his diminished reason. Outwardly cordial to Otero, secretly she contemplated the proposed marriage with horror and persuaded her to dismiss him and accept my father instead.

Otero pretended to accept graciously my mother's decision to break her betrothal, but I was to learn much later that from that very hour he conceived a murderous hatred for my father and behind his back did all in his power to harm him. Yet he ingratiated himself so skillfully with my parents that they named him godfather to me and held him to be their most trusted friend.

This intimate intercourse with our family afforded him many chances to worm his way deeper into my mother's confidence. He hovered about her, solicitous traitor that he was, ever ready to do her bidding. No favor was too small or large for him to do for her, no compliment too insignificant for him to pay her. Pretending to be my father's devoted friend, he availed every opportunity to make innuendoes touching on his flaws and slyly to impress on my mother's vulnerable mind the evil notion that he was unworthy of her love and trust.

Otero was abetted in his diabolical scheme by my mother's jealous nature, for no sooner did he hint of my father's infidelities than she took them to be fact. In truth, however, he was devoted to her and so startled and bewildered by her screaming accusations that in time he came to question her sanity and, worse, to doubt her love for him.

Sadly, these confrontations and damning suspicions became more frequent and violent. Finding no hope of remedy for her outbursts, my disillusioned father took to gambling his evenings away in the taverns. Soon his drinking was noticeable and rumors circulated of other women. Too late my mother commenced to realize the folly of her insane jealousy and promised time and again to change her behavior. But her native disposition and Otero's insinuations were too strong, and as she failed to curb her rages, alcoholism and gambling consumed my father.

Grieving over their unhappy son's vices, my grandparents soon declined and departed this life. The hacienda then passed into my father's hands, but so ravaged was he by the bottle that he neglected its maintenance and devoted himself entirely to dissipating its resources.

Meanwhile, Otero and his father, both cut from the same rotten fabric, plotted to gain possession of the hacienda. In this scheme, however, more adroit creditors outsmarted them. If there was any bitter satisfaction in the sad events that ensued it was in knowing that in the end the Oteros fell into the very trap they had laid for my family.

To the great consternation of my parents, from my earliest childhood I detested Mariano Otero. For all that he was my godfather and sought to win me with gifts and obsequious attentions, I loathed him for reasons I could not explain. Some say that children can sense the true character of a person. That may be so, but I suspect—and sometimes can nearly recall—that in my infancy I heard or saw unremembered things that shaped my morbid impressions of him. It was only because my parents urged me that I suffered his company at all. There were many unpleasant disputes between us as they labored to convince me of his goodness and I, to persuade them of his duplicity.

As my father sank deeper into alcoholism, my mother idealized her old feelings for Otero. In truth she had never loved him, yet now she gilded their friendship—for that was all ever it was at most—with such fantasies that she no longer remembered the difference. Then began she to draw unfavorable comparisons betwixt husband and suitor, and these tilted so in favor of the latter that she lamented aloud and to my father's face the mistaken choice she had made.

I was still a child, no more than ten, when utter ruin finally overtook us. Three somber officials in black attire and top hats came in a carriage to seize the hacienda with official documents and legal pronouncements. It was a day I shall never forget, though on my oath I would gladly give all the gold I have stolen to erase the bitter memory from my mind.

With the help of an old friend of my late grandfather, we took up residence—if it can be called that—in a miserable hovel in Torreón. There we subsisted for a time on the charity of the Sisters and the handouts of our remaining friends. But before long they tired of us and ceased their help, pointing to my father's drinking as the reason. In truth, our friends were few to start with, for no sooner spread word of our disgrace than without ado most turned their back on us. I cannot describe the shame and mortification I suffered as girls who were once my best friends now on instructions by their parents refused to speak to me or mocked me openly in the streets.

Then even the obsequious Otero abandoned us. Instead of befriending my parents and seeing to my welfare as he had sworn to do as my godfather, he announced to us that he and his father were leaving Torreón. He promised to help us as soon as he was established elsewhere, and for many months both my parents, but especially my mother, vainly awaited news from him. "The good Mariano will not abandon us. He will send help soon," she repeated. Yet all we perceived from him were long, tasteless responses to our letters in which he described his homesickness in Chiapas but made only indifferent references to our circumstances. Never was there any material aid or hint of help.

When it finally became evident to my parents that their last hope had failed them, their spirits broke and our family collapsed completely. One night as my mother commenced her daily tribute to Otero, my father, drunk as usual, suddenly rose from his chair and with a great bellowing cry, gave her a brutal beating, despite my efforts to stop him.

Neither of them ever recovered. My mother's reason began to evaporate and ere long she became insensible to reality. Eventually her physical wounds healed, but there were many times when she seemed no longer even to recognize me. Often she slipped out of the house to wander a vagrant about the city until I would find her and lead her home. As for my father, crazed by grief and drink, he shed the last pretense of shame and became a drunken street beggar.

I was left alone and desperate without means or friends. At fifteen the only assets I had left were my youthful looks and body. These I sold at a brothel, and as a prostitute I took a perverse pleasure in bedding the husbands and suitors of my former friends. Upon learning of my degradation, my father summoned a spark of his former dignity and attempted to rescue me from the brothel. It pains me to remember that I laughed him to scorn and threw up to him his many failings. In the end he hung his head and disappeared—though not before asking me for money. So bereft of reason my mother had become that I am certain she never knew what became of me.

Because I was much sought out by the men of Torreón soon I had enough money to leave the city and the bitter memories it held for me. My parents were beyond rescue in any case and all my thoughts were fixed on flying from the brutal humiliations I had suffered. One of my wealthy clients offered to establish me in a residence in the capital of the Republic provided I would reserve my favors for him. I agreed to his conditions and he took me to Mexico City. There I prospered, for in addition to the allowance he faithfully gave me, during his long absences I earned more plying my lucrative profession.

In this way eight years passed and my elderly protector died. I mourned his death with genuine regret, for he was always kind to me. Indeed towards the end I came to look on him more as a kindly uncle than a lover.

Thanks to his generosity and my own enterprise I had by then accumulated a tidy sum and my thoughts increasingly turned to Torreón and my parents. Furthermore, during the liquidation of my lover's property his family learned of my secret residence in Mexico City and demanded my removal. I left willingly, for I was tired of my life there and thought to establish myself in the provinces.

In Torreón I learned the sad news of my mother's demise. You may imagine the remorse I felt for having abandoned her. But my regret turned to outrage when I learned that only a few months earlier Mariano Otero also had returned to Torreón and, according to rumors, as a final act of hatred towards my father had murdered him with a bottle of poisoned wine. He even had the effrontery to pay for his burial. But rather than have my father lie in a tomb of infamy, I paid for his reburial next to my grandfather's pantheon. No one knew where they buried my mother. All I could do for her was to have a mass said in her name. Imagine my rage when they told me that the hypocritical Otero had requested a similar mass for her some months earlier. Otero, the very man responsible for her ruin and death!

That same day I swore vengeance and commenced to pursue Otero, as a hunter would stalk a wild beast, with the intention of killing him without contemplation. First I followed him to Chihuahua, then to San Cristóbal, only to learn that he had departed not long since for Santa Fe. There in the distant north at last I found him as he sat drinking alone in a tavern. So changed was I that at first he failed to recognize me as I called his name. It was only when I came near enough to plunge my knife into his black heart that his eyes widened in recognition.

"Why, dear Raquelita, why?" were his dying words said barely above a whisper.

Why indeed! As if he did not know that I had reasons to kill him a hundred times over!

Because Otero was a stranger without importance or consequence in Santa Fe the authorities readily accepted my claim that his death was in just retribution for a great dishonor done to my family and me. They asked only that I quickly leave Santa Fe. Having thus extracted vengeance, I departed at once to rejoin Bernardo and the band.

The bandidos bowed their heads politely at her story, for surely they knew it already. I then asked how she came to be one of Bernardo's followers, but she ignored my question.

"That, Padre Pedro, is another story," Bernardo whispered to me, "best told at another time. I would not ask her more questions about it. She will tell you if she chooses."

Likewise, Bernardo deflected my questions about his life, laughingly observing that he robbed because it was easier than working.

Two days later the bandits saddled their horses, gathered their guns and gear, and rode south for raids deep in Sonora, leaving only a lookout on the peak and Tacho to tend the camp. As for me, Bernardo thought that I would ill serve the band in Sonora and decided to leave me to aid Tacho and care for the remaining horses.

"We return in two or three weeks," promised Bernardo. "But if perchance fate has my name written on a ball, make provisions for yourself and I will await you in purgatory!"

"Ah, Patrón, you mock Providence too much," lamented old Tacho, shaking his graying head. "It is perilous to speak so disrespectfully of the Higher Power. And is it wise to raid so soon again in Sonora? We bled that land dry last year, and after so many raids, will they not be waiting for you this time?"

"Dear fretful Tacho, you worry too much about me and not enough about yourself," rejoined Bernardo, giving his miniature friend a rough hug.

Without the bandidos the nearly deserted mine became depressingly silent, and its confining walls seemed to close in on me like the miserable calabozo in San Cristóbal. I sought to relieve the oppression by engaging the fretful and ever bustling Tacho in conversation.

"Tacho, what can you tell me about Bernardo and yourself? Where are you from, and how did you end up as bandidos?"

"Ah, Padre, that is a long story and I have work to do," he answered me curtly.

I waited for a time but he fell silent. My mind drifted to other thoughts, and I began strumming one of the guitars.

"It is a story of a great injustice," Tacho said abruptly.

"What did you say, Tacho?"

"That the way Bernardo was driven into thievery was a great injustice and a series of injustices."

"How so?" I asked, laying the guitar aside.

"Bernardo was the son of don Matías Aguirre y Maldonado, a wealthy Spanish hacendado whose family owned vast properties on the Sonora river hard by the city of Hermosillo. I was a servant in his household and have known Bernardo since his birth."

"It does not follow from your description that Bernardo was the victim of injustice but a child of privilege."

"That is because you do not know his story," he responded disapprovingly to my hasty opinion.

"Then tell me so that I may correct my mistaken impressions."

"I will tell you only what is meet for me to say. Bernardo may relate other things if he chooses."

"Then tell on, good Tacho."

"Don Matías was a hard man, a tyrant to doña Eva his wife and daughters María and Maribel and a harsh taskmaster to servants and workers. And I know firsthand of what I speak, Padre. Yet he was a man of his word, honest in his dealings, and generally upright in his morals, though in his younger years perhaps not above occasionally taking his pleasure with the Indian maids. He was indulgent to a fault with Bernardo, his only son and the apple of his eye. And Bernardo repaid his father's affection with an obedience that verged on reverence for his sire.

"Father Hidalgo's cry for the independence of Mexico nowhere resonated louder than in our province wherein lingered the memory of ancient Spanish oppressions. Por favor, Padre of my soul, do not poke the ashes with your stick; it will mean more work for me! Everything is more work for me!"

"Pardon me, Tacho, I did it without thinking. But what happened to turn Bernardo from such a favored existence to the life he now leads?"

"As I said, our province was ripe for vengeance and independence. But would that it had been so simple a matter, for in truth, greed was mixed in equal portions with patriotism."

"How so?"

"Don Matías was the richest hacendado in the whole region of Sonora. Many envied him his fat cattle and abundant crops and complained that he enjoyed unjust advantages because of his Spanish birth. But that was pure slander, Padre. Don Matías left Spain a poor lad without advantageous family connections. Rather it was through perseverance and hard work that he was able to expand his hacienda from a small beginning to the great estate it had become at the time of his assassination."

"What was the manner of his death and who were those responsible?"

"Hear me, Padre, and you will learn. Hoping to confiscate his rich property under the cloak of patriotism, don Venancio Sorzano and his two sons recruited a hundred-strong company of marauders and Yaqui Indian scouts. Claiming to oppose the Spanish authorities (in truth already fled from our province), they plundered several ranches before beseiging our hacienda. But learning of their violent depredations and foul intentions, don Matías had prepared for the assault. Although the enemy more than doubled us in numbers, we had the better position and in two days our defenders killed or wounded fully twenty of the attackers, whilst losing only five of our men.

"Whereupon don Venancio requested a truce to remove his dead and wounded and to discuss an honorable end to the bloody conflict. Don Matías agreed to both terms and with Bernardo rode out beyond his gates to meet Sorzano and his two sons Abel and Fernando. But, alas, what he thought was to be a meeting of honorable caballeros was in reality a foul ambush. For no sooner had don Matías dismounted than Venancio Sorzano killed him with a pistol shot to the head, while his sons intended to dispatch Bernardo in like manner.

"But the cowardly Abel's hand so shook that he missed his shot entirely, whilst the ball from Fernando's pistol harmlessly grazed Bernardo atop his left shoulder. Then responding with grief and fury to their treachery, he outdueled the brothers with pistol and sword and killed both. Don Venancio himself escaped with his life but not before Bernardo dealt him a crippling swordstroke not a handsbreadth from his heart. He never recovered fully but lingered only for a number of months

247

obsessed with grief and vainly swearing revenge for the loss of his sons and the outrage of his daughter.

"For there is a sentimental side to the story of which I know much less, for Bernardo has always refused to say what happened. I know only that it was a part of what drove him to the life he has since lived.

"Before the tragedy of the false truce, he had won the heart of Clemencia, the beautiful daughter of don Venancio, and dreamed only of the day when she would be his bride. But when informed of the killings, she said through her tears that even though she would always love Bernardo and no other, honor would not allow her to take to husband the man who had killed her brothers and crippled her father. Nor could she permit Bernardo to wed the sister of his father's assassins.

"Bernardo was overcome by grief and rage over the loss of his beloved father and future bride. At no small risk to his life he outwitted don Venancio's guards and by night gained entry to Clemencia's room. When morning came the two lovers were gone and for a week eluded their pursuers. Then Clemencia reappeared at a home in Hermosillo and from there was spirited, so it was said, to Puebla, where she eventually took her final vows as a nun. Malicious tongues whispered of a child, a son, but how could they know? Never has Bernardo himself spoken of the matter, nor has anyone I know of had reliable news of doña Clemencia since that time, now ten years or more agone.

"But one certainty is beyond doubt: what Bernardo did was a fine vengeance for don Venancio's perfidy. For not only did he slay his treacherous sons in combat but by stealing his daughter from under his very nose also placed another ignoble stain on the Sorzano family honor. Don Venancio did not long survive the shame but died a painful, inglorious death not many months thence.

"Meanwhile the authorities—or at least the greedy men who now called themselves such—hastened to confiscate the Aguirre hacienda in the name of the new Republic, citing more legal pretexts for their theft than I have fingers to count.

"As I said, Bernardo never spoke again of Clemencia. He returned only long enough to make provisions for his mother and sisters and to collect me and a few other trusted men to ride with him. Since then we have lived as bandidos, yet not without a sense of gentlemanly honor. He is respectful of human life and often gives to those in need. Nor has he neglected the welfare of his mother and sisters. As you have seen, he shares none of my cares but is a man indifferent to danger and thus fears not to live life to the full. Yet at times I sense that he would welcome death."

Two weeks later Bernardo and the band, their ranks swollen by a dozen new recruits from Sonora, returned from their raid tired and dirty but boastful of their success.

"What has chanced here, Padre?" Bernardo asked as he ran his fingers through gold and silver coins in their booty. "Has Tacho taught you the ways of an obedient pinche?"[9]

"I fear that Tacho has despaired of teaching me anything. He says that I am fit only for singing, storytelling, and standing in his busy way. As for news, such as I have is too dreary to report."

"Well, Padre, unlike you I have momentous things to tell. Word comes from the east that the Americans settlers in Mexico, the Texians, as they call themselves in their tongue, have risen in revolt against the government of General Santa Anna."

"To what purpose and result?" I asked.

"It was not altogether clear at first, Padre. The earliest reports told how General Santa Ana annihilated the American rebels in San Antonio, at the Alamo Mission. But then reliable men told me that the Americans were victorious at San Jacinto further east and have formed themselves into an independent republic. This is good news, for I see advantage in it for us."

"How so, Patrón?" inquired Tacho, as mystified as the rest of us by the remark. "For all that we are outlaws in our own land, yet is it not unseemly to cheer the triumph of the foreign gringos over our own Mexican countrymen?"

"Countrymen! I have no country!" Bernardo snarled the words, his customary smile gone, and his face scowled with bitterness. "New Spain and its old oppressions or Mexico with its corrupt tyranny? I tell you, brothers, nothing has changed in this land! We thought to win independence and justice when in reality we but exchanged one set of brigands for another. It was in the name of Mexican Republic that I lost my father, my property, my Cle—for what the Republic has become under the tyrant, I spit on the name!"

"Forgive me, Patrón, I did not mean to offend you," offered the mortified Tacho, extending his hands in supplication.

Bernardo enfolded the dwarfish Tacho in his great arms. "The harshness of my words was not for you intended, old friend."

"You spoke of gain for us in the uprising," I reminded Bernardo.

"Yes indeed, Padre. But we shall need men and daring to bring it about. That is why I asked these brave friends from Sonora to join us."

"More to cook for, more work, always more work," grumbled Tacho.

"But no more work here, good Tacho," said Bernardo, giving him a healthy cuff to the shoulder. "This mine and these mountains have served us well, but save for our failure in San Cristóbal we have exhausted this sparse land. Tomorrow we ride south where a more lucrative prize awaits us."

Bernardo would not tell us more but bade us to sleep well and prepare to depart at first light. As dawn broke over the Mimbres Mountains we streamed out of the still dark mine and canyon, some twenty-five riders trailed by five or six panniers and a remuda of five horses under my care. For the better part of two days we traveled quickly and—save for an incident that I shall now relate—without events worthy of your attention.

Bernardo boldly led us southwards along the main river road. He was contemptuous of the poorly armed regional militia, which in recent years seldom ventured beyond its garrison walls.

"If they dare attack us we have enough men and firepower to send them running with their tails between their legs," he boasted.

At the Doña Ana crossroads we paused briefly at a posada for drink and food. There I experienced a momentary thrill of panic upon reading a posted notice that one Peter Prosper, marauding robber and suspected murderer, would fetch a reward of seventy-five Spanish dollars to anyone who should deliver him or his carcass to the authorities in El Paso del Norte. My agitation passed as I read a description much unlike mine and remembered that since Santa Fe I had used the name Pierre de Tourmoulin. Bernardo observed my keen interest in the posting.

"Know you the brigand, Padre?" he asked. "Perhaps I will shoot him myself if he crosses my path; it is men like him who give honorable thieves a bad name."

"The name I know not," I lied, "but the description aptly fits a man, an American, I rode with briefly on the road from the Plaza de Albuquerque."

"Names mean little here on the northern frontier. There is a saying in this God-forsaken land:

Many a man arrives here as Pedrito
And changes to the lineage of Juanito."

As I said, we reached El Paso del Norte without other incidents worthy of comment. Even though the local authorities had prudently absented themselves in the face of our large band, the ever-fretful Tacho

250

persuaded Bernardo to set up our camp half a league outside the town boundaries. There the rest of us soon learned that El Paso was astir with the rumor, now confirmed, that Bernardo had kept to himself. Colonel Pascual de Prados Vázquez, an aristocrat of Sonora and commander of a small contingent of General Santa Ana's defeated army, had disobeyed orders to transfer men, munitions, and gold from San Antonio to Monterrey. Instead he decided on a bold stroke of state. He counted on the weakness and ouster of Santa Ana following the American victory and believed that in consequence the Mexican Republic itself would soon disintegrate. In consequence, he set out for Sonora with the grandiose intention of creating a new state with himself as its head. His forces were small, no more than sixty or seventy bedraggled men and a dozen or so horses, but he had arms, gold, and considerable matériel and with these hoped to rally recruits to his cause as he went.

But the fatuous colonel had badly miscalculated the many hindrances and daunting hardships of the long march. Having at last struggled to a shallow ford a few leagues west of the conflux of the Rio Grande and the Conchos, his weak, desperate men refused to advance into the deeper deserts and mountains of Chihuahua. Instead they confiscated a small hacienda on the north bank and from there refused to move until they had eaten and rested.

"They are as defenseless as legless chickens, and we are the foxes that will devour them," Bernardo announced, gleefully rubbing his hands in anticipation. "We want only more men to assure our victory. And we must hasten before Santa Ana's soldiers overtake them and seize the booty for the tyrant. Spread the word quickly that I need seasoned riders and experienced fighting men, and that I will pay them handsomely in gold."

No sooner was the word released than commenced a stream of hard, disreputable men to our encampment, among them, much to my surprise and chagrin, Billy Wells and three other American ruffians.

Billy was greatly changed in countenance from the ignorant braggart I had known months earlier. His once vacuous blue eyes were now focused into a malignant stare, and a thickening beard and mustachios gave him a look of deviant maturity. He now sported a holstered pistol and rifle, and I saw a long knife sheathed at his side. The errant lad was now become a hardened felon. Once past our reciprocal surprise, I approached Billy to inquire privately about my horse and belongings.

"I don't take kindly to the drift of your words, whoever you are. They sound like an accusation to me, don't you know. My things are mine, good buddy, and my horse—my horse, mister—is tethered yonder, and if you know what's good for you, you'll let him be."

"But he belongs to me!" I protested, "And so do the things you took off me when the limb unseated me from my saddle."

"He belongs, my friend, to Peter Prosper, and that man is me. I have papers to prove it, don't you know. So they are my papers, my things, and my horse, unless you can prove otherwise. Or maybe you think you are man enough to best me fer them, do you. But just you remember this, good buddy, I have killed men before and I'll do it again if you push me."

Needless to say, I was not of a mind to push him, but returned angry and humiliated to my tent, his jeering comments about my manhood burning my ears. My cowardice was a stinging shame, but with a deeper prudence I reminded myself that for the moment it was better for Billy to masquerade as Peter Prosper and for me to continue in this life as Pierre de Tourmoulin. Pierre might be guilty of serious crimes in San Cristóbal, but Peter was wanted for a hanging charge of murder and, unbeknownst to Billy, for other capital offenses in Memphis.

(Perhaps, gentle reader, I have alluded to my lack of courage on other occasions. I cannot recall with certainty. Physical resistance was beaten out of me early in life. Forgive me in any case if I weary you with a recount of my weaknesses.)

I pressed the matter no further but distracted myself by grooming the horses and making other preparations for our impending raid. By sundown Bernardo counted sixty hardened and heavily armed brigands under his command, enough he judged to subdue the exhausted soldiers. As was his custom on his raids, he roused us at first light the following day and led us smartly eastwards along rutted roads flanking the north bank of the Rio Grande. I brought up the rear with a remuda of twelve horses.

After two days of hard riding we neared the hacienda where it was reported the broken soldiers had taken refuge. Bernardo sent two of his most trusted scouts ahead to reconnoiter. Within hours they returned with a report that confirmed our earlier intelligence: an exhausted company possessing not above two dozen horses in as poor condition as the humans. Despite three cannons they had laboriously trundled across the wilderness, it was the opinion of the scouts, that the wretched physical plight of the soldiers rendered them incapable of a significant defense, much less of any offensive threat against our men.

"They will surrender without a fight and would even join us, if they could, to put an end to the colonel who has so sorely abused them," observed Fabricio, Bernardo's most trusted scout.

To my great relief, Bernardo ordered me to remain with our horses. Thus I am relieved to say that I was responsible for no loss of human life that day. In truth there were few casualties in the fray to weigh on any conscience. Bernardo's men crept to the very walls unperceived by the haggard defenders. And no sooner did they force the main gate and break into the patio and adjacent corrals, firing as they ran, than the white flag of surrender was hoisted and the weary, drunken soldiers staggered, hands raised, from their quarters. Only the colonel's personal guards fired a few errant shots from the roof of house before Bernardo's expert marksmen dispatched them.

The colonel himself, his thin beard trembling in fear, was dragged from his quarters and stripped to his drawers, to the jeers of outlaws and soldiers alike.

Then began the assessment of the booty. Of usable arms there were few, for the haggard soldiers had strewn them along leagues of barren wilderness. Of documents, almost none, for they were the first items abandoned. Of gold, there remained a miserly sum. Bernardo and his lieutenants suspected that much of it was hidden or buried, and they entertained the colonel for hours with various scorchings and tortures. But beyond his screams and curses these had no measurable effect. Not until they resorted to the ancient bastinado and reduced his feet to a bloody mass did he break and, pleading for mercy, gasped out its buried location. In short order it was retrieved to the gleeful ovations of the band. Then to the indifference of most and the vengeful glee of those who had suffered most at his hand, a well-placed ball to the temple silenced the colonel's forlorn cries for mercy.

At the approach of the troops, don Lope Menéndez and his family had fled south in panic across the river, taking with them most of their valuables and supplies. Although they left little food for the usurpers, to their glee the latter discovered a well-stocked wine cellar. Moreover, the cattle herds were yet grazing on the nearby riverbanks. Bernardo and his men slaughtered and spitted two beeves over a roaring fire in the main corral, and soon was begun an orgy of eating, drinking, and celebrating.

By midnight outlaws and soldiers, now united in one body, had eaten and drunk themselves into a stupor. Thus it was that none noticed the stealthy approach and strategic deployment of the colonel's pursuers. Too late Fabricio sounded the alarm, for by then the federal soldiers were inside the walls, and our addled host looked up to discover cocked rifles aiming at them from all sides.

I make of myself an exception, for by an accident of fate I had absented myself some time earlier from the company in response to nature's old urgency. Having accomplished that private necessity, I then had the fortunate, albeit inexplicable, thought to inspect the horses. From my favorable vantage point on the slope above the hacienda I witnessed the bizarre carnage below.

It was not in Bernardo's nature to surrender meekly. Pulling his pistol and sabre and roaring orders, he rallied his men for a sally. Immediately most of these were cut down by rifle fire. But in the bedlam other outlaws took courage. One doused the fire with a large bucket of water, and in the sudden smoke and darkness the confusion and shouting increased.

A stray ball whining through the very space my head had filled only an instant earlier broke my fixated attention on the mayhem below and persuaded me that headlong flight was much the better of my choices. Even had I been of a mind to aid my companions—an option remote from any intention on my part—surely my insignificant person would have introduced little difference into the fray.

Firm, therefore, in this determination, hastily I untethered my horse and raced away in the night as my imagination presented images of murderous pursuers closing on me. Indeed, as these feverish fears subsided with distance, I saw a rider following in mean proximity. Panicked by thoughts of being overtaken by a vengeful enemy, I veered off the roadway into concealing foliage and prayed that he would not spot me.

It was Billy Wells, alias Peter Prosper, and by the looks of him badly wounded. I fell in behind him, glancing over my shoulder for other riders, and watched him sway and lurch in the saddle. Eventually his mount—my Comanche mount—slowed to a walk as he dropped the bridle rein, and I came up behind him.

"Billy, are you hurt?" I asked cautiously, bending to pick up the reins.

"Petie, is that you? Man, I'm ... worse than hurt, don't you know. I-I don't think I'm gonna make it. I'm bleedin' real bad, Petie."

In his agony and fear Billy seemed to regress to the lad I knew months earlier. His bravado and swagger were gone, and his voice had a pleading tone to it.

"We had best stop, Billy, and let me take a look at your wound. You need to lie still so the bleeding can stop."

He did not argue the suggestion but willingly accepted my help in dismounting. I could not see well in the moonless darkness, nor knew I much of gunshot wounds in any case, but from all that I could tell, Billy was right: From a raw wound high on his left side blood spurted with each heartbeat. His skin had the clammy feel of a corpse.

"Billy," I asked as I drew his shirt back over the wound, "is there anything I can do for you?"

"Petie, I'm real sorry I killed that feller usin your name. I just got afraid to use mine. And I'm sorry I spent Baldy's money. And, Petie, do you ... know how ... to pray for my soul? My momma ... knowed how to pray, but I ... never learned ... 'cause poppa laughed at religion. But, Petie, I don't want to ... die without some good words ... prayed over me, don't ... you know. Can ... you do that for me ... good buddy?"

With that he fell into a swoon from which he never roused in this world. There came to mind the many prayers I had said during my days as a bogus priest, but the one that stood out most strongly was the Paternoster Father Branigan taught me long ago. I recited it over Billy until his breathing died away and he was gone.

It required much doing to load and strap Billy's lanky body across the saddle of my horse. Then tying the reins to the saddlehorn of my newly retrieved Comanche mount I rode west towards El Paso. At dawn I paused to examine Billy's pockets and saddlebags. In the latter I found the familiar leather pouch with Caroline's cross, which I clutched to my bosom with emotions I could not now put into sensible words. With it was the letter of reference John Greenley had written on my behalf. In a pocket he carried, perhaps as an object of pride, a folded and worn copy of the posted notice of his crimes and reward for his capture. I pocketed the disappointingly small amount of money he possessed.

I rode all day almost without pause, for the weather was warm, and I was worried about the deterioration of the corpse. Pushing hard, I reached El Paso the next day, and let me say, not a moment sooner than absolutely necessary for the body was becoming disagreeably aromatic. Green flies buzzed tenaciously about the face and other exposed parts. I averted my eyes so as not to become nauseous at the sight. (Pardon the indelicacy of this description, dear reader.)

A curious crowd gathered as I made inquiries and was told that this was a matter for the Alcalde. They pointed me to the wretched structure they had the audacity to call an ayuntamiento, or municipal building, but there I learned that he was away from the town, but that in his absence his aide perhaps would attend me. I gave my name and explained to the obese, perspiring assistant that by chance having happened upon the notorious Peter Prosper, who then expired in my presence, and having dutifully delivered the body to the proper authorities, I was now here to collect the publicized reward.

"We will need an official notarized report of the circumstances," the skeptical assistant responded.

"I shall be happy to comply."

"But we have no notary in El Paso at the moment. Next week perhaps. You will need to return then, señor."

"That will be difficult, señor, for I had planned to continue my journey tomorrow."

"Señor, these are not matters to be handled quickly and lightly. There is a dead man here, who knows, perhaps a murder, and you cannot leave the city so long as this business is pending."

"There is a more pressing matter that must come first, sir," I reminded him.

"And what would that be?" he wondered as he inspected his fingernails.

"The corpse; it is stinking and must be buried at once."

"The man was not Catholic, by my report, and cannot lie in our cemetery. Nor can I summon a priest to conduct a heathen funeral."

"Be that as it may, sir, the body must be put in the ground. With your permission, I, though Catholic, will say words of respect over the grave of the heretic, if such he was, if you will provide a plot for the burial."

Despite a great reluctance to act at all, the fat assistant, one Manuel Cisneros by name, had no choice but to authorize the interment. The townspeople were complaining of the stench and demanding removal of the cadaver.

"Take it north of the river and bury it where you will, but away from the stream," he instructed two sullen employees assigned to the dreary task.[10]

"In a coffin, don Manuel?" one of them asked.

"Forget the coffin, *joder!*" he thundered with gross profanity, exasperated with the whole affair. "Just get the *cabrón* under ground!"

This they did and as the last dirt was shoveled over the corpse, I doffed my hat and said a short eulogy in the French tongue in Peter's honor:

"*Il n'était pas si mauvais qu'on croit, mais un homme pas plus bas* ... [He was not so bad as people believe, but a man no lower than his worst deeds and no higher than his best desires. I cannot say that I was his friend, yet I spent much intimate time with him and probably knew his short life better than any other. Of him I can say this in his favor: though often neglectful of the ways of Providence, yet at the end he placed his hope in the only good decision in his power to make: to die better than he lived. And so we commend his soul to the mercy of the Most High and commit his mortal remains to the earth. Amen."]

With these words we laid Peter Prosper to rest. I was so moved by the forlorn image of myself lying in the dark with suffocating dirt covering my face that tears came to my eyes. It was the first time I had died, and the experience filled me with the saddest of emotions. Yet upon further reflection, with Peter's death, I thought myself free of his turmoiled life. Even as I mourned for Peter, I was pleased to be Pierre de Tourmoulin.

The men reported my eulogy to Cisneros, who eyed me suspiciously.

"You are, then, a foreigner, señor? I gathered as much by your Castilian, which differs from ours. The men tell me you spoke unchristian words over the outlaw's grave."

"The words were French, sir, for such I am by birth, though a resident of New Orleans for most of my years."

"Then the matter we spoke of is greatly complicated. I know of no law authorizing the Alcalde to turn money over to Frenchmen."

"But, señor," I raised my voice in protest, "the notice specified that anyone might claim the reward for delivering the outlaw Prosper, alive or dead. And that I have done."

"That may be true, señor, but what proof have I that the dead man was Prosper? For all I know, you yourself could be the outlaw."

"You jest, of course, about me. I am a French gentleman of noble ancestry, and my features in no way fit the description of the American criminal. Besides, in his saddlebag he bore this letter of identity, which I leave in your hands as evidence."

"I never saw the face of the man you buried. Furthermore, do I know—and pardon me for saying so—that you found the letter where you say? There is much banditry afoot in this land, and one cannot be too cautious."

With that he leaned back in his chair, pleased with his sagacity.

"Perhaps we can reach an accommodation on the matter?"

"What do you propose, señor?"

"In appreciation of your trouble and the great efforts you exert on behalf of order and peace in this city and province, would you permit me to make a gift to you from the reward, leaving the notarization and other details to your able discretion?"

"It would offend my honor to be offered a bribe."

"Not a bribe, señor, but an earnest of my esteem."

"In that case, there may be a shortcut we can take through these official requirements. Return tomorrow, and we shall see."

I left in high hopes that the main portion of the reward for my death and burial would soon be in my possession. I took a room at a posada near the river, nervously trying not to call excessive attention to myself. But it was all to no avail, for word had spread quickly of the curious foreigner who had delivered the outlaw Prosper to the authorities and claimed the reward. Everywhere I turned, eyes were fixed on me. My nervousness increased upon overhearing gossip about the sensational skirmish between the soldiers and the bandidos.

"Sadly, don Hilario, many of the bandidos were killed in the ambush, if I heard the truth of it," said a bent, white-haired gentleman to his younger companion.

"Ah, don Eduardo, you are too kind as usual with the scoundrels," responded his black-bearded companion.

"Eh, what say you?" asked don Eduardo.

"I said, don Eduardo, that you think too kindly of these ruffians," he fairly shouted back to the deaf don Eduardo. "Would that the same justice overtake them all! Maybe then we could live in peace! And we must wish a worse fate for the malditos Americans who are greater thieves than our own, for they steal our very country from us!"

"But what is this new theft you speak of, don Hilario? I have not heard of any thieves stealing our corn."11

Don Hilario threw up his hands in exasperation and turned to me: "What opinion do you offer of these matters, my young friend?"

"I fear, señor, that I, having only just arrived, am so ill-informed in the matter that I cannot offer any."

"But are you not the man who brought the dead Americano into town?"

"Indeed I am, señor, but I chanced upon him at his dying breath and know nothing of how he received his fatal wound or other circumstances such as you speak of."

"Surely he was in the massacre at the hacienda of don Lope Menéndez," offered don Hilario with a knowing look at his befuddled friend. "You must have ridden hard by the site if you journeyed along the river. Yet you say you saw and heard nothing?"

"Nothing that I noticed at the moment; yet now that you draw my attention to it, I recall hearing gunshots one night, but they were at a great distance from my camp and of no concern to me, that is to say, I thought it more prudent not to make it my concern."

"That is strange, strange indeed," mused don Hilario as don Eduardo tried to make sense of his words. "Twenty men died while nearby you camped unaware of the battle. Very strange indeed."

"Twenty men!" responded I with amazement. "Would you, sir, be so kind as to tell me what happened?"

Don Eduardo suddenly reconnected to the topic, and both men launched enthusiastically into their respective versions of the massacre, whilst I, listening first to one, then turning to heed the other, was left to sort out the conflicting accounts. Both agreed that above twenty men had perished in the surprise attack, but their stories differed where Bernardo Aguirre himself was concerned. Don Eduardo told of the outlaw's death, but don Hilario described his escape into the Chihuahuan Mountains with a surviving handful of his stalwarts. Which account was true, I cannot say, but I hoped it was don Hilario's, for I kindly remembered the noble bandit's protection and generosity.

I excused myself from their presence, yet I felt their eyes following me and knew they were gossiping about my pretended innocence. I was resolved to secure the reward for my death, yet I sensed that the truth about me was pushing too close to the surface to conceal it for any great length of time. In order to distract myself and divert my thoughts from these morbid themes, I asked the proprietress doña Conchita whether by chance there might be reading matter in the posada.

"Alas, no, señor Torbellino," she responded, comically distorting my new surname. "You ask an impossible thing. Few of our guests read and no newspapers from the Capital reach us. Of books I have none."

As I was turning away, she brightened, and reaching in a drawer, pulled forth a torn newspaper. "I forgot this, señor. One of the gringos left it behind. I am told that it is not in our Christian tongue but in heathen English. How one tells the difference I do not know. For paper words make no sound, and to me they all look like the scratchings of a chicken."

Indeed, it was in English—and from Memphis—with the date of October of 1835. You may guess, gentle reader, which of the following items received my keenest attention:

We take up pen to remark that Mr. Hezikiah Turrentyne of our neighboring town of Sommerville of a certainty has set the record in these modern days for matrimony and fatherhood. A little above two years ago he wedded the blissful Miss Serepth Mahala Hathaway, his fifth wife, and in this short matrimonial span by her had two offspring, thus bringing his total progeny to twenty-eight. He often spoke of raising his figure to thirty but death cut him down even as he was striving to reach his aim at age seventy-eight. He leaves a large and disconsolate family and a bereaved widow to mourn their loss.

It falls our sad duty to report the untimely demise of one of Memphis's leading citizens and businessmen. Mr. Lucas Pollard, a Christian gentleman of upright aims and righteous conduct, lost his life trying to rescue items safeguarded in his burning residence. Mrs. Bertha Pollard, his grieving widow, reports that Mr. Pollard entered the burning funeral parlor, disregarding all sound advice against the action. The fire is reported to have erupted from a candle falling on spilled spirits, the latter being kept by Mrs. Pollard for medicinal purposes. Much property was lost, counting not least among the items the disappearance of the slave Antoine and his woman Poulette who were seen running from the burning building with their impaired daughter. No trace of them has been found and it is feared they may have escaped to the North.

Howard Fuller is in his grave and Henry Lawrence will go to prison for his murder. The facts are these: last Saturday Fuller ran Lawrence off his property with a shotgun and warned him to stay away from his wife. Lawrence returned an hour later with a pistol and called for Fuller to come outside. When Fuller stepped forth Lawrence shot him between the eyes. Fuller leaves a widow and two young daughters, and Lawrence likewise will abandon a grieving wife and four children. The two men are cousins and once faithful churchmen.

Mr. Rayford Summerford, heroic veteran of the last war and Indian fighter against the Comanches in the remotest west, has purchased the barbershop and remains of the mortuary from the widow of the late Mr. Lucas Pollard. Colonel Summerford pledges to the people of Memphis to keep to the same ethical standards as his predecessor.

We join fellow citizens across our Great State in mourning the passing of our illustrious senior Senator Horace McCurtain of an apoplectic seizure in Washington, D.C. His wife, the former Miss Caroline Thomas of our own Memphis, and their young son Wilbert are left to mourn their loss. We join our lamentation to theirs but take comfort in the certainty that he looks down smilingly from on high, and we are pleased to learn that the widow McCurtain has made known her intention to return to Memphis to establish her residence.

In the trial of Rufus Horton, a respected and intelligent colored man, for the theft of Homer Milligan's mule, a verdict was rendered Monday last. Horton was found to be innocent of the theft and released from custody after it came out that Ralph Milligan, son of the complainant, admitted that in an inebriated state he bartered the beast for whiskey.

We learn from a Shawneetown paper, that the steamers "Memphis Lily" and "Hudson", a few days since, came in contact with each other in the Canadian Reach, the former ascending, the latter, descending the Mississippi River. The boilers of the Memphis Lily were misplaced, and her guard kitchen and wheelhouse entirely carried away. The Hudson also received injury, but not so material as that of the Memphis Lily. The latter took fire and so rapid was the progress of the flames, that the passengers had merely time to save themselves, a part of them jumping in the River. The loss of baggage, cargo and vessel is total.

I pondered these and many other things far into the night. The next morning I gathered provisions, saddled my horse, and made my way to the ayuntamiento.

Manuel Cisneros greeted me with an affability formerly undetected in his character.

"Señor Tormolino, I have prepared the papers for you to receive your recompense," he announced with a broad smile. "You only need to affix your signature for the matter to be happily concluded between us."

I looked over the document, noting that sixty of the promised seventy-five dollars would remain with the ayuntamiento in fees for handling and services.

"I had not thought to donate so generously to the city, my friend."

"Would you prefer instead that we keep everything, señor?" he asked, his smile suddenly vanishing. "For that can easily be arranged. Furthermore, I can even offer you fine lodging in our facilities here until the Alcalde returns from his journey. He will have many questions for you. And believe me, my friend, he is a hard man, much harder than I who wish to be generous with you."

"No, señor, your point is well made and politely taken, and since my business elsewhere is pressing, I shall accept your generosity and be on my way, with your permission."

Cisneros eyed me cynically as he counted out fifteen dollars. "Now that the agreed-on division has been made, my friend, a donation from your share would be most acceptable for my trouble."

"But, señor, the city has already taken most of it," I protested.

"I remind you, señor, I can keep it all, if I choose."

I fumed silently and counted out three more dollars, but his palm remained open. I dropped another coin. He was unmoved. Another and another fell. At last when only five remained, he laughed and closed his beefy palm and deposited the coins in his ample purse.

"I thank you for your gratuity. Now you have my permission to leave, and my advice is for you to be far from El Paso when the Alcalde returns."

"In considering all things, though the division of the reward seemed harsh to me at the moment, I deem that you have dealt more kindly with me than many another with the advantage of office and power. I am in your debt. Allow me to shake your hand, señor, and if you will permit me, to give you an abrazo. For I look upon you as a friend."

He made no objection but was instead pleasantly surprised that I should find his repulsive person worthy of high esteem. Having demonstrated my feelings with a firm handshake and tight abrazo, I hastily took my leave of him.

My racing horse was barely past the last houses of El Paso when I heard his cursing roar and not long thereafter saw the dust rising from the hoofbeats of my pursuers. Whereupon I spurred my mount to fullest gallop, pleased by the jingling of the purse I lifted from him during the abrazo. I thought of the Spanish saying concerning Purgatory:

> *Quien roba a ladrón*
> *Tiene cien años de perdón.*
> (He who robs a thief
> Earns a hundred years of relief)

For hours I urged my speedy steed eastwards through the desolate, wind-ravaged country north of the Rio Grande, gambling that Cisneros would not pursue me deep into this inhospitable terrain. For he himself would have many questions to answer should I be overtaken and hauled back to El Paso. And luckily for me my reasoning held true and, as best I could judge, after a time the riders turned back. By late afternoon I ceased looking fearfully over my shoulder and began to consider what lay ahead. Before me receded immeasurable horizons to which I now commenced to sing high-spirited fancies of love and money. But in response I heard only the occasional mournful hum of the winds or the silence of the vast desert emptiness.

I was eager to leave this dangerous country. Visions of elegantly gowned ladies, silk shirts, civilized food, and fine wine held my imagination in thrall. Mexico had failed its promise of fabulous wealth. Yet I was not dismayed; fresh enthusiasms were already springing up to replace the ruins of my old dreams. It was, after all, a new day, and I was a new man. Furthermore, these assets I counted also in my favor: I was newly possessed of a sizeable purse, a sturdy horse with good riding furniture, and, most appealing of all, the resurrected though irrational hope of finding my Caroline, my one true love, in a city distant hundreds of leagues to the east. And thither I bent my steps determined to do or die for my love.

I hoped to find fellow travelers with whom to cross the trackless waste. But a week into my journey and many leagues removed from El Paso I saw not a soul. Benumbed by solitude and my ghastly surroundings, as I was about to ford a small river I was startled back to full awareness by the dust and commotion of several riders approaching from the east. At that moment they espied me and with whoops and pistol shots made in my direction with such speed and deliberate intent to intercept me that neither flight nor concealment was possible. In the cold chill of panic I wondered, who were they and what would be my chances with them?

But the answers to those questions and the telling of that adventure, so different from all the rest, dear reader, must await another day, for in what remains of this one I must take my rest.

Part VI: How Peter, now naming himself Pierre de Tour-moulin, became the slave of Baron Gustave de Thibaudet; how after a failed dash for freedom he was bested in a life-or-death gambling duel with the Baron; how in a final bid for his life, a singular twist of fortune saved him; how thereafter he returned to New Orleans in pomp and honor where he began a search for his lost love and brought his tale to a close

The riders I described to you yesterday, dear reader, were as hostile as their first indications threatened. They rushed to surround me and my nervous mount with drawn pistols and profanity-laced orders from their leader to dismount and stand clear of my horse. This I did without protest, hoping that a servile acquiescence to their commands would at least save me from an immediate pistol ball to the head. But my meekness seemed only to annoy the leader who, swinging down from his horse, strode forward and delivered a stinging slap to my face that sent my hat spinning into the dirt. As I bent to retrieve it, he gave a vicious kick to an unmentionable part of my anatomy that caused me to join my headwear in the dust.

As his men, a half dozen in number, laughed at my dilemma, the leader added threats to his actions.

"Mister, you have just bought yourself a death sentence! That's the Baron de Thibaudet's dirt you're chewing, and all trespassers caught on it are liable to pay for the violation with your life. If you're lucky you'll be hung or shot right away; if not, you'll die working in the Baron's mines!"

I proclaimed my ignorance of the Thibaudet boundaries and pleaded that I had wandered into these lands in complete innocence and without the least harmful intent. All to no avail; my horse was confiscated, my hands were tied to a rope trailing from the saddle, and I either ran behind it or, stumbling in the jagged scrub, was dragged on my stomach for stretches before I could get to my feet again.

Finally, bruised, bloodied, and winded, I was relieved to see that we had come to a long, wooden building with adjacent smaller structures constructed on a granite outcropping that abutted a low mountain. In the midst of these shacks was a mine adit from which occasional muffled booms could be heard, and a fine dust swirled about the entrance. Men with handkerchiefs over their nose and mouth pushing carts loaded with what looked to be crushed rock emerged from the mine to empty them in waiting wagons, then quickly reentered the dark adit. Guards with whips and rifles supervised the workers. It all resembled a busy ant colony.

I protested the brutal treatment I had suffered to a man on horseback I took to be in charge. For a short time he listened indifferently to my plea, then turning to one of the guards ordered me flogged. The sadistic underling was not slow to obey. Unfurling his bullwhip, he laid into my back and limbs, and indifferent to my howls—nay more, spurred on by my agonized cries—he did not stop until my clothes were in tatters and my body aquiver with pain. Espying my ample moneybag as the fabric parted under the powerful whiplashes, with a cry of delight he swooped on it as a hawk on a helpless dove. Only Caroline's cross that I carried in a smaller satchel escaped his notice. But the triumph of the underling was shortlived. The mounted man demanded the bag for himself. The other grumbled and vented his anger by giving me another pair of lashes.

Thereafter still moaning, I was pushed and shoved by a pair of burly stalwarts to the long building where they chained me to an iron rail.

"Better ye stop yer whimpering and save yer strength," one of them said. "Ye'll work the night shift, and if ye can't man up, Charron'll probably shoot ye on the spot. We don't 'low no shirkers in the mines."

"This man Charron, who is he?" I asked through swollen and bloodied lips.

He laughed. "Ye'll learn about that gent soon enough, and any time is too soon."

And I did. Charron was the Baron's partner and manager of the day-to-day operation of the mine and its crews of desperate men. Some men I learned had come purposely to the silver mines seeking work. Others, like me, strayed innocently into Thibaudet lands. But their fate was the same in all cases. Work they found, willingly or unwillingly, but not wages, nor ever the chance to return to home and family. So remote from towns was this precinct of Hell and surrounded by thousands of barren acres that on those rare occasions when a captive managed to make a run for freedom, he either died of thirst or hunger, fell prey to the mountain lions that prowled in the cliffs above the meandering river, or roving Thibaudet patrols hunted him down. In eight years, Charron warned us almost daily, although a few had tried, no man had ever escaped this place and lived to tell the tale.

After a meal of the most unpalatable gruel my tongue had ever had the misfortune of tasting—worse even that the bone and gristle soup the alguaziles served me during my imprisonment in San Cristóbal de los Frailes—I was placed in leg irons and assigned to the night crew as promised. By lantern light we dug into the rocky walls of the mine with pick and shovel, following the silver lode. Then with sledgehammers we broke the loose rocks and with scoops loaded the crushed debris into the carts. I was told that in other branches of the mine dynamite was used on the richer veins often with disastrous results. Occasionally I saw streaks of silver in the rocky debris.

It is probably needless to say so, but I was not accustomed to manual labor, and my flabby muscles soon trembled with exhaustion. Some of the other men, emaciated by age and malnourishment, were in a far more deteriorated state, and I could see they were near their mortal end. Yet the ever-singing whips kept us toiling until the last ounce of strength had been drained from our weary bodies. After twelve hours in the shaft we stumbled to our barracks where the guards locked our leg irons to the long iron bar and we slept the sleep of death. The daily gruel never varied, and a bucket of muddied water that passed from man to man was our only beverage.

It was a common sight for one or more of the men to be unable to rise when it was time to return to the mine. If the whip could not rouse them, the guards unlocked their leg irons and dragged them away.

"They dump the bodies—dead or still breathing—down by the river," Alford McKenzie, one of companions, whispered to me. "The big cats come to feast on them at night. You can hear them fighting and snarling over the bodies—and sometimes the men will scream out, too."

Charron was a man not far if at all above forty. I cannot now, as once I could, recall with certainty his distinguishing features, for I was eager to forget his face once I had the chance. I do remember, however, his intense, unblinking blue eyes, which seemed to take in every pulsation and current of life in a single glance. No emotions ever betrayed the evil tranquility of his youngish, unlined face.

Thinking that perhaps he was French because of his surname, I spoke to him in that language the only time I had a chance to do so. The overture seemed to earn me nothing; he repaid my effort with silence.

But a few days later one of the guards unsnapped my leg irons and led me on foot along a pathway leading to the top of the low mountain behind the mine. There I beheld a splendid residence, or so it seemed to me in contrast to the harsh and ugly conditions of the mine. Nearby where two smaller houses, no doubt the overseers' or servants' quarters.

The guard tethered me with a rope and we waited at the gate for nigh on an hour. Then I heard voices, and a man of middle years and handsome appearance, dressed as it appeared as butler, emerged from a side entrance. He addressed me in French.

"*On nous dit que vous parlez français. D'où êtes vous?*" (They tell us that you speak French. Where are you from?).

"Monsieur, indeed I speak French. I was born of French nobility in the Antilles," I answered, hoping against hope that this intelligence, though untrue, would provoke a change in my status.

"Here your nobility, if such was your previous condition, will not serve you in the least. The mineworkers are all of the same class: the lowest. But by what name do you claim nobility?"

"Monsieur, I am Pierre de Tourmoulin, descended from the Normandy branch of the family."

He nodded and responded in French, "The baron knows of the Tourmoulin family, if indeed you are descended from them. He is also from the North of France, and his family is remotely related by inter-marriage to the house of Tourmoulin." Then he turned and addressed the guard in English. "Return him to the mine, for his shift time is soon to begin. We do not tolerate slackers."

I was devastated, and my hopes were dashed. The loss of a small hope in the condemned is often more painful than the highest disappointment to a free man. But as we turned to go, the man said to me, again in French. "Work faithfully. The baron may wish to speak to you later."

Weeks passed, and nothing chanced to ameliorate my circumstances or offer any hope of regaining my freedom. Even though my muscles had hardened, my body had so shrunk in weight that I was reduced to a fair replica of my New Orleans days. Then unexpectedly I was summoned again to the baron's residence where the same man met me at the gate.

"The baron sends me to speak for him. He wishes to know what aptitudes and skills you may have."

I hastened to tell him of my studies (omitting my failed bid to become a priest), my musical talent, doctoring skills (but leaving out my barbering experience as something unworthy of a nobleman). On a whim I described my abilities as a gambler, puffing myself up as the greatest in New Orleans. Thereupon I was summarily dismissed and returned to the slave quarters and my leg irons.

These occasional visits to the baron's residence, from which the baron himself never emerged, seemed to be a fruitless venture. But it set me to thinking that perhaps they could offer a chance for escape. Obsessed with the possibility, I began to devise a plan.

My companions had not failed to notice my occasional absences. I explained the reason and hinted to a pair I trusted that if we worked carefully there could be a chance to escape.

Alford McKenzie, whose bunk was next to mine, reacted immediately and favorably. "I'm ready, Pierre. I've been here, unless

I've lost count, three years, and I know I won't last another three. I'd rather get killed trying to get away than die in this goddamned mine!"

"The same goes for me, men," whispered Tom Maddox. "I've got a wife and kids—leastwise did have—till they drug me here nearly four years ago. I feel just like Alford here. Dying out in the wilds can't be worse than dying like a rat in this hellhole."

My plan involved numbers. When next the guard came for me, assuming he came, the plan was for the three of us to jump him once my leg irons were loosed and then free the other slaves. Twenty freed men would create enough confusion and havoc to let at least some of us escape to open country.

Not two days passed before the guard, now familiar with the odd routine of my visits to the baron's residence, casually unlocked my leg irons. Then on my signal the three of us pinned him on the ground where we beat and kicked him into unconsciousness. Then warning the others to be silent, I took his key and freed the entire crew.

"It's every man for himself!" I whispered vehemently. "May God protect you!"

The prisoners streamed out of the barracks, running or hobbling in all directions. The general alarm sounded, shots were fired, and in no great lapse of time many of the men were, I suppose, back in captivity and worse off than before.

As for me, I had the presence of mind to take the guard's rifle and head for the baron's residence. I had my own plan that I had not revealed to my companions. I was sure that none of them would escape. Charron was right; exposure, wild animals, and starvation would finish those men the roving patrols might miss. My aim was to hide where no one would think of looking for me.

Reaching the residence, I warily opened the gate to the patio and entered the house by the same door from which the butler always emerged. Once inside I would devise further strategy as circumstances permitted.

At first all went well; the door was unlatched and I entered. But then calamity befell me. As I was searching for a hiding place, perhaps an attic, a woman opened a door, and, seeing me, let out a piercing scream before swooning on the spot. In an instant, armed men surrounded me and led me to the butler. Servants carried the fainting lady out of the room.

"Reasonably clever of you, Monsieur de Tourmoulin," the butler remarked, "but not nearly clever enough. Step slowly away from the rifle and do not resist or I will kill you on the spot. Your plot has failed; your fellow conspirators are even now being captured or killed. As for you, you have earned only one privilege that sets you apart from the other captives."

"And what is that?" I asked in a faint voice as I saw all hope fading.

"The baron himself will pass sentence on you."

With that he called other servants. "See that he is bathed and dressed decently. When you have completed the task return him to me. And guard him carefully at all times. Today he has done considerable mischief. See to it that he does not do more."

Two hours later freshly bathed, perfumed, decently dressed, and my appetite quieted by wine and delectable hors d'oeuvres, I was escorted by armed guards to the baron's quarters. Imagine my surprise upon entering to see the butler sitting at a grand mahogany desk.

"Monsieur de Tourmoulin, stand here before me."

"Monsieur, you led me to believe that I would meet the baron himself."

"And so you have. I am he. You will forgive me for pretending to be the butler, one of my quirks, but I have my reasons and my methods, and so far they have served me well."

He discoursed for several minutes on matters of little consequence. When he asked me to tell him more of my ancestry, I proceeded to fabricate a pedigree with a thread of fact and yards of fiction.

After a time he shook his head skeptically and declared, "Perhaps there is a straw of truth in what you say. Yet it is said that the house of Tourmoulin perished in the Revolution when the revolutionaries burned the Château, so your claims are unconvincing. Perhaps we shall speak more of this, but you understand, do you not, Monsieur de Tourmoulin, that nothing you say here can change the sentence I shall pass on you? You have conspired to do great harm to my enterprise, and this I cannot tolerate. You surely must understand my position, do you not?"

"Sadly, yes," I agreed, not knowing what else to say and waiting with great anxiety to learn of my fate.

"You said once that you are a master gambler, the greatest in all New Orleans. Do you still make that false claim?"

Wounded in my petty pride, I retorted, "Yes, monsieur, but it is no false claim I make."

"Think you highly enough of your gaming abilities to accept my challenge? If so, then we shall see the truth or falsity of your boast."

"Monsieur, for what stakes do we play?"

"Your life, in a manner of speaking, though not your freedom. Win and you will linger as my captive in the mine. Lose and I shall kill you myself. In either case, the sentence is death, late or soon. Which is your pleasure?"

"With respect, monsieur, I find no pleasure in either course. But since a man's hope of life extends unreasonably beyond facts and reason itself, I choose to live as long as I can. I accept your challenge."

And so the scene was set. Nanette, Madame Pauline's serving woman, fetched food, drink, cards, and chips to the baron's quarters and hovered by the gaming table to attend our every whim. On instructions from Monsieur de Thibaudet she distributed the chips to my disadvantage: a sizeable stack for the baron, a modest number for me. I dared not protest the unfairness of the arrangement. Besides I trusted in my ability to outgame the baron. Two armed guards took their position in the back of the room, and the game began.

Years of wandering and, latterly, the months of my captivity and hard labor had dulled my touch and perception, and it soon became evident that I was pitted against a master gambler. Nevertheless, I held my own until midnight was well past. Finally the baron extracted a watch from his fob pocket.

"It grows late, and we shall take our rest, monsieur. Sleep well, for tomorrow will be your last day in this world. And think not of escape. If you try, the guards will snuff out your existence tonight, as I shall surely end it tomorrow."

I cannot describe the conflicting dreads and laments that kept me awake and agitated until the night was far advanced. In the end I fell back on remembered prayers, always the last resort of the desperate. How I regretted that wretched night my betrayal of Father Branigan's trust and how bitterly I repented of my crimes and transgressions that had brought me to this pass.

At dawn a servant served me hot coffee with crème and French bread, butter, and marmalade. Very well, I said to myself, if today I must die, at least I shall leave this world having enjoyed a Louisiana French breakfast, a *petit déjeuner à la Louisiane*. I was stoically grateful for this small gesture of fate.

Then our game resumed, and by noon it was clear that the baron was the better gambler. In truth, I had never seen his like. Not only did the cards run consistently in his favor but also he seemed to read my mind and call me on every bluff. I, on the other hand, found him to be inscrutable, steady, and invincible. As we paused for a light midday meal, my mound of chips was perilously close to exhaustion. Then fortified with fresh food and drink, I made a modest winning run and believed ever so briefly that the tide was turning.

I was wrong. The baron was merely toying with me, letting me win a few hands to prepare me for the coup de grâce. It came not long thereafter. My last chips were lost, and I was bested.

"Your chips are now mine, Monsieur de Tourmoulin. What have you to say for yourself "?

"What else can I say? I bow to you as the winner and confess that I am the loser. You indeed are the better man at cards. But I accepted the challenge and the stakes and now I must bear the consequences of my loss. Anyway, as you said in the beginning, the sentence was death, win or lose."

"Manfully said, Monsieur de Tourmoulin. I had not thought you so plenteously endowed with courage and fortitude, but I am pleased to be surprised by your attitude. For that I congratulate you. You played with style and verve, and I am loath to see the game end. You, of course, have no other assets to bring to the table?"

One thing only had I managed to keep or retrieve throughout the misery and splendor of my travels and turmoils: Caroline's cross, now become the dearest thing to my heart and the memento of the only woman's love I had ever known. But to what avail would I bear it unto death? If life was lost so was my love. Slowly I retrieved it from my little satchel, thinking that with it I was surrendering my last ideal.

"I have this, Monsieur de Thibaudet. It is all I have left."

The baron paled when he touched the cross, and his hands trembled as his long fingers gently caressed it. Then he looked at me with rage twisting his face.

"How did you come by this cross? Tell me, did you steal it? Tell me or I will shoot you where you sit!"

I was astonished and so taken aback that I blurted out the truth to the baron. "It belongs to the only woman I ever loved. Circumstances prevented me from returning it when we were parted. I have kept it to honor her and our love."

"'Belongs', you say, does that mean she yet lives? If so, where? And how dare you speak of love! She is far too good for the likes of you. If you have wronged her in any way, I shall kill you."

Perceiving that I had a powerful bargaining chip, I turned coy with the baron and took the riskiest gamble of all. "We are agreed, monsieur, that she is better than I, or any man I know, for that matter. But if you kill me, you will never know who or where she is. Consider that, monsieur, before you act hastily. I am the only one who can lead you to her. But I shall not do so unless you tell me what she has to do with you."

The baron's face was a kaleidoscope of conflicting emotions and I was afraid he was ready to expunge my life out of pure rage. Finally, he regained control of himself, and caressing the cross, said softly, "She was—is—my daughter, Christine de Thibaudet, my lost daughter, my only child. These are her initials, CT, and this is her cross. I commissioned a master silversmith to design it at her birth in Rouen, France a year before we came to America. And if there were yet any doubt the emerald insert would dispel it. It has been in my family since the Middle Ages, one of many treasures our ancestor Guilbert de Thibaldet, as the name was written in former times, brought back from the Holy Land after the last Crusade. Now, monsieur, you must take me to her. I must find her."

"I will do so willingly if I can, monsieur. But it may not be an easy task. We have been separated these many years. Yet I had news not many months ago that she is alive. But first there is another matter we must settle between us."

"To what do you refer, monsieur?"

"The small matter of my life. I cannot help you if I am dead. And there is not enough torture in the world to make me tell what I know."

On the latter point I bluffed. But I hoped it would deceive the addled Baron.

"You win, monsieur, fate has dealt you the winning hand after all. You have my word that I will spare your life, and if you can lead me to my daughter, I shall see to it that you are rewarded with wealth and honor. From now on, instead of trying to take your life, I shall jealously guard it. You shall not be out of my sight until we find my Christine."

That very day I was installed in the baron's home. He instructed the servants to attend me and see to my every need. There I met Madame Pauline, the baron's petite and pretty brunette wife, or mistress perhaps, who appeared to be much younger than he. (I knew not her status and thought it prudent not to inquire.) I made my apologies to her for the fright I had caused her. She graciously forgave me and eagerly engaged me in conversation. It was obvious that she lived here in isolation and dreary loneliness and was eager for human contact and communication.

But amidst the newfound comfort, I was troubled and left in doubt about my fellow captives slaving in the mines. I asked the baron about them and interceded on their behalf.

"Most of them were caught before they made it out of the compound," he told me. "A few were picked up by my patrols. Two resisted and were shot. The men you asked about are, I think, uninjured, but I am not fully sure which ones you mean. Give them no further thought in any case; they are no longer your concern. Besides, in a matter of weeks we shall leave this place."

"Monsieur, I am not usually given to close friendships, yet if you grant these men their freedom you shall have my gratitude."

The baron looked at me disapprovingly. "Beware of sentimentality, monsieur, and friends you know not well. Both may betray you at the first opportunity or impose on you most inopportunely."

Nevertheless, I was pleased when he told me that same afternoon that he had freed the two and given each of them a horse. "I have no further need of the men. In a week or so all this is to become the property of Charron, fool that he is."

"Why do you call him fool, if I may ask? Will he not continue to extract riches from the mine?"

"Perhaps for a short time, but he does not realize that ominous changes are about to happen. Even before you gave me evidence that my daughter is alive, I was making plans to leave this place. As long as Mexico claimed this land, we ran our enterprise with only perfunctory bribes to a few officials who turned a blind eye to our methods. But with the recent rebellion this country has passed into the hands of the Americans, who have already begun to make disturbing inquiries. Charron expects things to remain the same and believes that he can simply suborn a new set of officials. But I dealt with Americans before I came here, and I know they do not think as Mexicans do. The Mexicans are satisfied with trifles and tokens; the Americans will take everything that is profitable and most likely find a reason to shoot those who stand in their way, including Charron. But his obtuseness works to our advantage. Soon we shall depart with my wealth, leaving him to answer for my actions. And the direction we shall take depends on you, Pierre. So lead well."

The more we talked the more Baron Gustave and I discovered our similarities. As our understanding deepened, I asked him where and how he learned his gaming skills.

"From my earliest manhood I was a devotee of the gaming table, but it was here in America of all places that I perfected my skills under a master gamester. I who thought myself nonpareil in France was but a neophyte in comparison to him. I shall flatter you, my friend, by telling you that you have some of his mannerisms and gestures, which greatly surprised me. But though you possess the native skills, you yet lack the polish and daring he developed into a high art."

"What do they call him, for surely such a man has made a name for himself?"

"His name, Pierre, is, or was, Joseph Prospère, or so he said, and there will never be another like him."

"Joseph Prospère. It seems that I have heard his name somewhere. Where is he now?"

"I know not, perhaps in hell or purgatory. At my urging, he stayed here for a year. I paid him handsomely, but he grew restless for new risks and left us two years ago. I know not where he went—we parted not on the best of terms. Perhaps he returned to New Orleans whence he came or to France where he was born. He lives dangerously and is not a man to linger long in the same place."

Assuming they were the same man, I thought it more prudent of me not to confess to the baron that Joseph Prospère was my father, if my mother could be believed. I knew not in what way the knowledge might hurt or help me, but I had learned even at that early age that secrets once uttered are no longer under one's control and direction, and God alone knows the unknown ways they may return to work one woe. There is a cruelty in fate that may be aroused by the mere naming of harmful things. Had I not suffered their effects in *carne propia*, in my own flesh, as they say in Spanish?

In any case, I had a greater concern. The thrill of seeing Caroline again was tempered by the fear of having to face accusations of the gravest kind. Fully I intended to honor my promise to lead Gustave to his daughter, if it lay within my power, for it suited my deepest and most personal desires also. But to do so meant returning to Memphis where a death sentence against me was still in force.

The dangers facing me were all too evident, but as I contemplated my chances I summed certain advantages that might work in my favor. I fled Memphis an all but beardless youth. Now I possessed a luxuriant, glossy, black beard, which though not yet grown to fullest manly thickness altered my appearance beyond easy recognition. To this feature were added several inches of stature, and with the baron's rich table to overcome my emaciated condition in the mine, the enhanced girth of a man entering into prime manhood. Some who knew me well in my earlier years might suspect the wayward Peter Prosper under the elegant guise of Pierre de Tourmoulin. Yet the world is filled with odd coincidences and inexplicable similarities, and my newly acquired condition of nobility and the appearance of wealth would surely douse any doubts. No one believes the poor when they make claims that would elevate them above their poverty, but people lend worshipful credence to the words of the rich. The poor are never wise in the eyes of world, whereas the merest banalities falling from the lips of the wealthy are taken to be the very oracles of God.

Meanwhile, the dissolution of the partnership and transfer of the mine to Charron having been completed, the day of our departure arrived and a long caravan of wagons, carriages, and carts stretching nearly half a league across the dusty hills began the long trek eastward. As I counted them, a mounted escort of nearly three score heavily armed men flanked us on all sides, and the drivers were no less prepared to repel hostile Indians, Mexicans marauders, and American outlaws. The baron himself carried a brace of pistols and a saber. Offered arms myself, I refused them at first, but after Gustave described the hazards we might encounter in this untamed land and remembering my terrifying captivity with the Comanches, I relented and accepted a rifle with which I was now passably familiar.

The full seriousness of the baron's determination to find his lost daughter was now made starkly evident to me, and the responsibility I bore to guide him rested on my shoulders like a heavy weight. I gave him only the preliminary instruction to wend our way to distant New Orleans. There I would give him more specific directions. This accorded with his decision to remove certain assets deposited in San Antonio. Time was crucial, he reminded me, for he feared that once their government was fully organized, the Texians would place an embargo on his property and confiscate it in the name of the breakaway republic.

These fears soon proved to be a reality. Arriving at length in San Antonio without unduly adverse incidents, the baron learned that the new regime had approved legislation forbidding foreigners to transfer significant capital beyond its borders without prior approval. Given enough time and bureaucratic signatures, the retrieval of his capital might still be possible, but time was precisely what he lacked.

But for the time being the wily Gustave was prepared to leave his capital on deposit in San Antonio and pursue another strategy. Even though he had already sold his share of the mine and transferred its title to Charron, he conveniently produced other deeds of ownership and offered to sell the entire property at public auction in San Antonio. Asked why he proposed to sell such a lucrative enterprise, the baron pleaded illness and homesickness. "*Accablé de maladies, je voudrais mourir en France.*" (Overcome with illnesses, I would like to die in France). In truth he was the epitome of healthy manhood.

His solid financial standing in San Antonio removed any doubt about his solvency and integrity. He further enhanced these qualities by producing a rich display of silver samples and several bags of gold dust, which he claimed he had recently discovered on the same property. This news created such a frenzy of excitement that before the auction could proceed, a consortium of eager speculators made him an offer that exceeded the worth of his embargoed holdings. At the same time other men infected with gold fever set out on horseback in hopes of tapping into the mythical lode. My admiration for Baron Gustave's maneuver was nearly boundless. In my best days I could not have conceived, much less carried out, a deception on so grand and profitable a scale.

As these transactions were unfolding, Gustave quietly sold most of his wagons and possessions, dismissed the drivers and sizeable escort in preparation for a race to the Louisiana border before the unpleasant truth about his duplicitous affairs could surface. He reduced his train to four wagons and a coach for himself, Madame Pauline, Nanette, and me. To these conveyances he ordered hitched the swiftest teams he could find. A dozen or so armed men escorted us. Without a true word, but many false ones, of his intentions to anyone in San Antonio, he ordered Madame Pauline, Nanette and me into the coach, and we slipped out of the city at dusk on a Monday. All that night and the better part of a week we raced eastward over dusty, primitive Texas roads, stopping only for a few hours to rest and feed the teams and catch sleep.

Our once prime teams exhausted and ruined, finally we reached the Sabine River without seeing pursuers or suffering unexpected inconveniences in our hasty flight from the Texian Republic. But not until the ferry had transported us across the river on a chilly March afternoon did we all breathe easier.

"Luck favored us, Pierre," Gustave confessed out of Madame Pauline's hearing. "In our last days in San Antonio I would not have wagered an adulterated Spanish dollar on our chances. Suspicion was spreading that my documents were, shall we say, not entirely legal. But it was my only profitable option under the circumstances. I believe the Americans were readying a warrant for my arrest. Only their obsession with the mine and the gold gave us time to escape. For while we were riding as fast as horses could run for Louisiana, half of San Antonio was surely riding west as quickly to claim property or stake claims. I would not want to be in Charron's shoes when he has to confront the Americans. No doubt they will declare his deeds of ownership false—for indeed they are as worthless as their own. My documents supposedly granted by the Mexican government were clever forgeries at the highest level, but it will probably take years to sort out the deception. In any case, I have reached La Louisiane with my fortune intact and my head still attached to my shoulders. I dare say Charron will not fare so well with the Americans."

Our arrival in New Orleans was an apotheosis, if not an epiphany, for the proud citizenry of New Orleans smarting under American rule and still yearning for the old days when the Catholic kings of France and Spain reigned over Louisiana. Word ran swiftly throughout the city that a rich French baron and a young enigmatic count had arrived to take up residence in one of the most spacious houses in the Vieux Carré.

It would be impossible to describe to you, dear reader, my dreadful state of mind upon returning to New Orleans after several years and twists of fortune. How well I remembered my life as street urchin and thief, my sordid dealings with DuClos and Patrice LaChaise, and the infamous affair with my brother Henri and deputy Downes. Was there still a price on my head? And would anyone recognize the aristocratic Pierre de Tourmoulin as the lowly mischief-maker Peter Prosper? Gustave took note of my nervousness and correctly surmised its cause.

"I doubt not, Pierre, that you have a history of misdeeds in this city, and that fears of retribution haunt you. Do not trouble yourself overmuch. As long as you bruit it about that you are Count Pierre de Tourmoulin, it is not likely that anyone will perceive the duplicity or suspect your former identity. It is no longer a matter of playing an assumed role, Pierre, and pretending to be another person. You must really become that person. Mere pretense and play-acting will fail you. From now on you must be fully and boldly Count Pierre de Tourmoulin or, failing, you will be nobody at all."

"But I really am Pierre Prospère," I protested, confessing to him for the first time my original name.

"Prospère? Then you are perhaps related to Joseph?"

"I never knew him, but my mother told me my father was so named."

"You slyly kept silent about that fact when I mentioned his name. But the kinship explains many things I noticed about you."

"But though he may be my father, my mother tells me that I am descended on her side from the house of Tourmoulin. I could be a count after all, even though I am really Pierre Prospère, once known here as Peter Prosper."

"No, Pierre, you were never that lowly Prospère, much less Peter Prosper. He was the false person. Few people ever really become themselves. Instead they pass their years captive to the fiction of themselves with only rare glimpses of who they really are."

It was not long before my new identity was put to the acid test. Before a fortnight had passed, the French Consul, his Excellency Honoré G ..., invited the baron and his household to the consular residence at which the social and business elite of New Orleans, including the American mayor, gathered to pay their respects.

Despite the baron's calming advice and indifference to possible dangers from the Texian Republic, I accompanied him to the gala event with my heart in my throat yet determined to play the charade to the full. Accordingly, I stood haughtily erect as beautifully gowned and bejeweled ladies curtsied before me and men shook my limply proffered hand, now thankfully almost rid of the hard calluses of captivity in the mine. Naturally I saw none of the riff-raff of my earlier life. By the end of the evening I knew that I was well on my way to establishing the character and manner that henceforth would form my identity as Count Pierre de Tourmoulin.

Baron Gustave congratulated me on my performance.

"Masterful, Pierre, masterful indeed! You fairly dazzled the worthies of New Orleans. As I watched you during the evening even I found it hard to believe that you were not born a count. But take care that your low antecedents do not betray you. And a word of caution: You would do well to polish your French a bit more. Your accent is genuine, but I cringed at one or two vulgar expressions that French nobility would consider inappropriate. But these are things easily corrected."

Later I made discreet inquiries about Mother and Monique, but all I learned was that they had left New Orleans two years earlier escorted by a Frenchman. Despite my determination to be indifferent to their fate, a wave of melancholy swept over me. And my father? I was not destined to know the truth about any of them until many years later.

This favorable moment climaxing an evening of adulation seemed the time to bring up the matter of money, of which I had not a disposable cent to my name. But Gustave rejected my request out of hand.

"Do you take me for a fool, Count Pierre?" he asked sarcastically. "I promised you money and honor when and if we found my daughter. Tonight you had a taste of honor, but do not let it swell your head. You will see no money until I find my Christine. With money you could easily revert to your old picaresque nature, and I would never see you again. As long as you are dependent upon me for everything, in everything you must be loyal to me. Find my daughter and I shall reward you, fail me and you shall have nothing, betray me and I shall kill you. Do I make myself clear?"

"Perfectly, monsieur," I mumbled, thoroughly chastised and put in my humble place.

No sooner had Gustave completed his business affairs and hired or purchased slaves and overseers to serve Madame Pauline in his elegant and spacious dwelling hard by the Convent of the Ursulines than he expressed his impatience with further delays in the search for his daughter.

"Now, Pierre, if you would keep your word and your life, you must lead me to my daughter. Where is she?"

"To the best of my knowledge she is in Memphis. After I knew her she was married and resided for several years in another city, but I received news months ago that upon the death of her husband she was returning to Memphis. There is where we must seek her, though I cannot attest to the reliability of my information about her."

"What name does she go by?"

"Do you think me a simpleton, Gustave? You and I both know that my only safeguard is information about her that I alone have. I shall share it with you bit by bit as circumstances unfold and the need arises. We are gamblers, you and I, in a game that proceeds one hand at a time, one card at a time. Neither of us trusts the other, but we have no choice but to play the game by the rules. Perhaps we both shall win, or perhaps one or both shall lose. But remember this, monsieur: Regardless of what you think of me, your daughter, if such she really be, is the only woman I have ever loved. She is, I know now, the love of my life, and even if I were tempted to betray you, I will not betray her. Few get a chance to regain a lost love. If we find her, a thing that is not at all certain, and her love for me still lives, I will choose her even over your money."

"I had not expected to hear such words fall from your lips, Pierre."

"Nor until now could I ever imagine saying them. But many things are becoming clearer to my understanding, things I never comprehended before."

"You mentioned that she is widowed. Does she have children?"

"A son, so it was reported. Whether she has other offspring I know not. Now a question for you: What of her mother and other relatives? Surely Madame Pauline is too young to be her mother."

"You surmise correctly. Her mother died in childbirth, and I left France to distance myself from the heartbreak. Most of the Thibaudet family, once numerous, fled or died at the time of the Revolution, but a few remain and some returned to our ancestral properties in Rouen. As for Madame Pauline, she has been the comfort of my middle years, but the tragic loss of Christine's mother is ever with me. If I find my daughter I shall have at least the fruit of my marriage."

Accompanied by young Creole Henri Ménard newly employed by Gustave, the three of us set out for Memphis by steamboat. I was annoyed by the intrusive and obsequious Ménard and made no effort to hide my displeasure at his presence.

"Why have you brought that fellow along?" I asked Gustave when we had a moment alone. "What good is he to us?"

"I will tell you exactly why I have brought him, Pierre. You know my English is somewhat deficient, and since you are not above slanting things to your advantage, Henri will see to it that everything is reported to me accurately."

I fumed and muttered that such a cynical ploy cast aspersions on my character.

"As if you had any character to begin with, Count de Tourmoulin," Gustave said with a sarcastic laugh.

I was indeed agitated but hardly because of doubts about my character. For all my brave talk earlier, the truth was I did not know of a way to keep matters under my control once we should find Caroline-Christine. What would prevent the baron from summarily dismissing me from his presence, leaving me penniless or dead? It was becoming plain to me that my fate rested in Caroline's fair hands. Only if we found her would I have a chance, but only then if she interceded on my behalf. And if she did not, then regardless of his promises to me, the baron would have no further reason to keep me alive, much less to enrich me.

We took the best lodging available in a hotel newly constructed on the main square. Memphis had grown greatly in the six years since I left it. The crude frontier town was beginning to take on the appearance of a settled city. Many buildings had disappeared, including Lucas Pollard's dilapidated mortuary and barbersop. In its place rose a respectable two-story structure bearing the rubric "Rayford Summerford Enterprises." I saw no need to mention that I had once known Summer-ford.

If Memphis had grown, the Thomas mansion had vanished. To our inquiries a neighbor woman described the horrific conflagration in which the Thomas family perished. My heart sank, and Gustave was visibly distressed.

"Madame," he asked in his heavily accented English, "please tell us, what of the young woman, the daughter, what of her?"

The woman stared at him, suspicion written across her face and displeased that he had addressed her as "Madame" in the French manner. "Why do you want to know, mister? You sound like some kind of foreigner. What do you have to do with the Thomases?"

"Mr. Thibaudet is from New Orleans," I hastened to explain, "and he meant no disrepect when he called you 'Madame'. His family is related to the Thomases on the maternal side, though he has not seen them in many years. "This gentleman and I are associates of Mr.

Thibaudet, who has a number of commercial enterprises. Without going into details, which I am not at liberty to do, I can tell you, ma'am, his visit involves a substantial inheritance, and from what you tell us, with the tragic passing of her parents, it will no doubt fall to the daughter, if we can locate her. Oh, what a terrible thing, what an awful thing indeed! Mr. Thibaudet came here bearing the happy news of the inheritance only to learn of this tragedy. Any information you can give us that might help us locate the daughter will be greatly appreciated."

"Well, I can tell you this, the daughter, Miss Caroline, when she lived here as a girl, was not living in the Thomas mansion when it burned down. And as far as I know, she lives somewhere here in Memphis, but I can't tell you exactly where, maybe in one of the houses her father owned."

We were heartened by this news. Despite its rapid growth, Memphis was still a small city, and now it was simply a matter of tracing her whereabouts amongst a few thousand inhabitants. Suddenly I remembered that Caroline had once mentioned the original Thomas residence, how did she put it in her quaint English? "... down there on Poplar Street round the corner from where you live."

"I think I know where she is," I confided to Gustave and Henri as we walked back to the hotel.

"Where?" asked Gustave, excited by my confident tone.

"Be patient, and I shall show you. I just remembered something she told me years ago. But if she's not there, she's probably in one of the other Thomas properties, as the woman said. We'll find her, Gustave, we'll find her."

Without stopping at the hotel we hastened to Poplar Street. We were nearly there when of a sudden I saw myself coming towards us. That is to say, as I once was. The boy was six or so with dark, curly hair, slight build, and sharp features that replicated in nearly every detail the street urchin I once was. Not that he wore the tatters of my childhood. No. He was dressed becomingly with buckled shoes polished to an attractive sheen, clean trousers and suspenders and spotlessly clean shirt with a snugly fitted collar. A black nanny who accompanied him constantly cautioned him about stepping into the muddy wagon ruts, reminders surely so often repeated that he paid them not the slightest heed. A few paces farther the pair entered a house.

For a moment I felt lightheaded and strangely dispossessed of myself. There could be no mistake; he had to be Wilbert.

"We have found her, Baron. That is her residence," I announced, pointing to the house where the boy and his nana had entered. "For I am certain the lad is her son."

"How can you be sure?" Gustave asked.

"Take my word for it. We must make arrangements to meet your daughter."

The task was more easily decided than done. The baron elected to send Henri to arrange a meeting, but he was summarily rebuffed before he could explain himself. It seemed that the widow McCurtain had many would-be suitors charmed by her beauty but even more bewitched by her property and money. Caroline had learned to be cautious.

We conferred about our next approach. It would not do to send the baron himself. His defective English and Caroline's odd accent would render communication between them on such delicate themes all but impossible. The task then fell to me.

"But, Tourmoulin, Christine knows you, or did, and likely has griefs against you. By what magic can you present yourself as a stranger and persuade her to meet with me without being discovered for the fraud you are?"

"Perhaps I shall try the novel approach of telling her the truth. Late or soon she must hear it. But in any case, you must trust me, and you must give me the cross. I shall need it to convince her."

The baron shook his head, but having no better plan, grudgingly gave me the necklace and his consent. "But mind you, we shall be in hailing distance of the house and watching your every move."

Never had I quaked inwardly so much as when I knocked on her door. When death stared me in the face during earlier episodes of my life, mere terror seized me in its fatalistic grip. But now fear and hope raged within me, creating a greater emotional maelstrom.

The nanny ushered me in and bade me sit and wait for her mistress. In an adjacent room I heard a woman's voice and the occasional complaining response of a child. Finally Caroline came in. I stood and bowed before her.

"Nanny says you want to talk to me. What can I do for you, sir. Please be seated," as she sat down across the room from me.

She was taller now, but fairer, lovelier, and more beautiful than I remembered her. Her English, though still slow, was noticeably less regional. My love for her, long submerged and sullied by a thousand turmoils and errors, surged to full vigor in her presence. It was all I could do not to fall on my knees and declare myself.

"Ma'am," I said in a voice lower than normal by a half octave, "my name is Tourmoulin, and I am here on a most serious matter, but one that is entirely to your benefit. I ask only that you hear me out. I shall not take much of your time."

"Then speak quickly of your business, sir. I am a widow and do not make a practice of havin gentlemen in my home."

I nodded and proceeded. "First of all, Mrs. McCurtain, I learned of your recent family tragedy. Please accept my sincerest condolences."

"Thank you, Mr. Touahmoulin. But if you would get on with the business that brought you here."

"Ma'am, I represent a gentleman of great wealth and social standing ..."

At that point she rose. "Sir, I do not accept such proposals from men or their agents!"

"Oh, no, ma'am. This has nothing to do with a proposal of matrimony, but with an inheritance that is due to fall to you."

"An inheritance?" she asked as she sat down again. "What sort of inheritance, sir?"

"Ma'am, if I may be direct, it has come to our attention that you were an adopted child. We have investigated the case carefully, for the gentleman I mentioned is a cautious, prudent man who does not want his estate to end up in the wrong hands."

"And just how did you learn that I was adopted?"

"It was a strange turn of events, but the information came to us by way of a young man who confessed it at his death. And he said that this would confirm his story if we could return it to you."

I took the cross from my vest pocket and placed it in her hand.

"My cross, my precious cross! I thought it was gone forever. Wherever did you get it, sir?"

"As I said, the young man confessed that he had taken it."

"What was his name, sir? Can you tell me that?"

"I believe they said his surname was Prosper, or some such. Does it sound familiar to you, Ma'am?"

Tears welled up in her lovely blue eyes. "Peter, Peter Prosper," she said softly. "Yes, sir, I know him, or used to. Did you say he has ... passed away?"

"According to our reports, ma'am, he was buried somewhere in Mexico."

"He lived an unsettled life. Did you know him, sir?"

"Only in passing, but I know from what I was told you can be sure that he has gone on to a better life."

"Dear, dear Peter. I shall mourn for him. Lately, sir, I have done so much mournin for loved ones."

"I am truly sorry that you must add yet another name to your list of lost loved ones."

"Thank you, sir. But I fail to understand what connection Peter's—Mr. Prosper's—death has with the inheritance you spoke of."

"The gentleman I mentioned has seen the cross, and according to him, it is the only one of its kind in the world. He commissioned it in France for his daughter Christine, his only child, who was lost on a journey to New Orleans. He always assumed she perished in the wilderness above Natchez, but this necklace gives him hope that she survived. In a word, he hopes that you, ma'am, are his long-lost daughter. And if you are, you stand to inherit an immense fortune."

"Sir, I don't rightly know what to say. This is sure enough the cross and gold chain I was wearin when my Poppa found me in the forest. But that's all I know. I was too young to have any recollection of who I was or where I came from."

At that moment Wilbert came into the room, stopped, looked at me, and then whispered loudly to his mother, "Momma, who is the man behind that big beard? He looks like a billy goat with all that hair on his chin."

"Wilbert, you hush up. This gentleman is Mr. Tour—I'm sorry, sir, what did you say your name was?"

"Tourmoulin, ma'am. You have a handsome son. How old are you, Wilbert?"

"Six, if it's any business of yours."

"Wilbert! What kind of talk is that? You be polite to Mr. Tourmoulin! Now you go back to your room and play, young man!"

As Wilbert darted back into his room, Caroline sighed and apologized to me. "I'm sorry, Mr. Tourmoulin. Please forgive him. He's a caution with that sharp tongue of his. I never know what he's going to say to folks. People probably think I've never tried to teach him manners."

"Don't give it a second thought. He's just a boy, and a sharp-witted one at that. But getting back to the matter of the inheritance, would you be willing to speak with Mr. Thibaudet, the man I represent? I can assure you of his good intentions, and you can understand his interest in meeting you."

"I'll talk to the gentleman, yes, but I must tell you right away that I could never think of anyone but my Momma and Poppa as my parents."

"Mr. Thibaudet understands your filial affection, Mrs. McCurtain. After all, they raised you and cared for you as their own. He would never try to take their place in your heart and memories. May I therefore suggest that you meet, get to know each other, and see where it leads?

Does that sound to you like a reasonable procedure in the matter?"

"It does, Mr. Tourmoulin, and I want to thank you for sweet and patient way you explained things to me. I've always wondered where I came from, even though Momma and Poppa could not have been better parents. You tell Mr. Thibau—what did you call him?—that he is welcome to come to my house tomorrow afternoon."

"Just one other thing, Mrs. McCurtain, would you be kind enough to let me return the cross to Mr. Thibaudet? He wants nothing more than for you to have it in your permanent keeping, but for the moment it is the only link he has to his dear daughter."

She graciously consented to my request, and no sooner had I stepped into the street than Gustave and Henri rushed to meet me. "She will see you, Gustave," I announced triumphantly as I handed him the cross, "but I perceive that three strange men in her house at the same time would be too much for her. Since I have already gained her trust, I suggest with due respect to Henri and in consideration of her sensitivities that he remain at the hotel whilst you and I call on her tomorrow afternoon."

"Then Christine did not recognize you?" inquired the Baron.

"Not in the least. I explained that the man Prosper died and was buried in Mexico, which officially speaking actually happened. With that idea planted in her mind it would not occur to her to identify me with the man she knew years ago."

My reasoning carried the day and persuaded Gustave to leave Henri at the hotel. It gave me a measure of satisfaction to push him aside and reassert myself in the matter. Indeed, I felt my own influence was growing and that I was beginning to shape the affair with Caroline-Christine to my advantage.

The meeting between Gustave and Caroline-Christine was difficult and emotional for the three of us, even though as soon as he met her Gustave was convinced that she was Christine. "Pierre, she is the very image of her beautiful mother," he whispered to me in French.

Gustave described how they lost her along the Natchez Trace Road. His Uncle Jacques de Proulx fell desperately ill during the journey, and they rushed to get medical help in Natchez. Unfortunately he expired despite their efforts. Then they confronted a greater calamity. They discovered to their horror that his two-year-old daughter Christine was missing from the carriages. The two women assigned to care for her each assumed that she was riding in the other's coach. Frantically they retraced the route but found no trace of her. After three days of searching and beseeching heaven with prayers and supplications, they came to the sad conclusion that she had perished in the wilderness.

"I was I inconsolable," Gustave confessed, "and would have taken my own life if my guards had not removed my weapons from me. I insulted the women with bitter words, though I knew theirs was human oversight and not malice. Never did I recover from the loss. Since then I have lived with a great emptiness in my life, which neither money nor power, nor adulation could fill. But now, dear, dear Christine, you are restored to me; after so many years I have found you again."

Caroline—or perhaps now I should say Christine—was shaken by conflicting emotions. The baron's unbounded joy and the story of his suffering moved her deeply, yet for the moment he could be no more than a stranger to her, much less a father. This she explained to him as he struggled to understand her English.

"I thank you, sir, for telling me what happened, and everything convinces me that it happened as you said and that you are really my father, my original father. But you must also understand that to me my Momma and Poppa, the wonderful people who raised me, are the parents I remember and cherish."

"Pierre," he said to me in French, "I am too overwrought to explain to her in English. Please tell her for me that it is as it should be. Naturally she must always cherish the memory of the good people who became her loving parents. I do not begrudge that love; on the contrary, I am grateful to them for caring for her. I only desire to add my fatherly love to her good memories of them."

I did as he bade me, but as I was explaining his view of parental love to her, something in my voice or my gestures caught her attention and she gave me a searching look. "Mr. Tourmoulin, I declare there is something familiar about you. I noticed it yesterday. Have we met before, sir, before yesterday, I mean?"

"What makes you think we knew each other before, ma'am?" I asked, startled that in some way I had revealed myself.

Seeing my dilemma, Gustave attempted to come to my aid. "Dear Christine, our visit has been long and trying for you. You have much to think about and assimilate. But before we leave you for the day, I understand you have a son and I, a grandson. May I see him so that his image is fixed in my mind until we meet again?"

Christine summoned Hettie, the black nanny, who brought Wilbert into the room. Gustave's eyes widened when he saw his features, and looking first at me and then at the boy, inquired of Christine, "He is a handsome boy but his good looks do not reflect your own beauty or the general traits of my family. Perhaps he resembles your late husband?"

Silent until now, Wilbert spoke up tartly: "Look like that old goat! No, sir, I don't look like him at all. He was uglier than a swamp frog and meaner to me than a sore-tailed dog!" Then turning to me, he added: "So the man behind the big beard is back. Why do you keep coming around here, mister whiskers?"

"Wilbert, don't speak that way of your father," the mortified Christine admonished him, "and you apologize to Mr. Tourmoulin for your rudeness. He is a guest in our home."

Gustave chuckled in avuncular approval. "He has spirit. Better to let him speak the truth than teach him to dissemble and lie. He knows his own mind. Come here, Wilbert, and let us shake hands like men."

Surprisingly, Wilbert complied, and from that moment he and Gustave became friends. But with me he was more reserved and would not readily accord me the same courtesy.

As we walked back to the hotel, Gustave took me by the arm and pulled me to a stop. Then he wagged a finger in my face and declared, "Pierre, two things are now obvious to me: First, it is settled beyond any doubt in my mind that Christine is my daughter, for which I give thanks to God. And, second, for better or worse it is evident that you are the father of my grandson. A man would have to be blind not to see the physical resemblance and dull indeed not to catch the same impertinent sharpness of wit and tongue. What I have yet to decide is what to do with you in consequence. On the one hand, I am indebted to you for leading me to her, but on the other, I shall hold you responsible for any mistreatment she suffered at your hand in the past. What little I know of her marriage and the boy's outburst tell me it was not a happy union. If in some fashion you contributed to her unhappiness you shall answer to me. Do I make myself clear?"

"Very. I shall await execution whenever it pleases you, Monsieur le Baron," I said sarcastically, tired of his repeated threats.

"It would not be wise to take my intentions lightly," he warned.

"And no wiser of you, monsieur, to disregard your daughter's feelings, for I tell you she still has a tender regard for the deceased Peter Prosper and, as you saw, she is coming close to perceiving that he and I are the same man. My best efforts will not deceive her much longer. And if she should learn that I have perished a second time, and at your hand, you might lose her for good. Think of that before you do something that cannot be undone."

"Like the gambler you are, you stake everything on her affections. Is that not so?"

"It has been so from the beginning, Gustave. It was the only hand

I had to play in this matter. Your promises to me meant nothing. You and I both know that."

Seeing that the dejected Henri had no role to play, Gustave dispatched him to New Orleans whilst he and I paid several more visits to Christine. The level of trust continued to rise, and before many days had passed she was able talk with greater ease about her life. She confided that indeed her marriage was a loveless union, one she regretted from the start.

"I acted, sir, out of a broken heart," she confessed to Gustave, "and suffered several years of hell as a result. Forgive me for puttin it in such strong terms, but it is the truth."

"Then you were in love with someone else?" Gustave asked. By now they were accustomed to their respective accents and were able to converse with only occasional help from me.

"Yes, sir, I was, but he deceived me."

"Was it the man Peter Prosper that Pierre told me about?" Gustave asked, giving me a hateful stare.

"Yes, sir, it was Peter, Peter Prosper. I thought we were going to get married. He talked about settlin his estate in New Orleans and a bunch of other stuff. But I guess it was all lies. People told me it was, and they told me other awful things about him and his mother. It was so hard for me when I realized he was playin with my feelins. I know I was foolish, but I loved him so much, sir."

"Do you still care for him, Christine?" Gustave asked, as we both leaned forward to hear her answer.

"Well, sir, I still treasure his memory, always will. That's all I can do, for now he's gone on to his reward. I just hope he made things right and didn't have to suffer. I wouldn't want that for Peter."

"If he walked through that door today, would you still love him?" Gustave asked.

"Oh please, sir, don't trifle with my feelins. Peter's an old dream now, a love that's forever impossible. I have to live in the real world and it's not easy. These past months have been so hard for me. I just want things to settle down so that I can raise Wilbert and mind my business. And that's another thing. I've been nearly out of my mind tryin to settle my husband's estate and Poppa's businesses. The senator's family and especially his children have been so hateful, threatening lawsuits and such. And Poppa had businesses and dealins goin on that I never knew about. I've got means enough, I reckon, but no peace of mind. And what makes it worse is all the men that come around, wantin to marry me, so they say, even though I've been a widow for less than a year. Why most

291

of them don't even know me. I reckon they're after my money and possessions."

"Christine, my dear daughter Christine," Gustave said, taking her hand. "You're not alone any more. You have your father to defend you and look after your interests. That is, if you'll accept my help."

"I thank you, sir, and yes I will accept your help. I know I can trust you. And I trust you, too, Mr. Tourmoulin, but in a different way, as you can understand."

"Of course, ma'am. I am happy to be included in your circle of trust."

On the other hand, my trust in Gustave had dwindled away, and I saw that I must end my charade and risk revealing myself to her. I was on very dangerous ground. Gustave no longer had any real need of me and probably would dispose of me under the next convenient pretext.

And perhaps there were other dangers. That afternoon I made discreet inquiries concerning the principals in my earlier troubles in Memphis. To my relief I learned that Bascom Harvey had left Memphis for Texas, so it was unlikely that my name would register with the present constabulary. Pollard was dead, of course, and his widow Bertha had returned to Natchez. Dr. Thurlow Cheatham had departed some years earlier for parts unannounced. Even Colonel Rayford Summerford had left Memphis within the past month, and no one I asked knew anything of my old nemesis Esmer Powell. With this favorable intelligence I breathed easier and proceeded to have my beard shaved in a new barbershop from which I emerged feeling strangely exposed and denuded.

Gustave laughed when he saw me. "So you have decided to reveal yourself to Christine. You look vulnerable, exposed, like a scared lamb readied for sacrifice."

"Perhaps I am, Gustave. But better to be sacrificed by her hand than slain by yours. Anyway, we shall see what we shall see."

We called on Christine the next day. I had asked permission from Gustave to speak first. As she came into the room, I rose and spoke these words: "Clever little Wilbert asked who the man was behind the beard. Now, Christine—or Caroline when I knew you—you can see for yourself. I am the man behind the beard. You knew me as Peter Prosper. Now I am Pierre de Tourmoulin. I have returned."

I cannot recall everything that was said or all that happened on that fateful afternoon. I do remember that she all but fainted away, and Gustave had to help her to a chair. There were tears and protests, accusations and recriminations, but one truth emerged and held constant:

She still loved me, though her love was wounded, wronged, and rendered tragic by events. Finally, Gustave spoke to her gently.

"Christine, my fatherly love for you is unconditional, and I want only your happiness, but tell me if you will, who the boy's father is, the senator or—"

She could not say the words for her sobs and tears but mutely pointed to me.

"I surmised as much by the strong resemblance. Now I have waited to ask this question before acting: What would you have me do with this man who abandoned you with child? Say the word and he will never lie to you or abuse you again."

"Oh no, sir—Father—I wish him no harm, only happiness and all that is good and proper in his life. He forced me into a loveless union and brought me the awful news that Peter was dead. I forgive him for that evil lie, but I'll not soon forget it."

"You heard her, Pierre, now what have you to say for yourself?"

"Only this, sir, I lay my life before her, declare my love anew, and dare ask her to be my wife. I loved her as Peter Prosper, but I could not marry her as Peter. Peter was a renegade, a pauper, a man with a scandalous ancestry and past. But when that man who bore his identification was mistakenly but officially buried in Mexico it freed me be a different and perhaps better man, a man of a much higher class. And with the wealth to which you have given me claim, sir, I shall be able to provide for her respectably as she deserves."

Christine dried her tears. "Peter, or Pierre, or whatever your name is now, are you proposin to me or to my father? You must ask me, dear man, if you expect me to give you my answer." Then smiling through her tears, she added: "and you must not fly off again in a balloon, as you did before, you naughty man. Folks around here talked of nothing else for weeks."

"On that you have my most solemn promise, dear Christine. Now, here is my proposal to you: I love you, have always loved you, and, as your father is my witness, if you will marry me I promise as your husband to make amends for all the sadness I caused you. Dearest Christine, will you marry me?"

She hesitated and my heart almost stopped beating as she rose and took a long moment to look into my eyes. Then she took my hand and spoke the words that gave me new life: "Peter, I know about your past and your family. I know you have done wrong things, but I believe that despite all there is goodness in you. And you are Wilbert's father. Peter, I love you, I never stopped loving you. That was my problem. So my

293

answer, Peter, is ... yes. Father, with your blessing I will marry this man, Pierre de Tourmoulin! And with the Good Lord's help maybe someday I'll even learn how to say all his new names!"

And so she did. A civil magistrate married us in Memphis. Gustave attested to my identity and bestowed on me a considerable capital to spare me the embarrassment of having to depend on Christine's wealth for a livelihood. Later, with Gustave's advice and a trio of capable barristers we negotiated Christine's complicated affairs in Memphis and settled ourselves in New Orleans. There we resided for a few months in Gustave's mansion but eventually removed to another house on nearby St. Phillip Street. Madame Pauline and Christine became fast friends. As for Wilbert, after some initial uncertainty and resistance, he accepted me as his father, and neither he nor Christine objected when I insisted that we change his legal surname from McCurtain to Tourmoulin. Even at that age I suspected he sensed the truth about his relationship to me. Within the strict limits that Christine imposed on us, his grandfather and I took turns teaching him card tricks and slight of hand maneuvers, which he learned as easily as a duckling takes to water.

Because the Thomases were indifferent to Christianity, Christine had grown up without religious instruction to speak of. But before long she reached the practical conclusion—no doubt encouraged by Pauline—that since everyone around her was Catholic she ought to be also so that we could be married in the Church. Gustave and I were delighted with her decision.

At the ceremony in Memphis Christine had whispered to me. "Darling, I married a man named Pierre de Tourmoulin. As far as I'm concerned, Peter Prosper will stay buried way out yonder in the West. I promise you I shall never mention the name or his ancestry to anyone. Anyway, I like this version of you better," she giggled.

"And so do I. You also have my pledge that I'll never mention him again," I whispered in return as we sealed our agreement with a kiss.

Some months later Christine scolded Gustave. "Father, you will never find a better or more beautiful lady than Pauline to share your life with, nor a more faithful one. She loves you dearly, and you must repay her loyalty and true affection by marryin her."

"But, Christine, can't we just leave things the way they are? I'm too old to marry," he protested.

"You're too old not to," she retorted spiritedly. "Now you must do what is right by her. And if you don't, I shall never forgive you, Father."

Gustave, who had faced down and outwitted all breeds of men and taken every risk, wilted before his beloved daughter's icy stare. Before the year was out he and Pauline were married in the Cathedral.

And so were Christine and I. In my case, however, my multiple betrayals of the Faith troubled me so much that before our wedding I sought to ease my conscience by confessing my failures and reconciling myself to the Church. In the confessional I poured my heart out in a lengthy recital of transgressions.

The priest gave me absolution, and as I rose to walk away, he opened the confessional door and called to me.

"Peter, wait a minute. I need to talk to you."

I knew the voice and recognized the lanky form of Lawler Adkins.

"Lawler, what in the world are you doing here?" I asked in astonishment. "When last I saw you, you were—"

"Running away like you."

"But what happened? How did you end up here? And are you really a priest or as I was, a counterfeit?"

He laughed. "No, Peter, I'm real enough. I'll tell you what happened. I was about to take the ferry for Illinois when I realized that as hard as it was for me to go back, I had to return to Perryville and face Father Branigan, our other teachers, and our seminary brothers. I had failed—we had failed—but I couldn't let that youthful failure keep me from being the priest I was called to be. So I went back, humbled myself, was forgiven, completed my studies, and was ordained. And here I am, assigned to the Cathedral in New Orleans. The Bishop transferred me here to assist Father Branigan."

"Father Branigan is here?" I asked as a guilty terror rose in my breast.

"He is here but not in the best of health. The Bishop transferred him, believing this warmer climate would suit him better. But even though his strength has declined, in mind and spirit he is as keen as ever. I know he would like nothing better than to see you. He speaks often of you. Come, I'll take you to him."

Although Father Branigan now walked with a cane, he threw it aside when he recognized me.

"Peter, *Petrus*, my son, how happy I am to see you!" he fairly shouted, giving me a bear hug. "I have thought often of you, and I could not count the intercessory prayers I have prayed for you!"

"No doubt, Father, your prayers are the reason I am here and not in the deepest pits of Purgatory."

"I see you are troubled, my son. Be at peace and tell me what has befallen you."

We talked long and earnestly. I explained how my name was now Pierre de Tourmoulin, and both agreed to respect my decision. In response to his questions, I told Father Branigan of my travels, travails, and recent civil marriage and impending Church ceremony and asked him to perform the ceremony. On other matters I generalized but took care not to contradict what I had said to Lawler in the confessional. Most of all, I apologized to Father Branigan for betraying his trust.

"My son," he said in his peculiar tone that always prefaced a gentle admonishment, "you have not betrayed me. You must understand that there are many ways to serve God. The priesthood, though I wrongly and selfishly believed it to be your way, was not God's way for you. That was my error, not yours. Now that you are married and a father, you must serve Him as a *Paterfamilias*. And far better a good husband and father than a priest without a priestly calling. Go your way in peace and may you prosper, but come often to see us. And bring your dear wife and family that we may know them, too. God willing, we shall have good times together, the good times of old and loyal friends. Is it not so, Lawler?"

"It is so, Father," Lawler said, "and I rejoice with you that Peter—Pierre—has come back to us."

Father Branigan's words turned out to be prophetic. Not only did he marry us in the Cathedral but also regained a measure of health. We were blessed with many years of his friendship before he left this life. As for Lawler, he has remained our steadfast friend and wise spiritual advisor to this day. Meanwhile, though there were dark moments of heartbreak, Christine and I saw our family flourish with the birth of three more children—two daughters and another son—in the first decade of our marriage. And once my attention turned from roguery and theft to legitimate enterprise, my fortune and influence commenced to grow as my early delinquencies faded into yesteryear. If any had doubts or suspicions about me from my former life, they died away to the spiteful murmuring of those envious of my rise in the world. Even though I prospered, as my old surname implied, ever afterwards I honored my pledge to Christine to be Pierre de Tourmoulin, for it was the name under which I came to know real happiness and prosperity. As the years passed and New Orleans became more American in character, I quietly dropped my pretense of nobility. As myself finally, I made the fulfilling discovery that I needed to be neither a rogue nor a count to make my way in the world.

By this time my distrust of Gustave had melted away, bonded as we were through our wives. In its stead, my feelings for him took on some of the coloring of a filial affection. But as it grew so did my fears that the vengeful Texians might still come for him.

Gustave brushed aside my concerns. "Pierre, I have enough money to suborn every official from here to Texas. And if that fails, more than enough loyal stalwarts to protect me from importunate fools who would risk their life by refusing my bribes. Remember also that I left considerable capital in San Antonio for them to squabble over."

Of my boyhood friends—if they can be called that—the only one I ever saw was "Pouches" Ducoeur, and remembering our unhappy association and seeing the miserable state into which he had fallen in manhood, I pretended not to know him.

This only remains to be said: Knowing that but for the grace of God I would have shared the fate of Ducoeur, DuClos, and the other ruffians of my early days, I awake each day with a heart full of gratitude that God gave me the chance to live my life with my beloved Christine and my children by my side.

Translator's Addendum

Proper source attribution of these items is impossible since the date and captions of the newspaper were not included with the clippings. Nor is there any way of knowing the connection these reports had, if any, with the life of Pierre de Tourmoulin. The internal evidence of the last item and the slight modernization of the journalistic style suggest that several years had passed since the events in the narrative.

Items

The heirs of Maxim desChesnes, lately deceased, who immigrated to New Orleans from the Isle of Martinique in the first year of this century, will hear something greatly to their advantage by applying in person to attorney Julien duBois, Esq., at 25 Orleans.

The public are cautioned about a trifling fellow, late from Paris, who calls himself Jacques Bonnefoi and pretends to be in possession of a large sum of money for the purpose of buying land and properties. He takes special care wherever he goes to decamp to eschew the courtesy of a formal adieu and settling up arrears.

True love still triumphs in these crass times. Betrothed to another suitor who was unable to win her fondest sentiments, Miss Celeste Frémont honored her pledge to wed. But at the final minute she chose as

297

her groom the man she had secretly loved since childhood, Mr. Daniel Montvert, at present a resident of Baton Rouge but a pleasant son of New Orleans. We learn that pistols were drawn and tragedy loomed. But in the end the bride's tearful pleading and the intervention of cooler heads tipped the scales towards happiness and the happy couple have sailed away to Europe to begin their matrimonial idyll.

We regret to learn the death of Mr. Edouard LaGarde, which melancholy event occurred at the residence of his brother, in Metairie, on Thursday ult. A respected figure in this city for forty years, he was stricken down with congestion of the brain, and the vacuum thus made in the community will be hard to fill. He was laid for his final rest next to the tomb of his sainted wife on Friday.

On Monday ult. the angel of death folded his dark wings over the home of Guillaume Fontanin, lifting from his loving embrace his wife Sophie, aged 29 years, 3 months.

Homicidal Slave: We learn with indignation and dismay that on Wednesday ult. an evil assault was made on the person of Count Pierre de Tourmoulin. The circumstances our informant provided are these: Count de Tourmoulin, a citizen of the highest respectability whom all admire for his commercial astuteness and conspicuous social standing in New Orleans, was engaged in the purchase of a sugar plantation on the Bayou Teche when a maddened slave called Henry burst his way into the room brandishing a knife, screaming menacing obscenities, and threatening the Count with death. The sure hand of Providence and the quickly reactive host and his servants prevented the monstrous deed, the Count suffering only curable abrasions. In his delusional rage the slave, surely intoxicated with rum, made the insane claim that he was the Count's betrayed brother and shouted similar absurdities, laughable had they been less serious. The mortified host gave order for the quick hanging of the servant, but Count de Tourmoulin interceded and recommended as punishment that the slave be whipped and kept under observant guard for a prolonged term, after which, barring other outbursts of his madness, his life might be spared. All were wonder- struck by the elevated example of Christian nobility of spirit the Count's request betokened. We lay down pen with the certainty that the Evil One never rests in his rage to work woe on the innocent yet are consoled by the happy assurance that the Count will suffer no enduring consequence of this wanton aggression. We regret that for want of particulars we cannot satisfy the reader's curiosity regarding the fate of the homicidal slave.

[1] The surnames "Prospère" and "Tourmoulin" do appear in the parish records but time and water stains have obliterated the given names (translator).

[2] Although some surviving Attakapas people deny their ancestors were cannibals, historians generally agree they indulged in ceremonial cannibalism (translator).

[3] Scholars still debate the site of the fort (translator).

[4] Here Peter is correct. Andrew Jackson did visit Memphis in 1832 (translator)

[5] In the Comanche nation the chief was allowed to take four wives (translator's note).

[6] The Arkansas River on modern maps (translator's note).

[7] The Atocha sank off the coast of Florida where it was found in 1985, its treasure of gold still intact (Translator's note).

[8] Fray Domingo seems to be describing a grizzly bear (Translator)

[9] Spanish for a kitchen scullion (Translator).

[10] The original El Paso was on the south side of the Rio Grande (Translator).

[11] Meaningless words unless don Eduardo confuses *maíz* (corn) and *país* (country) (Translator).

www.ingramcontent.com/pod-product-compliance
Lightning Source LLC
Chambersburg PA
CBHW020945260626
47169CB00006B/1827